MW00825322

The Snowbirds

Also by Christina Clancy

Shoulder Season
The Second Home

The Snowbirds

A Novel

Christina Clancy

ST. MARTIN'S PRESS
NEW YORK

First published in the United States by St. Martin's Press, an imprint of St. Martin's Publishing Group

THE SNOWBIRDS. Copyright © 2025 by Christina Clancy. All rights reserved. Printed in the United States of America. For information, address St. Martin's Publishing Group, 120 Broadway, New York, NY 10271.

www.stmartins.com

Library of Congress Cataloging-in-Publication Data

Names: Clancy, Christina, author.
Title: The snowbirds : a novel / Christina Clancy.
Description: First edition. | New York : St. Martin's Press, 2025. | Identifiers: LCCN 2024042891 | ISBN 9781250284952 (hardcover) | ISBN 9781250284969 (ebook)
Subjects: LCGFT: Novels.
Classification: LCC PS3603.L3514 S66 2025 | DDC 813/.6—dc23/ eng/20240916
LC record available at https://lccn.loc.gov/2024042891

Our books may be purchased in bulk for promotional, educational, or business use. Please contact your local bookseller or the Macmillan Corporate and Premium Sales Department at 1-800-221-7945, extension 5442, or by email at MacmillanSpecialMarkets@macmillan.com.

First Edition: 2025

10 9 8 7 6 5 4 3 2 1

For John, who is always there. Will you marry me . . . again?

We have stood
    from year to year
        before the spectacle of our lives
            with joined hands.

—William Carlos Williams, "Asphodel, That Greeny Flower"

The Snowbirds

Chapter One

Palm Springs
January 2, 2023
6:00 A.M.

The day after Grant went missing, I was still convinced that it was only a matter of time before he walked through the front door—chagrined, maybe a little dirty, certainly contrite. Others weren't so sure. When he didn't return from his hike, a pop-up command center topped by a satellite dish was set up in Indian Canyons faster than I could say REI. The park was buzzing with helicopters, drones, thermal sensors they called FLIRs, and rescuers in orange gear.

It felt as though half the population of Palm Springs was out searching the mountains, from the tribe's rangers to volunteers with the Mounted Police—I couldn't keep track of all the agencies or who did what.

What a spectacle, all for one man!

Yesterday, Grant had been planning to leave before sunrise for a New Year's Day hike to Cedar Springs with Hobie, his hiking buddy, and our neighbor. He was gone when I woke up. I'd expected him home by lunch, but the minutes ticked by, and then night fell. As our dinner grew cold and my texts and calls were met with eerie silence, I became increasingly concerned. Then again, I'd had a bad feeling all day. Things were not good between us.

When I saw Hobie in the courtyard of our condo complex that

night, I knew something was wrong. All day, I'd assumed they were together. But when Grant wasn't waiting outside by the Jeep in the morning, Hobie figured he was still sleeping off a New Year's Eve hangover. Hobie immediately insisted we call the ranger for help. Good midwesterner that I am, I didn't want to trouble anyone, and I thought there was some kind of twenty-four-hour rule that applied to missing persons. But Hobie didn't rattle easily, and his concern set off my own alarm bells.

Still, I assumed that the ranger, Brady, would think I was overreacting. Instead, after taking down some preliminary information about Grant's age, fitness level, and what he was wearing, Brady asked why I hadn't called sooner. "At this point, I'm afraid he's going to have to spend the night up there," he said. "I can't create an incident within an incident by sending people out in the dark."

At the crack of dawn, Hobie drove me to Indian Canyons to meet with Brady. I was expecting to retrieve Grant as though he were a lost dog picked up by animal control. That's when I discovered that the vast thirty-one-thousand-acre hiking area and ancestral home of the Agua Caliente Band of Cahuilla Indians, a major Palm Springs tourist destination with sixty trails that lead into the San Jacinto Mountains, was now closed to visitors. Hobie whistled, impressed. "Well, look at that. The entire canyon has been evacuated."

I cringed, worried I'd created all this missing-person hubbub for nothing.

Brady was studying a Google Earth map on a giant screen. "Did you find the vehicle?" Hobie asked.

Brady shook his head no. "We sent some guys up to Morris Ranch Road again. Nothing there, nothing here."

They followed the long red line running along the map with a circle in the middle to represent Cedar Springs, Grant's supposed destination. I learned he could have gotten there from above by driving about forty-five minutes to the higher elevations, parking at the top of the trail near Pinyon Pines, and making his way down the Jo Pond Trail. His other option was to park where we stood in Indian Canyons and walk up the West Fork Trail from below. On a map, it looked easy.

Brady pushed his readers down his nose and gazed at me over the lenses. "Without knowing where the car is, he could be anywhere. The first thing we do is look for shoe prints outside the vehicle. Then we create a radius to determine how far he could have gone. Without it, we don't even know where to start."

"What about his phone?" I asked.

"Not much reception where he is," Brady said. "Could be dead. Could be stolen. Maybe he left it in the car? Thieves can jailbreak or use activation unlock tools. We can ping it, but we need permission to get his info from his carrier. Could take some time. We'll need your authorization, too. Did you bring what I'd asked?"

I handed him a small bag with Grant's prescriptions.

"Xarelto," Brady said, looking at the label with concern. "He's on blood thinners?"

"Is that a problem?"

"I sure hope not, but could be. If he falls or gets cut, he could keep bleeding. On the other hand, if he hasn't taken a pill for a few days, he could throw a clot, especially up in the high altitude." Brady handed back the bottle of pills. "I'm sure he's fine."

I could tell that Brady had no such certainty.

The tribe charged a fee to use their trails, and Brady, while sympathetic, wasn't too happy that their daily operations would be disrupted to search for another lost weekend warrior. He said that when they found Grant (I took comfort in the fact that he said *when*, not *if*), he would be banned from the reservation for life.

I'd brought some photos so they could get a better sense of his appearance, prints that I'd made at Walgreens the night before. The picture of Grant on the top of the pile already seemed dated because he was no longer the pale, beardless, out-of-shape fiftysomething who'd left Wisconsin with me last fall. I'd taken the photo the day after we arrived in Palm Springs and explored the downtown for the first time. It was impossible to miss the giant twenty-six-foot-tall fiberglass statue of Marilyn Monroe from *The Seven Year Itch*, just off Palm Canyon Drive. The first thing visitors to the Palm Springs Art Museum see when they exit is Marilyn's bulbous rear as she's famously trying to hold down her billowing skirt as the wind shoots up from the imagined sidewalk vent. I watched some guys in baseball caps stand between the statue's shapely legs and look up at her panties. Whoever had approved the statue hadn't considered how uncomfortable it would make a woman like me feel to watch grown men openly point up at a female crotch.

"Perverts," I muttered, fully intending for the men to hear me, in the same way I intended neighbors with pesticide flags on their lawns back home to hear me say, "Poison," as I walked past.

Grant's interpretation of the *Forever Marilyn* statue was louder, less passive-aggressive, and more intellectual than emotional. "This isn't art. This is selfie trash begging to go viral. You know what this is, Kimmy?" He always had to sound like the professor he was. "It's 'Art in the Age of Mechanical Reproduction' beyond Walter Benjamin's wildest dreams. Talk about the decay of an aura. If we tried to put this eyesore on a college campus, can you even imagine the outrage it would spark? Tell me, why is it okay here, smack-dab in the middle of a small, supposedly 'progressive' city?"

He didn't notice that while he was gesticulating, I'd covertly taken that photo to send to our daughters. I knew they'd appreciate the odd juxtaposition of the mountains, palm trees, and Marilyn Monroe in the background, and sweaty Grant spouting off in the foreground in his New Balance sneakers, his windbreaker tied around his waist.

Brady frowned when he looked at that photo of Grant. It was not a good choice because it confirmed what I suspected the officer was already thinking—that he was just another stupid tourist.

"Let's get a better sense of the man we're looking for, okay, Mrs. Duffy?"

I am usually quick to correct anyone who assumes I share Grant's last name. Even though we've been together for almost thirty years and have grown daughters, we never tied the knot, at first because he was still married, and the prenup I'd signed with my first husband, Basil, had specified that my alimony would end if I were to remarry within a decade. When Grant's divorce was official and my alimony ran out, we thought about getting hitched, but never did. Weddings are expensive, and I didn't think we needed a piece of paper to show the world what we meant to each other.

Lately, Grant wanted to make our union more official, but our arrangement worked for me—especially the separate-but-together routine we'd established when we spent most of our time living in different places. It provoked so much commentary from friends and family that it felt brave, even, to remain together but unmarried for so long. When people accused me of being commitment-phobic, I'd point out that we'd outlasted most of our friends. How many of them, if they were in our shoes, would make the decision to marry each other at this stage of life after all these years?

I liked to think we were like Goldie Hawn and Kurt Russell, who insisted that *not* being married meant that every single day involved making a choice to be together.

I did not explain this to Brady because it wasn't anyone's business but our own, and I worried that if he found out I was Grant's mere "partner," I could be cut out of the whole search.

Brady asked a series of routine questions that ranged from easy to hard, the way wine is listed on a menu from lightest to boldest.

"How would you describe his appearance?"

"Oh, he's very appealing." I've always liked the way Grant looks.

"How tall is he?"

"Average height, about five-ten, although he'd tell you he's six feet. He's in much better shape now than in that photo. He was even starting to get a six-pack. His cheeks are always flushed, and he's very fair. He has to be careful here in the sun, although I suppose everyone does. His hair is more salt than pepper now, although I think of it as brown. He still has a lot of it."

Grant had a child's fear of getting his hair cut, so I learned how to use shears ages ago, but I did a terrible job because I didn't know how to work with his cowlicks and waves. Our new friends in Palm Springs, Thomas and Raul, aka the Husbands, were aghast and took matters into their own hands. They insisted on giving Grant an edible and took him to a barbershop called Daddy's, where they played Destiny's Child on blast and a man named Strap gave him a fade, leaving a shock of hair tumbling over his forehead. It was the best cut he'd ever had, and it made me sad for all the years I'd missed out on seeing this more clean-cut and angular version of him. Thank God he let Strap shape the full-on ZZ Top beard he'd started growing as soon as we'd arrived in Palm Springs.

I tried to describe it to Brady. "His hair came in silver by his mouth, like fangs. I told him that he looked like one of those shih tzus with different-colored muzzles." I've always been nervous around authority figures, and I was beginning to feel more worried about Grant. I overtalk when I'm nervous. I say stupid things I regret. "We used to have a shih tzu. His name was Milky."

"Eye color?"

"Milky's? His eyes were brown."

Brady didn't laugh. Instead, he shot me a look that said, *Don't you understand that this is serious?* The thing was, I did, but even though Grant was relatively new to hiking, he was obsessed enough for me to believe he knew what he was doing. He subscribed to a California topographical site and routinely pored over the Google Earth images Brady, Hobie, and the other volunteers were now studying.

"Is he nearsighted? Farsighted?"

"He's incredibly nearsighted, particularly in one eye." His glasses were often crooked, weighed down.

"Right or left side? This can help us figure out which direction he might have gone."

"Right," I said. "Oh, and his eyes are hazel, like our daughter March's. Dort's are blue like mine. The girls are twins, but it's easy to tell them apart."

Everyone, including Brady, looked as though they'd misheard me when I said our daughters' names aloud. When I was pregnant and we learned we were having twin girls, we couldn't agree on what to name them. Grant's mother had gotten pregnant in high school and was given no choice by her Catholic parents but to marry Grant's alcoholic father. She named him after the Serenity Prayer, so that every time she said it aloud, she would be reminded: "God *grant* me the serenity to accept the things I cannot change." When I asked my mother why she'd picked the name Kim for me, she shrugged and said, "Because it's easy to spell."

Grant suggested we each pick a name and keep it to ourselves until we filled out the birth certificates. One child would be a Hastings, the other a Duffy. I picked the name March because that was the name of painter Milton Avery's daughter, an artist herself. It was important to me to choose a name that was artsy and "different," and I thought March Avery was the coolest name I'd ever heard. I was certain Grant would love March Hastings, and he did.

Then it was his turn. Grant was bursting with excitement, overjoyed to be a father despite the obstacles we'd faced with my complicated and unexpected pregnancy. He lit up. With tears in his eyes he said, "Dorothy. Dorothy Duffy, Double D."

"Oh, honey. No." I wanted to clean out my ears.

"It's unique. Nobody names their kid Dorothy anymore."

"There's a reason for that."

"It's a family name."

Grant hadn't followed a trend in his life, and he was a sucker for tradition. He had a library of first-edition yellowed books that smelled like damp sawdust, and he refused to replace the cool-looking 1950s O'Keefe and Merritt oven that came with our house, even though it cooked unevenly and only two of the six burners still worked. He was incredibly uncomfortable with technology, and he often waxed nostalgic for times, and people, gone by. He once told me that he fell for me because he thought I was old-fashioned. He thought this meant that I was capable and unfussy, low-maintenance, and I've spent the last thirty years letting him believe this.

"We can call her Dort, like my nana," Grant said. "She wanted the name passed down. She asked on her deathbed."

I'd met the elder Dort shortly after Grant and I had gotten serious. Her name invoked the odor of the mothballs that had permeated her Victorian home in Virginia. She wore a hairnet when she cooked, and she once gave me a bag filled with her old nylons cut into pieces so I could use them to tie my tomato bushes to the cage. To me, the name sounded like *dork*, and *wort*. I thought it was ugly and strange, and I was convinced that our child would be teased relentlessly. But who was I to put up a fight? We had an agreement, after all, and I'd never felt more scared and vulnerable.

Our daughters had arrived early and with a great deal of crash-cart and ventilator drama. The NICU nurse called them *pollitos*, little chickens. The doctor explained we'd face tremendous risks if we wanted to have more children.

"At least you had twins," everyone said, as though we were begging for consolation.

We'd talked about risking it again, or adopting, but as the girls grew more capable and independent and our days filled with activities and obligations, we put away the plastic toys and donated the car seat and stroller, and Grant agreed to a vasectomy. With our lives taking place mostly in separate cities at that point, it didn't make sense to grow our family.

If only it were possible to pinpoint the exact moment when we'd moved beyond the luxury of being able to make a decision, when our uncertainty about raising more children calcified into gratitude or regret for choices we'd never actually made.

Once I was finally better, I told myself that the name wasn't important; all that truly mattered was that we were out of the woods. Still, I couldn't help but think that Grant and I were like two dented cereal boxes: we'd come from broken families, and we'd both been briefly married before we'd met. My pregnancy, only weeks into our relationship, had forced us together. As a new family, already we were weird.

But Dort made the name her own. She was squat and strong, the star of a Roller Derby team (they called her Dortorrhea). She accused her sister of being "basic," even though, with her long blond hair and obsession with makeup tutorials, March played competitive chess and graduated at the top of her class. Both girls did well in school—it didn't hurt that Grant challenged them with brainteasers and logic puzzles as soon as they could talk. When they were eight years old and wanted bikes, Grant bought bike kits and made them build them in the garage. They attended youth science and language institutes at the college because they were free for faculty kids. March was fluent in Spanish and French; Dort spoke Russian and Arabic and was studying for the foreign service exam.

I'd been missing the girls terribly. And now I missed Grant terribly, too, which seemed especially ironic because lately I'd been imagining what life would be like without him.

Brady tapped the photo.

"Oh," I said, as though I'd just remembered an important detail. "Grant has the most amazing eyelashes—the eyelashes of a child."

I wasn't yet afraid he was in real trouble, or, rather, I hadn't allowed myself to think it. What upset me was the argument we'd had the night before he left. I didn't want to mention this to Brady, who scratched his boot against the dirt like a horse anticipating bad weather. "Can you tell me what your husband was wearing?"

There it was, that word again: *husband*. "Sure, I can tell you exactly. A navy beanie, his navy sun hoodie, and a Montbell ultralight down jacket, also navy. And expensive."

Grant had never cared much about his wardrobe until he joined the "ultralight revolution." At first, when his shorts and pants had been torn up by rocks and cacti, he covered the holes with duct tape. After Hobie gave him a hard time, he joined a Facebook group of hiking gearheads and settled on a two-hundred-dollar pair of pants that were made out of a fabric called biomass balanced polyamide and had pre-bent knees, adjustable hems, reflectors, steel stirrups, and lots of pockets and zippers; they were his prize possession, along with his two-ounce backpack made of material called Cuban cloth. I often teased him about knowing how much his clothes and pack weighed right down to the ounce, but now I took comfort in the knowledge that he wasn't bogged down. His fancy pants with space-age fabric were keeping him warm and dry, and his gear was keeping him safe.

"Tell me, does he have any distinguishing moles, birthmarks?"

I pushed up my sleeve and showed him the tattoo on the inside of my wrist. "We all have the same one." The family tattoo had been Grant's idea, when he was looking for a way to celebrate March and Dort's eighteenth birthdays. "Grant's is on his upper arm, right here. Dort's is on her thigh, just above her knee, and March—well, she started crying because she thought it hurt too much. She's such a baby. She only has the waves."

The pier represented the memorable times our family had shared at Camp Jamboree, which my father had owned and run, and where I'd spent all my summers growing up. Grant felt it symbolized access, but also safety and security. "A pier is how you get out of the water when you're in trouble," he'd explained, "and how you get in when you want to swim. You tie your boats to it. You can rest on it. A pier, like family, is always there for you."

What could be more incongruous than a pier in the desert? The reminder of Grant's deep love for me, for the girls, brought me close to losing it for the first time since he'd disappeared. I hate crying, especially in front of other people.

Instead, I forced myself to serve up a false, cheery smile, in the hopes that I could charm Brady into working harder on our behalf (now that I was older, I had to work harder to charm a man). When my mother was briefly hospitalized after her stroke, I'd taped photos of her to the walls so that the nurses would know she was more than a patient, she was a person. Similarly, I wanted Brady to know that the lost hiker wasn't just some tourist, he was the man I knew right down to the sound of his sneezes and the shape of his pinkie toenails. He doted on Dort and March—and he would have doted on me, too, if I'd been the type of person to allow it.

Grant usually checked in with me a thousand times a day, a habit I sometimes found irritating because every text felt like a call for attention. He would tell me that the line at the post office was long or share a photo that had popped up on his phone in our family group chat of Milky with a Frisbee in his mouth. His texts on the trail were much less frequent and usually included photos of what he was looking at.

"I told Grant that he shouldn't go hiking that far away on his own," Hobie said.

"Grant never listens. You know how academics are." Did Hobie? I decided to clarify. "They always think they're too smart to get into trouble. Too smart for everything, actually."

Brady asked, "Is it possible he met up with someone?"

"I doubt it. He was into solo hiking."

Hobie gave me a look of pity. "He's asking if you think Grant has a sidepiece."

"Oh no," I said, defensive.

"Suspicion of foul play?" Brady asked.

Hobie laughed. "No way," he answered for me. "Not that guy."

"Hobie"—Brady was irritated that he always chimed in—"can you make yourself scarce?"

"Why does everyone always want me to make myself scarce? Fine." He sprinted to the trailer.

Brady got back to business. "Alcohol problems?"

"No. Grant only drinks occasionally. Both of his parents struggled with alcohol and drugs, and his dad died when he drove his car into a tree. He swore he'd never—"

"I don't need his family history."

I saw Brady's eyes linger on my naked ring finger. "Trouble in your marriage?"

For once, I didn't have a lot I wanted to say. I let out a nervous laugh. "I guess you could say we've been having some issues."

"Issues?"

I didn't like sharing the most intimate details of my private life with anyone, aside from my best friend, Octavia, and Basil. This guy was a stranger, not a therapist. Knowing that Grant and I were at a "hinge point" in our relationship, as Octavia called it, wouldn't help Brady find him. "Oh, you know, we don't really agree about how or where we ought to live and what our life should be."

Finally, I'd succeeded in amusing Brady, although it pained me to admit to our seemingly intractable problems.

"Was he unhappy at work?"

"He recently lost his job. The college where he taught closed, just like that." I clapped my hands together for emphasis. After years of declining enrollment and financial mismanagement, the president of the small liberal arts college announced at graduation that the lights were being turned off in the ivory tower. Everyone knew it could happen. Like losing a loved one after a long illness, it wasn't a surprise, but it was still a seismic emotional shock for Grant, who thought of his colleagues and students as family, and the campus as his home. His work had been his life.

"He was depressed?"

"I think *he'd* say he's been doleful. But being here has been good for him. He's seemed better the last few months. A lot better. He loves hiking. He's obsessed." I felt a shudder go through me when I realized what Brady was getting at. "You aren't trying to say Grant would— you don't think—?" Suicide was something I hadn't considered. "Grant wouldn't do that. Not ever."

I knew what Brady was thinking: *That's what they all say.*

The warden tucked her walkie-talkie in its holster and ambled over to where Brady and I stood.

"He'll be okay?" I asked, suddenly needing the assurance Brady seemed disinclined to offer.

She pointed out into the distance. The mountains, capped with snow, were reflected in her metallic sunglasses. It was an image I suspected was always there, no matter where she was looking.

"The farther back they go," she said, grouping Grant with all the other hikers who'd ever gone missing, "the more trouble they're in. Big, big trouble. It might be sunny and warm here, but you get as high as seven thousand feet and it's easy to lose a trail in the snow, or fall in an ice chute. There's hypothermia. Nights get very cold this time of year in the higher elevations. He's not exactly young." Grant would have hated to hear the warden say that. "He could have had a sudden cardiac event, a stroke. He could have slipped or crossed paths with drug traffickers. We see a lot of activity up there. Bobcats can be nasty. Mountain lions. Last week we found a young lady near Murray Peak, high out of her mind, naked as a jaybird. She thought she was dancing on the moon. She's lucky she's alive. Lots of kooks in the desert. You think it's bad now, just wait until Coachella."

The city of Palm Springs is tucked into the elbow of the San Jacinto range. From where I stood, the mountains appeared barren and rocky, dry and scabbed, like a scene from *The Flintstones*. I thought that it would be hard to get lost without dense foliage, but this is the steepest escarpment in the United States, rising to over ten thousand feet above sea level in just seven horizontal miles. As Hobie put it, the landscape "gets gnarly" the higher up you climb. As far as Grant was concerned, the gnarlier, the better.

Just then, some of the tribal members showed up on horseback, accompanied by an army of equestrian volunteers. This modern cavalry paused, and the ranger on the lead horse stopped briefly to consult with the warden. There was some pointing in the distance and discussion of trails, lots of stomping and whinnying, and then they were off. Despite the circumstances, I found it beautiful to watch the animals trot effortlessly from the Trading Post down into the crag of Palm Canyon and out into the rocky landscape. I thought of that Bukowski line Basil used to recite: *The days run away like wild horses over the hills.*

And there it was, the possibility now creeping into the corners of my consciousness, the voice I'd tried to hush because it was no less terrifying. Grant might be lost, as Brady and Hobie feared—or he might have run away. Again.

Had I manifested this situation? I was the one who'd felt restless, I was the one who'd pushed us to come here. Palm Springs had been my dream, not his. I rarely asked for much, and look what happened when I did.

It had seemed so simple: I just wanted to go somewhere warm for the winter.

Chapter Two

Madison, Wisconsin
August 25, 2022

My ex-husband, Basil, has a knack for reaching out in my most humdrum moments. While I'm scrubbing grout with a toothbrush or pulling mustard weed from the garden, he regales me with tales of his spontaneous trips to Paris to have matching suits made for him and his boyfriend, Greg, or of sitting at the chef's table in a Michelin-star restaurant. His texts are filled with photos of beaches, mountain chalets, cobblestone streets, dinner parties with celebrities, and late-night EDM shows, causing me to experience a sort of existential whiplash between what my life was like, and what it might be.

I'm not usually a jealous person. And I didn't want Basil's life—or, rather, I wasn't suited to it. I wouldn't know how to dress for awards shows and black-tie galas. I feel silly and self-conscious trying to put on airs. My idea of fun involves long bike rides around Madison lakes, planting vegetables, and going to dive bars with Octavia. After raising twin girls, I'm incredibly selfish about my sleep, and to this day I'll do just about anything to get to bed by ten at night.

Basil name-drops famous friends who don't impress me. All my life I swore I'd be different from my mother, Polly, but as I age, I find that I, too, don't get excited about money and status. She always had a flat expression on her face that seemed to say, *Thrill me, go ahead, just try.* Once, she saw a squirrel running up and down an old bur oak at

Camp Jamboree. She took a drag of her cigarette and said, in her usual droll manner, "He's a heck of a squirrel, but he's still a squirrel."

But Basil's dispatches from afar are constant reminders that my world is small compared to his. He's never dustbusted Cheerios out of the back seat of the car or hosed down the inside of the recycling bin, and I have no idea what it's like to play tennis with Bono or lie flat on an airplane.

That late-summer afternoon when Basil called, I could hardly make it to the kitchen to pour myself some kombucha. I was laid up on the couch in the den with my foot propped on a pillow, still swollen and raw from surgery. I wasn't raised to feel sorry for myself. Basil liked to say that Polly had originated the phrase *pull up your big-girl panties*. But my pain meds were wearing off, and my left ankle and foot radiated with an electric ache where the skin had been cut open. The minute I heard Basil's dear voice on the line, I couldn't help it—I began to cry (again, I almost never cry) and started blubbering about my surgery.

"Surgery?" Basil's voice rose with panic. "Tell me you aren't sick, Kimmy." I hadn't told him about the operation—nobody knew except Grant and the girls because I hated for people to fuss and worry over me. I'd broken my ankle the previous winter and this second surgery was to have the pins removed. While they were at it, the doctor convinced me to also have the painful knob on my foot shaved down. I didn't like to tell people about that part of the operation; I found the word *bunion* laden and ugly. It screamed middle age.

"I'm not sick, Basil. Calm down. God, you're such a drama queen."

"And I make a damn good living because of it, thank you very much." Basil was a lyricist for musicals. The girls and I loved singing along to "Hey, Daddy Daddy" and "Stop! That Tickles!" Some of his songs have become anthems, and we knew all the words. Even without his own success, Basil had come from ridiculous money. His father, Vandyke, had manufactured jet bridges that connect airports to airplanes, and his mother, Melody, was from an old Detroit auto family and worked as a fashion stylist. The Underwoods lived in the home formerly owned by William Boyd, who portrayed Hopalong Cassidy, and were fixtures on the Los Angeles social register. If they hadn't sent Basil to the north woods of Wisconsin when he was fifteen in hopes the experience might make him more rugged (and less gay), our paths would never have crossed.

He paused, suddenly serious, and said, "Please don't ever scare me like that again. I'm so relieved you're okay."

"I did not say I'm okay! My foot hurts like hell. I'm pretty sure I'll never walk again."

"Are you asking me to feel sorry for you? That's new. You *must* be sick."

"It's really painful."

"Oh, my poor baby. But at least you're not *dying*. That is expressly forbidden. My friends are starting to drop lately. I swear I'm going to end up like Vincent Price in *The Last Man on Earth*. You know I can't live without you, Kimmer. You're the keel of my canoe." He'd been saying that since the first summer we'd met.

Basil continued, "So, tell me, what was the surgery, really: boob job? Butt lift? Tummy tuck?"

"Shut up. You know I'd never do any of that."

"There's no shame in going a little *Real Housewives,* my love. A squirt or twenty of Botox can work wonders, just look at me. My face looks like it's been pumped with liquid concrete. I've been thinking about pec implants."

"Don't you dare—"

"Okay, maybe phalloplasty if we're being honest, but whatever. Tell me, what in the hell happened to you?"

I proceeded to explain how, just before going under, I'd told the anesthesiologist that I loved him, and I offered a detailed description of my incisions, knowing Basil couldn't stand it. My mother was a nurse at camp during the summers and at the private Chicago high school I'd attended. I'd spent my childhood watching her tend to rich kids' torn-up knees, poison ivy, period cramps, and stomachaches, but Basil lived as though he didn't have a body, joking that his insides were filled with stuffing. His skin was always scrubbed to a high polish, and he never stank of body odor, smelling only of his signature cologne,

Tom Ford's Black Orchid. I couldn't remember Basil ever even stinking up the bathroom.

"I hope our boy Grant is taking good care of you."

"He's not even here. Sasha found a baby raccoon in her living room just before her first open house. She needed him to help her catch it."

"What's Grant going to do with a wild animal, try to reason with it? He should be home with you, not with his ex-wife. And didn't you say she has a new boyfriend now? The German professor? Can't Ulrich handle the raccoon?"

"His name is Matthias. He's nice, actually, and they're moving to Europe. I told Grant it was fine to go."

"Of course you did, you idiot. It's okay to ask him to help you out every now and again, you know. You don't have to be so damn proud all the time."

Self-sufficiency was my religion. I never wanted anyone, including Grant, to feel obligated on my account. Grant knows this about me. Still, he had a history of disappearing when I needed him.

"My doctor said it'll be months before I'll be able to walk comfortably. And did I mention there's a pin in my big toe where they had to break it and put it back together again?"

"Stop! Heal fast and I love you and all that, but can we talk about Ibiza before I throw up? I'm on an oligarch's yacht right now. It could be seized at any moment. That buzzing you hear in the background? It's a chopper on the helipad delivering oysters flown in from Japan."

"How wasteful, all of it! The oysters, the yachts. Billionaires shouldn't exist."

"Okay, Karl Marx. You know, you're sounding more and more like Polly every day. Not just what you say, but how you say it."

When Polly got pregnant after a brief summer fling with Burl, who ran the camp, she thought she'd discovered how to have the best of both worlds—the child she'd always wanted, without the confines of marriage, an institution that she'd wanted no part of after observing her own parents' unhappy union. Burl was a confirmed bachelor twenty-three years her senior, who cherished his independence almost as much as she did. There was never a question that he'd move to Chicago, or that she'd move up north. They struck what they thought was the perfect compromise: Polly would continue working at the camp each summer so Burl could help raise me. The rest of the year, Polly and I would live in Chicago, and Burl would drive down for holidays, birthdays, and graduation ceremonies.

Basil continued carrying on about the yacht. "Speaking of waste, my friends just started popping bottles of Dom Pérignon and spraying it all over each other. At least I'm not part of that."

"You're only saying that because it's too messy."

"You're not wrong."

I'd known Basil since the day I stood outside the camp infirmary with Polly checking the heads of incoming campers for lice with Popsicle sticks (we never saw any nits, yet every summer there was still an outbreak). When a black Lincoln Versailles with a hired driver pulled up, Polly rolled her eyes and said, "Here comes the funeral procession." All the other campers had arrived with parents, but a tall, gangly, and shockingly pale teenager who looked like a young Art Garfunkel with a head of wiry white-blond hair stepped out of the car, alone. Time stood still when he smiled and waved at me as though we were already friends. I looked around to see if his greeting was intended for someone else. I was neither camper nor staff. "Neither" has always been my whole identity: neither married nor single, not fully a city dweller, not exactly rural. As the scholarship kid at wealthy Chicago Latin, I was virtually invisible.

I never thought I was very special until that moment I met Basil. I don't see him often, but we talk all the time and he knows me better than anyone else. Grant feels threatened by our intimacy, though there's no lingering physical attraction between us. In fact, I had never really desired Basil, even when we were briefly married, a commitment we rushed into because Burl was dying, and he'd always wanted to see us together—and because we were stupid, scared, and young. The world felt so big and dangerous after college, but at least we had each other.

I was convinced our tepid sex life was all my fault. I tried to come up with ways to seduce him, putting porn on the television and dancing around in baby-doll lingerie like a clueless idiot. I shouldn't have been surprised when, a few days before our first wedding anniversary, he tearfully confessed that he'd given a stranger a blow job in an airport bathroom and that all his life he'd been living a lie.

Over the last few months I'd been lamenting to Basil that I couldn't go anywhere exciting for my work sabbatical, a benefit that Go Green, my employer, had introduced for full-time staff as a way to make up for the low pay at the nonprofit. On his sabbatical, Vic, the charismatic and infuriating executive director, had climbed Mount Kilimanjaro. Wendy, the lobbyist who always had the best gossip about the misdeeds of state legislators, spent her time birding in Greenland. When my turn came up, I, too, wanted to go somewhere exotic. I thought about traveling with Dort in Eastern Europe, but Dort brushed me off. She said she traveled by couch surfing, and besides, she was too busy with her band.

What I'd really wanted was to sleep in a hammock in the Yucatán or trek the Cardamom Mountains in Cambodia, but my mobility was limited thanks to the first ankle operation, and I had a hard time seeing myself alone in an unfathomable environment. I'd never done anything so adventurous before or spent that long apart from Grant.

As my time off approached, life changed dramatically. Grant lost his mother, then his job. Sasha seemed to be moving on. Grant hated flying, and I knew that he wouldn't want to go exploring with me. How could I leave him when he was so despondent? Resigned to another long winter in Madison, I decided to undergo the painful but necessary surgery I could no longer put off.

"But this is *your* time, Kimmer," Basil had said. "Six months! You need to go far, far away. Let that tiger out of the cage." He disapproved of my feelings of resignation over my sabbatical. He knew how much I loved Madison, but also how much I hated winter and yearned to go somewhere warm. For years I'd complained about changing out the storm windows, replacing filters on the furnace, ice dams, salting sidewalks, and bouts of despair. Then, last February, I was carrying groceries into the house and slipped on black ice in our driveway. The pain was almost worse than childbirth.

After breaking my ankle, I didn't just hate winter; I was terrified of it.

Grant was happy to have me around. "Think of it as a staybatical," he said. He was quick to point out the irony of me being the one with a sabbatical when he'd worked in academia his entire adult life, making it, like everything else, about him.

"Is it ironic? Really?" I asked. "Madison must be the sabbatical capital of the world." Half the houses in our college town were rented by the semester through sabbaticalhomes.com. I tried to focus on the bright side, reminding myself in my daily gratitude practice that I was fortunate to have an opportunity to have some downtime to reconnect with Grant and find myself—whatever that meant. It was unsettling to feel so unsure in middle age—more unsure of life than I'd ever felt. I'd always thought this was a time when I'd stop struggling and striving and finally just . . . be. Instead, I was at loose ends. I was agitating personally and professionally, while Grant compared himself to Orpheus, looking back in hopes of seeing the life we used to have.

With Grant home, I was suddenly desperate to escape our house—and him. I wasn't used to spending time together except on weekends and in the summer. I began to think of him as an intruder who tracked dirt in when he didn't take his shoes off after he walked through the door, who dragged the tines of his fork against his teeth when he ate, and who left toothpaste spittle in the sink.

I knew I couldn't relax because to be home was its own kind of work. Grant didn't know the names of our plumber and electrician; he wouldn't snake the drain or check to make sure we had a new battery in the thermostat. He delayed fixing things, never seeing the house as a thing that needed to be taken care of. He bought expensive tools and we owned a too-big toolbox, but I was the one who learned to use them, who got bids and negotiated with contractors. I was the one who had to deal with the damage when we had an ice dam after Grant insisted that we didn't need to hire someone to rake the roof after a blizzard. I dealt with the insurance company and the workers when it came time to remove and repair the flooded drywall.

If our house were a city, I would be the mayor and the city workers, and Grant would be a visitor on vacation. It represented different activity-to-rest ratios for us. This was part of the reason I wanted to get away from our home, because everywhere I looked, I saw something broken or neglected that I knew Grant, whose life was of the mind, wouldn't see—and certainly wouldn't recognize as a problem.

When he did help—and in fairness, he'd do anything I asked (but I had to ask!)—he'd expect me to fall all over myself thanking him for caulking the toilet or changing out a storm window. I couldn't really complain. He wasn't great at houses, and, honestly, neither was I. We fought off entropy as best we could, but we fell into a different rhythm from our neighbors, who seemed as if they were born with an instinct for knowing when to trim rosebushes, plant tomatoes, and aerate their lawns.

"As it happens," Basil said, "Greg and I have decided to go off the grid. We rented a house on the island of Bonaire."

"Bonaire?"

"In the Dutch Antilles. I've been commissioned to write some songs for a musical about climate change based on Finnish mythology, my greatest challenge yet, my chef d'oeuvre. Greg wants to kitesurf and hunt for lionfish while I pray my heart out for inspiration. We're about to find out which one of us can go the longest without Bellinis."

Greg was Basil's lover, and I was irrationally jealous of him. I wanted to think of Basil as mine and only mine—he's the kind of warm, charismatic person who makes everyone feel that way.

This was the kind of exotic sabbatical I was supposed to have, and the life of creative purpose I'd always dreamed of. Never in all the years I'd known Basil had I felt more envious of him than I did in that moment—for the first time ever, I wondered if he was being cruel. Why would he rub in his fabulous trip when I was at a low point? I looked at my mangled foot and wondered if I'd ever go anywhere again when I couldn't even walk to the mailbox.

Basil continued, "I was thinking, why don't you and Doc Duffy spend the winter in Palm Springs? It's not fancy. I bought it way back in the day as a sunny little pied-à-terre so I could have my own space when I visited my parents at the Ranch. Le Desert is a quaint and odd condo complex, a real island of misfit toys. I'm hardly ever there anymore, so you'll be doing me a favor to give it some use. You can walk down the street in January without killing yourself. It'll be a great place to recover. Hang out and relax, maybe even get struck by a creative thunderbolt yourself. Didn't you say you wanted to get back into your art? The light in the desert is amazing, like in the South of France."

The desert? This caught me off guard. For some reason, all these years I'd pictured Basil in Florida when he talked about Palm Springs, but I must have confused it with Palm Beach. It didn't matter. Both places were interchangeable in my mind: rich, indulgent, inaccessible.

Basil's reference to my "art" was jarring. I didn't consider myself a great painter or photographer by any stretch, although Basil had always taken me seriously. He loved my modest creations and was incredibly supportive of my efforts. As a girl, I spent all my time in the camp's craft cottage, where I made pinch pots, bracelets, and stamp paintings. In college at Saint Mary's of Notre Dame, my free time was spent at the studio working with paint, then eventually I moved into other media, especially photography. When Basil and I married and moved to Chicago, he gave me a fancy new DSLR Canon as a wedding gift. That camera was the nicest thing I'd ever owned. He encouraged me to sign up for classes at the Art Institute, and I did.

I found myself drawn to non-spaces. I photographed back alleys, shattered neon signs, and abandoned railroad tracks overgrown with weeds. I tried to fix my camera on the parts of the world that everyone else overlooked. I had an entire series on sofas left by the side of the road, and another with loose garbage that had blown where it didn't belong. I liked it when the photos came out looking as if someone had just left the scene or was about to enter it again.

I turned my eye to the everyday because it seemed wrong and in-dulgent to lust for beauty. Polly had tried to steer me clear of any pursuit that involved passion and emotion, and that's what art was all about. She'd imparted to me that sanity, evenness, and control were the three legs of the stool that could prevent me from coming apart. It was best not to hope to become great at art—best not to want for or aspire to greatness with anything, even romantic love. "If you wait for exactly what you want," Polly used to tell me, "you'll end up with nothing at all." No wonder I settled for a passionless first marriage to Basil.

After we split up, I quit taking classes and devoted myself instead to a series of jobs in the nonprofit sector. By the time I met Grant and moved with him to Madison, I thought of art as a fun little hobby, occasionally indulging myself with a new project when the mood struck.

When we were first hot and heavy, I took some candid photos of Grant standing naked at the kitchen counter spreading butter on a piece of toast. In another, he was bent over the dresser looking for matching socks. I was sheepish about sharing my work. When I did, Grant was complimentary, but asked, "Is that how you see me?" He liked to be thought of as more, not less, than he was. It was hard for me to explain that I found Grant at his sexiest in the small, intimate domestic "non-spaces" of our relationship.

I was especially drawn to Alice Neel's paintings of her lover pissing, and of herself as an old woman in the buff with sagging breasts and stomach rolls. That got me back into it for a while. My painting began to change when the girls were little, when I allowed some sentimentality to sneak into my work. I fancied myself a regular Mary Cassatt, capturing March and Dort when they were sleeping, zeroing in on their sweet, dimpled hands and flushed cheeks. "This is amazing," Grant said. "Kimmy, you've got an eye, you really do."

I don't like attention, and I don't want anyone to think I'm expecting praise. "They look like they have rosacea," I said.

"Take a compliment for once. Maybe their eyes are a bit . . . rheumy. But you've really captured their unique sparkle. That's very, very hard to do. It's okay for me to like your work, you know. It's okay for me to think you have talent."

Still, I didn't believe him. I thought about switching mediums. I found acrylics plasticky and inflexible, but I used them because they were cheap, and because oil was such a hassle to clean. Painting is a messy endeavor, and I was too exhausted from picking up after everyone else to create more disorder of my own. I didn't have a studio to work in, and as a solo parent during the week, I didn't have time. I lacked the confidence to think of myself as anything other than a lowly amateur. How could I justify spending a lot of money on high-quality materials or fancy camera lenses when we needed a new garage door to replace the broken one? Eventually, I threw my supplies into a box and let my tubes of paint petrify. I put the fancy Canon, and my aspirations, back on the shelf.

But when Grant lost his job, I felt caged with him in the house, so I dusted off the camera and started a new project I didn't even tell him about. Weekends, before my surgery, I headed to Middleton and started a series of time-lapse shots in the parking lot of a strip mall. I couldn't explain why, after all these years, I felt an almost urgent desire to circle back to my old aspirations and younger self.

I propped my tripod on a construction berm overlooking the sea of cars and used a remote-control timer every five minutes from dusk to dawn. Now, with all the downtime after my surgery, I was teaching myself to upload the photos into a video. The movement of people in and out of the sliding doors, the loading and unloading of carts, and the backing out and pulling in of minivans and trucks had a lonely sort of cadence. It was eerie and industrious, all that stuff moving in and out, all the people like ants gathering clips of grass and breadcrumbs to take to the colony while the sun rose and set behind them. I could play it forward and backward, speed it up or slow it down, and it hardly made a difference.

Then it hit me: Was that my life lately? Was I, too, just going through the motions?

The condo in Palm Springs struck me as a way out of that kind of routine. I loved the idea of a warm escape, a return to creativity, a glimpse of other ways of living, and a chance to develop into someone better, someone with more purpose and focus.

It wasn't just a winter away from home that Basil offered, it was a bridge to a new way of existing in the world.

When we ended our conversation, I strapped my foot into the ugly bunion boot the doctor had given me and hobbled to the kitchen to prepare some snacks for Octavia, who was coming by for a visit. I was daydreaming about Basil's offer when I tripped on the decorative runner and dislocated my shoulder on the way down. I lay there for several minutes as the pain washed over me. Thankfully, Octavia never knocked.

"What the hell are you doing out of bed?" she said when she found me.

"I wanted to put out some snacks for your visit. But I fell before I could get to the kitchen." I winced from the pain.

"I don't need snacks. And besides, why couldn't Grant do it?"

"Because he's not here. As usual."

When Grant finally returned from Sasha's and met us at urgent care, Octavia read him the riot act for leaving me alone. "You really thought Kim would just sit in bed all day?" she said. "Do you even know her?"

"She said I could—"

"I don't care what she said! And did you even catch the raccoon?"

Grant grinned from ear to ear. "I came up with a great idea, actually. We cranked the stereo. Metal music. Then we started banging pots and pans together. He didn't like the noise and crawled back up the chimney—problem solved."

"There's your new career right there: pest control," Octavia said. She wasn't laughing.

After that, Grant was pretty good about taking care of me as my foot healed (fortunately, my shoulder popped back into place), although I still found myself not wanting to ask too much of him. He'd grab me a nearby hair tie and a glass of water that was hard for me to reach with my sling, but if I wanted a book from downstairs, I would wait another hour or two, wary of burdening him too much in that moment.

Before I had the chance to tell Grant about Basil's offer, a puffy gold envelope arrived in the mail. It reminded me of Willy Wonka's winning gold candy bars. My name was written out in Basil's loopy, old-school cursive that I recognized from the mixtapes he used to make for me. Inside were a few keys on a worn leather key chain, and a letter on monogrammed stationery. "The big one is for the gate, the small one is for Unit 1, the smallest is for the mailbox, and the one with the yellow tab is for the laundry room. PALM SPRINGS OR BUST, BABY!" Followed by a PS: "Don't burn the place down," a reference to how I'd accidentally started a small fire in our kitchen when I was making dinner for his parents on a rare visit by them to Chicago. Melody and Vandyke had eaten meals prepared by the finest chefs in the world, and there I was making my mother's famous deviled eggs and a shrimp scampi recipe I'd found in *Cooking Light.*

I was reminded that the Palm Springs condo came with a significant catch: Vandyke had passed away, and Basil had asked me to look in on Melody. My ex-mother-in-law used to scare me to death. But I'd do anything for Basil.

Grant felt so guilty about not being there when I'd fallen that he didn't have much choice but to agree to the plan when I ambushed him. We were really doing it.

When I worked up the courage to tell Octavia, she encapsulated everything I would miss at home. Our Thursday day-drinking club. Walks through Owen Nature Conservancy. Flirting with "hot apple guy" at the farmers' market. All the live bands we saw together at the Crystal Corner. Still, she approved of the trip because she herself had "itchy feet." "You have to change up your life every five years," she said. "Switch your job, your partner, whatever, or it gets stale. And, girl, you are long overdue."

What was holding us back? Our friends were starting to scatter like jacks, downsizing to condos, spending more time in second homes, relocating to be near their kids or grandchildren, or taking care of their ailing parents. The more I thought about Palm Springs, the more excited I became. But as our departure date approached, Grant tried to convince me that spending the winter away was not a good idea.

"Can't we just stay put? I never get to stay put."

"And I never get to go. I need a change." The word *change* felt razor-sharp. This was not a small change, like flipping the mattress.

"Honestly, Kimmy, I know it sounds great to you, but I just don't know what I'm going to do there." Then he began to enumerate, as he was prone to do because he was once told this was a sign of genius. "First, I don't golf. Second, I don't play tennis. Third, I burn easy. Fourth, I am not someone who enjoys indolence."

"Try?"

"We're going to experience a parasitic existence, sitting around gazing at our navels like we're part of the leisure class. Like Basil."

"Basil works hard. Come on, we're going to have *fun*," I said.

"Fun." To Grant this was a strange, foreign word that made him suspicious. "You know what Aristotle says about fun?"

"No, but you're about to tell me."

"He thinks there's a role for fun in our lives only insofar as it allows us to get back to finding purpose. 'Happiness is not found in amusement,' he says. You can't make amusement your point of life. It will only make you unhappy."

"We're not making it our point of life, Grant."

"People are starving. The planet is burning up."

"Us going to Palm Springs is not going to change that."

"What about our wedding?"

There it was, the knot in my stomach that formed every time he mentioned it. I adored Grant, I did, and we were basically married anyway—so why did this renewed talk of formalizing our vows make my eye twitch? Why had I begun to resent his socks tumbling out of the dryer and the whiskers he left on the sink after he shaved, or despair of the fact that he could spend an entire day in our crumbling house watching YouTube videos about how to repair Swiss watches when, everywhere I looked, I saw so much that actually *needed* repair? I wondered if my feelings for Grant were intertwined with my feelings about the house. Would leaving it help us to see each other more clearly?

I couldn't make sense of us in the house in Madison that felt more mine than his, and where we'd established our patterns of living. I liked the idea of seeing how we could function together in a more neutral space before committing to marriage. Was it possible to get a sense of your life from a different vantage, like adjusting the aperture on a camera lens to allow additional light to pass through?

I said, "We have a year to add you to my insurance before COBRA runs out. What's your rush? Besides, I told you I don't want a big wedding. We can plan something simple for when we get back."

"Don't you think we should go all out? Thirty years we've been together. If that's not something to celebrate, I don't know what is. Why do you want to keep kicking the can down the road?"

I wasn't prepared to answer that question. "Grant, either you join me in the desert for the winter, or I'll go by myself."

"You'd really go without me?" he asked, visibly hurt.

"Honey, I would." I was surprised and frightened by the sureness of my answer.

I was determined to enjoy my sabbatical. More than ever, I wanted to punch beyond the boundaries of my life, have fun, and realize my unmet potential.

"It's just better there," Basil had said about Palm Springs. Those words floated around my brain like an airplane banner message pulling across the sky. What if there was an unequivocally *better* place to be than where we were? A less conventional life to have lived, a more natural habitat, a whole different set of decisions I could have made when I'd had my future in front of me?

Was it too late to start over?

Was it?

Chapter Three

Palm Springs
January 2, 2023
10:30 A.M.

The hot ranger with the thick black ponytail and body shaped by an active life took a seat at the outdoor table next to mine. I'd left Indian Canyons to get a jolt of caffeine. I needed something warm to drink, and the coffee shop offered an escape from all the commotion Hobie had created by starting the search, perhaps needlessly.

There wasn't much for me to do, anyway. Brady had ushered me out of the trailer. "It's not conducive for you to be in here," he said. "We see things a normal person doesn't see every day." He told me that, once, a young woman was waiting for news about her lost boyfriend when she'd overheard someone radio in that a body had been found. She thought her boyfriend was dead, only it turned out to be someone else's body, and the boyfriend was just fine.

But outside the trailer wasn't much better. Everyone was shouting into walkie-talkies, and helicopters took off and landed right next to me. I felt I needed to be there to stay near the action, but I also had a strong desire to leave in case the action was happening (to my mortification) entirely somewhere else.

The ranger's eyes were a secret, covered in sunglasses that wrapped around his head and shielded by the wide brim of his hat. To spend time in an area where so many people were protecting themselves from the outdoors was like attending a masquerade ball.

In my bucket hat and sunglasses, I could be anyone, so I decided to start a conversation. "I didn't realize it got so cold here." I shivered, wishing I'd brought my parka with me. A few months in Palm Springs had thrown my internal thermostat out of whack. What was warm before felt cold now; what was good before was bad now; what was normal before was strange; what struck me as benign was now terrifying.

The ranger seemed as if he wanted distraction as much as I did. His must be a lonely job—almost as lonely, I thought, as mine, which was waiting. "Looks like it's going to dip below freezing again tonight."

He said *freezing*, but I heard *hypothermia*. Just when I thought the cold was my biggest worry (of the moment), he added, "Big storms coming in a few days."

"Storms?"

"Don't you pay attention to the news?"

Grant *was* my news.

"Then again, I don't need a weatherman to tell me when we're about to get it. I can always feel the pressure drop, makes me tired. Thirsty, too. My sinuses act up. It's already starting."

"Back home, I notice that the birds fly low when the fronts come through," I said. "That's how I always know."

He nodded. "Atmospheric river, they call it. The Aleutian Flow. It's a big front coming across the Pacific. In a few days, the clouds are going to wring out like a giant sponge over the San Jacintos." He pointed up. The sky was the usual solid blue. "The thing about the weather here is it curls over the mountains. It could be bright and sunny when you start out, and suddenly it's snowing up there. I hear people say we don't have seasons in the desert, and I say they aren't paying attention." He took a sip of his coffee. "Take a picture of the same thing every time you hike, that's what I tell them. You'll see, it always looks different, every time you return to it. This place changes as much as anywhere."

"I heard a hiker went missing?" I played dumb, figuring he'd tell me more if he didn't know who I was.

"Yup. He's been gone longer than we like to see."

I wanted to ask, *What if it's all a mistake,* but I held myself back. Would we be charged for all the time and resources they were putting into the search if Grant were really just on a long drive back to Wisconsin? Then again, maybe he *was* lost, stranded just a few miles away from where we stood, but so turned around by the rocky sameness of the mountains that he couldn't get himself home.

I asked, "What do you think happened to him? The missing guy?"

"Could be anything. You've got people who get confused, and people who ain't right in the head to begin with. We just had one of those last year, some guy who convinced himself he was training for something, the military, special ops, who knows. We caught him a few times camping out and banned him from the reservation, but he came back again and again. Only the last time, he didn't make it."

I realized that the most thrilling part of this ranger's job was the worst-case scenario of my life. "We had a guy here last summer, twenty-five years old. Healthy. Strong. From somewhere in Europe. Two weeks before he was supposed to get married, he and his fiancée decided to go for a hike. She came back alone. A week later, I knew it wasn't good. I saw a redtail hawk making circles in the sky, and that's how we knew where to look. The hawks, they find the bodies before we do."

I tried to tell myself that these were stories that belonged to *other* people—someone else's demise, someone else's fear and agony, like reading the news. I couldn't stand the idea that Grant had left, maybe for good this time. But the more I learned about the dangers he could be facing if he was lost, the less I wanted to think he was still in the mountains.

"Do you think he'll be found?"

The ranger shrugged. "Sometimes they are." He paused. "And sometimes they come out in a body bag."

Did I wince? If so, he didn't notice. He was looking past me, at the mountains in the distance. It was his job to look.

"You'd be surprised how many people go missing. Lots of unidentified bodies turn up every year. All you've got to go on are fingerprints and dental records, DNA from a strand of hair, a facial composite from the CT of a crushed skull. Only a quarter of people who get lost can get out without needing to be rescued."

"That . . ." My voice choked. "That can't be right."

"We're used to navigating all kinds of tricky situations and dangers in life, big and small. That's what we humans do. But the decisions you make in the mountains aren't like any others you're ever faced with, and that's when you get into trouble. Do you go high to find a lookout, or go low? If you go off trail or the snow has covered it up, there's nothing to follow, just a lot of scrub that looks the same everywhere you turn. Makes some people crazy; they start to hallucinate. I've been on rescues where we find someone and the first thing we do is we try to see if they're alert and oriented."

He took a sip of his coffee. "They're scared when we find them. 'I'm freezing,' they say. 'No, it's one hundred degrees out.' They think their arm is broken and it's just fine. They don't even know their name. You try to help them, and sometimes they run from you. When you're faced with a stressful situation, your eyes will narrow to pinpricks. Your ears will close up. A regular person doesn't know how to respond to the stress of being lost—like, really lost."

I could feel my earlier optimism leak out of me. But then his tone softened. "You know, it's nice to remember that sometimes they do come out just fine. Last week a little boy disappeared. It was only twenty minutes or so, but—you got kids?"

"Two."

"Well then, you know. Remember when you were little yourself? You're hiding under the racks at the department store and you think you see your mama's legs, then they're gone, and you don't know where you are, and you melt down? That's why fairy tales are all about kids wandering into the forest and never coming back. Must have happened all the time in the old days. They'd get eaten by bears, carried away by crowned eagles or giant condors. The old-timers here talk about skin-walkers. They're like witches." He smiled to himself, and said, "That sure was nice, seeing that family reunite. Real nice."

I thought of the stories Grant's mother used to tell of the times he'd run away when he was a kid and how angry it would make her, but also how relieved she was when he'd come home. Once, when he was six, she'd gone on a bender and he bolted out of the house when she'd lost her temper with him, something that happened often after his dad died. That was a stressful period when she was young and had to work two jobs. She looked all over the neighborhood for Grant. When she returned home from her search, there he was, sound asleep in bed, his shoes still on, clutching the journal his concerned teacher had given him to help him work through his feelings after some outbursts at school.

"How come you don't think they've found that lost hiker yet?" I pressed.

He shrugged. "You want to know the truth?"

"Yeah." I needed to be leveled with.

"Because finding people is hard—especially those that don't want to be found."

I walked to the edge of the patio, leaned over, and worried I might throw up. The hum of conversation stopped. I could feel all the patrons looking at me.

"Oh no," he said. "Hey, are you—?"

I couldn't talk.

He walked over to where I stood and rubbed my back. "I sure am sorry. You should've told me you're the wife."

The wife.

"I didn't mean to scare you. Now, you listen, he's going to be okay, got that? We're going to find him. We're going to bring him home to you."

He crouched down next to me. "Shit, me and my big mouth. I had no idea that was your guy."

I wiped my eyes with the back of my sleeve. "Yes," I said, my voice cracking. "That's my guy." Married or not, Grant was mine. It was important for me to claim him.

Chapter Four

Madison, Wisconsin
November 2, 2022

Palm Springs seemed impossible to imagine from our Madison driveway. It was a crisp late-fall day. The sugar maple in the front yard had exploded into a crimson burst, and the leaves on the birch trees next to our house were mustard yellow. A squirrel scampered up the neighbor's white pine, which was still decorated for Halloween to look as if a witch had slammed into it, her broomstick and curled-toed boots strapped around the trunk.

The leaves were just beyond peak. One storm and they'd be gone, a canvas wiped clean. I thought that maybe it was better to leave when our world was still pretty and vibrant, to hold it that way in our memories.

The midterm election was coming, and all the yards in the neighborhood were studded with signs advertising the same Democratic candidates. As everyone here loves to say, Madison is ten square miles surrounded by reality, the border marked by little free lending libraries like Radio Free Europe. Soon Grant and I would exit our liberal bubble and enter an entirely different political landscape.

The northerly wind picked up as if to shoo us away. I shivered in the puffer that Dortie jokingly referred to as my "teacher recess coat." Just as Polly had insisted towels couldn't be both absorbent and plush ("You have to choose one or the other"), I'd learned that winterwear cannot be stylish *and* warm. I was practical to a fault; I chose warmth.

My whole body vibrated with the prospect of change, but Grant stood as though his feet were bolted into the driveway, with his hands tucked deep into the pockets of his baggy khakis. He had an odd love for old T-shirts and sweatshirts, which he wore until they gave out. Most had misshapen necklines and tattered hems. But that morning he wore the new camel-colored alpaca sweater Sasha had bought for his last birthday (I knew Sasha had spent almost two hundred dollars on the gift because she purposely left the price tag on—a jab, I was convinced, at my thriftiness, and to show that she spent more money on Grant than I did).

When Grant was nicely dressed, he could almost fool someone into thinking he groomed himself without needing to be nagged to cut his hair, shave the back of his neck, and tweeze his nose. Recently, his eyebrows had become alarming, like the woolly bear caterpillars that, when especially thick, supposedly foretold the severity of the coming winter. From the looks of it, I thought, it would be a bad one.

Grant had taken special care with his outfit that day because we'd planned to make a stop overnight in Omaha to see James, his old grad school friend. Grant wanted James to help him find a new job, although we both knew that it was virtually impossible for an older white philosophy professor to move into a tenured position; Grant would be lucky to become one of the exploited adjuncts he secretly used to look down on while claiming he was their advocate. As Grant's career counselor suggested, it was time to "pivot."

"Pivot?" he asked incredulously. "Pivot to what? An open grave?"

I gave Grant a loving nudge. "C'mon, G. let's get going."

"What's your hurry? We have all winter."

"It's Sally. I want to leave before she gets here."

Sally was on the board of Go Green, and she'd proposed that she and her husband rent our house while they remodeled their mansion in Nakoma. I didn't like the idea of someone else in our home, but how could I say no? It seemed incredibly wasteful for a house to sit empty for almost half a year—so wasteful it should be illegal.

I wanted someone there in case we had leaks or burst pipes. I could tell Sally thought that, with Grant out of a job, she was doing us a favor by paying rent, and she was.

Sally and her husband were also empty nesters. At a time when most of our friends were downsizing or divorcing, the Connors were undergoing huge cost and extreme inconvenience to add to their already-massive house in anticipation of grandchildren. I found this baffling. At this in-between stage of life, I didn't want *more* bathrooms to clean, and more unused rooms to gather dust and remind me of how empty our house had become. Our lives were finally manageable. We hardly ever ran out of toilet paper. The sink wasn't filled with dirty dishes. We didn't even have a dog to walk anymore. If anything, I felt we should downsize.

I worried that once Sally was settled, she would discover that the house I'd shown her when she came to check it out was a big lie. Before long, she'd notice the cracks in the walls and the dents in the molding. She'd find that the bathroom tub didn't drain well, the cabinet drawers got stuck, and the fireplace belched back smoke if you didn't first warm the flue. Would Sally disapprove of my dated choice of paint colors from twenty years ago, back when everyone painted the dining room red, before that dreary, agreeable HGTV *greige* became all the rage? I suddenly worried that the pillows needed to be replaced. I'd read that an old pillow can contain over a million fungal spores. Was it possible that some of our pillows were as old as some of our spices? And why did I care so much what Sally thought? Didn't she, too, have old pillows? Don't we all?

Grant fixed his gaze on the jagged roofline of our old Frankenstein's monster of a house that had started out as a hunting lodge at the turn of the century and had been insulated and added on to at various times, most recently (and unfortunately) in the seventies. Aside from the stone fireplace, millwork, and some old light fixtures, little of the original charm remained, and repairs were never straightforward. Still, it was mine. I knew it like I knew my own body. Blindfolded, I could navigate every hallway, light switch, and footfall.

"It's just a house," I said, sounding a lot like Polly, who had a gift for flattening emotion. She once told me that the idea of home is really just a fantasy. When I prepared our space for Sally and her husband, I finally understood what Polly had meant. I could see the house for the first time as a jumble of plumbing, wood, electricity, shingles, plaster, and drywall—a space that was incredibly intimate to me, yet someone else could inhabit it or even tear it down and start fresh. The dream I'd had twenty-five years ago when we'd moved in was to raise our children here, and we'd done that. I no longer knew what I wanted from the house, except that it seemed wrong and indulgent for two people to take up so much space.

Grant sucked in a deep breath of the crisp air. "I don't know why we're leaving during the best time of year." Like most academics, Grant thought of fall as a new beginning infused with a fresh syllabus, nervous energy, and an explosion of pheromones. That's why he especially loved the season (he could make the word *autumnal* sound natural in conversation). It was plain to see how much it pained him to be away from the Midwest, and especially the college, when the campus almost looked as if it could be in New England.

Like my father, I sometimes struggled with the winter darkness. Burl would slip into brief eddies of depression when the cold weather set in, and the life was sucked out of the camp. He'd despair when it was time to haul the sailboats into storage and pull the canvas tight over the screen windows in the cabins. Fall was the dreaded harbinger of another fallow winter. But summer? That was when all the cells in my body, and Burl's, exploded to life. I couldn't imagine anything better than experiencing summer all year long, which, for me, was the promise of Palm Springs.

Our neighbor Trent, a professor at the Nelson Institute at UW who also served on the board of Go Green, rode past on his racing bike, vacuum sealed in his Lycra cycling suit. He waved and shouted, "Yo, Grant! Sorry about the college, buddy."

"*Yo?*" Grant said as soon as Trent was out of earshot. "*Buddy?* What does he think I am, some little kid he's going to take fishing?"

I liked Trent, even if Grant did not. Trent had an alarming laugh that sounded like a lawn mower when you pulled the crank. We cracked jokes when we sat next to each other at board meetings, and he'd volunteered to serve as the fast-talking auctioneer at the annual fundraiser at Monona Terrace that I helped organize. At the last event a few months earlier, I'd let it slip that Grant and I weren't actually married, and Trent's attitude toward me changed. I could tell that he thought this made me fair game (most people mistakenly assumed we'd remained unmarried because we had an open relationship). He texted the next day to say he couldn't stop thinking about me. I was flattered and shocked. It had been a while since a man my own age had looked at me with an expression that said something other than *Don't get your hopes up, lady.*

I didn't respond to Trent's text. I found the thought of an affair interesting, but two men in my life sounded impossible and wrong, not to mention exhausting. Although now that Grant was again pushing to get married, I occasionally found myself idly wondering if I was better off on my own, or if Trent, or anyone else, would bring out a side of me that Grant couldn't. I didn't usually indulge these thoughts because commitment is one of my core values. Besides, secrets were things I didn't want to live with. Grant and I had made it clear from the beginning that we needed to be faithful to each other—with or without a ring. We had a pact to be honest, no matter what. It was bad enough that Grant took off on occasion; I didn't need to worry that he was with another woman.

Grant squinted at the back of Trent's colorful cycling jersey until he was too tiny to see. "What a blowhard. He's always bragging about his 'well-endowed' chair."

It was hard for Grant to live in a town that housed the same world-class research institution that had turned him down for a full-time job after he'd finished his postdoc there almost two decades earlier. That's how he ended up on the faculty of a liberal arts school with an unfortunate name: College of the Mounds. Even though it was less prestigious than UW and the commute was over an hour from Madison, it turned out to be a better fit because Grant was the kind of person who thrived on being, as he put it, 'a big whale in a small cog." Mounds was one of the oldest colleges in the Midwest, and he loved it there, although he felt he needed to make excuses for the school, describing it to his University of Chicago grad school friends as "the Harvard of the Midwest," leaving out that it sat downwind from a massive livestock facility. He often touted its rankings in the *U.S. News* "Best Colleges" issue, where it had been recognized in minor categories, such as "social mobility" and "undergraduate creative projects."

I'd always dreamed of having a family all in one place after shuttling between Burl and Polly, but when Grant was offered the job at Mounds, we decided that it would be best if he avoided the daily commute and spent most weekdays during the school year in a modest apartment. Time and time again he pushed for us to relocate with him, but I refused, arguing that I loved Madison, and I didn't want to uproot the girls. The truth was, I found the central part of the state depressing, as though a permanent cloud had settled over it. Mounds had never fully recovered after getting its teeth kicked in during the Great Recession. The biggest business was a feed mill. There were some nice old houses left over from its glory days, a few cute shops, and a farmers' market, but Grant saw the place through his pink lenses, referring to it as the Bedford Falls of the Midwest.

I suppose I could have learned to love Mounds, too. But I couldn't bring myself to relocate for a man who might up and leave. To be fair, it had only happened a handful of times, but a handful of times is all it takes for you to know, on a gut level, that the rug can be pulled out from under you when you least expect it.

The girls were blissfully unaware of these blips in our relationship. They were used to Grant being away at the college; it was all they knew. With the constraints of domestic life lifted during the week, Grant approached his "professoring" with gusto. He advised students and attended colloquia and lacrosse games. He went to concerts, dance performances, talks. He chaired committees and organized the annual philosophy symposia. Once he became more involved in the administration, he attended evening fundraisers and met with donors, alumni, and the board. He ditched his big sweaters and wore a pullover embossed with the college's quirky mascot, the spiny hodag, a fictional animal from folklore that was supposedly formed from the ashes of cremated oxen.

While Grant was in Mounds, I worked and took care of the house and the kids. I attended band rehearsals and forensic debates. I packed lunches, shopped for groceries, wiped up the spills, and taught the girls to be resilient when their friends were mean. Grant would return home for the weekends like a king sitting at a buffet, the girls out of their minds with excitement. He'd say, "It's good to be home," and although I was always glad to see him, his chaos made me also want to scream.

I was naive to think that our nontraditional relationship would level the playing field; instead, I found our division of labor was just as uneven as it was for my married friends. Grant got to be the fun parent, while my "shift" (I knew I shouldn't think of it as a shift) was bogged down with logistics and chores.

By the time the weekends rolled around I was exhausted and handed everything off to him. Grant loved being a dad. He took the girls to campus to see films and talks. He'd espouse wisdom on walks through the Arboretum and sometimes surprise Dort and March with a trip to the indoor trampoline park he loved to hate. I was freed up to take yoga, go to book club and meditation groups, and see friends who were jealous of our arrangement. In their eyes, I'd figured out the hard stuff: I had the commitment of a marriage and the freedom of a divorcée.

I'd visited Grant at the college many times. There, I felt lucky to bear witness to the most fully realized version of the man I'd fallen for. Grant was completely at home among all the historic and severely neglected buildings. He was full of purpose, doing what he loved, surrounded by his people. Although the politics of academia frustrated him, his work was generally filled with variety, rigor, and challenge. He walked around campus in his battered suede shoes, waving at adoring students and stopping to chat with his colleagues under the scraggly oak trees. He'd occasionally look skyward at the Cooper's hawks in their nests and lift the binoculars that perpetually hung around his neck to get a better view. It was quaint, though I found it odd to obsess over a species you wouldn't want to see near your bird feeder. Hawks can be vicious. They hunt songbirds and small animals and snap their skulls with their sharp middle talons.

Dortie had been a student at Mounds to take advantage of the free tuition benefit extended to the children of faculty members. Unfortunately, March was not as practical as her sister; she went to Vanderbilt, where she would have racked up college loans if Grant's mother hadn't stepped in to help with tuition. March joined a sorority and began to fancy herself a Southern belle. She wore white gloves to football games, her hair hung in Utah curls, and she started to speak with a fake accent that made us cringe, saying *y'all* and referring to trucks as eighteen-wheelers.

The "freaks and geeks" vibe of Mounds was a better fit for Dort, with her bleached pixie-cut hair and nose ring, and she was always happiest when she was close to her dad. Because Dort wasn't far from home, I was able to see her often, going to her dance performances and improv shows. I helped Dort move from her dorm room into a series of musty off-campus apartments so run-down that I literally cried at the thought of my child living in squalor, with centipedes crawling up the shower drain and mice brazenly scampering out of the heating ducts at night, while March lived in a plantation-style sorority house that smelled like Kate Spade perfume.

The last time I visited Mounds, I witnessed how much the place had changed. Enrollments were low and Grant's colleagues were tense, which is what happens when people operate in an environment where everyone fights over scarce resources, a situation I was familiar with after working for fledgling organizations over the years. Vacated positions were left unfilled. The supply cabinet was empty. The department's admin assistant had been let go—all that remained of Cherise was the Post-it note she'd left hanging on the mirror in the copy room that said PROFESSORS: CHECK YOUR TEETH.

The college had changed, and so, too, had the world. Grant was desperate for his students to experience the magic of his own formative undergraduate years, but many were too glued to their devices to want to stay up into the small hours talking about the meaning of life. He was fond of the Socratic teaching style, which revealed that students didn't know what they thought they knew. This didn't appeal to the newest generation of young adults. He wasn't afraid to call out his colleagues, who he believed shared the same basic political views but split hairs over the finer points of their ideals. What was once inoffensive, even expected, now could get him into trouble with the department chair and the dean.

Grant often complained to me about the latest campus dustup. When I accused him of being difficult in order to get attention, he said, "Why does everyone want me to just be the guy in the corner reading Aristotle?"

And now the college was shuttered, and Grant was home all the time. We weren't comfortable with each other. I began to feel as if we needed to choose between two options I found equally hard to fathom: to be fully together—or apart.

A red leaf from the maple landed at Grant's feet. He looked as if he was about to cry. His nostalgia made him sad, and too much sadness, or too much of any emotion, could be destabilizing. I tried to coax him with my smile. "Honey, we're going to have the best time. I just know it."

He walked to the driver's side of our Prius and hesitated before getting in, a meaningful pause before our big adventure. I liked to think we were different from everyone else in Madison, but the bumper revealed how we fit in. Each family member had carte blanche to attach any stickers to it that they wanted, just as I'd allowed the girls to color with crayons all over the basement walls when they were little. I wanted to offer them freedom of expression. Now, the bumper was plastered with the names of every liberal presidential, judicial, and senatorial candidate from the past decade, stacked one on top of the other like annual vehicle-registration tags. We had stickers that said RECALL SCOTT WALKER, "COEXIST," a magnet from my yoga studio, the local theater, Go Green, and every organization I'd ever worked at. Grant contributed the Darwin fish feet, and he'd made sure that the College of the Mounds decal strategically overlapped the Vanderbilt logo. The Prius was part of our family, a visual history of our personalities, causes, and the dents and scrapes from when the girls learned how to drive. Because it had been Grant's trusty commuter car, it had some cracks in the windshield and a ton of miles.

In Madison we might have fit in, but would we drive into Palm Springs like a modern-day version of the Clampetts? I worried we could be wrong for a fancy and glamorous town—from what I could tell from my research deep dive, it was a retreat for boho chic TikTok girls and rich fun-seekers like Basil, who flitted from place to place. He owned homes in New York, San Francisco, Majorca. I was no stranger to feeling like an outsider, only this was far outside my usual life.

Once we were in the car, Grant said, "I still don't know why we're spending the winter in Palm Springs."

"I don't know why we wouldn't. Basil's offer to stay in his place is incredibly generous."

Grant groaned. "Why do you pronounce his name *Ba-zille*? It's Basil, like the herb. You're still hung up on him, aren't you?"

"Look at you and Sasha! You call each other a hundred times a day."

"Not anymore. Now she has Matthias. Besides, Sasha is just Sasha. But Basil, he's so famous, he's so talented, he's so funny, he's so successful. Let's watch the Tony Awards and—wow! There he is! *Baaz-uuul Underwood.*"

"Grant, we were married for about five minutes. He's my dear friend. He's your friend, too. He loves you."

"He says I'm *quirky*. Right to my face, he says that."

"But you are! Look, you're wearing one brown and one black shoe."

He glanced at his feet in front of the pedals, smiled, and shrugged.

California was two thousand miles and thirty hours away. We'd need a car, and we couldn't fly such a long distance since Grant was prone to blood clots. After a rare trip to Mexico a decade earlier, he'd ended up in the hospital with a pulmonary embolism the day after we returned home. Since then, we hadn't ventured much farther than Nashville to visit March, Chicago for "museum vacations," and a bus trip to visit every Great Lake within twenty-four hours as part of a fundraiser for Go Green.

I overpacked because it was hard to anticipate our needs for that long a stretch, and because we come from a place where layering is second nature. It is not unusual in the Midwest for the temperature to swing forty degrees in a day, so I never trusted the weather or that we had the right kind of (or enough) clothes. Because we didn't travel much, the giant suitcases Melody and Vandyke had given Basil and me for our wedding over thirty years ago were in almost new condition. Grant set them on the bottom of the trunk, with duffel bags on top for our overnight stays. My clothes were neatly folded into packing cubes, while he'd packed his duffel so carelessly that it wouldn't shut. His journal poked out of the top.

The back seat was a jumble of pillows, a cordless back massager, sunscreen, and trail mix I'd bought at the Willy Street Co-op, where, every Saturday in the summer in the parking lot, the staff used to act out the comment cards with sock puppets. Grant didn't care for healthy snacks; he insisted we should stop on the road. He loved any excuse to eat junk, even though he was getting a dad belly and his doctor said his cholesterol was "concerning."

Our bushes scratched the sides of our car as Grant backed out of the driveway. Before we got to the street, I saw Sally and her husband in their Tesla, waiting to pull into the driveway.

I rolled down the window, waved, and shouted, "Enjoy the house!" in my most cheerful voice, suddenly finding it hard to think of home as a thing to be enjoyed.

"Did you hear about Vic?" Sally asked.

"Another bike accident?" The executive director of Go Green was Madison's version of Ralph Nader. The organization ran mostly on Vic's reputation as a youthful, feisty and ferocious campaigner for the environment. He biked everywhere and was famous for his frequent accidents. His office was decorated with what he considered badges of honor: bent bike wheels with spokes sticking out in all directions and a twisted handlebar mounted to the wall like deer antlers. He staged dramatic protests at the capitol, where he behaved like a teenage boy, jumping on the table during legislative meetings, undercutting the important and serious work we were doing. He was what we called an "idea hamster," coming up with a million things for us to do but lacking the patience and commitment to follow through. After six years at Go Green, I'd had enough of Vic, and my job, and, frankly, the idea of work in general.

"Google it," Sally said. "It's the lead story in *The Cap Times*."

I was officially on sabbatical. What happened at the office was no longer of concern to me.

Grant was a good, if absentminded, driver. I always loved the sight of his strong hands on the steering wheel, and I liked his face in pro-file, even if it was marred by the thickness of his glasses. Without his eyewear, it was easier to see the features that had drawn me to him initially. He had a confident nose and a clean, if softening, jawline.

When we'd first fallen in love, I'd reach over and nuzzle him as he drove, grab him, try to make him crazy enough to pull over and find an abandoned parking lot or a remote dirt road where we could screw around. I wanted to absorb him into my being, merge into a single entity. My attraction to him was still there, but it felt much less urgent.

I settled into my seat, connected my phone to the car stereo, and scrolled around for something we could agree to listen to. Grant liked podcasts with conservative philosophers, not because he agreed with them, but because he found their ideas challenging and provocative, and he wants to flex his arguing skills by understanding how other people think. That was fine for his commute, but I'd heard enough about Hegel. I also didn't want to listen to the old jazz Grant liked—not because I didn't enjoy it, but because Grant wanted everyone to appreciate his knowledge of the form. He'd snap his fingers, hum along, and make funny noises with his tongue. March could do a great Grant impression. "That sure is some refined articulation of the snare," she'd say.

I loved dance music, but Grant made a point of disliking anything popular, and he insisted that he hated the sound of the synth. I hit the preset button for WPR instead, and we listened to *Simply Folk*.

"Octavia thinks this trip will be good for us," I said.

He snorted. "What does Octavia know? Didn't you say she's at that nudist colony in Viroqua? And poor Brian has become that divorced guy straight out of central casting. The Apple Tree condos are so depressing. He eats Hungry-Man dinners now. His freezer is stuffed with them."

"He's a big boy. He can learn to cook." I sounded just like Polly when I said that.

Octavia had left Brian a year ago and embraced singleness with frightening zest. She got a boob job, froze her muffin top with CoolSculpting, and told me about a torturous facial she'd had called microneedling. Octavia was pro-collagen, pro-vagina, pro-sensuality. She'd slept with a twenty-two-year-old Pakistani graduate student, then started up a "thing" with her UPS driver. Her latest love interest was a jujitsu teacher named Greta, whom she'd met at karaoke night.

Octavia was suddenly like a teenage girl, her appetite for intimacy and adventure so voracious that her numerous exploits became almost boring to listen to. But among all her talk of ritualizing sex and the perfect lube (she was obsessed with all the various properties of the product—sticky, wet, slippery, tacky, smoothing, cooling, heating, lubricating), Octavia said something that really got stuck in my brain: that the only thing worse than letting a good relationship die is letting a bad one go on forever.

I said to Grant, "If we're going to get married—"

"*If?* What's with the supposition?"

"Okay, *when.*"

"Is this a winter test that I have to pass before you'll marry me?"

I wasn't prepared to answer that question head-on. "I just think we have some work to do, Grant. We're not exactly in the best place."

"Peaks and valleys." This was the sum total of the philosopher's thoughts. He didn't want to try counseling. He believed our relationship had its own velocity—that we'd been in valleys before, and we'd somehow powered our way back to the peaks. As far as Grant was concerned, we were a constant. Our relationship didn't need work; the trick was to wait out the rough spots. "We're basically married anyway. Nothing will change, except I'll be on your insurance."

"Are you listening to yourself? That's the problem, Grant. I don't want us to be *basically married.* I want us to be *better.* We're not used to being together all the time and it's . . . weird."

"You know what this is really about?"

"What?"

"You're afraid."

"Afraid of what, exactly?"

He looked at me and grinned. "Me."

He wasn't wrong.

"We don't have to be like Polly and Burl, you know. We can live in the same city, the same house even. We can be a normal couple. We can finally be *us*."

That was the problem—I wasn't sure what *us* meant after so much time apart. I said, "We'll be together all winter. I think this adventure is going to be amazing."

"Does this really qualify as an adventure? It's fairly conventional to spend a winter away. If you can afford it, that is. We pretty much know exactly what to expect. Sun, palm trees, a pool, old people in golf carts . . ."

"Warmth."

"The cold reminds you that you're alive."

"So did my broken ankle, and my bunion. And my dislocated shoulder." I said the last part with extra emphasis.

"Isn't it shallow to want to go somewhere just because of the weather?"

"Shallow?" I groaned. "I'm tired of shoveling and scraping ice off the windshield with a credit card. The wind feels like rocks in my face."

"I like the cold. I mean, I don't just like it, I love it. My spirit animal is a Siberian husky."

"My spirit animal is a lizard, basking in the sun." We'd just left home, and already I felt an argument coming on. "Grant, I hate winter. I mean, I really, really hate it. Doesn't it matter to you that all these years I've been miserable?"

Hadn't he seen me walking around the house in my fuzzy wearable blanket? Hadn't he seen my face lit up by my happy lamp in the depths of February? "It's not safe. Remember your accident? The Civic looked like an accordion. It's a miracle you survived without a scratch."

"That was a long time ago."

"You know what?" I was feeling more passionate about this subject than ever. "I'd be fine if I never saw another snowflake for the rest of my life." I tried to put a positive lilt in my voice so we wouldn't fight. "Maybe you'll discover that you like escaping the cold. Look at all the celebrities who go to Palm Springs. Leonardo DiCaprio, Brad Pitt . . ."

"Ooh, Brad Pitt. Whoop-de-doo."

"I'm just saying."

"And I'm just saying that I don't know why you're making me go to the desert."

"You could have stayed back. It was your choice to say no."

"Not if I wanted to be with you."

"That's how I ended up in Wisconsin for the last three decades, to be with *you*. Is it really such a big sacrifice to spend one winter away?"

Living in Madison had been our first big compromise; I'd always dreamed of leaving the Midwest, believing there was a different life for me somewhere else. But then I met Grant at a party, and we were one. I didn't hesitate to follow him to UW–Madison when he got his postdoc, and besides, what was I going to do? I was pregnant. My only stipulation came a few years later when he was offered his job in Mounds. That was a bridge too far.

"You made a voluntary decision to come to Palm Springs. Would you please stop talking about me like I'm a dominatrix?"

"Dominatrix? Talk dirty to me." He grinned.

"Why can't you be more open to this?"

"What do you mean? I'm open enough. Look at me, I'm driving halfway across the country because you asked me to."

"And complaining the whole time."

He grabbed my hand and gave it a squeeze. "I'm sorry." Grant was like our dog Milky, who would cover his eyes with his paws whenever he did something bad; it was impossible to stay mad at him.

I said, "Don't you think we deserve this? We've worked our whole lives. You've devoted yourself to education, and I've devoted myself to every good cause imaginable."

"Nobody 'deserves' anything. Listen to you, spouting off like Herbert Spencer."

"Herbert Spencer?" I was afraid to ask because his explanation could become long-winded, but then again, we would be in the car for days.

"He famously coined the phrase *survival of the fittest* and championed laissez-faire economics. With your ideas about your right to pursue happiness, you're well on your way to becoming one of the libertarians you despise."

I hated being lectured by him and he knew it, but he couldn't help himself. Grant's mother had doted excessively on him as an adolescent to make up for the horrible mistreatment he'd suffered from his father as a child, and the guilt she felt over her own problems with neglect and addiction before she cleaned up. Mitzie set her mind to making things right. She married Stew, the wealthiest and most bland second husband she could find. Once she had the means, she determined that the right way to raise a boy was to make sure that he became a great student and grew up to be successful at school and work. Everything else was taken care of for him. She loved to show Grant off to the new friends she'd made when she'd become a country club wife. He wasn't afraid to look adults in the eye and challenge their ideas. He had a terrific memory and could banter about any topic, often taking controversial positions just to get a reaction.

He said, "You know, helping Basil's mother could be a pretty significant catch. Friendly reminder: you called Melody a 'walking migraine.' Your words."

"Grant, I think we need this change."

"Oh, man, there's been enough change in my life." He shifted into his professor voice, as he was inclined to do when he was emotionally uncomfortable. "Besides, we change our reality by changing our mind."

"Please don't quote Plato."

"How about Shakespeare?" We were passing Verona, a town Grant could never go through without saying, in his loudest, most dramatic voice, "'Two households, both alike in dignity, / In fair Verona, where we lay our scene. . . .'"

"I knew you were going to say that."

He reached for my hand. "And I knew you were going to tell me not to. I love you, Kimmy. Marry me."

"Maybe."

We were heading into the hilly Driftless region, the only part of the state that hadn't been flattened by a glacier during the Ice Age. Grant was originally from the northern suburbs of Virginia. He came to love rural Wisconsin in a way that only someone who wasn't from there could love it—he was always taking photographs of quaint red barns and cropping them to hide the political signs, manure piles, and ugly lawn ornaments. It was as if he were trying to convince himself that it was okay, and even cool, to live in a place that people from the coasts considered insignificant.

He continued, "We're too young for Palm Springs. That's the kind of place you go when you retire."

Retirement? That wasn't a thing for him; he'd never thought much about what old age would look like, planning instead to limp along with emeritus status until his demise. "Old professors never die," Grant would joke. "They just lose their faculties."

A jolt of fear ripped through me when Grant said that word. *Other* people retired. *Old* people retired. We were still young, weren't we? Then I felt a surge of pain at my surgical site and wondered if Grant had remembered to take his blood thinner.

Young*ish*?

The landscape flattened. The cornfields were reduced to stubs. We passed cars and trucks, on-ramps and off-ramps, budget hotels and truck stops, joining the miasma of people who were between here and there.

For years, I was made to feel guilty if I wasn't at home taking care of the kids and the house. I had to remind myself that at this stage in life, nobody would really care that much that we were gone. Lots of people do this. It wasn't against the law to leave, but it sure felt like it.

Chapter Five

Palm Springs
January 3, 2023
6:00 A.M.

I don't think Hobie ever slept. When I opened the door and saw him waiting for me, he looked like a burglar with his black beanie on his head, dressed for hiking. The air was crisp and the sky was still dark. He led me to his car in the parking lot. It was a Toyota Corolla from the eighties that wouldn't start unless he hit the engine with a brick, making a sound that went straight to my already-jangled nerves.

"He's fine, right? It's been two nights and two whole days now." Only once before had Grant ever been gone this long, and that time I knew where he was.

"That's a long time, but survivable," Hobie said.

That word, *survivable,* swirled around in my head.

"Thing is, the cold might not be the thing that gets him in the end. You can trip your mind into thinking you're going to die. It's easy to say you're not okay, to panic yourself to death. Fear can kill you before anything else does."

Hobie was the best and worst possible person to be with during a crisis. On the one hand, as an occasional volunteer with the Palm Springs Mounted Police, he knew the mountains better than almost anyone else, and he was committed to searching for Grant nonstop. On the other, he always said whatever was on his mind and seemed incapable of recognizing boundaries. At least now I understood he wasn't being malicious; he just couldn't help himself.

"I think today's the day they're going to find him," I said, trying to stay positive. "I have a hunch."

"He shouldn't have left without me. If I was with him, this never would have happened. Hell, I never should have taken him hiking in the first place."

"No, you brought Grant back to life. It was wonderful to see him passionate about something again."

"Passionate? You'd think I dipped the guy in holy water."

We drove past the mid-century modern homes in Canyon Estates, with their breeze-blocks and painted doors. It was the kind of neighborhood that could make you believe there was order in the universe.

Hobie continued, "I keep trying to remember how much I'd taught him before he started going out there without me. Did I tell him to find the rivers and roads? Did I remind him to pack matches? I know I didn't teach him how to make a fire, and he's no Eagle Scout, that's for damn sure. He's probably rubbing two sticks together at this very moment wondering why nothing happens. Starting a friction fire is a royal pain in the ass." Hobie took a sip of coffee from his thermos. "If he drinks the water, he could have giardia. That's a nasty little bug. Even if he's found, I'm just warning you, could be months before he's off the toilet."

The woman who worked at the entrance gate to Indian Canyons knew who we were by then. She checked our IDs because she had to and waved us in, her expression filled with pity. We parked behind the trailer, and Hobie reached into the back seat for his pack. "I've got extras of everything. Extra food, extra water, an extra headlamp. Portable charger."

I gave his hand a squeeze. "I can't thank you enough."

"Usually, I hike just to hike. Now I'm hiking with a purpose."

We walked into the command center as if we were about to punch the clock at work. I felt like the only woman in the men's locker room. Brady and a few trained volunteers were sticking thumbtacks into a giant map on the wall. They gestured for Hobie to confer with them while I stood by, useless. "Think he might have found the old switchback trail on the desert side? The one that hooks up to the PCT?"

One of the rescuers pointed at another part of the map. "We already checked the north side over here."

"How about going with us in the chopper?" Brady asked Hobie. "Thought we'd circle around, see what we see."

I stepped forward. "The chopper? Can I go?" I wanted a different vantage, wanted to be helpful. Besides, if anyone could spot Grant from a distance, it was me. He had a distinctive walk, a certain way of holding his shoulders.

"We need you to stay right here," Brady said firmly. "Promise me you won't go looking for him. One needle in a haystack is enough." I'd heard a lot about needles and haystacks since Grant went missing. I could just imagine Grant lecturing the rescuers about their need for new idioms.

"Don't worry." I pointed at my foot. "I had surgery. My foot is better but I'm still not ready for hiking. I also hurt my shoulder, but it's fine now."

"Your shoulder? When did that happen?" Brady seemed suspicious that Grant had done something to me, or that perhaps I'd hurt myself while trying to hide a dead body. He must have seen everything in his line of work. Anyone and everyone can be a suspect, even nice middle-aged white women from Wisconsin. A part of me loved being thought of as dangerous.

"I tripped on a rug. A few months ago."

"That so?" He eyed me skeptically, sensing that I had complicated feelings about my accident. "Do you want to tell me about that?"

"I just fell." I shook my head. "People fall all the time."

"And they get lost all the time, too. That's why I have job security."

Did Brady think that I had something to do with Grant's going missing? Did Brady think I'd messed with Grant's compass magnet or poked holes in his water bottle? Or—a new thought occurred to me—was I supposed to be hysterical? Was that how Brady thought wives were supposed to react? I did feel hysterical, actually, but I was hysterical on the inside. Brady couldn't know that; half the time even Grant couldn't tell how I was really feeling—I made sure of it.

Before I could explain any of this, Brady led me out of the trailer, reminding me I was an interloper. Outside, the sky was already lighter. A new day. It was still so cool we could see our breath in the morning air. The chopper was waiting.

"Did you find the car yet?"

"No, but that doesn't mean much. Cars get stolen all the time when they're parked by the trails, which is why you never leave anything inside. But regardless, an old truck like that is easy to hot-wire. There's a pipeline from here to Mexico. It's probably been painted black and had the bumpers stripped off it by now."

Hobie and some other rescuers ran to the helicopter. The blades began to spin wildly. The sound was deafening, but Brady kept talking. I missed half of what he'd said.

"—we have to track them based on what we know about how their mind works. I'm sure he knows the best thing to do when you're lost is to stay in place. You think he'd do that? Just wait to be found?"

"No. He'd keep going."

What I didn't tell Brady was that Grant always came back, eventually, although I'd sometimes worried that he wouldn't. That sometimes, I'd even wished it.

I imagined what Polly would say, if she were still alive. "This is why I told you to live your life on your own terms, Kim. You don't need to put up with this shit. Why do you think I stayed single?"

My former mother-in-law pulled up in her Jaguar. I worried that her car would give Brady the idea that we were extremely rich. When we'd first arrived, Grant would park by the Walmart near the airport and count the private jets that landed and took off in an hour. "This isn't a place where money is made," he'd said. "It's a place where money is spent."

Melody emerged, looking grand in her Russian Cossack hat and fur coat. She pulled a foldout table out of the trunk of her car and two chairs. She shouted, "Today, Kimberly, I will teach you how to play mah-jongg. You won't make it in Palm Springs unless you learn. Come." She patted the chair. "Let's arrange your tiles."

"It's not even seven in the morning."

Brady started walking away from us. He held his walkie-talkie in his hand the way teenagers hold their cell phones, as if it were part of his body. I began to panic. "But . . . But . . . Brady!" I called. "I want to *do* something. Anything. I can't just sit here and play a stupid game while Grant is in trouble."

The older woman looked at me with irritation. "Tell me, if this game is stupid, why was it banned in China for forty years?"

Brady clearly found Melody amusing. She cut quite a figure in all that fur, pushing tiles around a makeshift table with her long, elegant index finger, the mountains behind her, fiddling while Rome burns.

Brady said, "I know you want to help, Mrs. Duffy, but there's nothing for you to do. You may as well play a game if it keeps your mind off things. Just stay where I can find you. Here, or at home. Make sure your phone stays charged at all times. Now, if you'll excuse me, I need to get going so this search doesn't turn from a rescue into a recovery."

Melody chattered about the game to keep me distracted. I recognized this was an act of kindness, but I couldn't process what she was saying about jokers, flowers, winds, and dragons. I only heard her mention good luck and bad, and the strategic removal of matched pairs.

She said, "We have much to learn. Come. You must first sit in an auspicious direction."

I sat looking at the mountain, hoping I would see Grant climbing down.

She frowned. "Oh no, sit over there instead. This is no good."

"Why?"

She began sorting tiles. They made a wonderful sound clicking together, a sound that became spooky when she said, "You're looking west. West means two things: heaven, or death."

Chapter Six

Palm Springs
Friday, November 4, 2022

The Prius died in the middle of the Mojave Desert—it was a *real* desert, the kind I thought only existed in movies, like the old John Wayne westerns I used to watch with Burl when I was a girl.

The temperature hovered above 105 degrees—I could actually see the heat. But even with the abrupt end of air-conditioning, I couldn't really feel it at first, in the same way that, after taking the polar-bear plunge into Lake Mendota on a subzero January morning with my friends, I didn't truly sense the cold until the shock wore off.

Grant tried one last time to turn over the engine. Nothing. Exasperated, he slapped the dashboard and said, "Well, I guess every car turns into a shit can eventually."

This startled me. It was unlike Grant to curse—he thought swearing was lazy and verbally reckless, and he worried that if he swore in conversation, he'd start to swear in front of impressionable young undergrads.

Smoke hovered over the hood. "It probably needs a small repair," I said. In our relationship, it was my role to be hopeful, and his role to see the world as it was.

"Nah, it's dead. Put a fork in it."

I stared at our surroundings. This was what rural Wisconsin would look like after the apocalypse. Aside from a single pink flip-flop by the side of the road and some tire skims, there were few signs of human habitation. What looked like the rocky tips of stubbly ancient mountaintops emerged from the endless sea of sagebrush and sand. A few reptilian-looking Joshua trees grew miraculously out of a bed of rocks and dirt.

When Grant called for emergency road service, they said it would be over an hour for the tow truck to arrive. Reception was bad, and our phone batteries were low because the cigarette-lighter charger had stopped working years ago, just one of many broken things in our lives, like the missing closet doorknob and the busted ice maker.

Grant, shaking his head in disbelief, said, "You really let our AAA membership expire?"

"Octavia said they funded conservative political candidates."

"Did you guys even bother to check if this was true?"

I hadn't.

"You're always complaining about cancel culture, and look at you. A cut-from-the-cloth Madison liberal."

"At least I don't spend all my time going on and on about the problem of 'other minds.' That's all you and James talked about in Omaha. You acted like I wasn't even there at dinner while you had your little 'salon.'"

"It's impossible to act like you aren't there," Grant said. "You made sure of that when you sent back not one but *two* glasses of wine."

"The first glass had a chip on the rim. Did you want me to cut my lip? And the second glass was watered down."

"Nobody watered down your wine. That's the most paranoid thing you've ever said."

"Unlike you, I've worked in the service industry. I know what goes on behind the bar."

We weren't really fighting, and we weren't truly mad at each other, but our banter always had a dangerous edge, especially lately. Our relationship felt like a Jenga tower that was built out of both love and resentment. One small insult, one uncomfortable truth spoken aloud, and we could precariously wobble and come crashing down.

"You know what your problem is?" he asked.

"Oh, *I* have a problem?"

"You rely too much on luck. Luck is a perverse form of optimism."

"Don't turn this on me. You're the one who didn't want to stop for gas." Grant had said we'd be fine, not knowing that we were about to encounter almost a hundred miles without a place to charge or refuel. We had no idea there were still such long stretches without civilization in the United States. I'd hit the scan button on the radio and the dial just slid across the screen. If we hadn't coasted downhill almost the entire time, we would have gotten into trouble in the middle of Utah instead of here, which, I reasoned, would have been worse, because it was dark in Utah, and at least, in the middle of the day, we could be seen.

Suddenly I was overcome, unable to tell if the heat was getting to me or if I was having a hot flash—or both. I tore off my T-shirt and sat in my bra, drenched. My "personal summers," as Octavia called them, had become normal for Grant, who was used to my sudden disrobing. It was amazing how comfortable we'd become with each other. In our early days, I'd spend forever in the shower primping and preening for Grant. Now I sat next to him shirtless, unselfconscious about the extra flesh on my stomach rolling over my waistband, drenched in sweat. I couldn't imagine ever achieving this level of comfort with another man, and I treasured it. He'd bought me a mini-fan to plug into my phone—a joke gift, but one that I appreciated. I turned it on at that moment, not caring if it drained what little remained of my battery.

"Just going out on a limb here, Kimmy, but if hot flashes are a problem for you, why would you want to live in this heat?"

"It won't be this hot for long. Basil said it even gets cold in Palm Springs."

"But isn't cold what you're trying to escape? Don't you think this is a sign we should turn back?"

"Nice try. Besides, you don't believe in signs."

"Do I believe the universe is sentient? No. Of course I do not. Unlike you, I don't 'manifest.'"

I laughed despite myself.

Five minutes passed, ten. Already my lips were chapped and my skin felt dry. I said, "I wish we'd stopped in Zion. It's supposed to be amazing."

"Kim, think about it: What are you going to do in a national park? You just had surgery on your foot two months ago. You can't take a baby step without wincing in agony."

"Oh, *now* you care."

We'd had this argument several times and it always went like this: Grant would again say that we should get married; I would exclaim that it hadn't even occurred to him that I would need help after my operation, so how could I trust him to take care of me in our old age— which to me was the only reason to make our partnership "official" at this stage of the game. He then would remind me that I was the one who always refused help, and I'd *told* him he could go to Sasha's. I had a ton of friends, he would add; Octavia had been due to stop by, and then she walked through the door precisely when I needed her. But that wasn't the point, and I couldn't say what the point was be-cause it was too big and too painful to utter out loud: needing Grant terrified me.

"Can you please let it go?" Grant said. "I'm sorry, I'm sorry, I'm sorry. I've said it a thousand times over. Congratulations, you've once again achieved next-level moral accountability."

"We could have at least stopped in Vegas. I told you I wanted to see it. I feel like I'm the only person in the world who's never been there." I almost added, *I've never been anywhere,* but I knew he'd say, *Really? Look who's stranded in the Mojave Desert.*

In truth, I doubted I'd even like Vegas, the epicenter of all the excess I despised. When we passed it on the freeway, Caesars Palace and the High Roller Ferris wheel emerged from out of nowhere, completely inorganic. "Vegas seems like a place everyone should go at least once."

"According to whom?" He loved saying *whom.* And *thus.* "It isn't where any culture was created. It's where it's regurgitated and dies. Honestly, would you ever *really* want to see a magic show? Or watch some pop star from the nineties try to make a comeback?"

I actually did, and I wished he did, too. I wanted him to see concerts in an arena without complaining about going deaf or to buy surprise plane tickets to Paris for our anniversary. Sometimes I even wished that he'd watch football or go to poker nights like other guys. I wished he could just be lighthearted and *normal*, but instead he played chess and solitaire on his phone. He only liked to gather in small groups. When you grow up at a camp, there's always something to do outside, and I liked to get out of the house and stay active, accepting every invitation with friends to do outdoorsy stuff while he stayed back. Grant accused me of being an "ing-er" because when I was in good shape, I was always kayaking, biking, walking, rollerblading, skiing, or birding. I suspected that he enjoyed my recent incapacitation. He'd always dreamed of being with someone who wanted to sit with him at the table and read *The New York Times* all morning. Early in our relationship, he told me that he thought we had great crossword-puzzle energy together. I didn't see that as a red flag at the time.

"The sight of all those old people sucking on cigarettes in a trance in front of slot machines is a sickness unto death."

"You're a snob."

Grant shrugged and wiped the sweat off his brow with his T-shirt. "In the age of *FBoy Island,* we need arbiters of taste now more than ever."

"It's just that we might never come this way again."

He gestured at the barren landscape. A bead of sweat dropped from his chin onto his chest. "And that would be just fine."

I was gripped by a persistent, vague fear that felt suddenly more pressing since Grant had lost his job: Where would we go together in our old age? Without work, what would we *do*?

"Vegas is the third ring of hell," he continued, "and you shouldn't make me feel like a bad guy just because I have zero desire to go back."

I sat up straighter. "Go back? You never told me you've been to Vegas."

He seemed suddenly cagey. "Years ago."

"Why were you there? A bachelor party?"

He paused. "I went with Sasha."

It suddenly hit me. "You got married there?" I thought I'd known everything about his relationship with his ex. "Is *that* why you're in such a bad mood?"

"I'm not in a bad mood." His knuckles were white from clenching the steering wheel, and we weren't going anywhere.

I leaned in, curious. "So did you, like, have an Elvis impersonator and everything?"

Grant cracked a smile that was not directed at me, but at his own memory, which made me feel left out and alone. "Yeah, actually. We were in the Chapel of Crystals, the whole cheesy deal. Sasha always had to make a statement."

"That's for sure."

"She thought it would be funny, like the joining of two souls was one big laugh riot. And then, plot twist! It was me who didn't take our marriage seriously."

I was surprised that Grant had gone along with getting married in such a kitschy place, and surprised that Sasha had ever exhibited a sense of humor. How on earth had she convinced him to tie the knot in Vegas when I couldn't even get him to go to a comedy club with me? Did she have special powers, or a stronger hold on Grant, or was he different before I'd met him? Had Sasha brought out a side of his personality that Grant kept hidden?

Feeling the familiar need to assert my dominance in his life, I kissed Grant on his scratchy cheek. He hadn't shaved since we'd left Madison, and he swore he wouldn't use a razor until we returned home.

"Well, now you have me," I said.

He looked at me as though he were just realizing I was in the car with him. "You, who dragged me to the middle of nowhere so we could die of heatstroke."

"Life is funny like that."

Five minutes went by. Ten. Had Grant worn a tuxedo? What did she wear? Was there photographic evidence? Why hadn't he ever told me?

It made me feel shut out of his life, but then again, I'd never gone into great detail about Basil and me getting married, either. Vandyke had been pushing hard for Basil to move back to Los Angeles to work in the family business since he was having a hard time breaking into musical theater in Chicago. He felt crushing anxiety about the prospect of returning home. Meanwhile, Burl's health was precarious, and I got it in my mind that having a wedding to live for might keep him going.

To Melody's horror, we tied the knot in the Camp Jamboree dining hall. Everyone thought we were too young to get married, and there we were, celebrating our big day at the place we'd spent our childhood. But the camp was where we'd met, where we felt safest. Burl officiated because there's no better person than a camp director to stand in front of a crowd of people and make them feel special, as if they're part of something bigger than themselves.

At the reception, he led the crowd in boisterous and loud renditions of "Do Your Ears Hang Low" and "Father Abraham Had Seven Sons." That was the last time I could remember him being himself. After the wedding his health took a dramatic turn, and he died two months later.

Polly had seemed apprehensive about the wedding. "I love Basil, but you don't need to marry him just to make Burl happy," she'd said. What she didn't say, not until Basil left me, was that she'd known he was gay the whole time.

"Why didn't you tell me?" I demanded.

She'd looked at me with a mixture of pity and shock. "Because I thought you'd figured it out. Everyone else did."

"So," Grant said, changing the subject, "James told me he might be able to arrange for a visiting professorship next year. One of his colleagues is going on leave, a continentalist." In Grant's world, there were two types of philosophy scholars: continental and analytical.

"You really want to move to Nebraska?"

"It's not like it's on my bucket list, but you know how it is, you go where the jobs are. And Creighton is a great school, very prestigious, and it's in a real city. You'd like it."

Omaha? As much as I wanted Grant to get back in the swing of things, I couldn't get excited about moving there because I felt it should be *my* turn to choose where we lived. My mind had been racing with possibilities. I used to dream of renting a loft in Manhattan or Chicago, although a big city filled with concrete and noise didn't appeal to me the way it used to. Maybe the ocean would be nice. I considered the beaches of the Carolinas, but I'd grown spoiled and comfortable living in a relatively safe liberal bubble. In Madison, we were surrounded by lovely lakes, greenery, abundant parking, and neighborly strangers who said hello. I'd perhaps become too spoiled, too comfortable. Madison was the kind of town that could make you forget the world was big.

"You'd seriously want to move all the way to Omaha just for a visiting professorship?"

"It's not like everyone is punching holes in my professional dance card, you know. Why aren't you happy for me? You keep saying you want me to find a job and here it is, gainful employment."

"I *am* happy." I tried my best to sound excited. "I just, I don't know, you caught me off guard. I guess I was thinking maybe we were ready for a *change* change."

"Isn't that what this is?"

"We don't know anyone there except James."

"Well, you don't know anyone in Palm Springs except Melody, and that's not stopping you."

"This is just for one winter."

"And Omaha would be one year, maybe two if I'm lucky."

"I'm sure it's great there, but what about me? What about my job? Nebraska is not what I want."

"You could quit your job. If we sell the house in Madison we can live like royalty in Omaha. Start fresh. Isn't that what you've been wanting?"

What *did* I want? I was very conscious that I was now the same age my mother had been when she'd had her stroke. We'd already gotten AARP cards in the mail. Little things had suddenly become profound—like the time we bought a new bed, and when the salesperson mentioned the thirty-year warranty, I realized that it might be the very last bed we would ever own. I'd compromised in so many ways, big and small; now, I was less inclined to settle.

"This job isn't a sure thing, anyway," Grant continued. "I'd still need to interview. They haven't even posted the position in *The Chron-icle,* but when they do, I plan to apply. If it works out, will you give it a second thought?"

That's when I said something aloud that I wasn't even fully aware I was thinking, a thought that was too hot to touch. "Well, maybe I'm giving *us* a second thought."

I could see the words hit Grant like a body blow. For once, he was speechless. I was immediately afraid of what I'd done, like inspecting the damage after an accident. I'd always had the feeling that one moment, one sentence, could take us to the point of no return. Maybe this was it.

I reached for his shoulder, but he flinched at my touch.

"Honey, I didn't mean that," I said. But didn't I? The heat had loosened my tongue, but I'd been in turmoil for months. Lately, it felt as if my life had never really been my own. All of my adult decisions had revolved around Basil, Grant, or the girls.

"Is that what all of this is about, Kim? This trip? You aren't just looking for a change of scenery, are you?"

I looked straight ahead as if I'd been accused of stealing the thing that was already in my pocket.

"You aren't sure about *us,* really? You tell me this *now,* when we're two thousand miles from home?"

"I'm just tired and hot. And, you know, it's been hard lately. You don't do hard." A defensive edge crept into my voice. The sun was so bright that it seemed as if it were aggressively bent on revenge.

"I'm the one who keeps asking you to get married. Kim, I just had the cosmic tablecloth ripped out from under me. Besides, life is hard. We can weather the tough stuff together."

"But we're hardly ever together."

"Well, we sure are now."

This was true. Our car smelled like breath and sweat and the residue of our lives. I fought the urge to reach over with a napkin to wipe ketchup from the corner of his mouth that was left over from the Utah McDonald's. Grant had researched the town we'd stopped in and learned that St. George was where Howard Hughes filmed the old movie *The Conqueror,* and almost the entire cast died of cancer from the fallout from nearby nuclear testing, including John Wayne, who was terribly cast as Genghis Khan. It seemed especially tragic that he'd ended up dying from making the worst movie he'd ever been in.

"Don't make me keep auditioning for you, Kim," Grant said. "You aren't perfect, either. Part of commitment is allowing each other to screw up without having to apologize constantly."

"I'm just thinking maybe we could be different."

"After all these years together? How different could we be? I'm me, you're you."

"We don't connect the way we used to. And it just seems like we could be happier."

"Do you have any idea how fraught that concept is? We're like Epicurus and Epictetus. You think happiness comes from enjoying the good things in life, from avoiding suffering. I think we should embrace our discomfort to learn from it."

"That's rich, coming from you. Embracing discomfort has never been your thing. We see things so differently."

"We don't have a problem! We love each other, and we're just working through life." Grant pressed his hands against his temples. "You want to throw everything away? Throw *us* away? Our family?"

The heat was overwhelming; even the upholstery seemed to melt. Grant looked like a basketball player whose team had just lost on a last-second shot. He was shaken. He'd hurt me before, but had I ever realized the power I had to hurt *him*?

"Is it because I don't have a job? You think I'm a loser?"

"No! It's not your fault the college closed."

"I should have been an accountant, or a marine biologist. I should have opened a chain of coffee shops. I had the idea for Starbucks before it was even a thing. Remember when nobody knew what espresso was, when they thought you spelled it with an *x*? Now look at me, I'm washed-up."

"You're feeling sorry for yourself."

"Yeah, I guess I am. That's what happens to normal people."

A few minutes went by. Grant looked at me. "You're pretty." He sounded dorky and kind, which is what he was, and it got to me. "We're fine, right?"

He was trying to get me to give him the answer he wanted, and I obliged: "Sure we are."

"I love you so much, you know. I'm like a dog you give a little love to, and he loves you back a million times more."

"And I love you. I just think we have issues."

"We've been together almost thirty years. We *should* have issues."

He stepped out of the car, shut the door, and walked along the shoulder, kicking a rock out of his way. He had a heart-shaped sweat stain on the back of his T-shirt.

I felt anxious for us, for everything we'd left behind and the uncertainty of what was ahead. Would we survive this repotting from Madison to Palm Springs? I stared into my phone for a distraction, pleased to see a glimmer of reception. I checked my email and saw two subject lines that made my stomach turn: one said UNFORTUNATE INCIDENT, sent by Maggie, Go Green's marketing and PR person. I was already so disconnected from work that, at first, I wondered how she knew about our car breaking down. I groaned when I read the content.

No, no, no.

Stupid Vic and his stupid dick! He'd been caught late at night groping a legislative assistant at the Great Dane—not just any assistant, but a young woman who worked for "Toxic Todd" Griffin, the most conservative representative in the state, and Go Green's biggest foe. Now Griffin was having a field day calling out our "woke" organization's double standards. Maggie didn't say as much, but the writing was on the wall: Vic would have to go. And if Vic went, so, too, I feared, would our funding, and, eventually, the entire organization. There's a good reason businesses and nonprofits should never be built around a single personality.

I looked at the vast, cloudless sky. Maybe we would need that job in Omaha. Our lives suddenly felt like the time-out screen on a faulty Web page that read PLEASE START OVER. ALL CHANGES HAVE BEEN LOST.

Chapter Seven

Palm Springs
January 3, 2023
11:00 A.M.

At any given time, as many as a dozen trained volunteers could be at the command center. Brady didn't want the public in on the search because he feared he could have another lost person to deal with, or they'd stomp on the footprints Grant had left behind. I was incredibly grateful for the rescuers, although it was unsettling to see how they lived for these situations, jumping at the chance to head out into the wilds in bad conditions. It couldn't be just pure benevolence. Deep down, do we all have a great desire to be part of the action? Or, is the allure of a missing person, the prospect of being well and truly *lost*, just too irresistible? Are we all secretly longing to be utterly removed from the world?

Melody stopped by with some lunch and handed me a copy of *The Desert Sun*. "A souvenir from your winter here." There was the photo of Grant and *Forever Marilyn* that I'd given Brady. Now our hell was everyone's news. The headline: SEARCH CONTINUES FOR ISOLATED MISSING HIKER: NO SIGN OF MIDWESTERN TOURIST.

The word *isolated* struck me as especially sad. *Midwestern* rankled me—it sounded pejorative, as if it were put there to explain that he wasn't equipped to navigate this harsh mountainous landscape. Then there was *tourist*. We'd been in Palm Springs for a few months, long enough to find the best date shakes at Fruit Wonders, for Grant to log hundreds of miles hiking and transform his appearance, long enough to fill up Basil's condo with the junk Grant brought home from the resale shop. Long enough to learn the name of the reference-desk librarian at the Palm Springs Library. Long enough to make friends. Long enough, even, to be occasionally bored here.

We weren't tourists. We were snowbirds.

Almost instantly, the story proliferated online. I began to hear from everyone we knew. High school and college friends, former colleagues, flirty Trent, neighbors back home—even a reporter for the *Cap Times* in Madison wanting to know more. The emails were filled with bromides and well-intended messages of support. Even my acupuncturist had found out.

How are you holding up?

I didn't reply. I was touched that these people cared, but what could I say that they didn't know already? There are two kinds of friends: the cheerleaders, who think they can make you feel better with optimism, and the ones who acknowledge that you're in a bad situation and it just plain sucks. The latter style is how my mother had dealt with life's mishaps, and that was the form of support I'd come to prefer and insist on, even if it wasn't always what I needed.

I also appreciated the rare third category of friend, the ones who made me laugh because their humor revealed that they knew Grant better than anyone who was searching for him.

They'll find him, Octavia said. *And when they do, I'll let my cat pee in his hiking boots.*

Rodney, Grant's former colleague from the philosophy department, said, *The searchers just need to listen for the sound of him talking to himself.*

Melody must have told Basil. He wrote, *I know you've checked the jails and hospitals, but have you checked the libraries?*

Please let us know if you need anything, they all said.

What I needed was Grant. I never knew I could need him so much; or, rather, I did know, but I didn't want to. The only thing I found more terrifying than being needed was to need him.

The biggest surprise came from Celia, my college roommate. I

hadn't seen her since our Saint Mary's of Notre Dame twenty-year reunion. GET A LOAD OF THIS, the subject line read, followed by an email
filled with her trademark exclamation marks.

Kimmer, Did you know there's a "Find Grant" Facebook page?
We're all on it, that's how I found out he's missing. OMG that must
be so scary but I know he's fine, I can feel it!!! He's smart enough
to figure his way out of anything.

Maybe this isn't the right time, or maybe it's the perfect time,
but anyway, I've been meaning to send this email to you for a while
now. Remember how obsessed Fitzie was with his dumb cam-
corder when we lived in Chicago? He took it everywhere. We have
boxes of tapes in the basement, boxes and boxes! I was getting
ready to sell our house after the divorce. Did I tell you I'm single
now? Fitzie had been having an affair for four years with his dental
hygienist.

FOUR YEARS!!!!!!
He moved with "Boobs, Butt, Barb" to Ohio and left me with all
kinds of junk, including his tapes.

How come it couldn't have been Fitz who'd gotten lost on a
mountain? Life is so unfair.

I finally sent some out to be digitized. Not going to lie, there was
some amateur porn, like *Blair Witch Project* meets OnlyFans. Now
I'm glad we did it. At least I have proof of how young and hot I used
to be. At my lowest point, know what I did? I emailed one of the
videos to Barb, ha ha.

Look at the date on this one (don't worry, it's rated G): New
Year's, 1991. Are you thinking what I was thinking?!? Fast-forward
to the twelve-minute mark, and . . . well, you'll see.

I've had this for a while and kept meaning to send but then my
mom got sick and Anna had some mental health issues and Fitzie
fucked up our lives and . . . you know how life goes.

I'm thinking of you and Grant, Kim. We all are. I can't wait to see
you when you guys return home TOGETHER, but don't hurry back,
there's a polar vortex and it's freezing here! People are throwing

boiling water into the air to watch it vaporize and getting third-degree burns. You were smart to escape the tundra. I'm jealous. Sending hugs and good, positive vibes from Chicago! Love you!!!

The video took forever to load; the reception was bad from the Indian Canyons parking lot. Once it did, I entered the loud, grainy world of my past and encountered my "sliding doors" moment.

I was at a low point the night I met Grant, utterly heartbroken over the abrupt end of my marriage and lonely without Basil, who'd moved to San Francisco. I was working a miserable, entry-level job with an underfunded patient-advocacy organization.

I retreated back to my old friend group, who'd moved en masse from South Bend to Chicago after graduation, including Celia, who invited me to a New Year's party in Hyde Park.

Saint Mary's of Notre Dame wasn't a college I would otherwise have considered attending—in fact, I might not have gone to college at all, but my fate was decided the first summer Basil attended camp. When Melody and Vandyke picked him up on the last day, they were thrilled to see Basil sitting on the steps of the Pioneer cabin with his arm around my shoulders. I was crying because I knew how much I'd miss him. They noted our physical proximity and concluded that I had the power to make Basil heterosexual.

After that, the Underwoods went to great lengths and great expense to keep our relationship going. They sent Basil back to camp the following year, and the year after that. Vandyke had been a big donor at Notre Dame. He knew the only way to convince Basil to attend his alma mater was to make sure I did, too. He helped get me into the sister school, Saint Mary's, even though I hadn't attended a church service in my life—the closest I'd come to religion was in my late teens, when Polly became a Quaker. I joined her a few times for silent "worship" at the meetinghouse, where we'd quietly wait for "that of God" to speak to us. What I took away from the experience was that decisions can be made by waiting for the divine voice, or through a difficult process of discernment, where the right choice, the one that will lead to joy, gentleness, and peace, will rise up inside you when you are free of your personal agenda and ego. This gave me the flawed idea that I had to be moved by divine inspiration for all my decisions, big and small.

My Catholic college friends, such as Celia, were the same variety of cute-and-adored upper-middle-class suburban girls I'd known at Chicago Latin. My roommates slept in Lanz of Salzburg nightgowns and received extravagant care packages from home, while Polly sent me boxes of tampons, a twenty-dollar bill, and newspaper coupons held together by a crusty rubber band.

My preppy and ponytailed college friends were much more fun than I'd initially thought they would be. The thing about Catholic girls, I came to learn, is that they believe they can do anything wrong during the week because their sins will be forgiven on Saturday at confession or church on Sunday.

And there my Catholic friends were, preserved in Fitzie's video. It was dizzying to watch because I was bleary-eyed from exhaustion, and Fitzie was a poor documentarian, with his drunken grip and short attention span. The camera jiggled and swung wildly from scene to scene. I almost gave up until suddenly I spotted my younger self, like a different person, an old friend. Grant could have used this as a teaching moment about the personal unconscious, all the repressed memories and temporarily forgotten information surrounding an event. I could fill in what I couldn't see; I knew I was cradling my cheap beer with the pastel gloves Polly had bought at the five-and-dime. She'd stuffed Hershey's Kisses into each of the fingers, a rare show of affection.

Young me was wandering through a sea of my former classmates in their Notre Dame–logo sweatshirts. I was as anxious about my future then as I'd been feeling lately. I was surrounded by the usual midwestern party atmospherics: a bong, red Solo cups, a couple making out on the sagging couch. A grainy image of Times Square appeared on the screen of the giant console television. I could remember wanting to peel away from the undergrad friendships that had defined me and meet new people who had strong concerns about Operation Desert Storm, who worried about the homelessness that broke my heart every day, and who would attend talks with me at the Art Institute. I was craving new ideas, men, sex. I wanted to go to better parties, where guests could hear one another talk about something other than sports, and where nobody threw up in the stairwell.

And there was Grant. He didn't belong at the party any more than I did. He looked tousled, as if he'd been lost at sea for months. He was a few years older than the rest of the revelers, and he didn't dress like a jock. He wore a Joy Division T-shirt and a Scottish-plaid scarf that was hung long on one end. With his thick, wire-rimmed glasses, he could have been a poet from the twenties.

"Who *is* that?" I asked Celia, transfixed. He was rumpled and woolly, dark and intense.

"Some dude who lives upstairs. Kirk invited him for a drink so he wouldn't call the cops if it got too loud. He was talking to me about how the Chinese used to make paper out of old fishing nets."

"He's cute."

"I guess, if you're into the scruffy type."

I felt I was scruffy myself. I have always dressed in what might charitably be described as camp chic—all that was missing was a whistle around my neck and a clipboard in my hands. I worried that if I tried too hard to be fashionable, I might do it wrong. After Burl's death, I took to wearing his old Pendleton plaid shirts over tie-dyed T-shirts, Levi's red-tag jeans and canvas high-tops. I had leather and rope bracelets on my arm. I never wore makeup, preferring to look natural and outdoorsy, my long auburn hair swept up into the same easy ponytail I wore until just weeks ago. This was a natural look Grant would later say he found attractive.

I didn't think I had a type until I saw Grant. He didn't just appeal to me for his looks—it was as though I could see straight through to who he was, and I found him as endearing as a stray puppy. He seemed bruised by life, and in need of rescue. I whispered in Celia's ear, "I'm going to go home with that guy."

"I'll give you ten bucks if you do."

"Deal."

There was a burst of activity. Suddenly people were donning hats and blowing into noisemakers. The countdown to the New Year—and what would become my new life—had begun. Everyone screamed, "*Three—two—one!*" Confetti shot into the air.

That's when I did the most spontaneous thing of my life: I turned and planted a kiss on Grant's lips, and he instinctively kissed me back. This was not the kiss of a drunk frat boy. His lips were firm, his cheeks stubbly. He tasted new and sweet, sugary.

Grant pulled away, flustered. "*That* was one hell of a kiss. It's like we rehearsed it a thousand times." He leaned in to talk above the noise, his lips grazing my ear. "Who even *are* you?" His voice was gravelly and mature. I liked that he was different from everyone else at the party, and I was intoxicated by my own boldness.

"I'm Kim."

"Kim." My name, short and monosyllabic, had never sounded so special until it rose out of his throat and tripped off the tongue that just moments earlier had pressed into my mouth. "Where'd you come from, Kim? God, you're adorable."

Adorable is not a word people had used to describe me. I'm tall and broad shouldered like Burl. *Strong* is a word people use. *Capable.* "Who are *you*?"

"I'm Grant Duffy."

I liked the name Grant because it hit my ears like a declaration, and I thought Duffy sounded gentle.

I wanted to kiss Grant Duffy again; in fact, the attraction was so surprising and strong that it felt as though the kiss—sudden, achingly sweet—was still happening. His dark hair swung moodily over his eyes. Already he was visually imprinting on me, from the flush on his cheeks to the shape of his earlobes to the cleft in his chin, a feature I had no idea the girls would eventually inherit. He looked smart, and I liked that. He was also somehow more animated and alive than every other person at the party, like the single colored-in figure in one of those manipulated sepia photographs.

Grant said, "I want you to kiss me again, but only if you want that. Do you?"

I didn't think Grant could top the surprise kiss, but the second one was back arching, tender. Achingly sensual. My legs turned to jelly.

"Want to get out of here?" he asked. "We can go upstairs to my place."

"God, yes."

He placed his warm hand around mine and stealthily guided me through the crowd.

Fitzie's footage was almost unwatchable. I could barely make out the sound of Bob Marley's "We Jammin'," a soundtrack to the most consequential moment of my life. I pulled the screen right up to my face, and it was unbelievable. There we were, a blur of movement. We hadn't even kissed yet! It gave me the chills to see Grant standing behind me, still a stranger.

Here was the story we'd told a thousand times, playing out before my eyes. We joke about it all the time. People ask us how we met, and Grant says, "It was a one-night stand that never ended."

And I joke that it reminds me of an old *New Yorker* cartoon. There's a couple in a bedroom, and the disheveled husband is getting dressed after stepping out of bed. The wife says, "Look, you seem nice, and I don't want to hurt your feelings, but I was really drunk when we met, got married, and bought this house."

The kiss. I saw those ghosts of ourselves pull back from each other, and then the camera moved on. It was just a fleck in the action. I might not have noticed it unless I was really looking.

I reversed and watched that explosive moment again and again, visually flying backward to the seed from which my entire adult life bloomed. It felt especially wonderful with Grant being lost to see us find each other that first time, and to be reminded of the feeling that happens when you meet someone consequential. It's the feeling of being found.

There was Grant, his back a little straighter, his belly leaner, his skin fresh and unwrinkled, his hair thicker. And there I was, more attractive than I realized at the time, back when I wished I were delicate and small boned. I gasped aloud, seeing with my own eyes the bending of our futures. How many couples get to actually see that?

How I wished I could show Grant that there was evidence of that emotional rocket launch that marked our beginning. I was mesmerized by the moment we'd come together, but also by the space that once existed between us, and how I'd been the one to close it. And thirty years later, I'd been the one to open it back up again.

Chapter Eight

Palm Springs
November 6, 2022

We parked our new truck between a sign that said NO OUTLET and another that read SIDEWALK ENDS. The universe was telling us that we could go no farther.

In a nearby barren lot I spied a mangy coyote sitting under a date tree watching us wearily as we stood like abandoned orphans in the street.

Suckers, the coyote seemed to say.

When I began researching Palm Springs, I'd seen pictures of tennis courts, swimming pools, palm trees, martinis, caftans, and the Rat Pack, but this rustic corner of town was like a scene from *High Noon,* all rocks, cacti, and . . . brownness.

Two men with grizzled white beards sat on the hood of a jalopy drinking blue Gatorade that was the same pure color as the sky above them. I resented the men—not for being unhoused, but for creating a scratch in the cheery fantasy that had been running through my mind of arriving at some sort of sunny utopia.

"Nice truck," one of the bearded men said.

Grant smiled at me as if to say, *I told you so.* "Thanks. We just got her."

The tow truck took us to a town called Barstow, where the mechanic performed last rites on the Prius, and we went to have lunch at a place called Peggy Sue's '50s Diner, in a building that had been constructed out of rail ties from the Union Pacific. We retreated into our phones while we waited for our John Wayne and Milton Berle omelets. I texted the girls a video I'd surreptitiously taken of Grant trying to peel the bumper stickers off the car for keepsakes, and I emailed Melody to tell her we'd experienced a delay.

I blew through my omelet and ordered a short stack of pancakes. Grant said, "This is like our first date when you ordered two entrées. I was so happy I'd found a woman with a big appetite."

He told this story every time we ordered food, and every time I would say, as I did that morning, "I was starving!"

"You said, 'If you want me, I hope you can afford to feed me.'"

Our moods shifted, and our fight had been reduced to a vapor trail. He was rubbing my forearm with his thumb—Grant always had to touch me. He was desperate for contact, while I found it hard to get used to after growing up with Polly, who shunned physical intimacy. Sometimes, I'd run up behind her and pinch her, just to make that connection.

"I like this place," he said, staring at a mannequin with a beehive hairdo propped up on one of the barstools in front of the counter. "It hasn't been packaged and repackaged. It's what it is, like you."

"I'm just me."

"Exactly."

Not two minutes later, I received a reply from Melody. It had been so long since I'd heard from my former mother-in-law that the email arrived like a voice from the dead. *Come to Smoke Tree Ranch for lunch Wednesday. Noon. I'll leave your name with the boy at the gate.*

The *boy*? Apparently, Melody hadn't changed.

I typed a response—a title from one of Basil's songs, and I wondered if she knew it: *Sounds great, can't wait!*

On our way out, Grant was humming along to "Puff, the Magic Dragon" when we saw two cars in the parking lot with sale signs in the windshields: a dune buggy with a stuffed monkey clinging to the antenna, and a burgundy Jeep. Grant wandered over and ran his finger tenderly along the side of the Jeep. "Oh my God, let's buy it."

I thought he was joking. "Oh, sure, you can have that one, and the dune buggy can be for me. His and hers."

His gaze was stuck on the truck. "I'm not kidding."

I walked to the front windshield, looked at the sticker, and gasped. "This Jeep is almost as old as we are. It looks like it's from *M*A*S*H*."

"It's got a Safari Snorkel, Warn winch, ARB bumper, White Knuckle sliders. This isn't a truck, Kimmy. It's a rig. A rig with a story." He kicked a tire and walked around the truck, staring at it appreciatively like a guy checking out a hot girl at a bar. "It's been rebuilt. OME lift kit. It's got thirty-threes."

"I don't even know what language you're speaking. Since when are you, like, a regular guy? How on earth do you know so much about trucks?" It was both sexy and disconcerting to discover that he had a deep well of knowledge he'd never shared with me before. What else hadn't he told me? What else didn't I know? "We aren't car people."

"But don't you see? This is not a car, my love." It had stickers all over it that had nothing to do with the ones that he'd peeled off our dead Prius. This car was covered in dust, so I could just make out what a few of them said: IDAHO OFF-ROAD CLUB, RED ROCK 4-WHEELERS MOAB, and a pair of bear-paw decals. A SHIFT HAPPENS bumper sticker. "I want to be friends with whoever owns this. We could take her anywhere. Look at her."

"She? Her? Who even *are* you?"

"You don't understand how special this Jeep is. It has a cult following."

"So do pimple-popping videos."

His eyes were filled with want.

"Grant. Snap out of it. *Twenty. Thousand. Dollars.*"

"That's so much less than they normally cost."

"It has well over a hundred thousand miles on it."

"That's nothing. Jeeps don't die, not if you take care of them."

"This isn't even a legit car dealership. Who knows what kinds of problems it could have."

It didn't matter what I said; his mind was set. He gave me an excited squeeze. "I've always wanted a truck like this. Always, always, always."

"We should get an EV. How could you be okay with driving a car that gets less than twenty miles to the gallon? That's unconscionable in this day and age. You were the one complaining about this trip being indulgent."

"I'll buy carbon offsets. Don't worry about sullying your reputation with the Go Greeners."

He still didn't know about the organization's already-sullied reputation; I wanted to keep that to myself for a while. "Have you lost your mind?"

He ignored me. "They have great resale value." He ran his finger along the red stripe on the side and smiled like a little boy on Christmas morning. "You know, George had a Jeep. He took me rock crawling in Bald Mountain a few times. Those were some of the best days of my childhood."

Grant rarely waxed nostalgic about his youth, considering everything he'd been through. A bright spot was George, a kindly World War II veteran who took care of Grant whenever his parents had problems, and especially in the dark years when it was just Grant and Mitzie and Mitzie barely held it together.

"I know you loved George, but there are other ways to honor him."

"You don't understand. That's the best memory from my entire childhood. Kim, I've wanted a rig like this my whole life."

A rig! Who was I to stand in his way? If he didn't live out his fantasies now, when would he? And who was I to hold him back from what he wanted, especially if it didn't involve moving to Omaha?

But then he stiffened. "I'm not asking for your permission, you know."

What was that tone? He spoke to me not as someone he'd been with for thirty years, but as a stranger.

"I'm buying it with my own money. It'll be *my* car."

He *did* have his own money, that was true. With the sale of his mother's house, he was sitting on some cash. Yet at our age, I thought it would be prudent to save every penny. We had been floored by the monthly cost of assisted-living centers and personal caregivers, not to mention the price of Mitzie's medications. As far as I was concerned, no matter how much we saved, it wouldn't be enough. Grant, on the other hand, thought of his inheritance as mad money, and it was burning a hole in his pocket.

Our first decade together, we'd both relied on my alimony from Basil. My prenup was structured so that I could collect a monthly sum for a decade—provided I remained single. This, according to Vandyke, was the standard arrangement. Theirs was a world filled with gold diggers; they couldn't be too careful. I honestly hadn't paid too much attention to the details at the time because I couldn't imagine life without Basil, and I'd assumed we'd be together forever. Vandyke insisted we have an agreement in place, and he was the kind of person you didn't say no to.

I used that money for the down payment on our house. Seeing my name on the mortgage was incredibly empowering after sharing an apartment above an Indian restaurant in Andersonville with Polly. Still, I'd never truly thought of the Madison house as mine alone. More like 80 percent.

What was Grant's nonsense about *his* money?

I shrugged, annoyed. "Do what you want."

That's how we ended up driving the last leg of our journey from the high desert to the valley in a truck designed for deep-water crossings. I stared at Grant in the driver's seat and my anger began to wane. He looked good, and happier than he'd been in a while, which was the whole point of the trip, wasn't it? I wanted to figure out who I was; maybe Grant needed to do the same. Was this the "real" Grant?

"Look how high up we are," he said. "I can see three cars ahead of the one in front of us."

"I never knew this was your thing."

"My 'thing' didn't make sense before."

"It still makes no sense."

"We had the girls. And you never would have gone for it."

"I'm not exactly going for it now." I leaned forward—there was so much space between my seat and the dash. "I could take a yoga class in here. Do you hear that? That clicking? Is there a knock in the engine?"

"The engine is fine. You know why you don't recognize that sound? Because you're not used to hearing raw power."

"It's just so . . . male. This car smells of vinyl and testosterone."

"Don't call it a car." He was grinning from ear to ear. "This feels amazing after driving the patchouli mobile for the last decade."

I pretended to take umbrage.

We descended the rocky hills into the Coachella Valley, passing an army of giant white windmills, finally encountering civilization: supermarkets, golf courses, the airport, and funky mid-century complexes all tucked into an oasis of green. Beautiful palm trees stretched to the sky everywhere we looked. The streets downtown were all closed off. We could hear thumping dance music. We glimpsed parade floats, rainbow flags, and drag queens and cheering crowds. Traffic had come to a standstill. My heavy thoughts suddenly lifted.

A cop was directing traffic. I rolled down my window. "What's going on?" I asked him. He didn't look like the cops back home; he had a Mohawk and a giant diamond stud earring glittered in the bright sun.

He smiled. "It's the Pride parade." Crowds filled the sidewalks. There were floats, a sea of rainbow flags, pink tutus, motorcycles, and music. From that point forward, Palm Springs struck me as a place where we were always on the edge of fun.

A few minutes and a few miles later, all was quiet; in the corner of the desert where we'd ended up, you'd never know that just a few miles away the town was packed with people.

Grant had to help me step down because of my ankle. "Do you think he gave me the wrong address?" I asked. The air was hazy, and the mountains appeared to be made of smoke. Everything was so still and so weird that I felt as if I'd wandered into one of the old art films Basil took me to when we were young.

I found it hard to believe that just a few days ago I was covering our rosebushes with burlap to protect them from the coming frost.

Here, the bright sun pierced down from on high, like the spotlight an actor stepped into onstage; it made everything else feel irrelevant, as though we hadn't been anywhere or done anything that mattered until now.

In front of us, behind a row of ficus, stood a tall stucco-brick security wall that revealed only the angles of low-slung terra-cotta roofs in the distance. "Looks like this is the place," Grant said when he spied the retro cursive sign next to the gate, hidden behind a chubby dwarf palm tree. The top nail in the s had fallen away, so the letter hung upside down like a cedilla indicating a question. Grant flicked it with his finger and set it into a rocking motion. *"Le De-ert,"* he said, faking a French accent. Grant had been making dad jokes about Le Desert ever since I told him the name of Basil's complex. He put a *le* in front of everything: le freeway, le bunion, le road trip. Basil explained that there's a hotel in Palm Springs called Les Cactus, which he suspected had been a sister property, named after a song by Jacques Dutronc. "It's got the best lyrics," Basil had said. "I wish I wrote it myself: 'The whole world is a cactus / it's impossible to sit down.'"

I walked over to the large rustic wooden door built under an arch and set deep into a vine-covered wall. Next to it, nailed to the gate, was a Moroccan-style lantern. I reached into my shoulder bag and pulled out the metallic-gold envelope Basil had sent. It still made me feel as if I'd won something.

I held the vintage key chain in my hand. The leather was stamped with the logo of a cactus with a cowboy hat on top and a pair of boots with spurs resting at the base. Below it was the number 1. Basil's unit.

Grant's sunglasses were fogged despite the dry heat, and his hair was dripping with sweat. His body was a furnace. He flushed often and easily, but that afternoon his face, still boyishly adorable, was heart-attack red.

"I literally cannot breathe here, Kim." Grant often used the word *literally*, pronouncing each syllable distinctly, always emphatically. He reached for his toes but ended up in an L-shape—he had never been flexible and refused to try yoga with me. On instinct, I rubbed his sweaty back and wished that we could just be a "normal" couple and enjoy this moment.

The sun glinted off the key—such a slight object to have so much power. When March was little, she used to walk around with a giant plastic toy key in her chubby little hands. She said it was for her castle. She took it everywhere, always hopeful, believing even as a child that she was meant to live a grand life, while I'd always strived for getting just what I needed and no more. Polly's worldview could be reduced to two words: *make do.*

Grant reached for the key. "Want me to try?"

I did not. Grant was even less mechanically inclined than I was, which wasn't saying much. My hands were shaky.

A group of men walked past and eyed us with our big bags. I overheard one grumble, "Oh, look, the snowbirds are back. There go all the parking spots."

"And the restaurant reservations."

"The doctor's appointments. You should see the line for prescriptions at Walgreens."

"They're changing the city."

"Oh, I like the snowbirds," the third one said. "Stop complaining about the city changing. Frank Sinatra is *dead.*"

I slipped the key into the chunky antique iron lock and turned it counterclockwise. My stomach dropped when the bolt came loose. The hinges whined as they opened. We made a graceless entrance with the wheels of our big rolling bags thundering along the unevenly paved walkway.

The gate slammed shut behind us.

Chapter Nine

Palm Springs
January 3, 2023
1:00 P.M.

The first time Grant left, he went to Sasha.

Grant and I hadn't dated for more than a few weeks before Sasha became a presence in our lives. One auspicious morning, we were holed up together in his 1920s Hyde Park apartment near the University of Chicago during a raging blizzard. We'd just made love—again. We'd made love so many times that we'd run out of condoms, and it was too horrible outside to go get some more Trojans at the 7-Eleven.

He knew his way around my body. His desire for praise would soon drive me crazy, but his eagerness to please also made him a good lover. He wanted me to say, "That was great. How'd you know how to do that?"—and I did. Before Grant, I was fumbling and awkward in bed. It was as though I was discovering sex for the first time, and I couldn't get enough of it. We moved to the same rhythm; it was a language we were proficient in.

Snow whipped around beyond Grant's windows; dense, glittery stars of frost had exploded over the glass. The radiator hissed. The couple in the apartment next door made food that smelled of ginger and cardamom. Somewhere outside I heard the city plows rumble past. I never wanted the storm to end, never wanted to go back to the sterile Gold Coast high-rise I'd once shared with Basil, never wanted to peel myself out of the warm tangle of our limbs. We were melted together, love drunk.

Grant groaned and pulled me to him as I motioned to stand. "Don't go. Don't ever go. I mean it."

"I'll be right back. Promise." I looked down at my body. My skin was marked by the folds in his hunter-green sheets, my hair a mess. I walked like a cowboy to the bathroom in his bathrobe, smelling like him, feeling as if I was *his*. In the whirlwind since that New Year's kiss, we were so hot and heavy, so lusty and full of conversation and questions, that I knew, even if it didn't work out with Grant (it had to!), my marriage to Basil had really been a union between friends.

Never before had I felt so desired—and desirable. For the first time in my life, I believed I was beautiful. I'd taken on that glow that caused me to be noticed by strangers. As sad as I'd been when Basil came out, it terrified me to think that I could have gone my whole life without knowing this feeling. Grant was a revelation, a drug, a portal to a different life. I didn't just want to be near him; I wanted to absorb him into my cells.

We couldn't stand to be apart. I was useless at work, so distracted by the memory of the exact sound of Grant's voice when he said my name. I'd close my eyes and my spine would hum when I imagined his jawline, the soft bottoms of his feet, the arch of his eyebrows, the desirous look in his eyes. On my desk was my application to work as a gallery associate at the Museum of Modern Art in New York City, and another application for an MFA at the Pratt Institute. I threw them in the trash, deciding that Grant was my next and only destination. Just like that, my whole world narrowed around one man.

His varied interests were on display in his long hallway. He was easily fascinated by every little thing, from Civil War submarines to astronomy, speed skating to the grain of the wood on his kitchen table. He was a collector. Metal souvenir statues of skyscrapers lined his windowsill. He had at least a dozen pairs of vintage binoculars on his dresser, along with loose change and twenty-dollar bills wadded up like old Kleenex—hundreds of dollars. Money didn't mean much to him. After meeting the Underwoods, I saw it as a refreshing sign that we shared the same values: he wasn't materialistic. I believed his lack of financial vigilance was in sync with my values of austerity. Later, I'd see that his disinterest in money could make him careless about how he spent it, while I cared too much, operating from a scarcity mentality that made Grant crazy.

He'd framed several rare, signed letters from notable figures in history. Some were written on personal stationery, some on onion paper, others on yellowed heavy stock. They were all difficult to read. He had a letter from Ivan Pavlov, and one from Brigadier General Charles H. Morgan, which I tried to make out—something about officers at Alcatraz. Grant told me that in his free time he would go through his *Who's Who* book and write letters to scholars and celebrities he admired and see if they would write back. His favorite sound was the clanging of the mailman's chain of keys in the lobby. He never knew what might show up in his mailbox on any given day. One of my favorite qualities about Grant was that he could be fascinated by what other people might find boring. As my college friends said when they met him, he lived like an old man.

But there, among the framed-letters collection, I noticed a small, square painting on a piece of clapboard. It was of two lovers walking arm in arm on the beach as the sun set. The male figure looked a lot like Grant; the woman was a wisp, with short blond hair. He leaned over and into his lover, his hand around her tiny waist. Grant didn't hold me like that. Maybe because I'm tall, or because I generally don't like to be protected or possessed, even though, sometimes, I do.

Grant then joined me in the hall. His expression shifted when he saw me looking at the painting and just like that, the spell we were under was broken.

"Who's that?" I asked, my stomach knotted up.

The question pained him. "My stepsister Lisa did it." He didn't say she'd *painted it*. She'd *done it*.

"She's talented," I lied. I found Lisa's painting sentimental and poorly rendered. She'd used too much white, a problem for beginners, and she also stopped painting too early, another problem for beginners. The effect was especially troubling because it implied there was more to be done.

"It was a wedding gift."

"You're married?" I could feel my heart seize up. "Seriously?"

My friends had warned me. They said to be careful about rebound relationships and moving too fast. I didn't even know this guy, they said, but I insisted I did. In the first five minutes, I was convinced I knew everything that mattered about Grant.

I ran into his room and began angrily gathering up my clothes. I needed to get dressed and get the hell out of there.

He reached for my arm and tried to hold me back. "You can't leave. You'll never get home in this weather. Kim, come on. It's dangerous outside."

"It's more dangerous in here!" I was trying hard not to cry. Polly hated it when I cried. She hated any outburst of emotion. *You're fine,* she'd say. *This city is filled with people who have worse problems than you.* "I can't believe this."

"I was going to say something, but—"

"Why didn't you tell me about her? I told you all about Basil." I pounded his chest with my fists. "I should have never let myself fall in love with you."

Grant grabbed my hands to still them. His face lit up with a broad grin. "Did you just say you're in love with me?"

"What difference does it make?" I had no intention of showing my cards so early in our relationship, but I couldn't take the words back. I was dying inside.

"Kim, stop. Listen to me. Sasha and I aren't together anymore."

Sasha? I hated that she had a pretty name, an interesting name.

"You're divorced?"

"Not yet. We've been separated. The paperwork isn't final yet, but believe me when I tell you it's a done deal."

My emotions had been on an elevator ride that plunged and suddenly stopped before hitting the ground. I'd gone from losing Grant to getting him back in seconds.

"What happened? What did she do? How long were you married? Where did you meet her?"

"Hang on, slow down. Long story short: we wanted different things."

I was so far gone, and so scared of losing it all again, that I decided right then and there that if we were going to work out, I would try to want what Grant wanted. And that's what I did, at least at first.

He started to say more—and froze. "Actually, I'm not ready to talk about it yet, if that's okay. It's pretty fresh."

In those blissful first few weeks, nothing had been off-limits. Already, our first boundary had been erected. We weren't one thing anymore—we were on the path to becoming individuals again.

I reached for my jeans from his floor and set them on my lap. "I need to know what happened right now, and if you don't tell me, I'm going to walk right into that snowstorm and get run over by a plow."

"I'm afraid I'll scare you away. I was a first-class jerk."

"Tell me! You cheated on her?"

He was clearly in pain. "No. I let her down in the worst way. Honestly, we shouldn't have gotten together to begin with, much less marry. We met two years ago. We were in the same metaphysical rationalism class. I thought she was brilliant. She *is* brilliant, way smarter than me. She's very bright."

"I only have a BA."

"Don't compare yourself to Sasha. Please. Don't compare yourself to anyone. You're one of a kind, a singular sensation." And then, after saying that, he went on to compare me to her: "You're way more even-keeled than she is."

"I don't feel even-keeled at this moment. But go on."

"We started working on a paper together, and the paper became a book idea, and we're cowriting it. We had this weird sapiosexual relationship."

"A sapio—?"

"When a brain thing is romance, where the ideas are like the sex. We decided to get married—the most impulsive thing I've ever done.

I knew I'd made a mistake the minute I said, 'I do.' For two people working on Ph.D.s, we couldn't have been more stupid. We talked about the big stuff of ideas but never the big stuff of life. The futures we wanted were totally incompatible, like our philosophical interests intersected but nothing else. We didn't like doing the same things or even eating the same food. The kicker was that I wanted a family, and I assumed she did, too. She didn't. She's adamantly opposed to having kids."

"I want a family!" I interrupted. How bold I was! "It's always been just me and my mom, and my dad. . . ." It was still hard to talk about Burl's passing. He'd been gone two years at that point. "My dad was great, but he was only there for part of the year. I want a house full of kids, big family dinners, traditions, you name it."

Grant kissed each of my fingertips. "See? You're different. I'm going to make our kids feel like they're special and planned." Planned? Little did we know that we were becoming a family at that very moment: my egg had been fertilized and it was splitting into two, making its way down my fallopian tube, busily dividing and dividing again and again to create two new humans, binding Grant and me together forever.

Our kids? He'd said that so casually.

After all I'd been through, shouldn't this ramped-up discussion of commitment have terrified me? Shouldn't it have terrified him? Why were we talking as if we'd decided to spend our lives together?

"So, what happened with Sasha?" I was hoping he'd say she'd run off to Antarctica or thrown herself off a cliff. We sank back into bed, and he told me the rest of the story while staring up at the cracks in his plaster ceiling.

"I thought there was something wrong with me. She's smart, and she's a real knockout. By far the best-looking woman in the philosophy department, although that's not saying much." Did he need to mention her looks? "And don't get me wrong, I love attention. This was too much, though. She was always checking in on me. She bought me clothes. She wanted to know about my *feelings*. She was always asking if I loved her and how much and why, and what did I remember about the first time I met her, and when did I know—it was suffocating because I didn't feel the same way."

To me, this sounded like the normal stuff of a new relationship.

"One day last September, we hadn't been married half a year, and I was heading back from Madison, where I'd interviewed for a postdoc position. I was in a bad mood because I was convinced that I'd blown it and messed up one of the answers. I imagined Sasha waiting here for me—"

She lived in this apartment? Slept in this bed? Suddenly I saw the space differently.

"I knew she'd ask me how it went, and she'd want to know *everything,* and I couldn't do it, I couldn't go back and look at her or hear her voice. I couldn't admit I'd failed. My father used to tell me that I screwed up everything and ruined his life. When his voice gets in my head, I can't explain what happens. It's like he takes over, and I'm a little kid again. Instead of exiting the freeway, I don't know what came over me. I just kept driving until I reached Michigan. I ended up in a roadside hotel in Grand Rapids. I hadn't called to tell Sasha where I was, even though I knew she was worried sick. I hated myself. I was just like my dad. He and my mom would get into some major knockdown, drag-out fights, and the next thing I'd know, the door would slam shut and he'd take off. I'd spend hours sitting by the window waiting for him to come back."

Grant's eyes were fixed on the ceiling, refusing to meet mine. I tried to imagine what it was like to be Sasha, to have this man's love one moment and have it be gone the next.

"I had to face the music eventually. I thought she'd be pissed—she had every right to be. Instead, when I told her I didn't want to be married anymore, she understood. She felt the same way and had some of the same concerns I did, which was why she was always wanting to talk so much about our relationship. I know I did the right thing for both of us, but in the wrong way. You've confirmed that I made the right decision, Kim. I mean, we didn't even meet, we just . . . collided. In the last few weeks, we've shared more intimacy, body and soul,

than I ever shared with Sasha. It makes me feel guilty, but also lucky."
He kissed me. "So damn lucky."

I rolled over to look at him, my head propped on my arm, my fingertip tracing our initials into his chest hair, KH + GD. "So, where do you stand with her now?"

"Well, she ought to hate me, but she's weirdly fine about it and insists on being friends. She's actually very grown-up about the whole situation. We see each other all the time at the university."

"You *work* together?" I hated the idea of Grant spending time with someone he'd slept with, even if he claimed there was no lingering attraction.

"You know how some people split up and have to keep dealing with each other because they have a kid or a dog? Well, we have the book to finish. It's under contract with Fordham University Press, and it's really important for my career, and hers. What I'm saying is that I need you to respect that she's a necessary part of my life, and she probably always will be. But there's absolutely nothing between us, I promise."

"Nothing? You were married to her. You still are."

"Nothing but friendship. Really, that's it. It's like how you describe your relationship with Basil."

"You're for real getting divorced?"

He stood up, walked over to his desk, and held up a legal-size manila envelope. "It's already underway, and it's costing me a fortune."

A week later, I met him at his office on the University of Chicago campus to join him for lunch. I saw how his female students lined up to speak with him during office hours, how he loved to joke that Wittgenstein was hiding behind the fireplace with his famous poker. They adored him and laughed at all of his jokes. He was completely clueless that he was real estate with multiple offers, an auction item with several paddles up in the air.

We walked down the hall. I put my hand on his ass, and he stiffened. "What?" I asked. That's when I saw the nameplate on the closed door: DR. SASHA DUFFY.

Sasha.

Duffy.

And there she sat at her desk. Tiny. Blond. *Real.* Grant pulled away. "I should go talk to her."

I ate lunch alone.

Then the phone calls started. We'd get ready to head out for the day and Grant would say, "I have to take this." He'd disappear into his room, sometimes for hours, leaving me waiting, frustrated and angry and feeling unable to complain. There was always work to be done on their book, and they were obsessed with academia and loved to gossip about people I didn't know. They spoke about ontology and fuzzy logic, topics that meant little to me.

Sasha had wedged herself between us, not necessarily because she was manipulative or evil, but because we'd allowed her to become entangled in our relationship—me, out of fear that I'd lose Grant if I put too many demands on him, and Grant, because he wasn't great at saying no to her and, moreover, he liked having two women who loved him. Who wouldn't?

"Aren't you jealous?" My friends would ask. I was—although not because they had chemistry. I didn't see a spark; instead, I saw something I perceived as even more threatening than sex: a deep intellectual fascia that connected them. They weren't fully unmarried and never would be. I felt I had nothing on Sasha—until I found out I was pregnant.

There was never any question that I'd go through with it. I was emboldened partly because of the discussion Grant and I had had about having a family, and partly because I couldn't have asked for a better role model of independence than Polly. Not for a second did she doubt that I could be a mother; she didn't make me feel as if I'd made a mistake. Instead, she said, "If I could do it alone, you can, too."

"But Burl helped raise me. And I don't *want* to do it alone," I said. "I want us to be a family." That word seemed too special for me to even say out loud, reserved for other people.

"You get your ideas of *family* from television sitcoms, Kim. You hardly know the man, and he's still in cahoots with his wife. You can't get married anyway, not if you want your alimony, and you'd be a

fool to give that up. You don't even need him. You can end your pregnancy—"

"No, I can't."

"Okay, so don't. It'll be hard, but you won't die. You're not a teenager. Women have been doing this forever."

I didn't want having a child to be a solitary experience, but after
what Grant had told me about Sasha, I was terrified. "I'm worried he'll
think I trapped him."

"Don't be ridiculous. It takes two to make a baby."

"But I'm scared to tell him."

Polly sighed. "Kim, you're saying that you want stability, and yet
this is a man who walked out on his wife when things got hard. What
makes you think it's going to be any different with you?"

I didn't have a reason why I believed it could be, I only knew that I
wanted it to be true. I told Grant I'd meet him near the giraffes at the
Lincoln Park Zoo. As he approached, I saw not just my boyfriend but
the father of my child, a man whose destiny was now forever intertwined with mine. There we were, surrounded by animals in captiv-
ity, and I felt as if I'd built a cage he was about to step into.

His smile was so wide, and for a moment I thought this was going to
be okay. I was about to hand him the rattle I'd slipped in my coat pocket
when he exclaimed, "You'll never believe it, Kim! I got the postdoc at
UW–Madison after all; the other candidate dropped out."

"What are you saying?" I dropped his hand. "You're moving to
Madison?"

"I can't pass it up. It's a chance to study with some of my heroes,
and to teach, finally."

"Congratulations," I said halfheartedly. My heart sank.

He lifted my chin with his thumb so I could look him in the eye.
"It's just for a year. We could keep dating long distance, but I can't
stand the thought of being away from you for that long. Will you
come with me, Kim? I know we're new, and it's a big move, but I want
us to do it together."

In an instant, I knew my answer. I would have gone anywhere with
Grant. "We'd love to," I said.

"Since when did you start speaking in the royal *we*?"

I handed him the rattle. On the underside I'd written my due date, October 11, in Sharpie. He looked at me quizzically. I pointed to my stomach.

He rolled the rattle around in his hand as the words poured out of me. "I couldn't believe it either. I tested three times. It kept coming out positive. My doctor confirmed it." I tried to read his expression. "I'm keeping it—"

"Yeah, for sure. I mean, you should do what's best for you. . . ."

"Best for me?" Why was he speaking to me as if I were a stranger he'd met on the el? I could see that he still hadn't fully processed the news. He tried to smile, but his eyes were so confused and frightened that I wasn't sure how to take it. "It's just, this is happening so fast. I'm not even divorced yet. You're so sanguine about the prospect of becoming a mother."

"Sanguine? What does that even mean?"

"Like, you're okay with it."

"Oh, believe me, I freaked out, but I've had a few more days to process it, I guess." I paused. "Grant, I thought . . . I thought you'd be . . . sanguine, too."

How had I allowed myself to hope this would play out any differently? I knew it was a shock, and yet, I didn't count on what happened next. His eyes glassed over. He stared off in the direction of Lake Michigan and suddenly it seemed as if he weren't there anymore. "I'm sorry." He kissed my forehead. He began to walk away from me in the stunned manner of someone who'd been in a terrible accident.

"Grant?"

He didn't respond.

"Grant, are you just going to walk away?"

He didn't walk—he picked up his pace and began to *run*, and with every step I could hear the rattle shaking in his hand. He ran through chunks of old, dirty snow and melting puddles, past all those animals napping and grazing, barely looking up as he went past.

Then he was gone.

Shattered, I walked back to my apartment in stunned silence. I was too shocked for tears and too sad to be angry. How did that happen? One minute he was asking me to move to Madison with him, the next, he was gone.

A few miserable hours later, my phone rang. I'd left some desperate messages for Basil to call me back and was hoping it might be him; he had always been there for me. Instead, it was a woman's voice on the line. "Kim? Don't hang up. I know we haven't met. This is Sasha."

How could my day get any more uncomfortable? Was she going to stake her claim on Grant, tell me to back off? "Why are you calling me?"

"I know, I'm probably the last person you thought you'd hear from. Look, I'm at Grant's. He asked me to come over. He told me about . . ." I could hear the pain in her voice, but I could also hear the kindness. "Well, he told me everything."

I clutched the phone so hard it could have shattered in my hand. "I have no idea what's going on."

"I know you don't. Did he tell you about what happened to him when he was a kid?"

"Just that his dad ran off and died, and his stepfather was kind of a milquetoast."

"I guess that's the high-level version." Here I was deeply in love and pregnant, and I felt she was making a point that I knew little about him. She wasn't wrong.

"His parents were so young when they had him. His dad got drunk and took off all the time, and his mom started drinking, too. They got into some epic fights. Lather, rinse, repeat—well, until Richard wrapped his car around a tree and never came home again. His mom hit the bottle pretty hard after that, and she didn't do the best job taking care of Grant, at least for a while. He's a good guy, he is, but he can't deal with conflict, and he'd rather be the one who leaves than gets left, if that makes sense."

"I guess?"

"It was hard for me to hear your news. But I know that, as a woman, you must be pretty damn scared right now. And as Grant's friend,

I know he's scared, too. He's a good guy, he really is. He's just been through lots of turmoil. He's not the kind of man who would ditch you in your . . . situation."

"But, Sasha, he ditched *you.*"

"We weren't working. I knew we didn't have a future, and so did he. It was different. I've already got a new boyfriend. I've moved on, and so has he, obviously."

She didn't sound like someone who was emotionally unstable; she didn't sound needy. She sounded kind and generous. Did I not know the whole story, or had Grant misrepresented their relationship? Did he have a low bar for neediness? Did he build up his side of the story so he wouldn't scare me away?

She said, "Will you come talk to him? He feels terrible. You'll both feel better."

By the time I got to his apartment, she was gone. Grant greeted me with a tearful embrace that I needed so badly I almost forgot how angry and upset I'd been. "I'm so sorry," he said. He stroked my hair, ran the back of his index finger down my cheek. "You must have felt—"

"I did, Grant. I felt as bad as you thought I could feel, and worse. I thought you left me the way you left Sasha. I thought I was going to have to deal with this all alone. I've never felt so shitty or so scared. Never. Don't ever do that again."

"I know, I'm sorry, I know. But you have to believe me, you're the one. I knew it the minute we met. And your news was a total surprise, although we were pretty careless, so it shouldn't have been. Things aren't lining up the way they usually do, but we're adults. We're smart and we're in love, and we can do this. Come to Madison. We'll have this baby and make such a beautiful life together."

Part of me was still standing at the zoo, watching Grant's back as he ran away. The other part could hear Sasha's voice in my ears.

"Listen to me. This is crazy but wonderful. We're off to a wobbly start but we'll right ourselves. You are not in this alone. Forgive me. Please?"

I did forgive him, but forgiving and forgetting are two different things.

If I hadn't been pregnant, we might have moved slower, talked through things more, seen a couples counselor. Instead, shocked by first a positive pregnancy test, then the revelation that we were having twins, we were plunged into an entirely new future.

It turned out that Sasha was good at talking Grant through his issues when I was too stressed or exhausted. Again and again, Grant turned to her, and I turned to Basil. We outsourced our emotional needs to our exes, never fully showing the messiest parts of ourselves to each other.

Sasha became even more entwined with our lives when she took a tenure-track job at College of the Mounds, an hour away from us, and then he started working there. On campus, everyone thought they were married because she'd taken his name. She had Grant during the week, and I had him on the weekends. I told myself that it was for the best. With Grant gone part of the time, there was less risk of upsetting his delicate equilibrium.

People talk about open relationships, and in some ways that's what we had all these years, albeit without sex. I came to appreciate Sasha's role in maintaining Grant's well-being and felt lucky, even, that I didn't have to be everything to him, even as I sometimes resented that her presence was so necessary. We were both good for Grant. I could be a lot like Polly. I didn't have patience for wallowing when he was down, and I soon learned that I could off-load some of that emotional labor to Sasha, who was a more sympathetic sounding board, particularly when it came to his academic concerns.

She'd gone through a series of boyfriends over the decades. And then, about a year before the college closed, Sasha fell in love with Matthias, a visiting sociology professor from Germany. He had a clear-eyed view of Grant and Sasha's relationship that we'd normalized. He said they were "enmeshed," and while he felt for Grant, he made clear that boundaries needed to be erected, even before their big move over the summer. Grant wouldn't say so, but losing constant access to Sasha was harder for him than losing his job. "After thirty years, you finally broke up," I joked—although I wasn't really joking.

I realized that I couldn't text Sasha with this news; I had to call. She seemed surprised to hear from me, and before I could lose my nerve,

I blurted out that Grant was missing, that he'd gone off for a hike and hadn't come home. I explained that a search was underway, and it was all over the news, and that the whole situation was incredibly scary and dramatic. "You know him, Sash. Do you really think he could have gotten lost?"

In the space of her pause, I clutched the phone and felt my stomach churn.

"No." She said this with the certainty of someone who had been waiting for me to ask her that question for her entire life. And for the first time, I felt she was wrong, and that I was the one who knew Grant better.

"But he's never been gone this long before," I said. "And he's really into hiking now." It sounded as if I was pleading with her. "I really think he might be lost."

"He's not lost, Kim."

"He's different. He's changed since we've arrived. *We've* changed. We were . . . we were really good."

"That's great." Her enthusiasm was forced, and she sounded skeptical. "I mean, not if he's truly missing in the mountains. But change is good, that's what we've all needed. I'm focusing on my own life, which means I need to be less tied up in Grant's drama."

"But aren't you worried? He could die up there."

She took a sharp breath, the kind you take when you're trying to prevent yourself from saying something too harsh. "He runs when he's scared, Kim. He always comes back. I'm sorry, but I can't be part of this anymore."

"I wasn't asking you to be part of anything," I stammered. "I was asking—"

Her words were harsh, but she was not unkind. "Grant is fine. He's always fine. But he's not my problem anymore, Kim. You either need to be his safe space and marry him, finally—or you need to walk away."

Chapter Ten

Palm Springs
November 6, 2022

To enter Le Desert was to experience the world flipping inside out. The security wall that just moments earlier kept us outside seemed to suddenly embrace us, providing me with the false sense that nothing could go wrong here.

Despite Grant's initial skepticism about the place, I could tell he was as taken by surprise as I was, because the exterior of the Spanish Mission–style complex didn't even hint at the sort of lushness that existed on the inside.

It wasn't the explosive foliage I associated with summer in the Midwest, when all the green could eat you alive. Here, every bit of color stood out like a miracle. Leggy palm trees created a stark contrast to the crumbling mountains in the background. Hummingbirds, startled by our arrival, hopped in the branches of the lemon tree next to the entrance and then, like birds in a Disney movie, darted directly in front of our faces. The fancy orange and coral flowers were so bright it almost hurt to look at them. The ground cover beyond the paved walkway and courtyard was essentially a carpet of cacti, the names of which I would soon know: San Pedro, Mexican fence post, barrel, and Peruvian apple. Hammocks were strung between surprisingly fat, bearded palm trees. The courtyard was not groomed per se, but it was tended to and cared for, an arid Eden.

The main building had six or seven units on each side, judging by the rosy-pink doors, each with an adjoining walk-out patio, and formed a C-shape around the courtyard. Two squat, charming detached bungalow-style casitas with wide chimneys and shutters sat on the far side of the property. Bright purple bougainvillea smothered the stucco walls. The jagged profile of the mountains in the distance rose above the clay-tile rooftops as though they were part of the architecture. It felt as though Le Desert had been there for so long that it had become a natural feature of the landscape.

Beyond the courtyard was a garden that went back beyond my view. I could just make out a dilapidated tiki bar and a mini golf course in the distance. I scanned for unit numbers on the main building.

"I was expecting this place to be more . . . *Jetsons*," Grant said, pleased. He had an appreciation for old things. "I feel like we just got off the last train to Marrakech."

"This is old-school Southern California glamour," I said. "Do you think we'll be haunted by the ghost of some Hollywood director from the twenties?"

The pool in the center of the courtyard was the crown jewel, the vortex, accessorized with wrought-iron loungers and fanciful striped umbrellas dripping with hot-pink fringe. In the middle of the pool a woman was swimming laps, oblivious of our arrival. Her rear was perfect and round, two brown moons divided by the metallic-copper thong of her bikini bottom. Her stroke was propelled by her slim but powerful arms, and as she moved, floating blow-up flamingos bobbed spookily on the surface in her wake. As soon as she got to the edge, she changed direction with an expert kick turn, and then, as if she could sense us looking at her, she stopped. She swooshed the long dark hair like oil slicks from her eyes and ungraciously spit out a mouthful of water. "Yeah? Hello?"

"Hi!" I said, my voice echoing off all the hard surfaces.

She stepped out of the pool, revealing gloriously ripe breasts that were barely covered by the two copper triangles of her bikini top, like the flags you put in the ground to show where the electricity runs. She was utterly gorgeous and cool in her youthful fullness, and her skin glowed with health. I couldn't really blame Grant for standing there dumbfounded as a teenage boy at the sight of this estrogen bomb. I was dumbfounded, too. I nudged him with my elbow, almost knocking him over.

Even in my best years, I'd never felt that comfortable with my body, preferring Speedo one-pieces to bikinis, pants to skirts, high-neck sweaters to V-necks. As a teen, I'd tried to tamp down my breasts with Ace bandages from my mother's office in fear that they would eventually hang to my waist like those of the topless women in the photos I saw in *National Geographic*. When I was growing up, looking sexy could get you a bad reputation. I dressed almost exclusively in stretchy, comfortable clothing. Grant teasingly referred to me as "our Lady of Athleisure." How I wished I'd had this woman's body confidence when I was young—and now.

I held up the key chain. I felt I needed to prove that we weren't impostors, even if that's how we felt. I said, "We're guests of Basil?"

"Oh, I love Basil. He's a starseed."

"A what?"

"He's connected to the universe."

"Oh. Yeah. Well, he's my ex-husband. Who are *you*?" I didn't mean for it to sound like an accusation.

She smiled dreamily. "I'm Cassie." She said her name with importance, as though she were Oprah or Cher.

"We're Kim and Grant," Grant said.

"Awesome! Are you Canadian?"

"No, we're from Madison."

"Oh. You look Canadian." She seemed disappointed. "We all love the Canadians."

A man's voice boomed from behind me, "And we love you right back, Cass." I turned and saw an older couple slowly walking toward us. Their matching white hair was amazing in the sun; it was almost unnatural, like pearly-silver nail polish. Two angels; I loved them instantly. They were Grandma and Grandpa, people who seemed as if they were born asexual, sweet and old.

"Well, how about that. Basil was married? To a gal?" The man rocked back on his feet. "How'd that happen? He's gay as a three-dollar bill. Come on, we'll show you to his place. Just wait till you get a load of it."

The woman said, "We'll see you tonight for dinner, Cassie. Taco pie! We made it vegan and keto and paleo and all that jazz, just the way you like it."

"It's basically a pile of sand," the man said.

"Love you guys!"

The couple slowly led us to the detached unit with the 1 on the door. "You're going to be right next door to us. We're neighbors! We even share a patio."

It didn't surprise me that Basil lived in a condo complex when he could have afforded a house. He loved to be around people, and here it seemed he could be surrounded by all kinds. Even so, he wasn't exactly slumming. His was one of the largest, nicest units with the most commanding views.

The man said, "Tell me, how long are you here for? And don't say a week or two, there's too much coming and going as it is. We like people to stay a while, like back in the day before all these short-term rentals."

Grant gave me an *uh-oh* look. "We're here through March," I said.

The wife clapped her hands together and smiled. "Oh, we'll be good friends. Wonderful, wonderful! We're seasonals, too. We arrived last week and we'll be here until April—"

"Unless we crap out before then," the man said, giving his chest a pat. "Could happen. Lots of people around here arrive on their feet and leave on their backs."

"We started coming, oh, what was it, twenty-five years ago now, Gene? We've returned every winter since, aside from 2020 because of the plague. You're from Wisconsin? That's as good as Canadian. We're from Regina. As far as everyone around here is concerned, that may as well be Saskatchewan. One of these days we're going to have a geography bee and see who knows what's what." The woman nudged her husband. "That's a good idea, Gene, ya? Instead of canasta, we can find out who can name all ten provinces."

"She's Little Miss Social Director," he said.

"I'm Jeanie," the woman said. "And this good-looking guy here is Gene. Easy to remember. We are quite a pair—a pair of jeans, that is!"

"I always say we should be a band. We'd call ourselves Denim and DNA." The couple laughed as though they hadn't told that joke a million times. Everything about them matched: their accents, silvery hair, and large wrinkled faces.

Jeanie gave the thick wood door with the little window covered in decorative iron a pat. "This here's Basil's place."

"Hey, I don't mean to intrude, but do you mind if we have a peek inside?" Gene asked. "We've been in almost every unit except this one. Did you know Basil and Hobie have fireplaces?"

"Who's Hobie?"

"Oh, everyone knows Hobie." Jeanie gestured at the mountains. "He thinks he's the boss. He's always hiking or chasing the sheep or spending time with lady friends or whatever he does while the rest of us are up to our ears in a whole lot of nothing. He can be very rude."

"Doesn't seem fair that we don't all have fireplaces." Gene made me feel as if I'd taken something from him.

"Come in," I said, even though I knew Grant would rather enter our new space alone. It was as if I'd grown an emotional periscope into his brain. I was so familiar with his comforts, anxieties, likes, and dislikes that I swore I felt his feelings for him.

The four of us walked into the living room like aliens stepping off a spaceship for the first time. It was bigger than I thought a condo could be and so perfect we had to catch our breath.

"Oh, is this ever nice!" Jeanie elbowed me. "Two bedrooms! Lucky ducks."

The wall facing the courtyard had large windows that revealed million-dollar views of the mountains. The exposed wood of the beamed ceiling made the space seem church-like and airy despite the heavy furnishings. I'd read that a well-decorated room should not have a single focal point. That was the case here, with balanced and explosive bursts of saturated colors punctuating the white expanse. The Moroccan ceramic tiles framing the fireplace were blue and teal. The deep velvet sofa was green, and the Turkish rug was red and gold. A gleaming white baby grand sat in the corner next to neatly stacked LPs, a record player, and six-foot speakers.

On one wall was a giant painting of a McDonald's french fry container, and on the other hung a giant Asian pop art painting with a lacquered surface. I found myself getting lost in it—a floating pink iPhone shot out of a raging neon-yellow sea. Some people want to surround themselves with beauty, while Basil, who could have afforded an original van Gogh, was content to make himself laugh. I was touched to see a framed photograph of Basil and me from our younger days on his mantel. We were standing in front of the *First Down Moses* statue on the Notre Dame campus, pointing up at the sky. How young we were. It was another lifetime, and it could have been yesterday.

Grant walked over to the piano to pick up a gold statue—a real Tony. The plaque said BASIL UNDERWOOD, BEST SCORE.

Gene whistled. "Think that's a fake? You can buy those on eBay, you know."

"It's real," I said, feeling defensive. "Basil is a genius, and he's very well-known."

"I've never heard of him outside of Le Desert," Gene said knowingly. "Then again, half the people you bump into in this city are sort-of and used-to-be famous." He stepped into the recessed dining room, stopping to stare at a stark painting of a red cube. Below it, stamped in big red letters, were the words EVERYTHING, BUT DESPAIR. He said, "Weird."

I met Grant's gaze from across the room and saw a smile in his eyes. From this day forward, I knew that if I thought something was strange, I could call it "everything, but despair." Our lexicon was filled with phrases like that, some dating so far back that I couldn't even remember their origin stories. What would it be like to go through life without the ability to share that language?

Grant said, "Fascinating that there's a comma between *everything* and *but*." He loved to say things were *fascinating*. And to him, they usually were. "Do you suppose the message is meant to be hopeful, like 'do everything but despair,' or 'despair everything'?" Grant paused. "Or 'despair everything *but* despair'?"

"Beats me," Gene said.

"Grant is a philosophy professor," I explained, feeling funny about using the present tense, and genuinely annoyed that he had to show off for these people we'd just met; this was the Grant show, and I'd seen it many times. "He usually has lots of thoughts."

"Well, I worked at the power company for forty years, so what do I know? Go on, smarty. Tell me what you think."

Grant said, "You might not want to know. You see, I'm a rather pessimistic philosopher." He winked.

"Is there an optimistic kind?" I asked.

Grant pretended to ignore me. I noticed a little spark in him that hadn't been there in a while. He was always happy to have an audience.

"Schopenhauer—Arthur Schopenhauer, a German philosopher, and an even greater pessimist than me—believed we wander across the stage of life in a state of constant misery, driven only by desire. But when we're satisfied, our desire dies, and without desire we die, too. See? That pretty much goes against the ethos of a resort town. We might be relieved of pain, but that same relief destroys existence. In other words, the only thing that exists is the present, so why bother striving to enjoy it? Maybe that's what this artist is getting at, albeit backward. Ignore despair, even if it's baked into everything."

"Bet you're fun at a party," Gene said, slapping Grant on the back. "Well, thanks for showing us around. Welcome! Palm Springs is a slice of heaven. We're off to the Mizell Center for some bowling with dice or what have you. When you get settled, you can join us. There's plenty to do, and all the time in the world to do it. Come on, Jeanie."

Jeanie suddenly seemed confused. She looked around, baffled. "Do we live here?"

We all fell silent.

Gene was incredibly patient and kind. "No, my love. We live next door. Come on, I'll show you."

As soon as they were gone, Grant said, "That was terrifying. That'll be us someday."

We wandered around Basil's place, opening cabinets and doors, all the while taking in his full-throated sense of style. "This," Grant said, "is what a home looks like when a fashionable homosexual blesses it with his magic sword."

I loved it, even though it made me feel like a complete failure. I'd never had the luxury of designing a room from scratch, or the money and taste to make it look cohesive, or the guts to buy avant-garde artwork or pillows with tigers' faces on them. Decorating had never been a priority for me. Our Madison home had become a comfortable museum of our former life, filled with framed photos and artwork I didn't have the heart to let go of. Our rugs were stained, and our couch sagged from use. When Mitzie moved into assisted living, Grant held on to some of her fussy Victorian antiques because he didn't have the heart to part with them. Somehow, we found room, but I resented Grant's inability to let go. Our space felt even more chaotic and crowded, a clash between Nancy Reagan and the Olive Garden.

I'd begun to see our possessions not as things to enjoy, but as future burdens for the girls to get rid of when we downsized or died. I resolved in that moment to return home and get rid of everything, maybe even the house. Start anew.

Grant said, "There are no books here, Kim. None."

A coffee-table book called *Let's Get Lost* about bucket-list travel destinations sat atop the credenza. I pointed at it, reminded of the sabbatical, and the time alone, that I didn't have. "I saw some cookbooks in the kitchen."

"Those aren't *real* books. This is what I hate about California. Nobody reads. They just want to relax and . . . vibe."

"Grant, since when do you hate an entire state? That's a pretty harsh generalization."

"Sunshine all year long makes you soft."

"You think suffering through winter gives us moral superiority? More depth?"

He shrugged. "Yeah, I do actually."

I didn't want to admit that part of me agreed with Grant. "They have plenty of stress here, too. Droughts and wildfires. Earthquakes. Kim Kardashian."

Grant would not be swayed. "I wouldn't know Kim Kardashian if she rang my doorbell."

We walked into the larger of the two bedrooms. Basil's room was more spacious than our bedroom back home, where we slept in a wooden sleigh-style bed that looks as big as an SUV, a splurge from the early years of our marriage. Basil's headboard was covered in green silk, and the walls featured a pink, green, and red Chinese-pagoda and dragon pattern.

Exhausted, I flopped next to Grant on the bed and kicked off my shoes. His shirt was pulled up to reveal the beginnings of a belly. I was always after him to lose weight. Still, I found his body attractive. Irresistible, even.

I stared up at the vaulted ceiling and began to giggle.

"What are you laughing at?"

"It's just so crazy that we're here. We're like the pelicans that were found in Greenland."

He rolled over and wrapped his leg over mine and stared at me lovingly. "Does it strike you as odd that I'm about to make love to you in your ex-husband's bed?"

"No. Not at all." I ran the palm of my free hand over the tickly soft hair that ran down his belly.

"I've been going crazy sitting in a car with you for so many days. I always want you. I want you now."

"It's the middle of the day."

"What else is there to do?"

"A million things! We need to unpack. Grocery shop. I was about to reach out to Melody. I told Basil—"

"Melody can wait. I can't."

Our lovemaking felt less routine in a different bed, a different room. Grant was slower and more purposeful, intent on my pleasure. Octavia had told me that marriages fail for the same five reasons: the balance of power, work, kids, money, and sex. We struggled with the first four. Then again, people have sex for different reasons. Sometimes out of frustration, sometimes love. Sometimes to pin each other down.

Usually, Grant would call out my name, or tell me he loved me, or say that I was beautiful, but he uttered something different at the height of passion, and in a more urgent, even scared, tone of voice: "Oh, Kimmy, I *need* you."

In all our years together, he'd never said that out loud. He would never have dared, and neither would I. *Why,* I wondered, *did he say it now?*

Chapter Eleven

Palm Springs
January 3, 2023
2:00 P.M.

The second time Grant left, I decided that if I needed to, I could be a single mother.

March took longer to rebound from her early entry in the world than Dort, which is why I've always gone out of my way to protect her. She was born notably weaker, with a low Apgar test. In those early days in the NICU, she'd get this look in her eyes as if she weren't there, and she'd turn gray. It was no big deal for the nurses, who would joke that she was taking another trip to "the Great Beyond." She'd stop breathing, and they taught us how to flip her onto her stomach and smack the bottoms of her feet to bring her back to life once we got home.

March had always seemed mysterious and powerful because of these spells. She grew out of them, but when they were happening, I couldn't rest because I was so fearful that she could drift off forever while I slept. I checked her breathing a hundred times a night. That first year, the twins were terrible sleepers anyway, and they'd wake each other up with their crying.

Grant wasn't around much. He had a busy teaching load, and fall was the time when academics look for jobs, a process that consumed much of his time. He was flown out to a few colleges for interviews that didn't pan out. UW didn't have anything to offer him but a lecturer position. I thought he should take it and try again the next year, but he argued that it had always been his dream to be a tenured professor.

When he came home, he saw me at my worst, too tired even to close the flaps of my nursing bra. My hair was greasy because I didn't have time to shower. My shirt was covered in spittle and baby food, and everything smelled of diapers and wipes. Our apartment was a mess because my arms were always full; I couldn't bend down to pick up baby blankets or toys, and there was no way I could cook. I didn't have any friends in this new city. All day long I'd do the best I could, afraid to ask Grant for too much help because he was busy, and I was afraid to tell him how much I was suffering. We were still so new, and so fragile. I kept thinking back to how he'd run away from Sasha, and how he ran away from me when I told him I was pregnant. I couldn't deal with his running away now and leaving me alone.

I dragged myself through the days as if on a military crawl through a dark cave, blurry from attending to my two little birds with their beaks open, hungry always at the same time. Dort would pound my breast when I couldn't make enough milk. *More, more, more.* March had problems latching. She'd squirm and cry in frustration, and I worried constantly about her weight.

One awful late afternoon when Dort and March were at their worst, I walked to the front stoop of our rented duplex, the girls screaming in my arms. They were so cranky no matter what I did, and I was so burnt-out that I was truly afraid of what I might do if I snapped. I needed to be where people would see me to keep me from harming the twins. I'd been horrified by stories of mothers who'd shaken their babies; I thought those women were monsters. Now I had sympathy for them, pushed over the edge by colic, hormones, and sleep deprivation. Babies were fountains of need.

That was the moment when I knew I couldn't get through another minute alone. Instead of begging Grant to take a day off, I broke down and called Polly. I hated asking my mother for help. She'd been so confident in my abilities, so certain raising children was something any woman could do alone, no big deal.

I felt I'd failed. Big-time.

The next day she showed up with her suitcase like a grim Mary Poppins, took one look at me, and said, "You look like shit, Kim. Go take a shower. Then go to bed."

"But what if they're hungry? And March, you have to watch her—"

"I'm a nurse—well, a retired nurse now, but I was damn good." She pointed her finger in the direction of our bedroom. "Go."

Within hours, order had returned to our world—or at least something close to order. The girls somehow knew better than to mess with my mother, which made me feel like an even bigger failure, as though they'd been keying off my anxiety. They grew mercifully quiet, and after a few frustrating days they started taking the bottle. The laundry was done, and the refrigerator filled with groceries. We went on walks and explored our University Heights neighborhood and I started to fall in love with my new city. For the first time in months, I felt human again.

Polly said, "You need a job."

"I know, but the—"

"They'll be fine. That's what day care is for."

"Grant would help but he's so busy, and his postdoc is just one year. He wants to make a good impression. It means everything to him."

"Stop making excuses for him." Polly's lips were pressed together. "Although in his defense, you never ask for his help. I'll stay and give you a hand, but only until you get a job."

Grant appreciated Polly, but not in the same way I did. He didn't know her well and found her harsh and too direct. He felt our space was cramped, and he was outnumbered by all the women in the house. When he came home, she'd make him do laundry and dishes and send him to the store to buy diapers. If he was tired, she'd put a baby in his arms and say, "We're all tired."

It was nice to have her do and say to him what I wished I could.

One morning, Grant put on a suit and spent extra time with his appearance. He didn't say where he was going, only that he'd return late.

When he did, Polly was at the store, and everything had gone to hell without her. Dort had just thrown up and March was hollering from her bassinet, and the oven timer was dinging relentlessly. I was at my wit's end.

"Guess what?" He picked up March and held her like a football. He was grinning from ear to ear.

"Can you grab a wipe? I need to get this roast out of the oven."

He cleaned up Dort and I took the roast out, burning my hand.

"Don't you want to hear my good news?"

"Sure." What I really wanted was to hear nothing. I craved silence and sleep.

"Well, I had an interview today, and I got it. It's tenure-track, a three-three load. The dean asked me why I wanted to teach at a small liberal arts college. I didn't know what to say, but you know what? I think I'd like actually knowing the names of my students. Not just their names, but really getting to know them, get to know their thinking. The campus was so quaint, filled with history. I think it'll be a great fit, a place to have a career."

"That's wonderful. Where is this mythical place?"

He hesitated. I could tell his excitement came with a big *but*.

"It's just an hour away."

"Where, Grant?"

March started to shriek, a sound that went straight to my spine. And, of course, Dort had to join the chorus.

"College of the Mounds," he said.

I felt as if I'd been kicked in the stomach. "That's where Sasha just got a job."

"I know. And she helped pull some strings for me when they had an opening."

"You are *not* working with your ex-wife. She still has your name! No, Grant. There are other colleges and other jobs. You can lecture for a year and try again. No way."

I saw him take in the scene: the messy house, the crying babies, the cranky, out-of-shape wife saying no to his dreams.

"I told you, we're just friends. She's dating a guy there, they're serious. I met him. It's a really good job. The way colleges are starting to rely on adjuncts, I might never be able to find a tenured position. This is all I've ever wanted to do, and it's mine for the taking."

"I honestly can't believe you'd even consider it. You knew it would be a problem for me because you didn't tell me you were interviewing."

"I can't say anything, it's always chaos here."

"Oh, I'm sorry you have to deal with my reality for a few hours each day."

"Kim, you're being unreasonable."

"*I'm* being unreasonable? I was up all night. Look around!"

And he did. Even with Polly's help, our apartment looked like footage of a small town after a tornado with chunks of roof and siding everywhere and cars on their side.

Polly walked in the door at that very moment, let out an exasperated sigh, and lifted March out of Grant's arms. "What's going on?"

Grant got that look in his eyes. I'd seen it before, the moment I told him I was pregnant. He couldn't process, couldn't deal. "Nothing," he said. He hadn't even taken off his coat. He turned around and walked out the door.

After he left, my mother showed little patience for my tears—not that night, and especially the next morning when Grant still hadn't come home.

"Here's what you're going to do. You're going to get a job, and you're going to find a day care. And you're going to buy a house with that money you saved. You can love that man all you want, but you need to protect yourself."

And that's when the walls I'd built around my heart grew even higher, only to come crashing down all these years later as I braced myself for an update from Brady. I pulled my phone out of my pocket and checked for news. Instead, I saw that the twins had been texting nonstop.

Please tell me they found Dad, March wrote.

Dort added, *I'm headed to the Berlin airport.*

I rebuffed their efforts. *No need, he'll be found before you arrive.* I still wanted to protect them, even as I wanted to beg them to come. I missed them as much as I missed Grant.

I had thought about keeping news of this situation from them, to spare them my anguish. Melody said they'd never forgive me if they found out about Grant's disappearance later. "Believe me," she'd said, "I know what it's like to have a child who won't forgive you."

March said, *Why can't they find him??? Isn't this their core competency?*

Dort shot back, *Why do you always sound like you're updating a LinkedIn profile?*

Dort was tough—maybe too tough—but March was still fragile, or at least that was how I always thought of her.

I wrote, *Dad is going all out researching his next Christmas lecture topic: adventure survival.*

Each year before opening gifts, Grant made everyone in the family give a very short TED Talk–style lecture on something interesting he or she knew about. This started when the girls were seven years old. They would teach us how to mummify a carrot or argue that video games improve literacy, in hopes that we would break down and let them spend their time the way other kids did. As the girls grew older, their subjects grew more mature, from the environmental impact of "cruel cashmere" to chain particle theory.

This year, our family spent our first holiday apart; March was invited to the house of the parents of her fiancé, Simeon, in Houston, and Dort's band had some shows in Slovakia. Even though they had other places to be, they both seemed uncomfortable with the idea of their parents in Palm Springs instead of our Madison home. We were supposed to be planted in one place, like the backyard oak tree they'd swung on as kids.

Our Zoom connection was iffy, which made the annual lectures seem more distant. Dort told us about the counterculture in Berlin's Prenzlauer Berg neighborhood, and March, who worked as an "integrated producer" for a digital-marketing company, shared her "best practices for process," which left us even more baffled about what she actually did for work.

I usually shared moving stories from my job, but this year I spoke about Sunnylands, the modernist mid-century estate of Lee and Walter Annenberg in Rancho Mirage, which Basil's mother had referred

to as "the Camp David of the West." The Annenbergs, wealthy art col-
lectors and philanthropists, were as close to royalty as we had in the
United States. One day, Melody took me on a private tour of the home.
She explained that she and her parents had been there several times
as guests. Her mother had sunbathed with Nancy Reagan, her father
had golfed with Richard Nixon, and Melody herself had eaten off the
fancy Herend china when she dined with the queen of England.

For my Christmas lecture, I talked about Walter Annenberg's obsession with bird-watching, and how it had shaped the house. I explained that he'd even installed a microphone in his bird feeder and
had the sound of chirping birds piped into his bathroom so he could
listen to them when he showered. "Now there's an app for that," Dort
said, unimpressed by anything she considered bourgeois.

Grant gave a lecture on the dangers of altruism and got into another of the heated philosophical arguments he and Dort loved, which
ended when she accused him of becoming a fascist. He barked at her,
"You, my sweet, have a low bar for fascism."

March texted, *I'm never complaining about Christmas lectures ever
again.*

Dort said, *I wouldn't go that far.*

Don't worry until you need to worry, I had replied.

But now? I had a feeling it was time to worry.

Chapter Twelve

Palm Springs
November 9, 2022

It's almost impossible to come to Palm Springs and see it for what it actually is. You already have a vision in your head: angular mid-century modern homes with large, brightly colored doors, breeze-blocks, shimmering pools, vintage cars, and palm trees. By the time we arrived, we had a certain set of expectations, and anything that didn't conform felt off, such as when we spied boxes of rat bait or saw a sun-hardened person walking around carrying a spare tire, or kids doing skateboard wheelies in the parking lot glittering with broken glass adjacent to a closed-down bank.

We expected the city to perform for us, and at first, I felt let down that we were not going to spend the winter inside the iconic Slim Aarons photograph from 1970, *Poolside Gossip,* which popped up every time I'd searched "Palm Springs" back home in Madison.

In the foreground, two fashionable, well-to-do ladies in palazzo pants sit in metal loungers outside a glassy, boxy mid-century home. They chat amiably in front of a turquoise pool while a friend, sun-tanned and relaxed in a jaunty white sundress, walks toward the pair, her scissored legs reflected in the tranquil water. I'd hardly noticed the mountain towering in the background, although now I could appreciate how it supports the entire scene. The drama and rough edges create a sublime contrast with the cool composure in the foreground.

The photo is a mood: light and uncomplicated, free of laundry, errands, messes, and men—a world that is deliciously unattainable, which I suppose explains the ubiquity of the image. Few people can experience that life, but anyone can buy a reprint of that photo, frame it, hang it on the wall, and dream.

Where, I wondered, as I tasted dust on my tongue and my sun hat kept blowing off my head from the relentless wind, was *that* version of Palm Springs? This view was different, but it was also more interesting and fraught. Here, everything had been stripped away from the Slim Aarons photo except the background.

From what we could tell from our maps, this area, about ten minutes from downtown, was geographically contained, bordered on one side by busy Palm Canyon Drive while, on the other, it disappeared into the long tail of a mountain cove. An arroyo ran through the middle of it, dividing the flat part where Le Desert sat from the hills.

Grant said, "This feels like Palm Springs before it was Palm Springs."

"Do you like it?"

"You know what? I do. It feels . . . *real*."

In our neighborhood in Madison, the homes were mostly built for the same middle-class economic stratum, but it seemed anyone could live here, whether you slept under the bridge by the wash, inhabited a bohemian artist's shack in the middle of the cactus-filled lot, spent your time in a plunge pool behind a sleek new house with a Ferrari in the driveway, or wintered in one of the mid-century condo complexes from the fifties and sixties called the Coco Cabana and the Sandcliff. Some of the homes were old and made of fieldstone, while others were chubby eighties-style retreats. In the Midwest, houses had attached garages to protect you from the cold. Here, houses were designed for the outdoors, prioritizing patios and porches, and they were positioned to take advantage of the amazing mountain views.

Everything seemed inside out. It made me feel young again to be in a place so unfamiliar, where I hadn't yet oriented myself, where everything was a new discovery, where getting lost was to be expected— the goal, even. To get so lost that you couldn't even remember the life you'd left behind.

Much of the Palm Springs housing stock, like Le Desert, was hidden behind tall walls, security fences, and dense foliage. I was beginning to understand that visitors had a kaleidoscopic impression of the city because none had the same experiences of it. While I could see for miles and miles across the desert, there were all these surprising enclaves, entirely separate ecosystems, places I wouldn't know about and experiences I wouldn't have unless I was let inside the gates.

Grant and I turned a corner and discovered a long, raised gravel walkway that ran alongside a dried river basin. Several people were walking on it, but there was a tall chain-link fence with a DO NOT ENTER sign at its opening. That's the thing about being in a new place: you don't always know which rules you can break.

We saw a little dog prancing in our direction wearing a plastic Mohawk-style outfit. My eyes followed the leash to the dog's owner. The man's legs were fit and tan, limbs a sculptor would study to capture the anatomy of the muscles and tendons. He was slim and rugged, his skin as leathery as the palm bark shavings that littered the road. He wore a black skullcap and reflective sunglasses that bounced our images back to us. Despite his youthful physique, his face revealed that he was about our age or older. He could have modeled for Metamucil or Viagra ads. Middle-aged guys didn't look this way where we came from.

"Basil's friends!"

After several days on the road, it felt great to be recognized. It was the first moment I felt we were really *here.*

"I saw you chatting with the Canadians. I hear you're from Wisconsin," he said.

Grant said, "Word gets around fast."

"Coco runs Le Desert's switchboard. She probably knows your Social Security numbers and blood types by now."

"Who's Coco?"

The man smiled mischievously. "Oh, you'll hear her screaming at me. She drives the mobile spa that takes up two spaces in the lot. Basil told me you were coming. I'm on orders to look out for you. I'll show you around, tell you where to go and where not to go. This path here is our version of the New York City High Line. I'm Hobie, by the way."

He shook Grant's hand hard enough to dislocate his shoulder. When I reached my hand out, he ignored it and leaned in to kiss me, European-style, on both cheeks. I hate it when people do this; it makes me feel unsophisticated and awkward. I turned my head instinctively, whiffing his distinctive scent of eucalyptus and sunscreen, and inadvertently brushed my lips against his thin ones. The experience was not unpleasant, and I don't think he meant it as an accident.

"That's quite an outfit." Grant pointed at the little dog.

"She needs it to protect her from the coyotes." Hobie pointed toward the arroyo and we saw a few darting into and out of the sagebrush. "People come here. 'Oh, it's so pretty,' they say. They have no idea. Over there, under the viaduct? That's where the meth heads live. Next to the Araby Trail on the other side, they found a pipe bomb some nut-job hid by the parking lot. And, of course, the coyotes are more than happy to tear an animal to shreds. This is definitely not a place to let your pets roam freely. I won't even tell you about what happened to Mushman."

"Mushman?" Grant asked.

"My last dog. I named him Harvey Mushman because that was Steve McQueen's racing name. Steve lived up there on Southridge Drive." Hobie pointed at the ridge along the top of the mountain where palm trees stuck out along the ledge. "I rode across the desert with Steve on a motorcycle when I was sixteen, the year before he died."

"Steve McQueen, the *actor*?" Grant was as impressed as I was. "The King of Cool?"

Grant's posture was different, as it sometimes was when he confronted men who oozed masculinity. I could see him trying to take up more space, stand straighter, his chest puffed. Hobie was the human version of Grant's Jeep, representing a sort of alpha-dog manhood Grant could never aspire to. Instead of feeling threatened, Grant was flush with admiration. So was I, at first.

"Steve and my dad were friends. They got into all kinds of trouble. Good trouble." Hobie grinned.

"You're *from* here?" Grant's voice reflected his disbelief. Until that moment, we'd thought of Palm Springs only as a place people visit.

"Sure am. Born and bred. I went to Palm Springs High. My dad and his brother owned Le Desert way, way back when it was still a hotel."

"You're a Palm Springs OG," I said.

"I am that. Not too many around anymore, but if there's a place to find us, it's here in Araby. That's what this area is called. Home of the freaks, the artists, the oddballs, or it used to be. You'll fit right in." He pointed at the road that trailed off in the mountains. "Howard Hughes had a place over there. He kept his girls inside and covered up his windows in tinfoil. After he died, Smokey Robinson rented it, then Eva Gabor. Eva, she was like you, Kim. She had *zest*."

I blushed. He thought I had zest?

There was something off about Hobie that I couldn't put my finger on. His forthrightness made me wonder if he seemed different simply because he wasn't midwestern.

"You'd run into Lucille Ball or Sammy Davis buying groceries. This was their community. We treated them like anyone else. I sold Christmas trees to Frank when I was a Boy Scout. Up by Steve's on Southridge Drive is Bob Hope's house—the one that looks like a spaceship. You can see it better from the trail. It's huge, as in two swimming pools huge, as in way too fucking big huge. When Tony Randall visited, you know what he asked after he had a look around? 'Where's the gift shop?' And see over there? The one next to it with the round roof? Look familiar?"

Absolutely nothing looked familiar to me; I felt as if I were on Mars. He pointed at a glassy home that looked as if it were about to fall into the cove.

"That's the Elrod House. You probably know it from the Bond movie *Diamonds Are Forever*. If you think it looks great now, just wait until it's all lit up at night."

We walked down a sandy berm and headed in the direction of Le Desert; already it was established that wherever Hobie went, we would follow. What a snake charmer he was. I was on my guard. As Polly used to say, it was the men with charisma you had to look out for. Still, I felt suddenly vain, acutely aware of how I looked in my wrinkled clothes, comfy shoes, and bucket hat that reminded me of an Amish bonnet. Nothing could be less sexy. Less *zesty*.

Hobie continued his history lesson. "When I was a kid, this area was considered outside of town, Wild West and all that. Not many wanted to come this way. This was the outback. The settlers needed big lots to keep their buckboard wagons. There were no streetlights, no gutters, no curbs. I could tell you all day about the women who founded this town, the date and citrus farmers and fights over water rights. They used to hang blue lights outside the hotels and golf clubs that meant Jews weren't welcome. One of the finest architects in Palm Springs, Paul Revere Williams, was black. Nobody would sit on the same side of the table as him, so he had to learn how to draft his plans upside down. Just wind me up, I can tell you the good and the not so good. I pick up a few shifts as a tour guide in season. That's decent money—well, unless the Canadians are on the tour. Canadians don't tip."

"What else do you do?"

"I make jewelry." Hobie reached into his shirt and pulled out a black beaded necklace with a brown gemstone. "This is tigereye. It gives you confidence."

"You don't seem to be lacking in that department," I said.

He smiled. "I had a bad dune buggy accident in my twenties." He lifted the corner of his beanie to show us a spot on his forehead with a divot in it. "Ever since, I just say what comes to mind. That's why they only call me in for tours when there's an emergency. I tend to tank their Yelp ratings."

Someone started a leaf blower. A shirtless jogger went by. Men in pairs walked dogs of all sizes. I heard the clip-clop of horse hooves as a gorgeous brown quarter horse loped past, ridden by a man in a helmet.

"Now these lots are getting snatched up for millions. Don't get me started on the tourists who come here to go to splash parties, the idiots hanging on pool noodles drinking expensive cocktails. They don't care about the history."

"What's that?" I pointed at a fence that stretched for a quarter of a mile, maybe more, with desert on the other side. "It looks like a migrant border crossing."

Grant said, "Or a religious compound. An upscale Waco."

"Smoke Tree Ranch, one of the most venerable Republican institutions in the country."

"That's where Basil's mom lives," I said.

"You're visiting Mel?"

"You know her?"

"I've known the Underwoods my whole life. My daddy was their draper."

"Their what?"

"He made their curtains. His drapes hung in all the houses here, including hers. You'll see them. He hung drapes for Liberace, Dinah Shore, Frank, Elvis. Go to Sunnylands, his silk drapes are still there."

"Did you inherit the business?" Grant asked.

"Nah, people buy blinds now. As we say, it's curtains for drapes."

Grant laughed a little too loudly. Dort once said her father "laughed in Ph.D."

"You should consider yourself lucky to have an invitation," Hobie said. "It's where captains of industry play cowboy."

"I'm going there for lunch today."

"You didn't tell me you had plans," Grant said. I wasn't used to having to share my itinerary with him. It was disconcerting to have him know or even care about my every move.

Hobie put his arm around Grant's shoulders. "You hike?" Hobie spoke to him the way Trent had back home, as if he were about to call him *little fella*. "We could hit the trails while your wife meets with the queen."

"I'm not his wife," I said.

Hobie seemed curious. "You're his lover?" He looked at me as if picturing me in bed. "Nice job, man." He gave Grant a high five.

I could tell Grant was ambivalent about hiking; in all the years we'd been together, he'd seemed out of place in nature. He wasn't inclined toward exertion, and it was beginning to show. Unlike most men, he wasn't physically competitive and didn't need to work out his stress hitting or chasing a ball. His idea of exercise was a holdover from high school gym class and involved a smattering of jumping jacks and push-ups.

Hiking had never been something I'd imagined people did here. I don't know what I thought people did—float around in a pool all day? Drink Aperol spritzes until they keeled over?

"Where would we go?" Grant asked.

"He likes to have a destination," I said, talking about Grant the way I might to a babysitter when the kids were underfoot.

"We'll take Shannon, right there." Hobie pointed at a sinewy tan path I could just make out, winding its way up the face of a mountain that seemed as tall and as straight as a wall. "We can start you off with a baby climb."

It didn't look like a baby climb to me, or to Grant, who visibly blanched. "It looks hard."

"If you want easy, I can get you a Netflix subscription."

We rounded the corner, and I realized to my delight that we were back at Le Desert, thank goodness, because my foot was starting to ache. The homeless guys were resting on the grass between the sidewalk and the road.

Hobie scowled at them, but lit up when he saw our truck, already covered in dust, parked in Basil's spot in the shared lot. "Pickups aren't allowed in the lot."

"It's not a pickup truck, it's a Jeep."

"Same difference. But that's a nice adventure mobile, I'll grant you that."

"She's ours," Grant said, puffing with pride.

I hated that he kept referring to the truck as *she*.

"You can get into some good trouble with a truck like this, take it to Ladders and the Chocolate Mountains, explore some abandoned gold mines. Take her out to the Anza-Borrego Desert."

Grant was positively beaming. This was the happiest I'd seen him in ages, which made me happy. I had no idea it was the exact moment that would lead Grant to his great hiking misadventure.

"For sure. Anytime. I'm down with that."

Down with that? Never once had he used this phrase in my presence. It's funny how men need to connect over something external, an object or an activity. I wouldn't have imagined Grant and Hobie as friends; they were not two sides of the same coin. They weren't even the same currency.

"Does she have a name yet?" Hobie asked, kicking a tire.

Grant seemed alarmed. How could he have neglected to think of something so important? "I hadn't thought of that."

"It's bad luck to ride a horse with no name. Wait a minute, you know the Jeep comes from *general purpose*. It's like an army thing. So maybe a general. General *Grant*? That's what we'll call her. I hereby christen her the Ulysses S. Come on, let's go. There's a cairn at the top of the hill. You can throw a rock on it and all your wishes will come true."

A few minutes later, Hobie knocked on the door to pick up Grant. His little dog was on its leash and started humping Grant's leg.

I had changed into a dress for my lunch with Melody, brushed my hair, and put on mascara for the first time in weeks. Hobie eyed me up and down. "Why don't you dress sexy? You look like a teacher."

Grant's face was glowing with zinc sunscreen. His legs were white. I could tell he was nervous he wouldn't be able to keep up.

"You have hiking boots?"

Grant shrugged. "Just tennis shoes."

"The incline is almost four thousand feet. What if you lose your balance, or a rattlesnake bites you?" Hobie raised his two bent fingers to look like teeth for emphasis.

"A rattlesnake?" I asked, alarmed. I'd never seen anything bigger than a garter snake back home, nothing with venom.

"Not many this time of year. But come spring, you'll see them sun themselves on the trails in the morning." Was this supposed to be comforting? He added, "It's the baby rattlers you need to worry about. They move like Slinkies, no control. Come. Let's find you a stick for balance."

"I'm fine, really," Grant said.

"You're overconfident." Hobie's tone was scolding. "That's going to get you into trouble, my friend. And not good trouble. You're what, one hundred eighty pounds? Two hundred? That's about the same size as a bighorn sheep. The mountain lions eat sheep every day, so why wouldn't they look at you and say, 'Hey, there's a meal'? You're going to need a stick because it makes you *bigger*. Here's what you do. You walk a ways. . . ." He began walking ahead of us, stopped suddenly, and jerked his body to the right so fast that I jumped. "Then you walk a little more. . . ." He did the same thing, but looking back from his left. "That's what we call a crazy Ivan. I wear a pack even if I don't have anything to carry. I like to cover my neck because mountain lions always attack from behind. Still don't think you need a stick?"

"When's the last time you heard of someone getting attacked by a mountain lion around here?" I asked.

Hobie shrugged. "Years. Doesn't mean it can't happen."

We followed Hobie to the back corner of the property. He was full of swagger and bravado. All these dangers he warned Grant about seemed made-up, the product of his head injury. I thought he was just trying to look tough.

"See that back wall?" Hobie asked. "Can you read what's written on it?"

I squinted. The paint was chipped and it was hard to make out, but someone had written THE 121ST MINUTE on it.

"That's been there since the fifties. When Hollywood worked on a studio system, the actors weren't permitted to travel farther than two hours from the sets in case they were needed while in production. Where we are? This is the very farthest point on that circumference, the last stop. That's what made the town a getaway for the stars, and this area is as far as you could get if you had some funny business. If only these walls could talk. Speaking of talking, enjoy the commentary now because I don't like to chat much when I hike."

I almost laughed. Hobie hadn't shut up since we'd run into him.

"I don't like the sound of voices and, no offense"—he looked at me—"especially women's voices."

"Well, I've heard a lot of your voice this morning so I'm looking forward to some quiet myself."

"I like you," he said. "You're like Coco. She also doesn't put up with my shit." He nodded in the direction of one of the units and scowled. "She *hates* me."

He approached a tree, or really an overgrown bush. It had leaves that didn't even look like leaves, more like old, curly pubic hair, messy and soft, depleted of color. An owl hooted in the canopy. A worn sign nailed to the base read THE DEVIL'S PLAYGROUND.

Hobie plucked off a long, thin leaf and without any hesitation about personal space reached for my hand and rubbed my thumb against it. Grant had the soft hands of an aristocrat; Hobie's were hard and worn. I looked at the ground, embarrassed by the guilty little zip of energy that passed between us. Hobie said, "Taste it."

I did. "Salt."

"Exactly. This is the salt cedar, or tamarisk. The tree sweats, just like we do."

"It's a beautiful old tree."

He stopped and looked at me, serious. "Beautiful? Their roots go deep into the aquifer. They can go through three hundred gallons of water a day. They reproduce like rabbits. They're growing where they don't belong, sucking resources. This right here is a worthless weed, that's what it is, and you know what we do with weeds."

I jumped when Hobie whipped out his jackknife. He made a gesture in the air of cutting the tree in half. Grant seemed impressed, but I was suddenly worried about sending him out into the mountains with this guy.

"I'd take her down myself if it weren't for the petunia planters on the 'garden committee' who insist we preserve this tree because it's been here a long time. Makes no sense. Should I keep a tumor that's been growing for a long time in my nuts?"

With precision, he cut a long, straight branch off the tree and stripped it clean. He showed us a piece of the purple-blue bark before chucking it on the pebbly ground. "The tannins are used to tan leather. At least it has some use." He folded his knife into his sheath and tossed it to Grant. "You can have this one. I have a drawer full of better knives than this. It's another thing you'll need when you hike."

You'd think this guy was going to take Grant through a field planted with land mines.

Hobie grabbed his little dog, threw her into his backpack, and gestured at the gate. "You have water?"

Grant shrugged.

"Never hike without water, that's the first rule. Dehydration is a real thing here, no matter what time of year. You don't want to be like the Germans who came here in the summer and headed to Joshua Tree in their lederhosen. They never made it back. You can hallucinate if you haven't had enough water. You can panic. You can—"

I'd had enough. "Hang on, I'll see what Basil has," I said.

"Basil? I've only seen that guy drink bottled water from Australia."

I ran into the kitchen and looked in every cabinet. Nothing but fancy Italian barware. That's when I had an idea. I thought it was pretty clever of me to rinse out the box of chicken stock we'd used the night before and fill it up with water. I handed it to Grant.

"You midwesterners sure are resourceful!" Hobie couldn't stop laughing, and Grant blanched. He looked like a little kid whose mom had just shown up at school with a change of clothes in case he had an accident.

"Let's go, Swanson."

Was I worried? Not at all. The way I saw it, Palm Springs was a utopia where nothing could go wrong.

I followed the men out of the compound. It felt like walking out of a spaceship into a different world. Once again, balance had returned to our relationship. Grant had his thing to do, and I had mine. As Octavia said, "I like my men busy."

Soon, I'd head over to see Melody and face my past.

Grant waved to me. "Bye, Kimmy." My heart bloomed with tenderness in these moments when I could see the little boy in him.

Already my own wish had been granted. Grant had a friend, and for the first time in a long time, he had something to do.

Hobie flashed me a flirtatious smile. It was difficult to know what to think of him. Still, I was immensely grateful. This was like sending

Grant off to a rehabilitation center and putting him in the hands of a professional, someone who knew more than I did about coaxing him out of his funk since the college closed.

I had the sudden feeling that Hobie, this perfect stranger, had the power to save our relationship—or end it.

Chapter Thirteen

Palm Springs
November 9, 2022

Smoke Tree Ranch was less than half a mile from Le Desert as the crow flies. I decided to walk there, which wasn't the best idea because, by design, the entrance is not well advertised. The big-box stores that front Palm Canyon Drive act as a shield. It was hard to imagine that such rarefied wealth could sit behind the parking lot of a Petco, World Market, and Chipotle. I had the sense that many long-time residents of Palm Springs might not have any idea that Smoke Tree Ranch even existed. Judging from the barracks-like buildings and the guard at the entrance, it seemed more like a military base than a retreat, as if something clandestine were going on inside.

There was no way to walk around the giant redwood swinging gate. The man in the booth with what looked like a sheriff's badge on his chest seemed confused when I approached, as though I were the first creature to enter on two legs instead of in a car, like walking through the McDonald's drive-through. "I'm here to have lunch with Melody Underwood," I said. He asked for my name and my ID and began tapping into his computer. A car pulled up behind me, so close I could almost feel the bumper on my legs.

"Go on in," he said reluctantly, as skeptical as a TSA agent. With the touch of a button, the gate swung open. All I could see spread out in front of me was desert.

"Stay to the right," he said. It was the day after the election, and I interpreted this as both the route to follow and a political directive.

I walked and walked, feeling apprehensive about seeing Melody again for the first time in over three decades. Basil said their relationship had markedly improved since he was young. She'd been so slow to embrace his sexuality that he felt he had to marry me to get out from under her. Did I hold a grudge after all these years? I thought that was all behind us—until now.

The roads were not paved; they were made of gravel, and instead of curbs they were marked by stones. A tiny cyclone of wind picked up from out of nowhere and pushed dirt under my sunglasses, causing my eyes to feel as if they'd been sandblasted. I tried to pull up a map on my phone, but the entire ranch was grayed out on Google Maps. The sun was so bright that I could hardly see my screen, anyway. There was no grass, and the tamarisk trees Hobie had told Grant and me about were tall and planted in rows. They looked as if they'd been there forever.

At last, I saw signs for Ranch and Colony Road, and I passed a few simple-looking one-story board-and-batten homes with split-shake roofs. I saw perfectly maintained tennis courts behind the pro shop; they were empty, and so, too, was the pool, dazzling and elegant, with yellow sun curtains hanging over the eaves of the pavilion. Polly had trained me to think of wealth as slick and shiny; loud and ostentatious. Limos, golden toilets, Russian hookers. This couldn't be more different. Here, wealth was quiet, anonymous. Old money didn't have to try so hard; at Smoke Tree Ranch, it almost didn't try at all.

I came upon the main building, painted brown and shaped like an L. I walked inside and saw the dining room straight ahead, the lounge and library off to the side. In between was the reception desk, where they sold golf gear emblazoned with the ranch's initials in a logo that resembled a Chinese character.

With the beamed ceilings, stone fireplace, knotty-pine walls, and fine upholstery, the space was cozy and elegant; everything seemed both new and used. Once again, my mid-century ideas of Palm Springs were challenged. The atmosphere was not spare and minimalist; it was at once rustic and luxurious—tanned leather and thick silk curtains, BBQ on fine china. The ranch was meant to envelop you, an institution devoted to the fun you could have outside your usual life.

I walked to the front desk. Two young men exuding an air of entitlement breezed through the lobby in their dress whites. "Hi!" I said. "Where are you from?" This was my new Palm Springs conversation starter.

They seemed confused by my question. "We're Colonists."

I paused, feeling both stupid for not knowing what a Colonist was and surprised anyone would ever say that word aloud, and with pride. "I'm sorry, you're—what?"

They looked at each other and rolled their eyes. "You have a nice day," they said, flicking on their sunglasses. Off they went.

Someone tapped me on the shoulder. "Boo!"

I turned and there she was, Melody. That's when I did the unthinkable: I reached in for a hug, and the older woman froze. It was like hugging a lamppost. I backed away, feeling stupid.

"Why did those men say they were Colonists?" I asked.

"Because they are! And so am I. It's what original owners and their descendants call themselves. I'm sure that's a word that rings alarm bells among the professor class in the same way that the word *socialist* rings bells around here. Anyway, welcome, Kimberly. It's good to see you again after all these years."

Was it? Or was Melody just being polite? I reminded myself that she was no longer my mother-in-law, and I was no longer in my early twenties. The ground between us had shifted. If she didn't like me, it didn't matter, so why did it feel as if it did?

She wore a crisp white shirt with a blue sweater tied around her shoulders, a pair of tan slacks, and orange suede driving loafers with a gold chain across the toes. Basil had inherited his looks and his style from his mother. They were both tall and willowy, although Melody was noticeably shorter now, and she appeared gaunt, as though she'd been freeze-dried. While Basil was incredibly pale, Melody was tan. Not a fresh tan, but a lifetime accumulation of tans that never had a chance to fade.

"I was worried I wouldn't recognize you, but you still look the same," I said.

"Ha! Don't try to flatter me, I've got a mirror. You've also grown older. You're prettier than I remembered. Much prettier, actually. You're one of those women who gets better with age in the way some men do, like Vandyke. That man even looked good on his deathbed."

"I'm sorry about—"

Melody cut me off. She was eyeing me carefully. "You've got those broad square shoulders and a long neck. The neck, in my opinion, is the actual key to beauty. Just look at Angelica Huston. I used to dress her, you know, when she was one of the Halstonettes. You, too, are an unconventional beauty. You and Angie share the quality of *jolie laide*."

She turned on her heel and led me into the library. "We could have met at that burger place in the mall out there or had drinks at the Parker, but I wanted you to see the place I love best. In my opinion—and I have many—this is the beating heart of Smoke Tree Ranch."

"Thanks again for inviting me here." Then I blurted out, "When I saw the big fence, I thought it could be a prison."

"It's the opposite of a prison, really. The exact inverse. From here, you see, it's the rest of the world that's a prison. We engage in a more gracious way of living that I fear is in danger of extinction. Cowboy chic, we call it." She gestured at the fireplace. "This is where I learned that style emerges from contrast. Here the women are expected to be both cowgirls and ladies, and the men are both dude and dandy. We don't try to impress each other. It goes against the Smoke Tree Ranch way of life. As founder Maziebelle Markham famously said, 'Most who have come here have been everyplace, they've seen everything, and they've done most things. This is what they do after that.'" Melody cupped her mouth with one hand and said, as if telling me a secret (I'd forgotten this little tic of hers to speak in asides), "We repeat this congratulatory little phrase to ourselves ad nauseam."

She tugged on her Italian gold earring and stared at me as though she expected me to say something. Even though I'd known Basil since I was sixteen, she and I had never spent much time together.

"This property is huge."

"It is. Almost four hundred acres."

"It's like the real desert here, I mean what I thought the desert should look like. I guess I'm surprised it's so preserved and ecologically friendly considering it's so . . ." There I was, blabbing because I was uncomfortable. I couldn't stop myself. "Republican."

Melody frowned with displeasure. I remembered that she'd always been a keen observer of decorum and felt it was in bad taste to bring up politics in a social setting. "*Eisenhower* Republicans, my dear."

Above us was a framed black-and-white photo of Dwight D. Eisenhower himself. I imagined him winking at Melody. In it, he was sitting in front of the same patterned curtains (made by Hobie's dad?) that hung in the room we now stood in. "We've had some diversity of opinion over the years. Stuart there"—Melody tapped the man in the photo talking with the former president—"now, he was a Democrat, and he caught all kinds of hell for it. These days, a few of us have fallen off the edge in either direction, including myself."

I couldn't help but wonder which way she'd fallen, but I didn't dare ask.

She continued, "What I wouldn't give to experience this place for the first time! I've been coming my whole life; Daddy said I was even conceived here, and so, too, was Basil, even though he disavows himself of Smoke Tree, insisting on living over there with the heathens." She pointed in the direction of Le Desert. "That place is crazier than a bag of nails. What a hodgepodge of ruffians and misfits. I don't know what he finds appealing about a bunch of old people obsessing about barking dogs and the timing of the automatic sprinklers."

"I like it so far."

She smiled. "Of course you do. Basil loves it, too, even though he's hardly ever there. You two have always been of like minds."

I stopped to admire a massive gold-framed painting of a cluster of palm trees set against the vast desert landscape.

"That's right, you're an artist. You're looking at a painting by John Hilton. In my opinion, his paintings are simple, almost cartoonlike. I prefer Gordon Coutts." She pointed at a pair of gorgeous, smoky pastels featuring dreamy desert landscapes. There was one with a cowboy leading his horses, and another with a settler warming himself by a fire in front of a covered stagecoach. "See the shadow on that mountain in the distance? That was his trademark blue. Once you see a Coutts, you find yourself searching for that magical shade of smoky indigo everywhere you look. You won't find it on a Pantone chart or anywhere else but here in the desert when the light is *just so.* Which reminds me, do you still paint?"

"Not really." I was embarrassed to talk about my interests—they seemed impractical, fanciful.

"Our tastes diverge, but I must admit that Basil has an eye. He thought you were good. I'll bet you just needed more practice."

"I don't know about that. I've been too busy with life to focus on art. I was thinking I could get back into it while I'm here now that I have some time."

"Oh, you must! These days, most people don't care to capture the world beyond taking photos to post online to show what they've eaten or where they've been."

She shuffled over to the framed black-and-white photos of visiting presidents, square dances, pool parties, an old water tower, groups of men on horseback. They harkened to better, more simple times. "See there? That's Walt Disney, our most celebrated Colonist. That's our logo on his bolo tie. He called this his 'laughing place,' isn't that wonderful? He sold his first home here to start Disneyland, a personal sacrifice that certainly paid off. That's how we achieved dreams in the old days. Now you just sell short. He bought another home on the property, of course. Here he is at a gymkhana."

"Gymkhana?"

"It's like a rodeo with timed events. We'd race horses around barrels in the elimination heats. Oh, we had the most fun!"

Practically every photo on the wall had a horse in it.

She tapped another photo of men in cowboy hats and little scarf ties. "Here's Walt heading out to the trails with the Rancheros, and that's Daddy on Darby, his horse. You'd think Walt was the only person of note to call Smoke Tree Ranch his home, but he is not the only celebrated Colonist. I've proposed we update some of the photo displays, and at least one, so help me, will be of my husband. He looked so very handsome in his Stetson."

I tried again. "I'm sorry about Vandyke. I heard—"

She waved her hand to dismiss my sympathies. Her skinny arm was covered in a thick stack of vintage melamine bracelets. "Did Basil tell you what killed his father?"

"Was it Parkinson's?"

"Nothing so pedestrian. He suffered from Creutzfeldt-Jakob syndrome. It's a disease linked to people who eat their ancestors."

"Wow." What does one say?

"Leave it to Vandyke, dramatic to the end! His diagnosis, terrible as it was, positively thrilled him. This was where he wanted to die. We came for the winter last year, as usual, but then we stayed through spring and summer, and I watched as his mind became a fun-house mirror. Everything changed shape. He hallucinated that I was an ant one day, a giant the next. Small and then large. It would have been worse the other way around, don't you think?"

I hadn't remembered Melody being quite this chatty. She seemed desperate to have someone to talk to.

"I'll tell you, it was very lonely in the offseason with nobody around to carry on with. Just me and the sagebrush and poor, miserable Vandyke. I can see why the town empties out in May. At night the heat isn't so bad, but it plays tricks on you during the day when you become the frog in the boiling water. He hopped out of the proverbial pot on the hottest day of the summer. It was a hundred and eleven degrees when he passed. Even with that impossible heat, I simply couldn't go back to Los Angeles, or anywhere. Most of my friends were in Montana or the Hamptons—if you can live here, you can live anywhere. Me? I simply lack the desire to leave. I may stay here until *I* die, too. Who knows." She led me back to the reception desk. "We have much to discuss. Oh, Davey!" She waved at the manager. "We're ready to sit. By the window, please."

We followed Davey around the long wooden tables with their tall-back chairs. "In my day, you'd come running when you heard the dinner bells. You'd grab a napkin and they'd score your clothespin."

She pointed at the wall of clothespins with Colonists' names marked with the number of times they'd dined.

Melody waved at a pair of men reading *The Wall Street Journal,* her bracelets jangling. "Mornin', dudes," she said in a faux-Western accent.

They looked over the tops of their newspapers. "Mornin' to you, Mel."

We sat at a table on the far side of the room next to a window with a gorgeous view of the mountains. She dramatically pulled out her napkin and snapped it in the air before setting it on her lap. "Those fellas thought I was really something in my day. Now I can tell they think I'm a sad, desperate, old widow—there's a word that puts years on you, *wi-dow.* But I'll let you in on something. It's terrible to lose a spouse, it really is, but now I can get together with friends without worrying how the husbands will get along. Not everyone liked Vandyke, you know. You probably didn't."

"I—"

"He didn't like you, my dear, but don't take it personally. He didn't like anyone who didn't attend boarding school or winter in Bermuda, and there's no reason you should have liked him. I'm sure Basil told you that he made our son's life very difficult because of his *sex-u-ality.*" She said the word as though she'd just learned what it meant and she could finally say it aloud.

"I honestly didn't know Vandyke all that well."

"A lot of the time, I didn't either. But he got better in old age. That happens. The hospice nurse said people die the way they live. Not Vandyke. He became very confused and very kind. So, tell me about your husband—Grant, right? Basil says he's a professor. What's he up to while you're here at the wax museum with me?"

"He's not my husband. He's my partner."

Melody rolled her eyes at that word. "*Partner.* Oh, I hate that. A partner is someone you work with."

In truth, I hated the word, too, because it always raised eyebrows. It seemed to shave something off the emotion and commitment in a relationship.

"Tell me, why not get married? What's the big deal? I have friends who've tied the knot to four, five, six miserable men, and they just keep running to the altar like the priest is handing out pills. As Zsa Zsa said, she was a personal friend, 'A girl must marry for love and keep marrying until she finds it.'"

"Well, you have something to do with that."

"Me?" She put her hand on her chest.

"We didn't marry at first because of my prenup."

She seemed confused.

"Don't you remember?" I was taken aback; this legal contract had dictated my life, and she didn't seem to know of or care about it. "After Basil and I broke up, I could only collect the alimony if I remained unmarried."

"That was all Vandyke's idea, I'm sure. I vaguely recall him working something up with his lawyers. Tell me"—she put her elbows on the table as if we were two old friends gossiping—"how much did you get?"

I felt so greedy. I hated talking about money with Melody because it was hers. "Fifty thousand a year for ten years."

She seemed shocked. "That's all? That's what some women collect in a month. You let that pittance stand in your way?"

"It was a lot to me, Melody. It was . . . it was my house. It allowed me to continue working in the nonprofit sector."

She waved this away as though it were of no consequence. "You should have just asked us for a payout. Are you telling me that even after the alimony ran out you still didn't marry Grant?"

"We talked about it, but we never did. I think we will now, though. He needs my insurance."

"Insurance. Listen to you, Kim. That's no reason to tie the knot. There's more to this story, I suspect. Does he cheat on you?"

"No. We promised we'd always be honest with each other no matter what. I'm not worried."

She cocked her head, confused. "Then what's the problem? Is there someone *you've* been pining for?"

"No, there's no one else."

"Maybe there should be. Nobody needs to know. I certainly won't say a word. If you're having second thoughts about Grant, just take a little advice: If his nail beds are purple, hang on. He doesn't have much time left."

I almost spit out my lemonade. Why did I feel inclined to share with Melody one of the most private, painful details of my life? "Grant can crack under pressure."

"Most men do. Vandyke would fly out of the house at the slightest provocation."

"That's what Grant does. Sometimes when he's too stressed-out or upset, he leaves me. It's only happened a few times, but I'm always afraid he'll leave for good."

"He comes back?"

"He does."

"Kimberly, haven't you ever just wanted to get in the car and keep driving? We all feel that way. Perhaps it's *you* who needs the space, you who needs to run on occasion to clear your head. Speaking from my own experience, I will say that there's an upside to feelings of ambivalence in a relationship. It gives you room to fall in love again and again. Falling in love is the best feeling in the world, and I intend to feel it a few more times."

She picked up her phone. "Should we invite him to join us? I'd like to meet this *partner* of yours. I'm a terrific judge of character."

"He's out hiking with a guy named Hobie."

"Hobie? Oh dear. Watch out for him. He's a cat in a rocking-chair store. He stops by from time to time to check in on me. He brings me flowers, offers to take me places. I suspect he's after my money and he thinks I'm too stupid to know it. I think he's a walker."

"A walker?"

"Oh, there are plenty of those in Palm Springs. A handsome man who ingratiates himself with rich, lonely old widows like me so we won't have to go to events alone." She leaned in and whispered, "Between us, I suspect Hobie is a gigolo. How else can he afford the

HOA dues selling his jewelry to tourists at the street fair on Thursday nights?"

I wanted to learn more about Hobie, but she changed the subject, pointing at my nylon cross-body purse on my chest. "Do me a favor, Kimberly, and take that thing off. I don't care to look at it."

I slipped out of it, suddenly hating it for its comfort and light weight, practical qualities I'd valued before. I set it against the back of the empty chair, where it hung like a dead cat.

"You don't want to walk around Palm Springs looking like a terrorist who's about to blow herself up in a crowded marketplace. Let's buy you a nicer one, or tell you what, you can have one of mine—I don't need bags the way I used to. I have some original Birkins. I'll just give one to you."

"It's okay, I don't really need—"

"And I have boxes and boxes of sandals I bought in Capri. I'll bet they'd fit you. Many have never been worn. And, please, will you let me take you to Galen to get a haircut? Nothing says 'I give up' like a woman your age with a ponytail."

But Melody was right, I *had* given up on my hair, starting during the pandemic. It was fun at first, like a science experiment, to see how my color grew out. I figured I'd cut it all someday for Locks of Love, or to celebrate some sort of important achievement or milestone, but it was easy to pull it back when I exercised. I started braiding it, and it hung like a rope on my back. Grant would pull on it as if he were ringing a church bell and sing, "Ding-dong!" Sometimes, when it got too heavy, I'd hack off a few inches with the same scissors I used to debone chicken.

"I'd love to dress you, too, but you're not there yet."

"I'm okay, I'm—"

She reached across the table to put her hand on my arm and looked into my eyes. "Do you have any idea how much money some of the most beautiful women in the world used to pay me for my services? But we'll wait until you're ready for a makeover. What a woman wears on the outside reflects who she is on the inside."

"I have a pretty good sense of who I am," I said, feeling brave. This was the most I'd ever stuck up for myself in front of her.

She smiled weakly. "Nobody knows who they are at your age. You're in a transition, and so, too, am I. A very different transition, but a transition all the same. I'm not being critical, you know. I'm being *helpful*. This was my occupation, one that started right here in Palm Springs when I was a little girl and met Lady Slim Keith herself, back when she was married to Howard Hawks."

I had no idea who any of those people were, and she could tell.

"She was the most stylish woman in all the world, and he was a director of note. Ever heard of *Scarface*? Hawks died after tripping over his dog at his home in Las Palmas. That's the way to go, nice and fast. My poor Vandyke should have been so lucky. He'd always wanted a dog and I said no."

A server came by and filled our glasses with water. "Pour us some martinis, Rosie. Citadelle. Extra dry. No ice chips. And we'll have the scallops in cream sauce."

I wasn't accustomed to someone ordering for me, but I didn't dare say anything. The drinks arrived almost instantly. I could have thrown back my cocktail in a single gulp, but I sipped like a lady, thinking this would be my new drink the next time I went out. I was growing pleasantly drunk, happy to hear Melody serenade me about Sinclair Chassis, the Detroit company her grandfather had started, and how he'd come to learn about Smoke Tree after the Lindbergh kidnapping, when the ranch was meant to be a place where well-to-do families, most from the Midwest, could feel safe, without worrying their children would be stolen.

When the food arrived, she said, "Vandyke would have ordered the scallops, and I would have said, 'Dear, your cholesterol.' Now I think of every time I prevented him from enjoying himself, and for what? He's dead now. Be nice to that fellow of yours. He won't be around forever." She took a quick draw of breath. "Oh, here we go with the waterworks. Pardon me." She dabbed her eyes with her napkin. "I get overcome in the strangest moments. No warning whatsoever." She offered a wan smile that was surprisingly endearing and sweet. "This is my treat, of course." Melody leaned in as if letting me in on another secret. "The food here is good, but it's no Paul Bocuse. Paul was a personal friend."

I could see that Melody was shifting into a conversational mode that made her feel more comfortable, and which had nothing to do with dialogue.

She picked up a silver spoon and fingered the logo etched into the end of it. "Look at me, trying to throw my weight around. It was once my job to be threatening, even to my clients, the very people who came to me for my services. The Hollywood A-listers don't trust you unless they think you've got something on them. I apologize."

As we ate, I prattled on about life in Madison, my job at Go Green, and Grant's job at the college. Ours was a world she knew and clearly cared little about, so far removed from her world. She cut me off when I mentioned the girls.

Her voice slurred a bit when she said, "I'm sure they are delightful, but I find it so tedious to hear about other people's children and all their *fabulous* accomplishments. You think it's bad now, just wait. This town is filled with grandmothers."

I found Melody's honesty refreshing. It was so different from the polite small talk I was used to. She put her hand on top of mine.

"I felt uncomfortable about you showing up here, Kimberly. Very, very uncomfortable."

"About me? Why?" Here I thought I had the corner on discomfort.

"What a dark time in my life you represent! You must have thought I was a monster. I wasn't good to Basil, standing in the way of who he was. And I wasn't good to you, either. I've thought about it a lot over the years. I'm not asking for you to forgive me, although I'd like that. It's just—I would like you to try to understand. It was a different time. I knew plenty of gay men from spending so much time in fashion, so of course I knew about Basil since he was a little boy, one simply knows. But I am his mother. I wanted to protect him from the stupid bigots and all the sickness. AIDS was bad everywhere, but it just gutted Palm Springs, gutted it! This was where the men came to die. It was so heartbreaking, all these wonderful, lively, whip-smart, talented, beautiful men I knew, the very best, smartest, funniest men, dropping like flies. I was terrified that even if I accepted Basil, nobody else would. I wanted him to be straight not because I cared about who he loved, but because I thought he'd be safer. You have children now, maybe you understand. I don't think that makes me the world's worst mother. But what it did make me was the world's worst mother-in-law because I watched you walk down the aisle knowing full well what you didn't—"

She paused and looked at me, then threw her napkin across the table and laughed. "But honestly, how on earth could you not have known? What straight man gets a subscription to *Variety* at thirteen?"

I couldn't help myself—I laughed, too, although her comment hit a nerve. That was something I'd wondered myself all the time. If I'd been so clueless about Basil, what might I be missing about Grant? "I guess I saw what I wanted to see."

"We've all been guilty of that. Basil values your friendship tremendously. You've been very grounding for him."

"Everyone always says that about me, that I'm grounding. I don't feel very grounded."

"I'll tell you a little secret: nobody does. I know Basil has asked you to check in on me while you're here, make sure I have a pulse. You can probably guess that he has asked me to do the same for you. But I will say right here at the outset: You owe me nothing. I used you once. I was a regular Geppetto, manipulating you from behind the scenes. I understand if you'd prefer to never see me again. You can enjoy your martini and your scallops and go on your merry way back to the nuthouse over there. You're off the proverbial hook." She made a J with her skinny finger.

I could see that Melody was saying one thing, but there was a note of desperation in her voice. She was lonely. I reached across the table. "Melody, I like you. It's okay."

A few days later, she responded in her own way. A huge box with my name on it showed up at Basil's door. It was filled with sketch pads, craft books, oil paints, pencils, expensive brushes I would never have splurged on myself, canvases, and gesso. Melody included a little note with a quote from the painter Robert Henri: "All real works of art look like they were done in joy."

Chapter Fourteen

Palm Springs
January 3, 2023
3:00 P.M.

The third time Grant left, it was unequivocally my fault. The girls were still young, maybe seven. Grant was on his way home from a week of teaching at the college. I'd been feeling agitated and insecure for days. It was silly—March had had her first soccer practice earlier that day. I'd brought her a Rice Krispies snack, and one of the mothers, Donna, acted as if I'd packed heat. "Friend, don't you think your daughter should eat something healthy?" She pulled a bag of carrots out of her purse and offered it to March instead.

I looked around at the mothers intently watching their children run up and down the field, when I didn't see why it was necessary to spectate at a practice—it wasn't even a game. These women seemed so much better at parenting than I was. They arranged playdates, met at the Children's Museum, watched jugglers at the capitol on weekends. Their children seemed perfect, while Dort was famous for her epic meltdowns, and March could behave like a real prima donna. I worried Dort was headed to the life of a criminal, and March would become a spoiled mean girl, and it would be all my fault.

Like Polly, I had a limited bandwidth for their emotional outbursts—I didn't care to negotiate or have conversations about *feelings*. On top of everything that week, I'd also been passed up for a promotion at the Veterans' Aid Society, where I'd been doing the work of two people. I didn't have time for exercise, and I worried my body would never bounce back. It was one of those days when it felt as if the universe were conspiring against me. I wanted a partner to offer comfort. I wanted Grant, but I was always afraid I'd burden him with my troubles or push him over the edge.

I went to our room to make the bed, and that's when I did something I'd promised him I would never, ever do: I opened his nightstand drawer and pulled out his journal.

January 23, 2002
Fresh snowfall, big fat flakes. White lights on the Christmas tree. Kim in the next room making a scrapbook. Photos everywhere. Dort finally asleep after much protest. She insists on making everything difficult. Kim thinks she's getting another ear infection, I think she's just being Dort.

March 11, 2002
Marianne is up for full professor. Went to evaluate her class this morning and she didn't show. Found her in her office, asleep at her desk. She told me she just started chemo—I had no idea she was even sick. Doesn't look good, she said. I subbed her class. Wrote an evaluation and said she knocked it out of the park.

April 14, 2002
Forgot how draining but rewarding student conferences can be. Semester is fully kicked in. Happy I get to do what I do. Pinch me.

"What are you doing?" Grant asked. I hadn't heard him come home. I slammed the journal shut. Busted. "I was just—"

"Can I have that please?"

He grabbed the journal from me, turned around, and left without another word.

He wasn't gone long that time, just four or five hours, although it felt as if he'd been gone forever. My stomach was in knots. I could hear him saying "Can I have that please?" over and over. I cleaned the house from top to bottom.

I called Polly, who sympathized with Grant this time. "Of course he's upset. How would you feel? He'll come back from Timbuktu or wherever it is he goes."

I fell asleep feeling more alone than ever. When I woke up, he was in bed next to me. In the dark, I rolled over to face him. He was wide-awake. "I was wrong to read your journal. I just missed you, and I wanted to—"

"I refuse to hide it," he said quietly. "It's not like I write about things I don't want you to see. It's for me. I've kept it since I was a little boy. It helps me process. Do you understand? If I know you're reading it, I'll start writing like it's for you, and what's the point?"

My cheeks flamed red. "I'll never do it again. It was the only time. I promise. I'm so sorry, I really am."

"I'm always honest. If you want to know what I'm thinking, just ask."

Now, in Palm Springs, I would have given anything to ask Grant what he was thinking—and where the hell he was.

He could have driven all the way back home by now, but he'd have needed gas. We shared a credit card, and I got an alert whenever he made a purchase; so far, he hadn't charged a dime. The Grant I knew never carried cash. But how well did I actually know him anymore?

Instead, I googled "missing hiker" and discovered countless tragic headlines. The people who seemed to go missing were mostly day hikers like Grant. There was a couple who'd hiked the Cactus to Clouds Trail on one of their first dates and got lost, only to be saved by taking refuge in a dead hiker's tent. Or the guy who'd fallen to his death after a cardiac event. A hiker who'd suffered alcohol withdrawal and never came home. One young man I read about didn't answer his phone because he thought the rescuer's call was spam. A dead tree fell on a woman who thought she'd found a good place to take shelter. There were stories of the victims of serial killers and deranged individuals. Bodies recovered, remains found—or, worse: remains never found.

I walked to the entrance of the trail and stood next to the sign that said EXTREME CAUTION: RATTLESNAKE HABITAT. I'd often overhear tourists talk about the desert the way Grant had at first, as though they were discussing a cilantro aversion. "It just isn't my thing," they'd say. I was convinced that the dramatic, almost unreal beauty of Palm Canyon would change any skeptic's mind about that. There are fifteen miles of California fan palms growing along the trickle of a river, with the slumped shoulders of ancient mountains rising up on either side. According to Cahuilla legend, an elder named Maul, anticipating his death, stood still in this spot and turned himself into a palm tree in order to leave something his people would value.

Now, alone, I did what I'd wanted to do for days: I walked to the edge of the valley and screamed his name. The sound came out of the deepest part of me, the depths of which I hadn't even known existed. I screamed so loudly that my voice ricocheted off all the stone surfaces, sank to the bottom of the gorge, swirled around the palm fronds, and rose to the tops of the mountains.

"Grant!" I hollered again, wishing he could hear me. "Come back! Come home!"

But where was our home anymore?

Chapter Fifteen

Palm Springs
November 14, 2022

We'd been in Palm Springs for more than a week, longer than what would have been a normal vacation. I began to feel unstuck in time; I had to think hard to figure out where we were in the calendar. There was no such thing as Wednesday hump day, TGI Friday, or sad Sunday night.

What day was it?

Who cared?

Not me. I was sitting outside drinking coffee, aware that I was living every midwesterner's fantasy. Coffee! In the morning! In November!

I inhaled deeply. In the moist, mossy world we'd come from, I'd thought of smells as heavy and pungent. Here, the air smelled clean, crisp, and dry, with hints of loose dirt and wood chips.

I recorded a video of myself holding Basil's Craigslist mug (that was his first Tony Award) to send to him. I let it pan out to Grant's yellowed paperback copy of *Riders of the Purple Sage*, which sat beside me. He'd bought it for a quarter at Revivals, the consignment store filled with casserole dishes and luggage left over from last season's snowbirds. Jeanie and Gene went there every day to treasure hunt and talked about the store as if it were the biggest attraction in town, and it did yield some scores. I'd never been to a thrift store where you could find Ferragamo flats or a Louis Vuitton bag for ten bucks. With Thanksgiving coming up, along with a visit from March, Grant and I had stopped in to buy some essentials for Basil's bachelor kitchen. When we paid for a whisk and a Crock-Pot, the guy at the front desk didn't even bother to ask if we qualified for the senior discount, which kicked in at fifty-five there.

Grant looked at me, baffled. "Are we seniors?"

"Only in Palm Springs," I said.

The volunteer and Grant struck up a conversation that ended with him suggesting Grant pick up a few shifts. To my great surprise, he took an application.

Jeanie calls me the Box Queen because every day there's a delivery. A mattress pad because the bed is too hard. A television—Basil doesn't have a single TV. You couldn't cut through water with his dull knives. I bought shelving units for the kitchen cabinets so I can see what we have. One morning, I shrieked when a gecko slithered out of our Raisin Bran box. Now we have a full set of airtight containers. You'd think a guy with so much money would have good sheets, but even the cheapest set we ordered are softer than his.

"Here's what we did," Grant said. "We drove two thousand miles in order to turn another person's house into the home we already had. Brilliant."

In my video I next zoomed in on Jeanie and Gene sitting in matching zero-gravity chairs on the neighboring patio (the proximity of Le Desert's units was hard to get used to after living across the street from a nature preserve) and panned to Grant swimming laps in the surprisingly large pool, setting into motion a dozen blow-up flamingos floating in the pool's west end. I found the flamingos haunting. When they bobbed up and down, usually in clusters, it seemed as if they were gossiping about me. Cassie was practicing yoga on the pool deck, which might explain why Grant was putting extra effort into his stroke. She was playing Indian sitar music on her tinny portable speaker, and her expression was incredibly focused and intense. She'd stop periodically to rub her mala beads, or to take photos of herself in her glimmering yoga shorts and bra, rays of sunlight bouncing off the diamond in her belly button. She'd set up a camera on a tripod and posed first with some groovy sunglasses, catching every angle, then she took selfies holding a container of what looked like candy perched on her outstretched hand, and more with the candy between her perfectly white teeth.

I sent the video to Basil, then to my group chat with Octavia and the girls. *Just another day in paradise.* Octavia responded two seconds later with a screenshot of the weather forecast in Madison: thirties and clouds. *I hate you. I love you. It's complicated.*

In Vienna for the weekend, Dort wrote.

We weren't always the best at communicating, but Dort and I shared an appreciation for art and often sent photos of work we loved or hated. She attached a photo of Egon Schiele's nude portrait of himself. It was amazing how he made the viewer's eyes go straight to his balls, raw and red. *I'm at the Leopold, where I'm supposed to admire (!) the art of a child molester.*

March posted a GIF with the art museum scene from *Ferris Bueller's Day Off* and a sad-face emoji. *Work jail. Huge project. I'm not going to make it to Palm Springs for Thanksgiving, Mom. Sorry.*

My mood instantly deflated. Sometimes it seemed perfectly normal for the girls to be out in the world on their own, doing their thing. That was what we raised them to do. Other times, like that morning, I couldn't understand how they could be so very far away from us, living their own lives. Now, at last, we had all the freedom I used to dream of when my life was mired in sippy cups and naps, dance recitals and shopping in bulk.

Grant emerged from the pool, shaking his wild hair like a dog, and sat down next to me. Already I could see the effects of the almost daily hikes he'd gone on with Hobie. He'd lost a few pounds, and his legs and torso were starting to show more definition. Driblets of water were stuck in the beard he'd insisted on growing. I wouldn't let him kiss me because it felt as if he were sanding my face.

"Who needs a therapist when you can swim?" Grant asked.

"I'm glad you find it relaxing."

"I wouldn't call it relaxing. That was quite a workout."

"I'm sure Cassie was impressed." His blush always gave him away. "I've been looking for things for us to do." It felt strange to plan activities for us to partake in together, as though we'd just started dating. "We can go to readings at the library, talks, the theater . . . They have their own film festival, and modernism week is in February."

I wanted to impress him with the array of cultural and recreational activities available in the area. I needed to undermine Grant's belief that our winter here would be as mindless as the time his mom and stepfather used to spend in Florida, where they napped all day, watched television, drove around in golf carts, and broke out the sherry at four o'clock. No, Palm Springs was like a beautiful starlet, so pretty you might think she's not very smart until you learn she has actual interests.

Hobie's little dog started to yelp hysterically from the pen Hobie had made when he'd strung some chicken wire between the shrubs that flanked his sliding doors.

"Oh, hi there, Audrey!" Jeanie waved, and the little dog grew even wilder. It was as close to a scream as a bark could get. "She's a soprano! Did you know Hobie named her Audrey because he thinks she looks like Audrey Hepburn?"

She did. She had skinny limbs and big, sad eyes.

"Bless his heart, Hobie drove all the way to San Diego to get her after what happened to poor Mushman. She's a rescue."

Gene said, "He didn't have to go all the way to San Diego. There are so many Chihuahuas in this town you'd think they sell them at the dollar store."

"She's our hiking buddy," said Grant. "She stares at me from Hobie's carrier. I swear she can see right into my soul."

Jeanie leaned forward to speak in a hushed voice. "A few people around here aren't too happy about Audrey. There's going to be a war over that dog, mark my words. There are wars over everything."

Gene said, "This nice couple just got here last week, we don't want to scare them."

"Cassie!" Jean waved her hand. "Stop spending so much time upside down or you might get stuck that way."

"I'm shedding my goddess skin."

"If I had your skin, I'd keep it. When you're done, come on over here."

A few minutes later, Cassie stood, brushed herself off, and walked to the patio carrying her phone and her mesa. She'd explained this was a traveling altar filled with special rocks and totems. The older couple fawned all over Cassie. She was so earnest and sweet, but she remained a mystery to me. In all the time we'd been here I hadn't seen her go to work. How she lived her life was none of my business, but she must have been around the same age as the twins, so I couldn't help but feel a motherly worry over her.

"I'll make you an egg," Jeanie said. She had good and bad days. So far, this was a good one.

"No eggs! You know how I feel about eating animals. Peace begins on your plate."

I'd had this same conversation about veganism with Dort a thousand times. It was strange to live in Madison, where half the residents were vegan but the restaurants served up offerings that were almost exclusively pork based.

I returned to my compulsive planning. I was in search of the very best of everything Palm Springs had to offer—happy hours, museums, day trips, activities. I felt like one of those people with big eyes and empty stomachs standing in line at the buffet. On the one hand, I didn't want to miss a thing, but I also loved being at Le Desert and felt little desire to leave the premises.

"We could see a show at the community theater," I said. "They even have a bookstore here."

"A bookstore? We have more bookstores than bars in Madison."

Even though we'd come here to relax, I worried that one too many naps by the pool could push us down a slippery slope. Already I knew exactly what time the mail carrier showed up, which day the gardeners came by with the dreadful leaf blowers, when the pool guy would dump chemicals in the pool. I watched Hobie survey the premises each evening, picking up any stray bit of garbage and making sure the pool umbrellas were cranked down. If we weren't careful, we might discover that we actually enjoyed relaxing, and we would become lazy and . . . old.

I continued, "There are drop-in, pay-what-you-want workouts in the park. There're also tai chi, drum circles, pickleball tournaments, bike rentals, hot springs, the tram. We could go to one of those pot bars with 'budtenders.'"

Grant said, flatly, "Hamster, meet wheel."

"Tomorrow there's drag bingo," Gene said. "We go every Wednesday." It was hard to picture Gene in his T-shirt that said WORLD'S BEST GRANDPA in a room with a drag queen. "We love Barbara Ganush. You should see the room light up when she calls out O-69!"

A hummingbird darted into and out of our airspace, its beak as big as a fingernail clipping. The bird's feathers were iridescent purple and green, her energy limitless. She was less bird, more Tinker Bell. She finally paused for a moment on the branch of the loquat tree, whose genus and species I'd learned when Grant and I had toured the botanical garden the day before. We learned that desert plants have adapted to the dry conditions by becoming succulent and spiny, growing only tiny stems. Their roots do not reach very deep and instead extend out and out. I wondered if the metaphor applied to the people who lived here, too: if the environment changed them on a cellular level; if it was changing us, and we were learning to adapt. Already I felt different.

Grant said, "I miss my office at Mounds."

I waved. "Hello? Can you just be here with me for five minutes?"

"I waited years for that office to be mine. Years. The door had my name on it. It had a fireplace. And those huge windows looking out into the tops of the oak trees. I could see everything. I knew all the squirrels. One had a mangled tail. I named him Hanson." Grant took a sip of my coffee. He told people he gave up coffee to prove he had discipline, but, really, he just drank mine. "It was a very nice office."

Witt Hall had once been a Carnegie library. It was easy to imagine what it must have been like there over a hundred years ago if you could look past the institutional furniture, flickering brass light fixtures, drab paint on cracked walls, and posters advertising speakers, shows, and study-abroad opportunities.

"I thought I'd die of a heart attack at my desk, just like Garvin did when he'd had the office before me. When they discovered his body, a red mark was running down the page he was grading. That's every professor's dream, working right up till the end."

"You hated grading."

"Still, that's how I thought I'd go. They kept that paper in the college archives. I've seen it."

"Oh, Grant." I reminded myself that Grant had always been supportive of me when I was unhappy with my job.

"What do you think they did with the archives? All the old yearbooks and newspapers, the photographs and diaries? Do you think they just loaded the college's entire history into a Dumpster?"

"It's gone. It doesn't matter."

"It matters to me, Kim. I spent twenty-six years of my life there." A small breeze rustled the pages of his book, a western by Zane Grey. Grant said, "His real name was Pearl."

"Whose?"

"Zane Grey. Pearl was his actual name."

"Grant, that book smells like cat pee. I can smell it from here."

"Fine!" He threw it across the patio. Gene, Jeanie, and Cassie looked at us with alarm. Our hummingbird flew away. Audrey began to bark. A few of the yellowed pages escaped the binding and flew loose. It was like a living thing.

In my quietest voice I said, "What is your deal?"

"I'm trying to have a conversation, Kim. Sometimes you remind me of your mom, wanting other people's problems to just go away. I want you to care, and to listen. You aren't listening."

"Are you kidding? I do care, Grant, and I *am* listening. I've been caring, and listening, and loving you for a long time. But I've got issues of my own, you know."

"Issues like what?"

"Well, I really don't like my job. I mean, I care about what Go Green does, but Vic makes my life miserable." Wendy had emailed earlier that morning and said we'd lost funding from the Schufro Foundation. I knew Go Green would probably cut some staff positions as a result. How could I tell Grant that I might not have a job after this sabbatical ended? Instead I said, "Who wants to hire someone my age?"

"Trust me, I know how you feel."

"I push folks around in wheelchairs at the airport," Gene piped in. I was mortified that he'd been listening to our entire conversation. "You could do that. I meet the nicest people."

Jeanie added, "I'm a wonderful nurse. I never have to stick a person twice when I start an IV."

"Honey, you haven't been a nurse in almost twenty years," Gene said gently.

She smiled, baffled. "Is that right?"

I could see Gene's heart breaking. Jeanie's slipping memory put our own drama into perspective.

"How about picking up a hobby?" I said to Grant, lowering my voice. "It seems like you're enjoying hiking. I started painting again. I was just making a sketch." I'd begun what I thought might become a series of scenes from our time here. I'd already painted Cassie sitting cross-legged, meditating. The one I was currently working on was of Audrey standing up on the fence.

Cassie chimed in, "The trouble is, you're blocked, Warby."

"Warby?"

"That's what we call you," she said. "Warby Parker, those glasses you can buy online."

Grant said, "Who needs an education when everything you need to know is on Instagram?"

"Careful," Jeanie said. "Cassie here says she's an influencer."

"Yeah? What do you . . . influence?" I asked.

"Everything that matters, and some of what doesn't. Like hair twisties and gummy vitamins that make your skin glow."

"You wouldn't believe the money." Gene whistled. "When I worked for the power company, I could light up a whole city for what you make posting a photo online."

"That's not my true calling, of course. It just allows me to share my message about integrating heaven and earth to exit the matrix."

I waited for Cassie to laugh. When she didn't, I said, "I honestly have no idea what that means."

Gene said, "We don't get it either. It's all blah-blah-blah to us."

"That's because you're still part of the matrix," Cassie said serenely.

"What matrix?" Grant asked, genuinely intrigued.

She lit up. "The mental construct your mind gets stuck in. You need to awaken and question the nature of the virtual reality you're in. That's how you become liberated. Then you can find other liberated souls and escape. You achieve freedom when you find truth and autonomy."

"You basically just described what I taught my entire career," Grant said, sounding appreciative, as though at last someone finally understood him.

"You need to exist in the world of possibilities instead of probabilities. Maybe it's probable that you can't teach again, but what are the possibilities that exist for you? You can change your story."

Even though I wasn't entirely clear about what Cassie meant, it felt as if she was describing our whole reason for coming to Palm Springs, and it actually made sense. "What's your *thing*?" I asked. "You know, that makes people follow you?"

"I'm a shaman." She became somber. She lowered her voice. "A pampa mesayoq." Cassie looked like someone who worked at lululemon.

"Yeah?" Grant said, always the encouraging teacher.

I would have thought Grant would find this all laughable. I thought we'd joke about it later the way we joked about Denim and DNA; instead, he found it fascinating. She started talking about following your heart path, being brave, and expanding your line of vision. I could feel a little fuse blow in my brain. "You can live your own calling through the heart."

Grant asked, "Okay, but how?"

"Start by journaling."

"I already have a journal. It's where I share all my tender thoughts and feelings."

This was a joke I'd heard before. Judging by Cassie's response, she wasn't any more amused by it than I was. "This is different. Try auto-writing for twenty minutes a day about what's in your heart." Octavia and I used to have a drinking game when we watched *The Bachelor* where we'd take a shot whenever someone said the word *heart*, a word that felt co-opted, so cheapened and overused it meant nothing. "It doesn't matter what you say," Cassie continued. "You write differently when you plan to burn the pages in a ceremony."

"I'll do that. And maybe I should learn how to meditate. Can you help me with that, Cassie? Because you know what I do when I swim?" Grant paused and looked right at me. "When I'm underwater, I scream. I scream my head off."

Chapter Sixteen

Palm Springs
January 3, 2023
4:00 P.M.

The fourth time Grant left I really thought he might be dead.
Polly had her stroke in mid-December 2008 and died after a short stay in the ICU. Her sudden passing left me utterly gutted. Just a month later, I was still too sad to want to have fun with Grant when he returned home from teaching a JanTerm class. On top of everything, the girls had hit a difficult teenage stretch I'd been hoping we could avoid. Dort was surly and got high all the time—she didn't even try to hide it. March was so involved in school, activities, and her possessive boyfriend that we hardly ever saw her. She treated me like an innkeeper.

Grant walked into our home simmering with tension and grief, expecting to be wrapped up in a warm embrace. Reunions were always poignant for Grant. Instead, we virtually ignored him. "Anyone up for an ice cream at the Chocolate Shoppe?" he asked.

No takers.

"How about a walk to Picnic Point to look for owls?"

"Dad, no. It's freezing."

"Sorry, homework."

A few minutes later he tried again. "There's a talk about human rights in Southeast Asia at the Union tonight. Anyone?"

"Not now," I said. "I have to take March to debate, and I told Octavia I'd meet her after."

"Why do you always make plans with Octavia on the weekends? Can't you see her when I'm not here?"

I was already running late. "She works, too, and so do I. We're busy during the week. What's the big deal? I'll only be gone a few hours."

He sulked, feeling neglected. "I just found out I didn't get the job as dean, in case you care."

"I'm really sorry to hear that, but you said you didn't really want it. You hate doing administrative stuff."

"That's just what I said. I was starting to like the sound of Dean Duffy."

"Well, sorry."

March was already waiting in the car and blared the horn. It was raining, and the rain was beginning to turn to sleet. I grabbed my keys, threw on a scarf, and tied my bootlaces.

"A little sympathy would be nice. Why do I even come home?"

I was at my wit's end. "Then *don't* come home. We're all busy, Grant. My mother just died. You want us to drop everything the minute you walk through the door. It's like you expect a marching band to parade down the stairs to celebrate your return. We're all just living our lives."

I met Octavia at the Weary Traveler feeling sorry and on edge the way I usually did on the rare occasion when I lost my temper with Grant. Octavia was still married to Brian, and they, too, were having some issues. Sometimes you need to feed off another couple's dysfunction to make your own feel more normal. The more Octavia talked about Brian's snoring and porn addiction, the better Grant sounded.

When I came home prepared to apologize, Grant was gone. I told myself it was possible he'd found something to do. Maybe he'd sat in on the lecture after all? I went to bed alone. It had been so long since Grant had walked out on me that I'd almost—just almost—let myself believe it wouldn't happen again. Grant had become good friends with the spiritual-life adviser on campus. They went for long walks and talked about the mental health issues the students faced, and eventually Grant opened up about his own past. Bill was a thoughtful listener, and he provided Grant with strategies to work through times of conflict. Their talks helped—it had been over a decade since he'd walked out after finding me with his journal, and I had allowed myself to believe that it would never happen again. Yet that night, I had a sixth sense that he'd driven back to the house in Mounds. Hadn't I basically pushed him out the door?

Nothing good happens after one in the morning. Just a few months earlier, some boys from Dort and March's high school were killed in a drunk-driving accident. The car had flipped over with such force that the hood had melted into and become part of the pavement. When my phone rang, I thought of them.

"This is Officer Schumann from the Columbia County Sheriff's Department. Is this Kimberly Hastings?"

"Yes." I could barely get the word out of my throat. I was frozen in fear.

"Can you please confirm that you drive a blue Honda Civic?"

"Yes, that's . . . that's our car."

"I'm afraid there's been an accident with your vehicle."

My heart was racing. It was all I could do to ask, "Which . . . which passenger?"

"Grant Duffy."

"Is he okay? Is he hurt?"

"I'm afraid I'm not at liberty to discuss his medical condition." The officer provided me with phone numbers and instructions to go to Prairie Ridge Hospital. I was a mess on my drive there with no idea what I was about to face.

When I walked into Grant's room, still raw from my last visit to a hospital to say goodbye to Polly, he was sitting up in bed with a trail of dried blood coming out of his nose, his hair disheveled. He saw me and lit up, then his eyes filled with tears.

"I'm so sorry I snapped," I said. "You just wanted to spend time with us."

He held my hand and put it on his chest. "No, Kimmer. I'm sorry *I* snapped."

"You need help, Grant."

"I tried. I got help. It was working. But then, tonight, it was the tone of your voice that got to me." His expression was confused, childlike. "And then you walked away. You walked right out of the door, and when I heard the door shut behind you, I felt like you'd cut me in half."

"I'm sorry. I know I could have been kinder. But we have lives, Grant, and parts of those lives don't include you—just like you have a life in Mounds that doesn't include us. And that's okay, it works. At least most of the time."

"It works for *you*."

I brought him home, and the next day we bought the trusty Prius.

And now here I am in California, about to talk about our latest car with a different member of law enforcement. Brady had called while I was trying to work off some nervous energy on a short walk along the main road that ran through Indian Canyons. Before he could say hello, I felt my heart race, and my face, hands, and feet began to sweat. "I'd like to ask you some questions about your vehicle."

Hearing the word *vehicle* set off alarm bells again. "Did you find it?" Any news about the car could help unravel the mystery of Grant's whereabouts.

"Why don't you come to the command center, Mrs. Duffy? We'll talk when you get here."

When I arrived, Brady was waiting for me in the middle of the road, arms crossed over his chest. I tried to read his face. This man held all the power in my life. He could open his mouth and tell me that Grant was alive or dead, the two most different possible and momentous outcomes in the world, but I'd never know it from his face.

"Mrs. Duffy." I could detect that something about his attitude toward me had hardened. I felt that I was in trouble.

"You can call me Kim. It's fine."

No response. "I'd like for you to tell me a little more about the vehicle you purchased."

"The Jeep? Grant bought it, I didn't. I didn't want to have anything to do with it."

"Why's that? Was there a problem?"

"Well, yeah. Poor fuel economy. A bumpy ride. Two seats. It's loud. The whole cool-guy vibe. It's not my kind of car. Like I said, I didn't buy it. We keep our finances separate. He bought it with his money."

"Okay, so when did *he* buy it?"

"Early November. We were on our way here, and our Prius broke down. Now that was a good car, right up to the very end."

"Where did you buy the Jeep? At a dealership?"

"No, in Barstow. Some guy."

"Some guy. Did this guy have a name?"

It seemed like a lifetime ago now. "I don't remember. We were stranded, and Grant saw it sitting in the parking lot of a diner. He said he'd always wanted a Jeep, which was totally news to me, so he called the number and Tony—that was his name, Tony—was there within five minutes."

"You had a Prius, and then you bought an off-roading vehicle? That's a pretty big change."

"It's what Grant wanted."

The more I talked, the more I saw us the way Brady did. We were complete idiots. "How'd you pay for it?"

"Grant went to the bank and wrote a check to cash. I know, checks. Old-school. He talked the guy down to eighteen thousand from twenty thousand dollars. He thought he got a great deal."

"So, you're telling me you gave eighteen thousand dollars to some yahoo you met in a parking lot?"

I shrugged. Brady was right, it was ridiculous. "Grant did."

"And the title?"

"He, um . . ." I'd never felt more stupid. "Well, Tony said he'd mail it to us. I thought maybe Grant got it? I didn't ask."

"The title is in the mail," Brady said this with excruciating slow- ness. "And you were okay with that?"

I paused. "Why are you asking so many questions about the Jeep?" I stuffed my hands in my pockets and braced myself for whatever was about to come next. "Did you find it? You did, didn't you? Can you please just tell me what's going on? I feel like you're laying a trap."

"Mrs. Duffy, the vehicle you reported missing was recovered."

At last, one part of the mystery of Grant's disappearance was closer to being solved. "So you found it? And was Grant in it?"

Brady continued as if I hadn't spoken. "I should have known where it was before now. Sometimes the agencies don't communicate very well."

"But—this is good news, right? I hope so, because I could really, really use some good news right now."

"Well, it's not great news, because you either stole the vehicle, or you bought it hot."

I began to laugh, until I realized Brady was serious. "Oh, come on. Do I look like someone who steals cars? I mean, look at me." After days of worry and little sleep, I looked strung out or crazy, or both.

"I've seen it all, Mrs. Duffy."

"Where did you find the Jeep?"

I held my breath in anticipation of Brady's answer. Whatever he said would tell me whether Grant had gotten lost or run off. This, I felt, was a tipping point.

"It was parked where you thought it would be, on the side of Morris Ranch Road near the trailhead. Someone had called about their car getting broken into, and while the police were there, they ran the plates on all the cars. When they saw it was stolen, they towed it."

I was so floored by this revelation that I didn't think before I said, "So Grant really was hiking?"

I watched Brady's face change. "Mrs. Duffy, are you telling me everything? You suspected that he might *not* be hiking?"

"No. Yes, I mean, it was just so strange that we didn't know where the Jeep was, that's all," I stammered.

Brady's voice rose. "I've got a whole team out there risking their own safety, at least for now. If there's something more we should know, Mrs. Duffy, if there's some funny business, you should tell me now."

"There's nothing to tell."

He stared at me a good long while, waiting for me to crack. "You don't want me to risk people's lives up there, do you? I can call off the search." He pulled out his walkie-talkie as if he was about to.

"You can't do that! If you do, what happens to Grant? He could . . . he could . . . he could die out there."

Brady looked at me as if I should have known this all along. "It's been over two days now, Mrs. Duffy. We've closed the canyon and activated tremendous resources. I wish I could assure you that he'll be okay. But this isn't an amusement park. If it were up to me, I'd cover the mountains with signs that say HIKE AT YOUR OWN RISK."

He pulled some breath mints out of his pocket and popped one into his mouth. "Want one?"

I declined. "Do we get the car back? What happens to it?"

He thought I was crazy. "That car was never yours to begin with. Next time, do your homework before purchasing a vehicle."

He turned and walked back into the command center. Alone, I felt suddenly lightheaded as the enormity of the situation sank in. I put my hands on my thighs and stared up at the mountains knowing for the first time that Grant really was a lost hiker. The mountains were so big, so vast, spread out in all directions, and now I knew how dangerous they were.

How on earth could they find him? What if they never did?

Chapter Seventeen

Palm Springs
November 19, 2022

Grant was so tired when he came back from his first long hike that he passed out on the patio chaise with his shirt off, and his socks still on. He wore socks over socks and shoes over mini-gators. Still, he'd worn holes through the toes, and his feet were covered in painful blisters.

It was late afternoon, the time of day when I noticed that all the desert birds and animals came to life. Roadrunners skittered seemingly straight out of cartoons and across the lawn, ravens swooshed dramatically across the sky, and brave rabbits approached me where I sat on the porch reading—or trying to read—my book club's latest selection, about reindeer habitat. I wasn't excited about the topic, but I was tackling it in solidarity with my beloved group. I was feeling down because I'd miss the discussion that night with my friends, most of whom were moms I'd met when our kids were young. For over twenty years, we'd gotten together without fail every month. We generally choose books that make us better people for having read them. Our last book was about the petroleum industry in Brazil, and the one before that was a fictionalized story of a woman with one arm who'd lost her entire family during Partition.

We'd show up at one another's houses to discuss these weighty topics armed with our own slippers in plastic bags. We'd talk briefly about the latest selection and move on to our spouses or divorces, our kids, our aging parents, and whoever had the latest bad diagnosis.

I'd been so excited about our winter away that it hadn't occurred to me that I'd be struck with pangs of FOMO for my Madison routines. I felt this way as a kid, when I'd go to the camp and worry that all of my friendships in Chicago would fall apart while I was gone, and here I was in my fifties feeling as if I had two lives: this one, the one that still felt fake, and the one that was real and was going on without me.

I heard my name from beyond the bushes. "Kim? Is that you?"

Then a higher voice: "Kim-a-lim-a-ding-dong?"

It was as if a bomb of sunshine and energy detonated when two men stood on our patio. Before I knew it, Grant was awake and we were all caught up in a flurry of hugs and conversation. I couldn't even keep track of who was speaking. *Oh my God, oh my God! You're here! Basil has told us so much about you!*

"I'm Thomas," the tall, blond, older man said, forcing a bottle of prosecco into my hands. "Welcome!" He was pale and clean-cut, in a nice suit and bow tie. He looked as if he could play a doctor on television.

The younger, smaller man wore tight yellow pants, a muscle tee, and a gold chain with a giant cross. He gave me a big hug. "And I'm Raul, your new best friend." He pointed at Grant. "And *you* must be Dr. Duffy. Look at that hairy chest! Basil didn't tell us you're a bear. We looked you up, you know. Now I see why you have almost as many red-hot chili peppers on Rate My Professors as I do."

"I do?" Falsely, Grant tried to appear modest. His chili peppers were a point of pride for him. He challenged and provoked his students, but some still found him dorkishly adorable and often developed schoolgirl crushes on him. It's easy to fall for someone who tickles your brain when you're young, when you get excited about all these new ways of thinking that make you feel impressive and deep. The thing about philosophy, according to Grant, is that it's better when you first get into it, when you consider the big existential problems that could puzzle anyone, the wealthy or the impoverished, the young or the old. *Who am I? Why am I here? What's the meaning of life?*

And here I was in middle age, still wondering the same things.

Grant would never admit it, but a big part of what made him feel terrible about losing his job was the loss of his legion of admirers. Off campus, there were no chili peppers, no blushing students at office hours, no adjuncts who would have given their eyeteeth for his tenure-track position. Now, he was just another guy.

"Where do you teach?" he asked Raul.

"Pomona. And then I come here to have fun."

Thomas looked me over in a generous, completely uncritical way. "And look at you, girl, so tall. Like Basil. You're strong! You can lift a school bus, can't you?"

Raul studied me. He said to Thomas, "Doesn't she look a little like Sigourney Weaver? Remember that queen we met at Oscar's?"

"Sigourney Beaver? Oh yeah, she does!"

Raul picked up my reindeer book from the coffee table and scrunched up his nose in displeasure. "Eew! What on earth are you reading?" He skimmed the back and dropped it back down like a dirty diaper.

Thomas said, "You and Basil? I can't see it. But you two? You look good together." People often said that about Grant and me. What they meant was that we were equally attractive, or in March's parlance, there was no "reaching" or "settling."

"Grant and Kim," Raul said. "We'll call you . . . Grim."

"Or, Kant, as I prefer to think of us," Grant said. "He was one of my favorite philosophers, although he was a virgin his whole life."

"He wouldn't last one night on Arenas."

"Arenas?"

"Otherwise known as *Uranus*. It's the street with all the bars. We're going to take you there."

Grant was overwhelmed. "Can we back up? I'm sorry, but . . . who are you?"

"The Arnold-Littles," Raul said, "Everyone around here calls us the Husbands."

Raul squeezed Thomas around the waist. "I love us."

"We put the *fun* in dys*fun*ction."

"Basil asked us to show you around and clobber you with our

charm, so here we are, all sparkles. But seriously, we're very sorry we weren't here when you arrived. We had a trip to New York and we spent the last few days at the monument."

"The what?"

"Joshua Tree. Are you finding everything okay?"

"Yes, everything is great," I said. "Basil's condo is awesome."

Raul collapsed dramatically in one of the rotating chairs next to the table, crossed his legs, and spun around a few times. "Basil could live anywhere—Mesa, the Movie Colony—but he chooses to be here with us. It's like the real estate version of being held back a grade."

"I wish he'd let *us* stay in his place for free all winter. He's hardly ever here. This is the nicest unit. Well, this and Hobie's." Thomas said Hobie's name with spite.

"Our place is over there. We're in eleven. It's tiny, but you won't hear *me* complain about a two-butt kitchen." Raul had a way of creating intimacy when he spoke, making us feel that we were part of an inside joke. "We'd buy something bigger, but prices are through the roof, and there's no way we're moving to DHS."

"DHS?" Grant asked.

"Desert Hot Springs. It's come a long way, but it's still filled with tweakers."

I'd never heard of DHS. I was just beginning to learn about the various towns in and around the area, which was a little like trying to remember the order of the planets from the sun outward: Cathedral City, Rancho Mirage, Palm Desert, Thousand Palms, La Quinta, Bermuda Dunes, Indio, Indian Wells, Coachella. Before, I thought it was all just Palm Springs.

Thomas eyed the bungalow like an appraiser. "Do you have any idea how much it costs to rent a place like this? Thousands for a week in South Palm Springs, never mind an entire month. Three months? Four? In season? Are you kidding me?

"We should have bought right away when we moved here from LA in 2010. This town was tumbleweeds after the Enron fiasco. But now the whole world has fallen back in love with Palm Springs, and why not?" Thomas pointed at the mountains in the distance and gestured for us to step out into the courtyard. "Everywhere you look you get an eyeful of wow. Especially my umbrellas."

Raul said, "Baby, don't get started on Umbrellagate, please, not again."

Thomas said, "The ones we had before were *so* tacky."

Raul added, "Tacky tacky tacky."

Thomas said, "So I ordered new umbrellas and paid for them out of the HOA reserves. I had them custom designed. And in fairness, they were a little bit more expensive than your average umbrellas, but they're fabulous, right? The stripes are so elegant."

"And the pink fringe!" Raul added. "The pièce de résistance!"

"Old-school glamour all the way. Hobie wants us to pay for the extra out of our own pockets and bend to his pedestrian taste. I designed dresses for Angelina Jolie. Please. Hobie says the umbrellas remind him of Candyland, and I'm, like, explain to me what on earth is wrong with that? *Everyone* loves Candyland. What is wrong with *whimsy*? This is Palm Springs, not San Quentin—"

"—where we're sure Hobie has served some time."

"He covets the enormous power of the HOA," Thomas said dryly. "Just wait until you see him walking around the place like the superintendent visiting a school."

"He has a clipboard," Raul said. "And a checklist."

"And a lot of rocks loose."

Raul said, "You'll see. People here have too much time, that's the problem. They're willing to battle to the death over trivial nonsense. It's Armageddon if someone leaves a sock in the dryer in the laundry room. We all complain constantly, but we love it here *too* much. Le Desert is so special, it's like a baby being passed around a bunch of old aunties who just squeeze it to death."

Grant and I were learning that the complex was not the utopia it had seemed at first. The place had layers of history and tension. It reminded me of the summer I was twelve when I overheard the counselors complaining about the camp—how little the staff were paid, how hard they had to work. Until that moment, I'd thought of Camp Jamboree as the most perfect place in the world.

"Look, there's our spirit guide."

Cassie approached our patio, utterly gorgeous and cool in her midriff-baring top, flowing low-slung pants, cowboy boots, and beaded bracelets. I felt so plain in my jeans. Up close, I could see that she had delicate little tribal tattoos on the pads of flesh above and below her knuckles, and a large one running up her forearm said BELIEVE in a fancy script adorned by snakes, skulls, and flowers. I once framed a photo of our family and hung it in the dining room with the word FAMILY engraved in the frame. Dort moaned with disgust when she saw it. "Oh God, Mom, how *cheugy*." Was Cassie's tattoo cheugy?

Raul hugged her and laid his head on her shiny shoulder. "Mmmm, Cass." He was dramatic, open, and adorable. I already had a soft spot for him. Thomas hugged her from the other side. Cassie didn't mind a bit; her body seemed as if it belonged to all of them.

"Cassie performed a healing ceremony for me," Thomas said, "and at the end, she touched my feet and said our baby was coming to us. The next day, we found out we were taken off the surrogate waiting list."

"Don't call her a surrogate," Cassie said. "She's a bridge to life. A loving vessel."

Thomas said, "Our baby is due in March. We can't wait."

"A Pisces," Cassie said. "Astrology is limiting, but in my experience, Pisces swim deep. He's going to be a soulful mess."

"Which one of you is the dad?" Grant was clearly fascinated.

Raul was visibly offended. "We both are! What a question!"

"Sorry," Grant said, embarrassed. "This is just new to us."

"Compared to most of the people around here, our relationship is as perfect and boring as they come. You swing?"

"We don't do that," I clarified. "Swing."

"We more like . . . stand in place," Grant said, in a way that made clear it wasn't really a joke.

"Too bad. See how all the doors have little brass pineapples next to them?" Raul tapped the one next to Hobie's door. "They're from the old days when this place was rocking. Some are upside-down. That's how you know who's up for some fun."

"Whatever, we've all got our kinks. Speaking of, Basil told us we had to show you a good time, which is why we're here," Thomas said. "We're about to hit up some happy hours with Cass. Want to come?"

Grant said, "Kim does. I'll pass."

Thomas pointed at Grant's eyes with his index and middle fingers, then his own. "I feel you, Grant. This town is too much for me sometimes. But Raul here loves to mix it up, and I figure I'll indulge him before I become a Little League dad. Come on, we'll give you a Jell-O-shot taste of Palm Springs nightlife."

"Smells nothing like teen spirit, I'll tell you that much." Raul grabbed my hand. "We're going to have the best time."

"I think you'll have more fun without me," Grant said.

I groaned inwardly. Couldn't Grant just try?

"One drink," Thomas said. "I promise, this is a very straight-friendly town."

I looked at the reindeer book and felt my homesickness lift. Maybe I wasn't missing out on anything at all.

We walked down Arenas, eyeing the bars on both sides. An incredibly built man in a G-string danced in the front window in one of them. Another bar was called Dick's. It was next to a store called Bear Wear, where they sold tight netted shorts, leather, and armor. The music was thumping, and Cassie swayed with the skill of a natural dancer, loose and unencumbered. She noticed that Grant seemed uncomfortable. "Don't worry," she said. "Streetbar is more chill than these other places. You won't have a dick wagged in your face just yet. You have to work your way up to the Tool Shed. That place is rough."

"Rough?" Thomas rolled his eyes. "Oh, please. A bunch of old queens in leather harnesses standing around discussing china patterns is not *rough*."

It was all so new to me, and so thrilling. Back home, I loved going to bars. Octavia and I went dancing a few times a month while Grant stayed home because nightlife confused him. He didn't understand the fun in being packed together with so many people, and with so much noise you couldn't have a decent conversation. He preferred small groups, cozy dinner parties, or, better yet, probing one-on-one conversations. He often pointed out the irony that we met at a keg party.

We went inside, and I snapped Grant's photo with my phone, thinking the girls would find it funny to see him next to a threesome in matching metallic jumpsuits while he stood with his hands stuffed deep into the pockets of his safari shorts.

Grant liked to think of himself as open-minded and progressive. He and Basil got along well. When he found Dort fooling around with a girl in our basement when she was in high school, he was supportive of her sexuality to the point of embarrassment, ingratiating himself with her and her girlfriends. He developed an appreciation for the micro-aggression training he initially didn't think he needed. He sat on the transgender student alliance, and he volunteered at Cooking with Gays, an event that Dort had organized when she was at the college to protest an inflammatory guest who ran a private militia who was giving a talk at the same time. Grant signed off his emails *Dr. Grant Duffy, him/his.*

Now, he was taking in the scene of this particular experience like a tourist. We both were, but I was trying to act cool, as if I went to the bars on Arenas all the time.

Thomas went to get us drinks, and Raul gestured for Cassie, Grant, and me to follow him as he weaved through the crowd looking for a table, stopping briefly to kiss a bald man with massive biceps—Raul *really* kissed him, tongue and everything. Their hips pressed against each other. Grant and I exchanged questioning glances: Weren't Raul and Thomas married?

Neither of us cared whom the men had sex with; what was disconcerting was such an open display of desire. Where we're from, sex happens behind closed doors, and promiscuity usually comes with a high social price. We'd landed in a place where you could be horny in public, and it was just fine—welcome, even. You could sleep with whom you wanted, young and old, and invite new people into your relationship. It all seemed very adult and open. It was disorienting to not know what was appropriate, to not have even known that our lives, to that point, had been governed by so many rules, and here we'd thought of ourselves as unconventional.

The ambient noise suddenly struck me as strange. It was low and deep, like the hum of a men's choir. Then it hit me. Aside from a drag queen in a bright yellow wig and sequined dress, Cassie and I were the only women in the whole place. Not even at a Packers game had I been so outnumbered.

"It's all men here," I said to Cassie, whose hair swung gently as she swayed to the music.

She smiled. "It's all men *everywhere* in this town."

To Grant I said, "I feel so safe. Do you have any idea how liberating this is?"

"Not at this exact moment. I think someone just gave me a prostate exam."

I started to shake my shoulders to Bananarama's "Venus." "I love this song!"

I felt so young again—until Cassie, looking ethereal with her shimmery gold eye shadow glittering in the blue lights, said, "I've never heard it."

"Look at us!" I smiled and gave Grant a kiss in the hopes it would loosen him up. He seemed as if he were made of cement.

"Yay." He waved his finger in the air, feigning excitement. "*Woot woot.* Can we go now? I'm still beat. Murray Peak was my Mount Everest."

"But we just got here." I loved being in a place that was so new and so different, so lively and bright. I gathered energy from all the activity, but I could see that it drained Grant. If I hadn't gotten pregnant just weeks after meeting him, would our differences have emerged organically and ended us?

"Our bars in Wisconsin are nothing like this," Grant said to Raul. "We have free popcorn machines. Meat raffles."

"Meat raffles? I don't know what that is, but maybe we need to reverse-snowbird and spend the winter in Wisconsin."

A group of older, shirtless men in leather vests, chaps, and captain's hats stood next to us, and the bar smelled suddenly of a tannery. "Why do I feel like I'm in a Village People reunion?" Grant said. "Is there a dress code?"

"Some holdovers from Leather Pride."

"What's Leather Pride?"

"An entire weekend of meat and heat," said Raul. "There's always something. Pride, the White Party, Outfest. If you're hard-core, you can go to Burning Man."

Cassie said, "Stagecoach. Coachella."

Raul said, "Coachella? Girl, please. You're better than that."

She shrugged.

Thomas arrived and set some red drinks in front of us. "This is the Rose Kennedy, the official drink of Palm Springs. Careful, they make them strong here."

Grant nudged his glasses up his nose. "Tell me, is fifty the minimum age?"

He was right. Almost every man had gray hair and bald spots. And they all seemed smart, interesting, and successful.

"Oh, that's Palm Springs," said Cassie. "Boomer gays."

"Gay and gray, baby," said Raul.

"Silver city," said Thomas, who planted a kiss on his younger husband's lips just moments after Raul had kissed the owner. "Except for us."

Cassie leaned in and looked intently at Grant and me. "Basil told me something about you guys."

"Yeah?" Grant was curious; I was nervous. Basil had a big mouth, and he loved to gossip.

"He said that you don't want to be here." She looked at Grant, and then she looked at me and added, "Grant likes winter, and you hate it. You two are like two different elements. It's hard for fire and water to coexist. You need to find a common ground so you don't become steam." She reached for our hands and squeezed them tight. Her rings, one for each finger including her thumbs, most with moonstones and exotic rocks, cut into my skin. "You can do your inner work separately, your shadow work. Then you can open up in a new way and validate each other's needs."

"What *exactly* did Basil tell you?" I asked.

"Just that I should help you."

"We're good," I said.

"That's not what you said on the way out here," Grant added.

"I can be your guide on a loving journey," Cassie said. "Let me know when you're ready." She was so confident that it was hard not to believe we would be in good hands.

Raul said, "People used to come to Palm Springs to recover from tuberculosis, asthma, skin disorders, alcoholism. Now they come here to trip in the desert and become totally new people."

Cassie said, "Creating novel experiences is a really, really great start. Congratulations to both of you for taking the first step. You're on the right path."

"I don't know about that," Thomas said, raising his glass to make a toast Grant did not participate in. "You'll have a hard time working on your relationship in a place where everyone starts drinking at three in the afternoon."

After Streetbar, we went across the street to Hunters, although Raul peeled off for a place called the Barracks because it was "underwear night"—he explained you pay twenty-five dollars and strip at the door. You can wear underwear, a harness, a jockstrap, or fetish gear. "Sorry," he said to me and Cassie, as though we were begging to join, "I don't think women are even allowed."

Hunters was packed wall to wall. The room was lit with neon, and a DJ wearing giant angel wings and a SAY KGAY hat (KGAY was the radio station that played everywhere) was remixing Donna Summer's "Bad Girls." I ordered a tequila sunrise, a drink that tasted sweet and stupid, and lost myself in a crowd of dancers, emerging a while later—an hour? Two? I had no idea—to find Grant.

But he wasn't at the table where he and Cassie had been sitting. The Husbands and I looked everywhere for Cassie and Grant—at the bar, in the bathrooms. They weren't waiting for us outside. I hadn't received any texts, and he didn't return my calls.

By the time Thomas and I Ubered home, I discovered, to my relief, that Grant was propped up against the headboard, asleep, looking so dear with his messy hair and his reading glasses on the tip of his nose. I walked over to him as I usually do in the evenings, took off his glasses, and put them on the nightstand. I didn't dare touch his journal. Without opening his eyes, he said, "You're back."

"Where were you? Why did you leave without me?"

"Cassie wanted to go. And so did I."

"Why didn't you tell me you were leaving?" I started to hiccup.

"I *did* tell you. I guess you couldn't hear me over 'It's Raining Men' or whatever."

I vaguely remembered Grant shouting something in my ear that I hadn't thought was important.

"You were dancing with the blond drag queen in fur boots."

"Oh, that's Mariah Scary, isn't she great? Raul says she's an institution here. She taught me how to waack."

Mariah told me that the dance was big in the underground LGBT club scene in the seventies but died out during the AIDS crisis. Now, thanks to TikTok, its popularity has surged again.

I tried to impress Grant with my new moves, starting in my shoulders the way Mariah had taught me, waving my arms in a propeller motion. I accidentally knocked a paperweight off the desk and onto the floor, where it landed with a thud. Grant groaned. "Kimmy, I was sleeping."

For Grant, the night was long over, but it was still happening for me. The woofers were vibrating in my ears, and my poor mangled foot and ankle were beginning to throb from dancing—I knew I'd pay for it tomorrow.

I was still a little wasted and I wanted Grant's mood to soften. Usually, this was easy. I swung my arms in front of me. "Take up space!" Mariah had told me. I never took up space, and there I was, drunk and abandoned. I had the best time. I was just another dancer, not a middle-aged woman with relationship issues, grown children who didn't need me anymore, a future that terrified me, and a job I didn't care to go back to. It felt amazing to let go, to be somewhere, and someone, new. "Be confident, honey!" Mariah had said. "Pretend you're an old Hollywood star. Look at you! You're a natural!"

Grant wasn't amused. "Would you stop it?"

"You never go dancing with me."

"I went tonight, Kim, and you ignored me the whole evening."

"I didn't ignore you. We just did our own thing. Like always." I spun around and stopped, dizzy. I wondered if I might throw up and sank down on the edge of the bed, my back to Grant, staring at myself in the mirror on the opposite wall. I was a mess.

"Getting drunk and going clubbing? That's not you, Kim."

"How do you even know that? What if it *is* me? What if it's just not who you want me to be?" I wondered what my life would be like if I were in Palm Springs alone, just as I'd gotten used to being in Madison alone. "Your idea of fun is talking with Sasha about bourgeois idealism."

"Why are you bringing up Sasha? Every time we have an argument it's Sasha this, Sasha that. I haven't called or spoken to her since we arrived."

"I'm entitled to resent Sasha, Grant. Our whole life you've run to her for everything."

"Our whole life you've pushed me away!" He slammed his journal shut and set it on the nightstand. "For years, you complained that I was gone all the time, but do you have any idea what it felt like to come home and have you shoot out of the house like a bat out of hell? And now, ever since the college closed, you look at me like I'm an intruder. I feel like you resent my presence."

"That's not true." But it was, and knowing that he'd picked up on it made me feel terrible. And yet if Grant was gone, I didn't have to worry about his leaving. It was the logic that had made our semi-long-distance relationship work. It made no sense, but without that framework, I was worried that *we* made no sense.

"And since you bring up Sasha, let's play fair. Should we talk about Basil? Look where we are right now. I'm sleeping in his bed. He seems to know everything about our lives. What did you tell him? I swear, Cassie is a virtual stranger and she knows more about us than I do."

Everything he said was true. I tried to deflect. "You're not really mad, are you?" I peeled off my clothes and slid into bed. "I'm sorry." I nuzzled my face in his neck. I tried to tickle him. Nothing. "Is it because everyone was gay? As a straight man, I could see how you'd be—"

"I spent the last two decades at a liberal arts college. I've spent more time with gay and trans people than you've ever known in your life. How many of your friends are Black?"

"My best friend! Octavia!"

"That's one. Aside from Basil and Greg, how many are gay, Kim, huh?"

"I just meant that you were outnumbered tonight. As a woman, I know how it feels to be in a room full of men."

"Like at a gay bar? You were outnumbered, too."

"Grant, I'm trying to be sensitive."

He rolled his eyes. "Sensitive? You didn't even care that I was there tonight. Admit it."

"You could have stayed back if you didn't want to go. You're an adult. Just because I want to do something doesn't mean you have to do it."

"You just said you want us to do more together! And I could tell you wanted me to go. What do you want, Kim? Tell me! Please, throw me a bone. I can't win."

I rolled off him and stared at the fan hanging from the dramatic sloped and beamed ceiling.

"Did you only bring me with you to Palm Springs because you felt sorry for me? Are you unhappy with me, Kim? Did you tell Basil we're unhappy?"

My head was spinning. *Was* I unhappy? What did I want from Grant? "I just told him that we needed a change, that's all."

"You keep talking about change. We're here, this is change. This is different. Tell me, how big of a change do you want?"

I said nothing.

"You're scaring me."

I paused. "I'm scaring myself."

"What if I want change, too?"

"We could talk about that." We lapsed into a tense silence.

"Maybe Cassie *can* help us," Grant said.

"She doesn't even have a partner. How much could she help? She's all about the divine feminine and she hasn't had the whole experience of being a woman. She's never had a kid or a hot flash. I like her. I mean, who wouldn't? But she's, like, fourteen."

"Even if she's young, so what? Young people are smart. They have the energy and focus we lack. Look at my students, they amaze me. Look at Dort and March."

"Grant, listen to yourself. Would you trust our girls to be your life coach? Remember when we were watching that news story about the guy who cut off his finger while he was snow blowing and they used leeches to keep his finger alive, and March asked how leeches got into the snowblower?"

But Grant was already asleep.

I rolled out of bed and grabbed Basil's silk smoking robe from his closet. He'd emailed earlier that day to thank me for having lunch with Melody.

She said you need a haircut, Basil wrote in his last email. *Buckle up, Kimmy. You're about to get the treatment.*

I slid open the patio door and stepped into the courtyard. The breeze was warm and forgiving. I had had no idea that the temperature would drop dramatically in the evenings. This still felt pretty nice to me, but we'd seen California hipsters sporting massive puffers as soon as it dipped below seventy. In Wisconsin, we had a different coat for every ten-degree temperature difference. Here, it was either tank tops or goose down.

I sat at the edge of the pool with my legs submerged to my knees. The water was surprisingly warm and felt great on my sore foot. Grant was right, I *had* acted like a jerk tonight. The fight we'd had was uncomfortable, but it also felt necessary, like the small earthquakes that release some of the pressure before the big one hits. I closed my eyes and tried to let go of the guilt and frustration I felt, which was easier than it would have been if my blood were running clear of alcohol.

The mountains were dark. Their tops were jagged and raw, as if they'd been ripped from a piece of paper. Off in the distance there was howling, a sound that was eerie and menacing but also beautiful and wild.

Was it too soon to say I loved it here?

I wanted to swim but didn't have my bathing suit. I didn't see anyone, so I slipped the robe off my shoulders and lowered myself into the pool. There was nothing more sensual than the feeling of water against my skin. I swam from one end to the other. I stopped and practiced the water ballet moves I'd learned at camp when I was little: the clam, the crane, the fishtail, and the knight. Emboldened by my nakedness and the privacy, I floated on my back and stared up at the sky. It was as if someone had poked thousands of holes in a giant black sheet with brilliant light behind it.

I stopped, stood in the shallow end, and tilted my head to clear the water out of my ears. That's when I saw Hobie sitting on a lounge chair watching me. He had a drink in his hand and casually waved as I slowly slipped back under the water, saying, *Oh my God, oh my God,* in my head. I propped myself up on the edge of the pool close to where he sat so that I could use the wall to cover my body. There may as well have been a million miles between me and my robe, sitting on the ground just out of my reach.

I had no choice: I maneuvered myself out of the pool, butt in view and boobs swinging, reached for the robe, and wrapped it around my wet body. I was too drunk to be mortified—but drunk enough to be titillated.

"Do you hear that?" he asked. There was that mournful howling in the distance again. "That's the coyotes." He said *ky-oats,* reminding me that I was no longer in the Midwest, where everyone lingers over their vowels. We say *ky-oat-ees.* "You can hear when they make a kill. Some mornings I'll walk along the wash and find rabbits with their guts torn out."

"I didn't know you were here." I felt embarrassed.

"Relax, people swim naked all the time, especially at night."

"What about Gene and Jeanie?"

He smiled. "Oh, hell no. In the summer, when this place is empty, the guys outside who sleep in their cars hop over the back fence and wash themselves in our hot tub. There's a lot that goes on here when nobody's paying attention. That's why I make it my job to notice every-thing. It's pretty thankless, I'll tell you that much. Nobody appreciates me." He paused and jumped to the next thing he was thinking about. "You've got a hot bod. I don't know why you cover yourself up all the time. Really nice tits."

"Hobie, you can't say that. It's inappropriate and totally offensive."

"It's a compliment. And honestly, I can't help it. Ever since I hit my head, I've had a bad case of the mouth runs. I might say too much, but I always speak the truth. I enjoyed watching you goof around in the water. You wouldn't believe how much we pay to maintain this pool and it hardly gets used. You're still like a kid. You haven't let the world break you down."

"Oh no, believe me, I have."

"Nah. Even just now, when you looked at the stars, you were in awe. Some people lose that sense of wonder. Let me show you some-thing." He stood behind me, put his arm over my shoulder, and with his other arm pointed at the sky. Part of me wanted to melt into him; the other part wanted to roll away. "There's Taurus the Bull above the hori-zon. And up there"—he turned me gently to shift my gaze—"there's the Seven Sisters. Pleiades. Want some water?" He handed me his giant Nalgene that went everywhere he did. I wouldn't normally share some-one else's water bottle, but I was thirsty all the time here.

"I've been meaning to thank you for taking Grant under your wing," I said. "He hated hiking at first, but now he really connects with it. He seems like he's more, I don't know . . . balanced."

"He's never going to be a Zen master, but he's coming along. And now I know enough about Heidegger to be dangerous."

We sat back on the loungers facing each other. Hobie looked an-noyed, stood, and walked over to a glass sitting on the table. He held it in his hand, scowled, and pointed at the pool rules sign. "No glass in the pool area, says right there. Did you know that if a glass breaks in the pool, we have to drain the entire thing to clean it out? That's a state law." He walked over to the garbage, tossed the glass, and rejoined me. "I'm on fire watch the next two weeks."

"That's your job?"

"Nah, I volunteer. I like to look for smoke—and shenanigans. It's wet on the other side of the San Jacintos. Hardly anyone goes back there, but sometimes you'll encounter the cartels. Their operations are more sophisticated than you might think. They sprinkle these blue-and-green pellets around the perimeter of whatever they're growing to keep the deer away. Looks like fertilizer. Stuff is outlawed in most countries. Any warm-blooded animal will have their nervous system shut down if they touch it. People here playing golf and pickleball have no idea how much goes on in the places they can't see."

"What will Grant do while you're gone?"

"There are hiking clubs. There's no shortage of retirees and tourists he can head out with—not to mention the tech bros looking for a new thrill after they've made their billions. When they aren't in Madagascar or Majorca, they're hiking the most insane terrain in Death Valley. Why are you so worried about Grant? He's a big boy. He'll figure his shit out. What about you?"

"What about me?"

"Grant says he wants to marry you, but you aren't so sure. You've had a lot of time to think that one over."

"We have our issues, like every couple. Have you ever been married?"

"Have I ever. Three times."

"Why'd you split up?"

He held up three fingers and folded his index finger down. "First one, drugs. I hardly remember being married to her. Second one?" He folded down his other finger. "Now, she was loony tunes. Crazier than I am. That lasted about ten minutes." Finally, all three of his fingers were folded into a fist. "Last one was Coco."

"You were married to Coco?" I was astonished. She'd given me a pedicure in her RV the other day, the best pedicure of my life. "What happened?"

"I couldn't keep it in my pants. There are so many women—and men—looking for a good time in this town. I can't say no. Coco could put up with me and all my bullshit, but she didn't want to share. She was the best thing that ever happened to me, but my doc says I have impulse-control issues. I'm basically like a four-year-old boy." He reached for the tie on my robe and ran the silky fabric through his fingers. "A very naughty boy. How about a nightcap, Kim?" He tugged the tie. "No strings attached."

I'd slept with four men in my life. Keith Turnbaum, whom I'd lost my virginity to in high school. Basil. Some guy I hooked up with twice before I met Grant, and Grant. All these years I'd watch characters in movies and television shows fall into bed with each other, and I'd wonder, Was it really so easy? Did that happen in real life? I found hookup culture unfathomable. Octavia's stories about sleeping with people she hardly knew struck me as strange. At my age, spontaneous sex seemed laughable, and Grant was the only man I'd ever wanted to be with.

But Hobie wasn't joking around. It felt good (if wrong) to be desired. I was in a new kind of world where moments like this were possible.

"If you want to have some fun," he said, "it'll be just between us. I won't ask for anything from you but pleasure."

Suddenly, the spell was broken. I burst into laughter. "A naughty boy? You won't ask for anything but *pleasure*?"

"I'm not going to take that as a *no*, but a *not right now*." He smiled, let the sash go, and stood up. "Look, I don't mind if you laugh at me. I don't mind if you don't want to sleep with me. But I do mind if you don't believe that I find you attractive."

I shrugged.

"You can come by my place anytime. I won't say a word to anyone. No commitment, no entanglements. I'm really talented."

I tried to compose myself. "I'll keep that in mind."

"Please do."

He reached for my chin with his two fingers, tilted my head, and gave me a kiss so light it reminded me of the "butterfly kisses" the girls gave me with their eyelashes when they were little. "Enjoy the stars, Kim. It's a great time to see the Taurid meteor showers. If you think that's cool, just wait until next month when the Geminids peak. Look!" He pointed at the sky. "A fireball. Just for us." He brushed my shoulder with his fingertips ever so lightly.

And despite myself, I felt a bit of a thrill.

Chapter Eighteen

Palm Springs
January 3, 2023
5:00 P.M.

Never in my life had I been so attuned to the sun as it arcs across the sky. By late afternoon, it slips behind the rough outcroppings and blankets the valley in a growing shadow, setting beyond view. The closer you are to the mountains, the sooner the day ends. And when the day ends, so, too, does the search.

Grant had already spent two nights alone on the mountain; I didn't want there to be a third. Brady said the third day was the tipping point; you could only go three days without water.

Cassie had brought me to this dramatic spot at the Trading Post shortly before Christmas. She wanted me to photograph her for a "collab" she was doing with a company that made antibacterial lotion. She needed a dramatic setting; if she could get enough engagement, the company would offer her a thousand-dollar bonus.

She wasn't the only Instagrammer who'd recognized the photographic possibilities of this location. Next to us were some girls in heels and skimpy dresses taking selfies. This was a scene we saw all over town. Young people were always snapping photos of themselves in front of cheesy glowing signs intended not for the moment, but for the virtual online confetti. They say CHILLAX, POOL TIME, and PALM

SPRINGS. "Look, an entire generation suffering nostalgia for the present," Grant would say.

Cassie stretched out her arm to take a photo of herself with her phone, testing out the background. "Selfies always make me feel funny," I told her. "My mother was not one for vanity."

"Well, I hope I look like you when I'm your age. Here, hold this." She handed me the bottle of lotion. "Squirt it into your hand." She fiddled with some settings, held her phone out, and leaned against me. We smiled. "That's good!" She pressed the button on the side of her camera and expertly snapped a few photos.

"This makes me so uncomfortable," I said through my grin. "Why doesn't anyone use the word *conceited* anymore? When I was young, it was a great insult to be seen as full of yourself."

Cassie put the phone down and looked at me. With great sincerity, she said, "But don't you see, Kim? If you aren't full of yourself, who are you full of?"

To my horror, that was the photo she ended up posting to @spiritguidecassie. The company loved that we gave off "mother-daughter vibes" and that the product implied you could be close to the people you loved if you had the right kind of protection. It didn't look staged, but natural. She did get the bonus—and with it, she took me to Sephora downtown, where she bought me a ridiculously expensive tube of sparkly blush, and then she made me get a makeover so I would know how to use it.

That same day at the Trading Post with Cassie, I'd snapped some photos of the posers, and also the hikers covered in dust emerging from their adventures. I tried to capture the look of gratitude that washed over their faces when they saw that they were back at the gift shop, which sold water and souvenir trinkets. Even portable toilets, under the right conditions, can appear to be blessings.

Now, not even two weeks later, here I was again, allowing myself to fantasize that Grant, too, was making his way back just before dark. He'd smile and wave when he saw me as though he'd expected me to be there all along. Or he'd emerge from the other entrance and surprise me with a kiss—that was our running joke ever since we'd met, the surprise kiss.

We'd get in the car and return to Basil's place and soak in the hot tub. He'd regale me with stories of coyotes and canyons and explain how he'd miscalculated his route. Or I'd return to Basil's and he'd be there, waiting for me, and we'd both apologize the way we always did, and everything would be fine.

Our relationship had worked up to that point because it was fueled by our cycles of absence and reunion—from the planned to the unpredictable. The longer he was gone, the more powerful the emotions when we saw each other again, the more emphatic the apologies, and honestly, sometimes, the better the sex—we were so much more acutely aware of each other's bodily presence.

I kept trying to tell myself that just because the Jeep had been parked near the Jo Pond Trail, it didn't necessarily mean Grant was lost in the mountains. But I didn't really believe that.

I felt a tap on my back that scared me to death. I screamed, turned, and saw Hobie.

His face was lit up with excitement. "There's been a development."

Hobie pulled the backpack off his shoulders and held it up; it was Grant's, and in that moment, it was as precious and meaningful as the girls' baby bootees I kept in a box in the basement. Grant's spirit and energy seemed to radiate from it with such force that I felt it could knock me down. I could see something poking out of the front pocket: his Moleskine journal. For all his concerns about the weight of his pack, he would never have hiked without it; he said he did his best thinking on the trail. Since Cassie's "assignment," he wrote more than ever. He found it freeing to burn his pages in the gas grill next to our unit when he was done, while I wondered what thoughts and fears he was so eager to torch.

Seeing his backpack, one of my questions—perhaps the biggest—was finally answered, and I wasn't sure how to feel about it. Grant actually *had* gone hiking, which meant that he was really and truly lost. At least, before, I could comfort myself with the thought that even if he had left me, he was at least physically okay. Now, I understood on a visceral level that he might not be.

He was in danger.

"But how would he have lost his pack? He needs it." I stuffed my nose in the fabric, my eyes welling with tears. I tore it open. "He still has a protein bar in here. What's he going to eat?" My hands were shaking.

"It was just sitting there next to a boulder," Hobie said. "Who knows what happened. But at least we have an idea of where he's been, and we can send some trackers to follow him."

"You should have left it," I said, my voice sounding hysterical even to my ears. "You should have stayed. He's trying to find it, I'll bet. He's hungry. He's hungry, Hobie!"

"We search in a given radius. He wasn't anywhere near it. He was long gone."

I reached for the journal. "Maybe he wrote something that will tell us—"

Brady appeared from out of nowhere and snatched the backpack out of Hobie's hands. I grabbed for it, and Brady pulled it away. "That's mine," I said, sounding like a petulant child. "What's Grant's is mine."

"I'm very sorry, Mrs. Duffy, but I need to keep this for a few hours. He might have written something that will help us find his coordinates." Brady's voice was soothing but firm. "I know it's important for you to see it, and you will, but I'm going to look it over. I promise I'll get it back to you. For the moment, we have to treat this as evidence."

That word *evidence* made me feel exposed. What would they find in that journal? Now everyone would know about our whole relationship, our complicated history.

To me, it was evidence of us, and who we were.

Chapter Nineteen

Palm Springs
November 29, 2022

L e Desert seemed quieter with Hobie gone. The power structure had shifted, like when your boss goes on vacation.

With Hobie on fire duty, Grant went by himself to Painted Canyon in Mecca. He said you can only get to the parking area if you can off-road. "See," he said, "I told you we'd need the Jeep."

It seemed unfair that Grant was having big athletic adventures when I was the one who loved and embraced the outdoors. I swam in the lake into October most years. I was always trying to rally Grant and the girls to go to state parks or on canoe trips where we'd sleep on sandbanks in the Wisconsin River.

I suppose I could have ventured into and around Palm Springs, too. I kept telling Grant we should check out Joshua Tree, about forty-five minutes away, but he suggested we wait until I could get around more comfortably.

It's hard to tell the difference between inertia or contentment. To be at Le Desert, for me, was to feel that I was already where the action was. The communal, almost dorm-like experience reminded me of my childhood. I saw Coco, braless under her pajamas, as she fixed Jeanie's silver hair next to the pool. I could hear what Gene was watching on television—then again, the television was so loud it could probably be heard all the way in Los Angeles. Cassie was chanting, and I could smell Thomas grilling chicken next door.

There was no room for washers and dryers in the smaller units, so everyone shared a communal laundry room. Basil could have found a way to add machines in his place, but he never did because he used a service and suggested we do the same, but I'd never pay for someone else to do my laundry, not ever, so I headed to the laundry room with a basket filled with Grant's workout gear. Sharing washing facilities was one of the bigger psychological adjustments to group living. I hated doing laundry at home, but here I didn't mind because it wasn't a solitary activity.

Gene and Jeanie hogged the machines; they were always seemingly midcycle. They'd run a whole load just to wash a pair of giant briefs. If I was even a minute late to get my stuff out of the dryer, someone would leave my clothes neatly folded on the table, which was the California version of a neighbor shoveling your walk for you back home.

That morning, I saw that someone had hung cheesy paint-by-number cat paintings across one wall—cats chasing balls of yarn, cats sleeping, cats looking out the window. On the other wall was the famous print of dogs playing poker.

"Looks like someone decorated," I said to Cassie, who was the only other person in the room, which exploded with the scent of her jasmine body oil.

"Oh, Coco bought those at Revivals. She's trying to piss off Hobie."

At that very moment, as though she'd heard Cassie's voice, Coco walked in with her laundry in a rolling basket.

"Hi, Queen," Cassie said.

Coco's voice was gruff. "Hobie's damn dog kept me up all night."

"She's just a puppy," Cassie said.

I could tell that even when Coco was talking about something that bothered her at Le Desert she lit up. The complex was home. It was her family. She loved it, and I had a feeling she still loved Hobie.

She pushed her laundry in the machine I was about to use, slammed the door shut, and said, "That yappy little shit won't stop barking, so you know what I just did? I walked over there and fed her an entire can of baked beans. She's going to fart her way to the moon."

And then Coco was gone, her clothes and her anger still swirling in circles.

I'd heard from Thomas that, during COVID, Coco's business at the salon dried up. She barely got by hustling the residents at Le Desert for services. Thomas and Raul had come to her rescue, loaning her money for the RV. Now she drove it all over town and parked outside the resorts. She'd long since paid them back. "That good deed paid off in unexpected ways," Raul said. "Free back waxes for life."

Cassie said, "There's a lot of love but also a lot of bad energy between Coco and Hobie. I offered to do some candle work to remove their blockages. They're twin flames, but they have entities between them. And bad energy. Like you and Grant."

"We don't have bad energy," I said, feeling defensive. "But I think we do have entities."

She nodded. "Like I said, bad energy." She was folding some shirts on a piece of cut cardboard with flaps. She could work for the Gap. It was hard to believe someone so flighty could also be so precise, and it seemed wrong for a woman as gorgeous as she was to have to engage in such a menial chore.

"You know," she said, "Grant's a good guy, but he's an energy vampire."

"A what?" I wished Cassie came with a translation guide.

"That's his mode, to feed off the energy of other people. I could see it the minute you guys got here. Energy vampires and energy mirrors aren't always a great combination."

"I'm an 'energy mirror'?"

"Well, yeah." She said it as if I were stupid.

"What does that even mean?"

"It means he looks into you, and you only let him see himself reflected back."

I was shocked. She'd basically summed up a relationship dynamic that would be hard for me to describe to a therapist. "What do I do about that?"

"There's a way to fix it." She brightened. "I'll show you how. But, Kim, you need to be one hundred percent congruent with your yes, that's all."

"Cassie, I'm sorry, but what does that even mean?"

"Anyone can see you're really blocked in your relationship. A wall rises up around you whenever you're with Grant. It's a force field so powerful it's like he gets electrocuted every time he comes near. If you want to let him in, you need to start saying yes. He told me the same thing."

She folded another shirt in a few deft movements. I'd been folding shirts all my life and they never looked like hers; this gave me some confidence in her therapeutic abilities.

"Cassie, when did you talk to Grant about us?"

"On our hike."

"You went hiking with Grant?"

"We went to South Lykken last week. Yesterday I took him to the Bump and Grind."

"The what?"

"In Palm Desert. That's my favorite trail, but he hated it. He said there were way too many people. But we had some really great, soulful conversations. It sounds like you guys are stuck in the abyss."

"What did he say, exactly, about our 'abyss'?" How could Grant get upset that I talked to Basil about us when he'd been blabbing to Cassie about our problems?

"You each have individual healing work to do before you can come together. He needs to look into his shadow spaces from his past, and you need to awaken to an embodied existence with him." She lifted her pile of clothes and set them in her basket. We were like old-fashioned wash maids in a weird, new world. She smiled, and it felt as if the light in the room grew brighter.

"'My embodied existence' with him?"

"Just like it sounds." I watched as some of the goddess veneer stripped away and we were back to being two women in reality. "And be careful of Hobie."

Had she overheard our conversation the other night? Sound traveled across the pool, and the desert.

"Why?" I asked, pretending to be clueless.

"Because if it has wheels or a dick, it'll give you trouble eventually."

Chapter Twenty

Palm Springs
January 3, 2023
7:00 P.M.

As I left the command center, all I could think about was Grant's backpack and the journal inside, pulsing like a beating heart.

How on earth had he become separated from his things, and when? I wanted to break into Brady's office and steal the Moleskine back. I was desperate to see what Grant had written, although after glimpsing his journal years ago, I had good reason to suspect it might reveal nothing at all.

Inside Le Desert's courtyard, a massive spread of appetizers, cheese, and a huge spiral baked ham were waiting for me. A feast to keep my spirits up, but I had no appetite for food.

The Husbands made a specialty cocktail they called the Absent Professor. Everyone wore neon-green RESCUE T-shirts in solidarity with the many volunteers. Raul's was cut at the midriff, and he'd paired it with bright orange booty shorts. "Sister, we put the *party* in search party," he'd said, giving me a warm hug. Later, he pulled me aside, serious and sweet, and looked right into my eyes. "You okay, my girl?"

"I'm fine," I lied as I downed my third drink, my hands still shaking. "Actually, Hobie found Grant's backpack today. Before, I was honestly worried Grant might not even be hiking. We'd gotten into a fight the night before and I thought he might have stormed off. At first I was relieved to know he's actually up there, but now another day has gone by and it's also, like, the worst news possible."

Raul gave me a hug. "Do you think it's strange that of all those volunteers, Hobie was the one to find his backpack?"

"No, he's been out there searching every day. He looks harder than anyone, and that's saying a lot. These rescuers, they're amazing."

"You know how arsonists stick around to watch a fire burn?" Thomas asked. "Raul and I, we were talking, and we think Hobie might have had something to do with Grant going missing. Maybe he's hidden him somewhere out there and he's about to ask for ransom."

"Thomas, your imagination runs wilder than mine does."

The girls and Octavia were due to arrive the next day, and I was dying to reunite with them. In the meantime, I looked around the firepit and realized I wasn't going through this alone. These new people I might never have met were part of my life now, and because of Grant's drama, they would be forever.

Coco ran to her unit and returned with another giant pitcher full of greyhound cocktails made from grapefruit juice squeezed from fruit that grew on the property's trees. California grapefruits weren't sour at all, or perhaps the magic was in the old trees. The drink tasted like candy, which made it a little too easy to sip.

A week or so earlier, before all the drama started, I'd gone for a walk near the Sandcliff condo complex and noticed that the air smelled of citrus. Dozens of grapefruits rolled down the street like errant bowling balls. "Why was that tree cut down?" I asked the landscaper after he'd pushed the trunk through the chipper and turned the machine off. With so much fruit, I couldn't imagine it was diseased. I felt as if I'd happened upon a heartbreaking crime scene.

He shrugged. "Nobody wants citrus trees on their properties these days. Too messy, and they use too much water. Ever heard of fruit rats?"

Coco walked around, with a cigarette stuck to her bottom lip, to refill our glasses. It drove everyone crazy when she smoked in the courtyard, but she was the grande dame of the complex; nobody was going to tell her what to do, and she'd been here so long, none of the rules pertained to her.

"This vodka tastes like lighter fluid," Melody said. "I'll bring you some Chopin next time. It's distilled from summer potatoes. It has a very mellow taste."

"'Summer potatoes.' Listen to Little Miss Smoke Tree. As long as it makes my hair curl, it's good enough for me." Coco leaned forward to ash in the firepit. After a long exhale she said, "Kim? I'll be delicate here—"

Melody let out a hoot. Was it possible that Coco and Melody were becoming friends? "My dear, you're about as delicate as a jackhammer."

"That's part of my charm."

"What's the other part?" Melody asked.

"This." Coco stood up and pointed to her ass, covered up in metallic-silver leggings.

The mood changed abruptly when Hobie walked through the gate and took a seat with us by the fire; he'd gone back in the helicopter after I left to show the rescuers where he'd found the backpack. At last, he was commanding the respect he'd desired.

"Any news?" I asked.

For once, he had little to say. "I looked high and low. Nothing. I thought for sure we'd find him."

This was the first time I'd seen him totally exhausted. Finally, his age showed. Coco pushed a glass in his hand. "Drink. Relax." For the first time, I could imagine them as a couple.

She continued, "See, I know people. You wouldn't believe the crap I hear when I'm picking at their cuticles. I'll just come out and say it because I have a feeling we've all been thinking the same thing: Do you think Grant might be having an affair?"

"He's *not* having an affair," Cassie said. "His heart is aligned with Kim's."

Coco seemed skeptical. "I don't know. Remember that young mom who went missing at Zion and it turned out she was in San Diego? She staged the whole damn thing so she could get away from home for a few days and sneak off with her ex-husband. Could Grant be with an old sweetheart? That's what men do at his age. They go looking for the women who used to think they were hot, relive their sexcapades, try to rekindle some old flames. Grant wasn't much when he arrived, but he was looking good lately. I'm sorry to say it, my dear, but it's possible he was up to something. Men don't change like that for no reason."

"He wouldn't need to sneak off with his ex," I said. "Sasha is already very much part of our lives."

"Hold up," Thomas said. "Sasha? Who's Sasha?"

"His first wife. When I met Grant, she kind of came with the territory. The three of us were practically a throuple all these years."

"Throuple! Nice job, Laura Ingalls Wilder. Our work here is done."

"I think," Cassie said, "that Grant pursued hiking because he is a seeker at his core. He's been trying to locate the map within, and that is ultimately what will guide him home."

Hobie sank back into his chair and closed his eyes, his mind still on the hike. "That's just a fancy way of saying he's lost. And it's a terrible thing to get lost."

Everyone became silent and entirely focused on Hobie. The firelight played up his features from below, so he was lit up like a figure in a Caravaggio painting. "See, it's an emotional experience. You have to ask yourself, What does someone do when they are in a state of profound darkness? Profound. Fucking. Darkness. You're supposed to sit still. That's what everyone tells you, as soon as you realize you don't know where you are, just sit down. But who can do that? Not me. I've been lost before, and I kept going. What are you supposed to do, jerk off? Daydream? We're animals, man. Pack animals. We're not good alone for too long. The problem is our nature. Your phone doesn't connect, you're hot, you're cold, you're confused. You're really going to . . . sit? Maybe it's not safe. And even when you realize you've lost your way, it takes a while for it to dawn on you that you're actually lost. *Lost* lost. It hits with a sudden shock, a deep way of knowing. You freeze, take inventory, and *then* you are truly afraid. The adrenaline kicks in. So you move, that's what you do. The blood flows out of your brain and into your limbs so you can fight, punch, run."

Thomas put his hand on one of my shoulders, and Melody put her hand on the other. Cassie set her mesa in my arms. "Hold this close to your heart for comfort," she said.

"The problem with Grant? He thinks he's smart. But it doesn't matter if you're a boy genius when you're out in the mountains. Even the most experienced hikers get punch-drunk without a map, without GPS, without a fixed object to focus on—a water tower, a tree. The landscape is very deceptive. You hike in the middle of the day when the sun is directly above you, it's not easy to see where the trailhead is. Or you see the lights in the distance and think you're not far away from civilization, but you have to go across boulders or down cliffs to get there. There are no guardrails, just a dirt path, and it disappears or comes back and makes branches. Nobody learns to tell time by the sun anymore, nobody knows their cardinal directions. Nobody even gets lost, not when they can see the little blue dot on their phones telling them where they are."

Hobie paused, his eyes fixed on the fire. I didn't want to hear his monologue, and yet I felt I needed to know what Grant was up against now that I knew where he was—approximately, at least.

"I tried to give him some pointers. And maybe he *did* do everything I told him to do. But he's one of those guys who gets in his own way. Even if he was wearing bright colors, and even if he did carry a book of matches and extra food and half his weight in water, he might not be in the right state of mind to make the best decisions. The minute you realize you don't know where you are, your brain and your body begin to disconnect. It's like what happens when you're sitting in the doctor's office and they're giving you a terminal diagnosis."

Coco said firmly, "Hobie, stop scaring Kim. She's right here. Maybe you should tone it down—"

"Me? You were just telling Kim that you think Grant was having an affair. How is that any easier to handle? You're in no position to talk about protecting Kim's feelings."

"You know all about affairs, don't you?"

I interrupted their argument. "It's not like all these possibilities haven't been running through my mind. It's all I think about. For the past three days, I've been trying to put myself in his shoes. That's what's so exhausting, not knowing what he's thinking, or if he's okay."

"I'll tell you one thing, Kim," Hobie said, locking eyes with me. "This will change him for good. Because the thing about fear is it's also a form of pleasure. You produce dopamine when you're scared. It's a natural high. The darkness becomes desire. To get lost in the landscape is like getting lost in emotion. Something bad happens and it becomes a place in your mind, a place you don't want to return to, so you avoid going back to it, even if it's the only place you really can be found, the only place that makes sense."

I realized he might as well have been talking about Grant's earlier episodes, and I became aware for the first time, on a deeper level, that when he ran, he wasn't running from me; he was running to a place he could feel safe.

"You can take just a few steps off the trail, and you might never find your way back again. It all starts with the sense that something might be wrong, but you ignore it—and then it's too late."

"That's enough for me," I said. "Thanks for dinner, you guys. My daughters are coming tomorrow and I need to get the place ready." As I stood to go back to Basil's condo, Hobie said, "Oh, wait. I have something for you."

"For me? What?"

"When I left, Brady asked me to give you the backpack. He doesn't need it anymore."

"Hobie, are you kidding me? You've had it this whole time and you're just telling me now? It's been sitting in your car?"

"I'm giving it to you now." He shrugged. "Look, I'm beat. I hiked fourteen miles today. I picked it up at the ranger station for you, and this is the thanks I get? Do you want to read it or not?"

He held out the tattered Moleskine. I knew that whatever was inside would either hold the answers I'd been desperate for—or leave me with even more questions.

Chapter Twenty-One

Grant's Journal

December 28

I meet the most ordinary people on hikes. Trader Joe's cashiers, Uber drivers. They tell me they don't want regular jobs because their real life is up here. They reject capitalism not as a philosophical principle but because they learned the secret nobody wants us to know: we don't need it. Everything we need in life can fit into a fifteen-pound pack.

Hiking makes us feel like heroes to ourselves. We can do hard things. We can disconnect and focus on one step in front of the other.

I'm on the new trail in Indio. It's not hard, pretty boring until you get to the badlands, but that's when it starts to pay off. I walked through narrow slot canyons formed by tectonic uplift and time. The rocks are torqued and twisted like Silly Putty. I just climbed to the high point. From here I can see the Coachella Valley, the Salton Sea, and the San Gorgonio Mountain. I stopped to get away from a yammering group of hikers. Now I know why Hobie tells me to shut up—Hobie of all people. The only time that guy doesn't say what's on his mind is when he's on the trails. I get it now. I've spent my entire career wanting other people's words in my head. Now, with every step, I push them out.

Everyone talks about the same thing out here: their relationships—who they love, who they used to love. Who let them down. Who they want but shouldn't. Who they don't want but should. It's where your mind goes for some reason. It's where my mind goes, that's for sure.

All these people sound crazy to me. What could they know about love?
What do any of us know?

December 29

Thank god I can come here to escape being part of everyone else's vacation.
The horror stories I hear when we meet the new snowbirders who arrive at
Le Desert and start random conversations . . . One guy, first thing out of his
mouth—"How much snowpack you got back home?" They love to tell sto-
ries of massive blizzards, curling . . . an ice arena that collapsed under heavy
snowfall. All we talk about is the winter we left behind.

Then there are the rental horror stories. The place that had only plastic
silverware, no toilet paper, moldy carpets, rusty baking sheets. Barking dogs.
That time their unit was double-booked, or they were scammed with a fake
listing and the police could do nothing. The house that looked nothing like on
Airbnb. Schlubby furniture with springs sticking out. Last-minute cancella-
tion mishaps. The old man who died while swimming laps in the pool in the
condo complex where they rented last year. Pulling open a dresser drawer
to find a month's supply of adult diapers. Some guy from Winnipeg told me
they'd gone out for dinner, returned, and found their place had been broken
into by members of a gang and the word ZEDA was spray-painted on the
wall. "That's when you know it's time to go home," he said.

I miss being around people who are living their normal lives.

I'd planned to go to Joshua Tree and didn't feel like it. I'm at DeMuth Park
watching pickleball games instead. I guess it does kind of look like fun.

December 30

I climbed Araby this morning so I could be back in time to take Gene to the
Air Museum to see the first F-117 stealth bomber. Hard to imagine that being
reminded of war days in Vietnam could be a break, but poor guy sure needs
one. He's not in great shape himself on top of taking care of Jeanie.

Talking to Gene about war pushed a memory loose. I was little, five or six
years old. This was about a year after my dad died, and a few years before
my mom met Stew. Too broke for a babysitter (too broke for bologna), she sent
me to our neighbor George's place across the hall when she wanted to hit the
town. I thought he must have been a million years old, but he was probably

close to the age I am now. He didn't know what to do with a kid, so he put me in front of a pile of books and told me to read while he knocked off.

The minute his head hit the pillow I was out of there. At first, I'd go to the corner. Then the next block. Eventually I started to learn some shortcuts around the neighborhood. I made it as far as Great Falls Park almost a mile away, where I discovered the trail that led to the ruins of Matildaville, an old ghost town. All that was left was a tavern chimney and the corners of houses and some fence posts. I'd pretend the town was still there, and I was in charge of it, or I was a bad guy on the lam, or I was a war hero like George, returning from the battlefield. From there I'd walk on the bluffs by the Potomac near Mather Gorge.

Imagine if the girls were allowed to leave home by themselves at the age of six and hang out by a river that dropped over 75 feet in less than a mile. Anything could have happened to me back then—it already had happened, as far as I was concerned.

One day I saw a man—or I could sense him. He gave off this aura. When water is at the edge of the waterfall, it gets darker than the water around it. That was him, this swirling, kinetic, dark energy. He was sitting deep in the woods, cross-legged, staring into space. I thought he was meditating. It was foggy. Very early. Something was very not right. I walked closer and saw his eyes were opaque, like Milky's eyes when he got old, when you could see yourself reflected in them.

"Hi," I said. What a dumb thing to say.

He nodded very, very slowly. More like his chin dropped to his chest and he couldn't lift it up again. I knew I had to run, but my feet felt like they were stuck in quicksand. That's when I looked down and saw that he'd sliced his arms lengthwise from his wrists to his elbows. They hung open like flayed fish. There was a knife in his lap and blood everywhere, so much blood I could smell it from where I stood. I can smell it now, just thinking about it.

I felt his death. He was on that edge, scarier than any monster or ghost. I could have screamed or tried to get help, but if I did, George would find out that I'd left the house, and he'd tell my mom, and those days, who knew what she would do. So I bolted. I ran as fast as my legs would carry me. I ran and ran and ran all the way back to George's apartment. He was still snoring loud enough to shake the walls. He had no idea.

From then on, I stayed put. The next time I sat in front of a pile of books, I turned every page, read every single word.

I never, ever told anyone about that man, not even Kim. I bet she thinks she's heard all my stories.

That experience left me with so many questions: Was I responsible for his death because I didn't get him some help? Was what I'd done unethical? I'd prioritized my own well-being over his life. Say I'd saved him: Would that have interrupted some sort of divine plan? Was there a divine plan? He clearly wanted to die, look what he'd done to himself. It was his right to end his life, wasn't it?

I was just a little kid, and I was musing about the morality around human agency before I'd ever even heard of Sartre.

That single event changed me forever. It was the moment I really started thinking. That was when I became a philosopher.

And this? This is when I stop being a philosopher. That event taught me how to think, and hiking is teaching me how not to think. I'm learning how to simply exist in the world with the wind between my ears, not a thought in my head. I need Kim, I do. But up here, I feel like I don't need anyone. I don't need anything.

December 31

Whoa. Thought Kim and I were finally finding our way back to each other. Now what?

Chapter Twenty-Two

Palm Springs
January 3, 2023
8:00 P.M.

The fifth time—the last time—that Grant left, I really thought we might be through.

Hobie said that experienced hikers know they'll inadvertently walk in a circle when they're lost, so they'll scratch a line in a tree or on a rock and scratch it again the second, third, fourth time they've found themselves in the same spot. That's what I've been doing in my head as I wait for news—marking the same painful spot where I hurt Grant; going back again and again to the only other time when Grant had been missing this long.

Camp Jamboree had changed hands, and the new owner purchased giant inflatable water toys that Burl would have hated. Still, I wanted the girls to get a taste of the same childhood I'd had, so every year they spent several weeks there. Grant and I had a long stretch of time to ourselves, and we'd hole up in Burl's house on the other side of the lake—he'd passed it down to me.

The cabin wasn't worth much. It was old, and without Burl to maintain it, it had fallen into neglect. It wasn't on the water but accessible via a footpath leading to the no-wake lake. Our quiet wasn't interrupted by Jet Skis or the trolling motor on a fishing boat. The only sounds we could hear were the hiss of cicadas, the belching of bullfrogs, and the voices of children laughing, playing, and singing on the other side of the lake.

The roof shingles were moldy, the lawn was always damp, and the foliage was so dense it could have gobbled up the house. Inside, it smelled like soil and fish and dead mice and musty carpeting. The cushions on the wicker furniture were damp and heavy with mildew and made Grant's eyes water. Every year I'd drag the furniture and cushions outside to let them bake in the sun, and I'd open every window even though the no-see-ums and mosquitoes could sneak in through the holes in the rusty screens. The tap spit out rusty brown water that smelled of sulfur. It was the kind of place most people would reject, but I loved it, at first because it reminded me of Burl, and over the years because it contained happy memories of the time I spent with Grant.

The cabin had the same ingredients that made Camp Jamboree so special for me when I was a kid: water, sun, warmth, and, most important, no adult responsibilities. It was the place where Grant and I were at our best, tucked away from the world, grateful for every minute without interruption.

Part of the spark of our relationship was the time we spent apart during the week. Weekends, we came together with the passion of reunited lovers. In the summers, we fell into a lazier, easier rhythm. Grant cooked pancakes on the skillet for breakfast. In the afternoons, we'd sit in the golden light of the sunporch, my head in Grant's lap as he read, his free hand tracing the outline of my eyebrows and the bridge of my nose. There was no Wi-Fi, and limited cell reception. Nothing beckoned. We had only each other.

I didn't try to fill up our time. We played Yahtzee and charades. We explored the trails. When it rained, we watched old VHS movies on the black-and-white television. We ate and drank wine in the flickering candlelight and talked about all the drama we experienced at work with our colleagues, our concerns and hopes for the girls, our dreams for the future. Burl had taught me how to play guitar—no campfire is complete without one—and at night I'd strum along as we harmonized (badly) to "Take It Easy" by the Eagles.

Every year, our most romantic tradition was to paddle out to the middle of the lake, jump in, and "marry" each other. We recited vows to give back rubs and not leave dishes in the sink; to eat crunchy food out of earshot, to be patient and kind, to always love each other. Without the slightest hesitation, we'd shout "I do!" at the same time, our voices skipping off the lake's surface. I felt more married to Grant in those moments than I might have felt in a church wedding.

There's a pine forest nearby, a relic from Depression-era WPA projects, when the workers planted the pine trees at neat intervals. Sometimes, we played a game I'd learned at camp where Grant put a bandanna around my eyes and hid while I counted to ten.

"Grant!" I'd called out when I finished counting.

"Here," he whispered.

I walked through the forest with my hands out in front of me, touching the soft bark of the trees. "Grant!" I'd call again.

"Over heeeere. You're getting warmer." His voice would grow a little louder with each reply, letting me know he'd soon let me find him. "Warmer, so hot, you're burning up." Then I'd touch him, and we'd tumble onto the ground.

By the end of our blissful time together, as we began thinking about our return to normal life, Grant would begin with his annual entreaty. "Move with me to Mounds. We can be a campus family. We can sell our house in Madison for a good price and buy one of those big old Victorians with a turret on Cherry Street. They cost next to nothing." He was right. Before NAFTA, Mounds had been a thriving manufacturing community. The executives had lived near the college, leaving behind grand homes that were practically free for the taking.

"That's because nobody wants to live there," I said. I was determined never to give Mounds a chance. It represented his other life. In truth, it was because that's where Sasha lived, and even though I liked her—loved her, even—the town would never be big enough for the two of us. Or was Sasha just an excuse? Did I think that the only way I could keep Grant was at a distance?

"Mounds is really coming back. Some tech guys from San Francisco moved their business to that old warehouse by the river. They call it the Silicon Valley of the Midwest."

"That's what they call every small town."

"You wouldn't even have to work if you don't want to. You can pick up painting—there's a studio on campus you can use anytime."

"No way, Grant. I like my job enough. I like our little house. I love Madison. It's always rated a best place to live for a reason." I'd been looking forward to finally enjoying my freedom, and the space and time to figure out what to do next. I'd made my life in Madison, and I wanted to reap the benefits. Not move.

"Come on, Kimmy. My students can babysit. We can go out all the time. We can have parties."

"Parties with all your faculty friends? And Sasha? No thanks. All we'd talk about is intersectionality."

He'd launch into his arsenal of arguments as if counting them off on his fingers. "Dort will be there. The girls can come to campus after school and do homework in my office. You've always wanted more children. We could adopt or become foster parents. In Mounds we can be a real family."

"We already are a real family."

But were we?

His line of reasoning was always the same, and so was my answer: no, no, no. "The commute isn't ideal, but it works for us."

"Easy for you to say because I'm the one doing it. I'm lonely, Kim. It hurts me to go to bed and wake up by myself. I miss band concerts and teacher conferences and homework. Look how we are here. We're so good together, Kimmy. You can trust that. We could be good together *all the time*."

"We're on vacation! It wouldn't be like this if I came to Mounds. We'd have laundry and—"

"How do you know that? I admit it isn't the sexiest place. It isn't on anyone's list, but there's a river. A park. The town has a history. It has a heart."

"It has vape shops. A uniform store. Liberty Tax. Giant tents where they sell fireworks."

"What's wrong with being exposed to some diversity of opinion?"

"Gun stores."

"We could have a good life."

"But we already have a good life."

"We're only half-together. What are you afraid of? Just because your mom and Burl lived apart doesn't mean we have to."

We covered the same ground again and again and again. The more Grant asked, the more I dug my heels in without realizing how much it hurt him.

Our last summer there, Grant lobbied harder than usual. With the girls entering college, he knew this was his final opportunity. I'd always argued that I needed to stay in Madison so as not to disrupt the girls; now that argument was moot.

We went out in the canoe and jumped in the lake to say our vows, but it felt more as if we were performing. "I promise to laugh at your dumb jokes," I said.

"I'll wipe the sink after I brush my teeth."

"I'll always be honest with you. Always."

"And I'll be faithful. I will never, ever cheat on you."

"I will be true to you forever."

I knew something was up because he grew quiet and tense.

Once we got back to shore, he ran into the cottage and returned to where I sat in an Adirondack chair. I assumed he was about to ask me to marry him. My alimony had run out years earlier. We talked about marrying occasionally, but I didn't see the point, not when we could seal our relationship with our annual ceremony at the lake.

"I have a surprise for you," he said.

I'd expected a jewelry box. Instead, he handed me an envelope. "What's this?"

Inside I didn't find a ring; I found an old key with a pink ribbon tied to the end of it. It felt heavier than it should have.

"You know that house on Cherry Street that Erika from the dance department owned? The one you said was your favorite? Well, Kimmy, I bought it with some of the money I'd inherited when Stew died." He was grinning from ear to ear.

"You did *what*?"

"Erika took a new position at Grinnell. She sold it to me for a song. No Realtor fees, no nothing. The mortgage is basically what I pay for rent anyway. We'll hardly notice it. You'll love it, Kim. The kitchen has been redone. There's a coffered ceiling in the living room. Stained glass. Marble in the bathrooms. She just had it painted."

"Grant, do you mean to say that you bought an entire house without even telling me?"

"Well, *you* bought a house. I don't recall you consulting *me* first."

"But I bought it for us when we needed a place to live."

He paused. "That's what I did, too. Kim, the girls are done with high school. As of September, Dort is going to be at Mounds, too, for Christ's sake! You don't need to be in Madison anymore. Why wouldn't you want to be with me, with us?"

I turned the key over in my hand, over and over. "I'm not moving to Mounds, Grant. That's not what I want. I have my job, my friends, my book club, my gym membership, my volunteer—"

"Would you just think about it for two minutes?"

"Why do you do this? Why do you make us have the same conversation again and again? It always comes to the same conclusion." I was boiling with the frustration I was afraid to show because I was always so afraid he'd snap, but I had my breaking point, too. "You never listen to me when I tell you that I am never moving to Mounds, not ever."

That's when I did something that haunts me now: I threw the key into the lake.

He said nothing as we watched the ripples spread and flatten. A tear slipped out of his eye, a leak springing from a giant aquifer of pain. "You'll never know how much I adore you, or how much this hurts me," he said. Grant went inside, packed up his things, and walked out the door.

I didn't see him again for a few days. I wasn't worried about where he had gone—I knew he would have walked to the county highway and hitchhiked all the way back to his new house. What I worried about was that the great, enduring love of my life was over, not because we couldn't get along, not because we didn't love each other enough, but because we couldn't agree on where to live. I thought for sure this was it, and I was so sick about it I didn't know how to go on. What would I tell the girls? How could I explain that my stubbornness—and his—broke up our family?

When Grant showed up in Madison two days later, we held each other and cried. There were no apologies, no more entreaties. The fever broke, and life went back to its old patterns. The girls moved out and I was left alone in Madison, and Grant moved all by himself into that beautiful old house where he said he rolled around like a pea in a bottle. I'd visit occasionally. We'd paint and wallpaper. We decorated it with furniture we'd found at garage sales. He shared it with an occasional visiting scholar, or he'd rent the guest rooms to adjuncts, and Dort liked to join him for dinner on occasion. When the college closed, one of his renters bought it from him.

We never went back to the cabin because the roof collapsed from the weight of the snow that winter, and the whole thing had to be torn down. Grant never asked me to move again.

Now, I'm haunted by the decisions I made—and didn't make. I could have shown some flexibility. I could have moved, if that would have made Grant happy. I thought I was being the type of strong, independent woman Polly had raised me to be. Maybe I *was* right that Madison had been best for the girls, and best for me, but had it been best for our family to be separated the way we were? My friends always tried to cultivate their own lives within their marriages, but how much independence is too much? Is it possible to achieve deep companionship with a ton of freedom?

Since he's been gone, I keep remembering the time we'd spent in the camp pine forest. The trees, planted in their orderly rows that defied nature, crowded out the sun. I saw only a bit of light creeping in from under my bandanna. I felt dead pine needles under my feet.

"Where are you?" I shouted.

"You're getting warmer," he called back.

I waited and waited for the sound of Grant's voice to call out to me again, but it only grew more faint. I could just barely make out him saying, "I'm here, Kimmy. I'm over here. Come find me."

There is a part of me that forever calls out his name, that always seeks to find him.

It's hard to believe now that we could have turned losing each other into a game.

Chapter Twenty-Three

Palm Springs
December 4, 2022

I couldn't hike with Grant, but my foot was getting better. I could easily handle my morning octogenarian walks with Jeanie and Gene along the wash. We moved slowly to adjust for our infirmities. I watched how loving Gene was with his wife, waiting patiently if she fell behind, holding her arm, never rushing her, always attuned to the subtlest changes in her demeanor. The couple had become like second parents to me, and role models for what Grant and I could become if we could get our acts together.

The wash was always active with dog walkers and runners. I'd been in Palm Springs long enough to establish a routine, and to begin to recognize people who were on the same schedule. Eighties sunglasses guy, the stylish lady with the standard poodle with its tail dyed pink.

Jeanie told me about her job as a nurse, and Gene told stories about working in a coal-fired power plant. During his lunch breaks, he and his coworkers would feed arsenic to the rats behind the building and place bets on when they would die. "The air in the plant was so thick with asbestos that you couldn't see across it."

"Some of my friends died from asbestos just from washing their husband's laundry," Jeanie said. Mornings, you'd never know her memory was causing her problems. By afternoon and evening, she could get lost in her own mind.

"My lungs feel like they're made out of cheap plastic. Listen to this, kid." Gene inhaled deeply so I could hear a cracking sound.

I couldn't stand the thought of Gene being sick. He reminded me of Burl, always kind and interested.

"Gene, are you . . . okay?"

"Today, I sure am. Sun is shining. I'm with my sweetheart. We're in this beautiful place. You know, at our age, anything can get us. The stuff we know about, the stuff we don't. We're just happy to be here. How old are you?"

"Fifty-five."

"Start counting your winters, my dear. You've only got so many." A pit bull running alongside an old ponytailed man on a bicycle darted past us. "This is probably our last year here, so we're really trying to enjoy it."

I heard countless stories about their kids and grandkids, whose names I couldn't keep straight. Jeanie said one had the voice of an angel when she sang. Another had gotten addicted to heroin and lived on the streets in Alberta. Because of this, Gene jumped every time his phone rang, worried about bad news. They were lonely without all their good friends who used to spend the winters here with them; they'd all either gotten too old, were priced out, or had passed away. Gene and Jeanie said they were closer with their snowbird friends than their friends back home because they spent more quality time together.

I thought these glacial walks would prepare me for "pep stepping" with Melody. That's what she called her long, fast walks around the inside perimeter of Smoke Tree Ranch, adjacent to the tall fence with scrappy jumping cholla cacti hugging the posts as if begging to be let in. It felt as if the fence weren't there so much to protect the ranch's residents as to remind the rest of the world that they are on the outside of all that wealth, history, and power—it was like the divider between first class and coach.

Melody wore a crisp white tennis skirt, a white polo top with the Smoke Tree insignia, and a Smoke Tree visor. She did not wear sunscreen. "Good lord, at my age, who cares?" If I'd seen her from the wash, I might have thought she was a young woman. Her body was shaped by a lifetime of vigorous use and excessive pampering. Maybe Grant was right. It wasn't the geography and climate of Palm Springs that made older people here look so young—the secret was that so many had so much money.

"Tell me, is Grant hiking again?" Melody asked.

"Every day." I was still rattled that Grant hadn't mentioned that he and Cassie had gone out together—twice. "He's super into it. I'm so grateful he has something to keep his mind off things. He's been in a rut."

"I can tell you what his problem is. He's got a case of the fifties."

She waved at an older man who drove past in a golf cart and smiled flirtatiously. "This happened to Vandyke. Men just barrel through life and suddenly the kids are grown, and the productive years of their careers are behind them. That's when they start to think about all the decisions they've made and they are shocked—shocked!—to realize their futures are shorter than their pasts. It's hard for them, poor babies. But women? We constantly assess. We talk with our friends. We're always checking in with ourselves and each other, like us. Look what we're doing right now."

Melody stopped to catch her breath. Behind her was a simple ranch home painted white with the traditional shake roof. "Come, Kimberly. Join me for lemonade on the palapa."

All the widely spaced homes in Smoke Tree were one story and the same general size, although some were campy and older, like Melody's, while others looked more as if they belonged in Florida, with coral siding and pink shutters. There were newer houses from the eighties, some that were a multitonal explosion of beige, and others had Polynesian-style roofs and recreated a more faux-tropical environment. We even passed a home in severe disrepair, a sight I found somehow reassuring. All of the homes were worth millions, and they hardly ever came up for sale to the public.

Melody's house was more lived-in and dated inside than I'd imagined it would be. "I keep waiting for a Svengali of the design world to come work his magic," she said. It was both laid-back and elegant, with lots of fine upholstery and western-style antiques.

She pointed at a dresser against one wall. "The credenza belonged to Walt." The surface was covered with trinkets and framed photos of Melody, Vandyke, Basil, and yesterday's celebrities. They were at parties, playing tennis, goofing around by the pool, riding horses. "The fun we had!"

She handed me some lemonade in a crystal goblet. "Vandyke's aunt Nell stole that glass you're drinking from out of Gloria Swanson's house. She thought it was possible Joe Kennedy drank out of it—she always had a thing for the Kennedys. As far as she was concerned, they were East Coast royalty, and we were the royal family of the West Coast. And do you want to know something? Jack winked at me in 1962, when he visited Bing Crosby's Silver Spurs Ranch in Palm Desert. I found him sickly and rather tragic, which of course made him attractive." Melody paused. "Bing, you know, he was a personal friend. Lovely man. I met him at dinners with Dolores Hope. Dolores loved her antipasti."

I was afraid I'd drop the glass, so I set it down and walked around to admire Melody's artwork; it was everywhere.

"This is amazing." I pointed at the painting above the brick fireplace. "A real Mark Rothko? That orange is so . . . emotional."

"I hate it!"

I almost jumped. I couldn't imagine hating something so clearly valuable. I wandered to the dining room, where I laid eyes on an authentic Joan Miró. Melody's house could have been a museum. I wanted to live a life where I, too, could be surrounded by so much beauty and art.

"Now Miró, he was better, but not my favorite. Vandyke's taste trended much more modern than my own. He preferred saturated colors that rise out of nowhere. Modern art is like a punch in the nose." She picked up a throw pillow to fluff. "I've always preferred the French impressionists, but Vandyke found their work frilly and feminine. When we married, without my consent, he moved all of my parents' 'splotchy' and 'soft' paintings—his words—off the walls here at the ranch and into our Hancock Park home. He especially hated Renoir's overly sweet greens. I was far more upset about the paintings than I was about any of his affairs. 'How could you?' I asked. They were *my* paintings, *my* history, *my* preferences, *my* taste! The tears I shed over that man!"

Basil had often recounted his father's infidelities, which was part of the reason I never liked Vandyke. I'd always wondered if Melody knew. "That must have been painful."

She pulled on her earring. "I suppose it was. I forget."

"How did you find out?"

"Vandyke was careless. But also, I think he wanted me to be jealous. His dalliances were legendary."

"Melody, didn't it bother you?"

"It bothered me that he had such poor taste. Carol LaGrange—that woman couldn't find her way out of a paper bag, and she was married to a real Casanova herself. My husband's taste in women, present company excluded, was no better than his taste in art."

She threw her sun visor on the mahogany dining room table. "Honestly, I was much more upset when I returned to Los Angeles and discovered Mother's beloved Pissarro painting of peasants picking apples hanging in the guest bathroom above the *toilet*. Now that was a true betrayal. She'd bought that when she was overseas at an auction with Lee Annenberg. You see, Vandyke did not know his place, that was the problem. *I* was the chatelaine, the keeper of our castle. But I got the last laugh, as I usually do. Now the painting is on permanent display at the Palm Springs Art Museum. I worked with a woman named Sherri over there. I told her to make sure the little sign next to it says, 'From the *Vandyke* and Melody Underwood Collection.'"

"Why don't you move your artwork back here to Smoke Tree?"

"Because up until now I haven't had anyone to help me do it. That's where you come in."

"Me?"

"Come."

She led me down a hallway and opened one of the doors. I couldn't believe my eyes. There were piles and piles of papers, manila file folders, boxes, unopened letters. The air-conditioning kicked on and the paperwork near the vent fluttered as though it were alive. It reminded me of an art exhibit I'd seen where you walked into a room filled with hundreds of reams of paper being blown by industrial fans. "It's not just the paintings that need to be moved, you see. I've let all my affairs slip." She frowned. "Our financials have been arriving in the mail and I just can't deal with them, so I throw them in here and shut the door. Out of sight, out of mind. It's sadly beyond my control."

"Can I help?" Sure, I'd made a promise to Basil, but this didn't have anything to do with him. Melody had become a friend.

She smiled. "I'd like that very much. You can assist me until I find my new husband. I'm determined to marry again. Most widows my age say they prefer to be on their own. Even my married friends prefer to be alone. It takes a long time to break in a gentleman of advanced age, but I'm up for the challenge."

If something happened to Grant, I liked to think I could manage. It even sounded a tiny bit appealing to me—not the part about something happening to him, but the idea of forging my own way in the world. Of making the food I want to eat, of cleaning up my own messes, of going—and living—wherever I desired, whether to escape winter or to start a totally new life. I got a taste of that here.

She put some lipstick on, bright red, and smacked her lips together. Then she looked at me. "Forget about widowhood and that horrendous mess. Come here, Kimberly. This would be a wonderful color on you. Chanel's Rouge Allure."

"Red? I never wear red."

"I know. It's because you don't want people to look at you, and it's time for that to change. May I?" She led me to a gilded mirror and told me to pucker. "Women excel at remaking ourselves because we do it all the time."

"My friend Octavia said that as women get older, they want men to change, while men just want women to stay the same."

"We change all the time because we actually think about life as we go through it, and we respond to it. We experience many renaissances. I'm having one right now. I can feel it. And look at you, Kimberly."

The color did look great—dramatic. "What about me?"

"You're here, aren't you?" She squeezed my shoulders. It was reassuring that she could see what I couldn't. "You're experiencing a renaissance right now."

Chapter Twenty-Four

Palm Springs
January 4, 2023
7:00 A.M.

Brady instructed me to come to Indian Canyons with a bag full of Grant's dirty laundry—just Grant's, no other smells. It was for the bloodhounds, as if he were part of a Sherlock Holmes mystery. Bloodhounds! I distracted myself from my worry by imagining the good laugh we'd have about that when they found him, those poor dogs smelling the damp socks and frayed boxers that reeked of hiker funk when I'd pulled them out of his hamper.

I was allowed into the trailer briefly to hand the bag to Brady. The mood inside had perceptibly changed; it had gone from feeling like a busy office to the situation room during a nuclear threat. The rescuers were tense and hyperfocused. I would never be able to fully express my gratitude for all they'd done, and as much as I hated knowing Grant was lost on his hike, I felt so much less guilty knowing I wasn't wasting their time.

But with the storm approaching and the situation growing more dire, everyone was all business.

"Now that you've read his journal, do you think it'll be easier to find him?" I asked, embarrassed that Brady had gotten a glimpse into our relationship and our issues.

He ushered me back outside where I belonged. "I guess it helped us narrow the search area, but every step he takes means we need to widen our radius of all the possible directions he can go. We suspect the lights he thought were coming from Cathedral City were actually coming from Palm Springs, which means he's probably headed north, or what he thinks is north. He's new to orienteering. I don't know if he knows that north doesn't mean north—true north and magnetic north are two different things. He might not know that you need to hold the compass flat or you might not get an accurate reading. We still have a big area to work with. I've got helicopters dropping my guys off at three thousand feet to work their way down. Let's hope he didn't get confused and start climbing again."

"You'll find him, right?"

"Mrs. Duffy, we're doing everything we can. We even mobilized San Bernardino County. We've got dogs and drones. But I must be clear with you: it appears we've gone from a lost hiker to a critical situation."

"'A critical situation,'" I repeated. "What does that even mean? Hasn't it been critical this whole time?"

"It's protocol, something we do anytime someone is missing more than three days. After this much time, we begin to shift resources from rescue to recovery."

I looked Brady straight in the eyes. "Are you trying to tell me that you think he's . . . dead? Because he's not. I can feel him."

"I'm saying that I think it's time to gather your family."

The girls were flying in that morning. I couldn't wait to be reunited with March and Dort, couldn't wait to see Grant in their looks and their gestures. They'd inherited his wild hair, his wry smile. Even Octavia offered to come out. "You know I'm your ride or die whenever Grant takes off."

"Isn't there anything I can do?" The helplessness was what really got me.

"You can excuse me because I need to get back to business. Every minute that ticks by is a minute it's less likely we'll find him."

Chapter Twenty-Five

Grant's Journal

January 1, 2023

*W*hat time is it?

That's the first thing Kim asks me when she wakes up, and I always say, "It's early." Why? Because I want her to roll into me and sleep some more. Her back is as soft as baby skin.

God, her back. I know it too well. Sometimes it's all she lets me see.

I feel like I'm running my hands on her back right now. The exact topography of her body exists in my brain. Now I'm into maps. I'm learning how to read them like an old-time explorer, looking for the contour lines, summits and spurs, saddles and reentrants. I learned Kim with my own body. The same way I'm learning the landscape here with my feet. Every knob of her spine, every rib. The soft baby hairs that spring from her hairline. The tan lines from her bathing suit straps. She has seven little moles on her right shoulder. One-two-three-four-five-six-seven. They form an upside-down J. A candy cane. A hook.

She hooked me.

Now she wants to throw me back.

Tell me, what use is this map without the terrain? It's about as good as a map of the lost city of Atlantis. A mythical place just out of reach.

I wish I were under the covers in a warm bed with Kim right now. I want to pull her close and become one thing. I miss the ease between us, the way it was when we met. We ought to celebrate our anniversary today. Instead, I'm seeking clarity about us on my own.

Lately, Kim has been looking at me like I'm a decision that needs to be made.

When she wakes up this morning, I won't be there to tell her it's early. But I don't want to stick around for her to tell me it's too late.

Maybe she'll think I'm gone again. Maybe she'll think I'm hiking. It's the same thing now.

I'm going to have an old-school adventure. Hobie says I need to become more self-reliant, so I ditched him. Today I need to hike commando, purposefully going off-trail without a phone. No Garmin. Just a compass and a map.

I'm on a solitary journey.

He warned me about winter hiking. What does he know about winter? Snow and ice? No problem. No such thing as bad weather, just bad gear. I have a base layer, a mid-layer, a shell. A balaclava that makes me look like an earthworm. Gloves, my pack, some protein bars, and a water bottle. The key is to stay dry.

I'm doing an out-and-back that'll save the sweaty stuff for the end. An out-and-back. Story of my life.

This is a new story now.

Three miles down to see Cedar Springs.

When I get there, I'm going to create a sacred space the way Cassie suggested. And then I'll meditate and decide if I can go forward in our relationship as the partner I need to be.

Then I'll hike back.

Easy and then hard.

I've got a thermos full of coffee. The Jeep is nice and warm. Sun is rising. There's nobody else here that I can see. I'm about to go. I'll stop writing now, not because I don't have things to say. I always have things to say. I've got everything I need. I'll begin.

I used to feel lost when I was gone. Now, this is where I feel found.

Chapter Twenty-Six

Palm Springs
December 9, 2022

Hiking quickly changed Grant. Gone was the man who made wry remarks about Jeanie and Gene's all-day grocery-shopping adventures ("My God, they hit every store in the Coachella Valley to find the cheapest yogurt"). Gone was the man who rolled his eyes at the guy practicing his golf swing while waiting in line for his prescription. The new Grant was a lot less critical of everyone else around him, and a lot more focused on getting into shape as quickly as possible for a previously sedentary fifty-nine-year-old.

He wore a weighted backpack everywhere he went. He tried to clap his hands while on the high point of a push-up. He even got a membership at a gym! I couldn't stand the idea of being inside a packed, smelly building when the whole reason we were in Palm Springs was to be outdoors. I went with him once, and that was enough for me. Almost every machine was taken, and, again, I was one of only a few women; it was like the daytime version of Streetbar.

Now, he couldn't brush his teeth without doing calf raises. Basil's condo smelled like a steak house from Grant's every-three-hour need for calories. I was awoken at five in the morning by the Vitamix tearing into ice, bananas, protein powder, and raw eggs. This man who hardly ever cooked now made his own power bars. Grant was exhausted and exhilarated, grunting and groaning about his stiff hips and sore back. He left ice packs on every surface and slept like a baby. Hardly a day went by when he wasn't on a hike with Hobie, or with strangers he'd met in a hiking club, and, lately, by himself. When he came home, he brought along a Ziploc bag filled with dirty toilet paper.

"Grant, no," I said.

He smiled, amused by my disgust. "LNT. My new religion: 'leave no trace.'"

Hiking seemed like such a simple subject, yet Grant researched it with even more passion and intensity than he'd studied philosophy. He learned about the right-of-way rules between uphill and down-hill climbers, horses, mountain bikers, dogs, solo hikers, and large groups. He bought and made sure he packed his (new, expensive) bag with the "ten essentials," including sunscreen, socks, first aid, and extra food. He stressed the importance of finding your rhythm, keeping a pace, and taking breaks at planned intervals instead of waiting until you need them.

He had goals.

He wanted to go farther, longer, higher, taking it to the "next level," as he called it, which meant going into the backcountry. He followed YouTubers who explored the gold mines that Hobie had told him about. Some, like the Cerro Grodo Mine in Death Valley, still have bodies in them. With almost seven hundred abandoned mines in Riverside County alone, there was a lot to explore.

As far as he was concerned, the fewer people he saw on the trail, the better.

Was I worried? Never. I'd gone on my share of hikes through state parks. The way I saw it, hiking was just walking with a gradient. And from where I sat in Palm Springs, there were people everywhere and everything seemed safe.

Honestly, I was relieved that Grant had his own thing; that was how we operated. I needed a break from so much intense time to-gether after years of being apart. Even during the pandemic Grant had his own place to go part of the time. My petty complaints could add up, from the sound of his spoon clicking against the bowl, the strings of dental floss that never quite made it into the trash can, the cadence of his feet on the tile floors. He hummed without realizing it. He left crumbs everywhere. I'm certain I bothered him, too.

Then again, we started to fall into activities together. We planned meals and cooked, eating by candlelight at Basil's table and catching up on our days. We finally had time to take care of things we'd been putting off, like moving some money around in our IRAs and redrafting our wills. I had Christmas cards made with a photo of the two of us sitting by the pool, and for the first time ever, Grant wrote the little notes on the back and helped address the envelopes. He did the grocery shopping and ran to the hardware store for hummingbird nectar and descaler for the coffee machine. We invited Gene and Jeanie over for dinner; after, we played some of Basil's albums on his elaborate stereo system while the four of us slow danced in front of the fireplace to Nat King Cole.

We watched the same television shows and went to movies together. We had new things to talk about with each other—for a long time, our conversations had revolved almost exclusively around the girls. Now, I told him about my adventures with Melody to the Parker for cocktails and to the polo grounds. Grant told me about hikers and explorers like himself who'd drowned in the mines or had breathed toxic gases. He showed me photos on his camera of stuff he'd found: broken china, spoons, metal detectors, and old chunks of jade. Instead of Socrates and Aristotle, his heroes became the old miners who'd slept perched on the edge of a mountain and endured tremendous hardship.

"Look—" He reached into his pocket, pulled out a rattlesnake skin, and set it in my hand.

"Show-and-tell is over. Let's throw that away." I handed it back to him.

"You won't believe this. We were up in the Chocolate Mountains and this guy in army fatigues comes out, and he's got a crossbow, and he—"

"A *crossbow*?"

Grant was more animated than I'd seen him in a while; this was what made him such a great teacher. He spoke with the energy of a kid relating an exciting dream he had the night before. "It was no big deal. I think he was just trying to scare us."

I couldn't tell if what made this new Grant appealing was that he was different from the man I knew, or if he was more like his old self, happier and more focused. I, too, felt happier—with Grant, with myself, with life.

"I learned how to shoot a gun."

"I feel much better!"

"There are guys up there with AR-15s. You can shoot anywhere you want. One of them let me try. I've never even held a gun. Did you know a bullet can travel for miles?"

"Grant, that's—"

He ripped off his shirt. He was starting to have actual abs.

"Bet you've never made love to a man who's shot a gun."

"No, and I've never wanted to."

I didn't need to sleep with Hobie or Trent to find out what it was like to be with someone else. This was a new Grant, no longer the man who screamed underwater. For someone who was basically retired, the outdoors had provided him with an enviable sense of purpose. A spark, a mission. I began to wonder if his new love for solo hiking would make him so independent that he wouldn't need me anymore.

But then, one afternoon, I found my own spark. I sat in a lounge chair chatting with a couple from Minnesota who'd just arrived and had rented unit seven for a few months. They were making plans to see a Liberace impersonator at the Purple Room, where the Rat Pack formed, and where Frank Sinatra famously pushed the piano into the swimming pool behind the club.

Already I felt like an expert on Palm Springs. I was telling the couple about all the things to do here when Grant returned from a hike covered in a film of dirt, as confident as an action-movie hero as he walked through the tall gate. He wore his new ultralightweight sunglasses with side shields. Hobie had given Grant one of his skullcaps. He took it off and his bangs were drenched. His beard was full. He was more mountain man than barista. The Terminator. He carried his water bottle like a weapon.

I took his photo and instinctively sent it to Octavia and the girls.

Dort texted back, *Holy shit! Dad looks like he just returned from a special ops mission.*

Never thought I'd say this, but Grant looks kinda hot, Octavia replied. *Rambo.*

March wrote, *Beast mode.*

Dort said, *GRAMBO.*

Octavia said, *You're never coming back, I know it.*

Chapter Twenty-Seven

Grant's Journal

January 1

I started hiking along the desert divide, on the ridge of the Santa Rosa Mountains. I was more than a mile above sea level. I looked at my map: the trail runs parallel to East Canyon Creek. Some switchbacks, not bad. The first part was mostly in the sun and offered vistas to the west of Thomas Mountain, and Joshua Tree and Palm Springs to the east. Not much snow at the beginning on the open part of the trail. Windy up here. I like the wind.

I had to walk through four gates to get to the springs, like checkpoints in a video game, through an oak grove and a meadow. Yucca grows on the side of the mountain up here. The trail was well marked, didn't even need my map and compass. Put them away. Saw some campers from the Pacific Crest Trail—I'll do that someday, the whole PCT. I met a guy up here who said he's been gone three weeks. He's done it before and he's scared of reentry. Once you live like this, he says, it's hard to go back.

Cedar Springs is beautiful. I loved being around trees that can provide shelter. I thought I'd miss the house, my job. Nope, it's the trees I miss the most. I found my ecosystem.

I touched the bark like a blind man. This, I decided, was my "power place."

I closed my eyes, meditated, and formulated my intention. Then the big question. Cassie said to keep it simple, to ask for only one thing. She said to imagine that I was boring a hole into the center of the earth, and when I climbed out of it, I'd be met by a spirit animal or guide who would help me find the answer.

I asked my question about moving forward and felt the answer in my bones. I could have been in Cedar Springs five minutes or five hours.

Made pretty good time getting back. Everything was going according to plan. I had a great time and felt the satisfaction of having accomplished what I set out to do. I was busy thinking about the answer, about what I'd eat for lunch, congratulating myself for what I considered a successful outing. I thought about what I'd want to say to Kim. I came back to Morris Road and the Jeep . . . is nowhere. It's gone.

GONE.

I thought maybe I'd come to the wrong place, but there was the dead crow I saw when I started my hike, looking even more dead. The spot where I'd parked was empty. There should be a German word for the disbelief you feel when you realize your car isn't where you'd left it. It couldn't be. Then again, who wouldn't want to steal my magnificent Jeep?

I'll bet the Ulysses S. is at least three hundred miles away by now. Kim manifested this. Now she'll never have to complain about needing a ladder to climb up into the cab again. I guess it was fun while it lasted.

A wiser man might have walked the four miles to Highway 74 and tried to flag down a car and hitchhike back to Palm Springs, asked for help.

That's when I started thinking . . . I'd just made my way to Cedar Springs. Wasn't bad. The day was still young. I could go back, and instead of turning around, I could keep going and find the West Fork Trail, take it back to Indian Canyons. In about five hours I'd be back in time for dinner. I could pick up the conversation we'd had. Figure out what to do about the Jeep. Talk about the future now that I have clarity. I'm a different man, secure in what I now know.

Why not hike back? If people can live out here for weeks at a time, so can I. I have water, some protein bars. I saw a bunch of hikers in the morning. Less now. I'm bound to run into someone. I'll ask them to call and let Kim know I'm okay or I know what she'll think.

I'll hike as far as I can before dark.

I can do this.

SHIFT HAPPENS is right.

Chapter Twenty-Eight

Palm Springs
January 4, 2023
12:30 P.M.

"The oranges here are amazing," Dort said. Juice dripped down her chin, and she left chunks of rind in a pile on Basil's coffee table next to her bare feet.

"They're from that tree right there." I pointed out the window, but all I could see was the mountain, and when I saw the mountain, I saw Grant.

Her messes usually made me nuts, but I didn't care.

All that mattered was that she'd flown halfway around the world to be here. March was here, too. Our girls had somehow managed to land at the Palm Springs airport within minutes of each other, just like when they were born.

I tried not to get too comfortable. Having grown children can be destabilizing; you're with them, everything is perfect, then they're too much, then they're gone. Part of you is glad, part of you misses them terribly.

"Coco picked the oranges for us," I said. "The best tree on the property is behind the hot tub."

Dort tore into another wedge. "I'm so sick of schnitzel and cabbage soup, I can't even tell you. And speaking of oranges, you know what else I'm sick of? Old Eastern Europeans telling me stories about the communism days and how they had to wait in line for three hours to get an orange from Cuba that was hard as a baseball. I'm also sick of airplanes. This guy who sat next to me from Paris to LAX took his shoes off, then his socks, and I was like, *Oh no, no no no*, you don't . . . but he *did*! Dude crossed his legs and put his nasty gangrene foot on his lap and caressed it like a pet ferret. And when dinner came, he picked up his roll in that very same hand. Then he gave me his number! Men are disgusting."

I hadn't seen Dort in almost a year, but she was refreshingly, maddeningly, the same. Like Grant, she took up all the oxygen in the room. Her bag sat open on the floor next to the couch, with the entrails of her nomadic existence scattered about.

One minute she sounded light, the next she was sad. "I thought that when my flight landed, I'd check my phone and everything would be fine again. How can Dad be missing still?"

"He's not missing," March said, "he's lost."

"Same thing, fact-checker."

March paced around the room in her kitten heels, which click-clacked efficiently on the terrazzo floors.

Everyone was so casual in Palm Springs that her outfit made me uncomfortable, and the sound of her shoes went straight to my spine. "Take off your shoes," I said. "Please. I feel like you're a Realtor." She'd left Houston straight from work and was still dressed in a blazer, low-cut silk tank, and tight leather pants. Her long dyed-blond hair, thick like Grant's, was parted down the middle.

"Oh, I almost forgot." March jutted her manicured left hand in front of our faces to show us her giant diamond. "You haven't seen my ring yet."

We didn't know Simeon well, but we liked him when she'd brought him home over the summer. He'd moved to the United States as a refugee from Sierra Leone, and he clearly adored March, allowing her to dress him, photograph him for social media, and generally lead him around.

"Wow, look at that," I said brightly, thinking about the ring I'd found in Grant's underwear drawer the week we'd arrived. It had been Mitzie's wedding ring, with a pear-shaped diamond set in a filigreed platinum band—a ring that, to her, said, "I made it," and to Grant said, "I settled." He'd never been a big fan of Stew's, although he grew on both of us as he aged. After everything Mitzie had been through with Grant's dad, I could see why she chose stability and security over love, companionship over being alone, steadiness over chaos.

Dort stood and hugged her sister. Only when they were right next to each other could you tell they were twins. "You and Simeon look good together. You're the kind of couple that stars in a reality television series about bosses who fire people."

"He's a recruiter. He actually helps people *find* jobs. He could help you, in fact, when you're done doing whatever it is you do all over Europe." March's composure began to dissolve. It was amazing how I could see her at seven and twenty-nine in the same moment. "Mom, what if I get married and Dad can't walk me down the aisle? What if we have kids and they never meet their grandpa?"

"Stop!" I said, a shrill edge to my voice.

Dort's arms were still wrapped around March. "It's okay for us to be scared. We have feelings, Mom."

"*I* have feelings."

"Well, you never show them. The past few days you're like *he's fine, he's fine, nothing to see here,* and you know what? He's not fine. He left for a hike three days ago and he hasn't come home."

"I didn't want you to worry, that's all."

Dort snorted. "Of course we worry. It's right to worry."

"As we speak, there's a swarm of rescuers and helicopters flying all over the mountain. They are total pros, they know what they're doing."

March began pacing around the room, then stopped to look at my paintings propped up against the wall. The one on top was of Cassie on her yoga mat, her mala beads in her hand. "Mom, this is actually pretty good."

"Thanks?"

"Wait, is her name Cassie? I think I follow her. Is this the shaman?

I bought some pants at Target because of her. They're actually super-comfortable. How in the world do you know her?"

"Cassie lives here. In Le Desert. We're friends. I took some of the photos she posted. Dad is especially close with her."

March flipped the canvas forward and saw my favorite painting so far: Grambo. She caught her breath. "Oh my God, look at Dad. That's him. It's like he's in the room with us."

Curious, Dort walked over to look. "This is good, Mom. I see you've entered a new artistic period. You moved on from garbage, parking lots, and abandoned couches. This has more soul, like you're tapping into—" Out of nowhere, Dort began to cry. For someone as tough as she was, Dort could be an ugly crier. "That's Dad. God, this really makes me miss him."

I thought back to the moment I snapped the photo of Grant as Grambo. I had been overcome with a wave of creative inspiration unlike any other I'd ever experienced—I felt an urgent need to paint him; I could see the finished product before I'd even begun. I knew I could work from the photo, sure, but I felt a desire to discard it and capture him in the space between what I saw and what I felt when I looked at him—really looked.

I had excused myself, run into the condo, and made a quick drawing. I took notes about the colors I was looking at and the feelings I wanted to capture—of the day, of the place: the temperature, the mood, and my feelings about Grant. How proud I was of him for embracing this new activity, how respectful he was of Cassie's beliefs, how kind he was with Gene and Jeanie, driving them to their doctor's appointments and helping them get around, how friendly he and Thomas and Raul had become. I wasn't sure if he'd always been this man and I hadn't seen him in whole, or if he'd changed, or if both of those things were true.

I felt a pleasant flutter in my gut when I thought of Grant. Melody was right: after thirty years together, we really could fall in love again. I'd assumed it was too late for that. I thought our feelings for each other would, at best, continue to deepen and evolve—or at worst, go away entirely. I never imagined that they'd be new.

And I never imagined that it would be just as thrilling and terrifying to fall in love now as it was when I was young. Or that these new feelings were setting me up for even greater heartbreak if Grant didn't make it off the mountain.

I went over to hug Dort and March. The three of us were in a slobbery huddle when the door flew open and Octavia marched in without knocking, as usual.

"Make room, bitches!" Dort and March considered Octavia to be a "sister mom." She showed up to all of March's Model UN and mock-trial events, and to Dort's concerts and Roller Derby competitions. When the twins graduated from high school, she gave them subscriptions to *Ms.* magazine. She was someone they could turn to when they were too embarrassed to ask me about how to treat a yeast infection, and she offered additional comfort when they went through breakups or suffered from friend drama.

Melody had picked her up at the airport. Melody stood in the doorway staring at the big, teary mess. "Get over here, Mel!" Octavia said. "Give it up."

I closed my eyes and tried to savor the feeling of being surrounded by everyone I loved most.

All except for one.

Chapter Twenty-Nine

Palm Springs
December 15, 2022

When I'd first moved to Madison from Chicago, everyone talked about "downtown," and I didn't know what they meant. I figured there was an area somewhere I hadn't yet been to with tall office buildings and busy streets, a metropolis like the one in the Superman movies. It didn't take long for me to figure out that what everyone considered the heart of the city was the square around the state capitol building on the narrowest part of the isthmus. Palm Springs was a bit like that, too, but I resisted thinking of it as a small town; *Mounds* was a small town. This was California. Celebrities vacationed here; it was a place that was known.

It was yet another blue-sky, sunny day, and we were walking along Palm Canyon Drive, the main street that ran through Palm Springs. Grant's thick sunglasses were secured with an elastic band that kept them from sliding down his nose. It divided the back of his head into two clumps of wild hair, top and bottom.

Until we spent time here, I hadn't realized that weather was such a big and defining part of our lives, even our identities. We tracked it, planned around it, talked about it, anticipated it, united over it. It was the source of our small talk.

I couldn't believe how much I missed having a dramatic front come through. Without the Christmas decorations strung along the light posts, it could be any time of year. Even the holidays felt strangely performative in a place where so few people lived full-time. Jeanie and Gene rented a storage unit where they kept their seasonal decor. When we got here, their front door already had a fall wreath and a floor mat that said HAPPY THANKSGIVING. The minute Thanksgiving was over, they'd set up an artificial tree covered with their cherished ornaments. They were like refugees celebrating an old tradition in a new land. It was their last Christmas in Palm Springs—perhaps their last Christmas ever.

Grant and I walked from the more touristy area to the design district on the north end of Palm Canyon Drive. We held hands—I couldn't remember the last time we'd held hands in public. The sidewalks were mostly empty, and the street had plenty of parking.

We were looking for a place to eat dinner before meeting Coco, Cassie, Gene, and Jeanie for show-tunes bingo, but after perusing the menus posted next to a few restaurants, Grant was still unsatisfied. "In Madison we have Nepalese. We have Taiwanese street food. This is the land of Cobb salad."

"I *like* Cobb salad."

"They still have bananas Foster on the menu. What is this, 1987?"

We took a detour closer to the mountains in a neighborhood called Old Las Palmas. I'd read that Elvis and Priscilla had honeymooned in the House of Tomorrow, and I wanted to find it. This was the slick, groomed version of Palm Springs that I'd originally imagined. Any home we passed could grace the cover of *Architectural Digest*. A few were of the same vintage as Le Desert, but most (at least those that weren't tucked behind gates and bushes) were more modern. The houses had brightly painted doors, big windows, butterfly roofs, decorative cinder-block brick to provide both privacy and light, and angles that made room for sneaky little clerestory windows. Cool vintage cars were parked by the entrances.

"It's cool here," I said. "Very *Mad Men*."

Grant wasn't so sure. "When you make a whole city all about one aesthetic the design just replicates itself."

"At least it *has* an aesthetic. It's what makes Palm Springs Palm Springs."

"When Baudrillard came to America, he felt we were presented with a synthetic version of reality. He's the one who coined the phrase 'the desert of the real.' He meant—"

"Honey, I'm not one of your students."

"But what am I supposed to do with all my knowledge? I've spent years and years pouring books into my brain, for what?"

"For the enjoyment? Aren't you glad you learned what you did? Do you regret it?"

He paused, as though I were a student offering a right answer, but not the answer he was thinking of. "I guess that's one way of thinking about it."

We walked another block or so, and I raised the question that had been nagging at me for days: "Why didn't you tell me you went hiking with Cassie?"

"Didn't I?" His reaction was swift, and sincere.

"Not a word."

"Cass wanted to come along."

He called her Cass now?

"You don't mind, do you?"

"I just thought it was strange you didn't mention it."

"Honestly, I was probably just beat from trying to keep up with her. She's a good hiker, and she has all kinds of relationship advice for us. She said she learned some couples techniques in an ecstasy workshop."

"If you have to take a workshop on ecstasy, maybe you're doing it wrong?"

Grant grew serious. "I told her about how I short out. About my dad, my mom. My issues."

"You did? Even the girls don't know about that. You hardly talk about it with me." For years, it had been something we'd lived with.

"She's dealt with some pretty heavy stuff herself. She said she came here as a runaway ten years ago. Coco found her squatting in one of the empty units. Instead of calling the cops, she took her in. Now she's got her own place. The people at Le Desert are the only family she's ever really known."

"And here I thought we had the corner on family dysfunction."

"I don't know anything anymore, Kim. What's crazy at home doesn't seem so crazy here. Cassie is kooky, but I'm trying to keep an open mind. Even Carl Jung was into shamanism. He could drop into a deep state of meditation and exist in a fairy world with other creatures."

"Well, if it's good enough for Carl Jung."

"On our second hike, Cassie said something that really blew my mind. She said that a spirit came to her and said that I have always been safe. I've always been protected. I can't really express how important it was for me to hear that."

"That's great," I said, halfheartedly. "You aren't interested in Cassie, are you?" Where did this insecurity come from? I had worked hard for years to keep jealousy at bay, seeing it as another form of neediness.

He stopped, held my hands, and gave me a kiss. "The only woman I'm interested in is you."

"An emotional affair is still an affair, you know."

"She's just a friend, like Sasha. Kim, we promised each other we'd always be honest. Remember when I was at that conference in Philadelphia and the grad student from Rutgers got drunk and tried to kiss me in the elevator? I was so sick about it I almost threw up, and I called you at two in the morning to tell you. Do you really think I could be untrue to you right under your nose?"

"I don't know. Because you're changing."

"I thought you wanted me to change."

We started walking back to the main drag. I said, "Since we're being honest with each other, I feel I should tell you something. Hobie hit on me. He said I can sleep with him anytime I want."

Grant froze. "He said *what*?"

"I'm sorry. I know you think he's your friend. But since we're being honest."

I watched him turn the idea over in his mind. I waited for him to get upset, waited for him to even turn around, run off, and leave me feeling that familiar abandonment and dread.

"Did you think about it?"

I didn't answer right away in hopes of provoking a reaction, testing his boundaries, seeing if he really was better. But then a grin emerged on his face.

"What are you smiling for?"

"That's actually pretty funny."

I gave him a playful nudge. "You're supposed to be jealous."

"Hobie? He's not your type. He's, like, everyone's type but yours. I'll bet you laughed in his face."

I gently punched him in the arm. "How did you know?"

"I know you." It felt good to be known. "Besides, he's no match for me. Just look." He made a fist and pounded his biceps. "Someone called me 'hot dad' the other day."

"You're insufferable."

The smaller streets led us back to the swankier end of Palm Canyon Drive. "Let's go look in this store," I said, even though I didn't love shopping. When I was growing up, Polly used to hustle me past the boutiques on Michigan Avenue as though she were shielding me from a gruesome scene. She'd scold me if she caught me gawking at the mannequins or staring in awe at the women in fur coats emerging from Neiman Marcus with bags on their arms. She'd remind me not to give in to the seductive power of objects. "Don't want, Kim," she would say. Those words became my mantra, and they applied to my feelings about more than just the things you can buy.

That's why it felt like an act of rebellion to push open the spotless glass door into Trina Turk's Albert Frey–designed clothing boutique. It was the embodiment of the joyful Palm Springs aesthetic called optimistic style. I definitely felt optimistic as I fingered the silky caftans with bold block prints and gazed longingly at the aggressively bright clothing.

I normally dress in whatever came my way during my clothing swaps with friends—we called it *hokey couture*. I suddenly saw myself the way Melody did; how schlubby I looked in my pilled T-shirt and baggy shorts with an elastic waistband. When was the last time I'd owned something new? Shouldn't I try to dress up while I still had a figure for it? I suddenly wanted what Trina Turk had to offer—not just the clothing, but the promise of a sophisticated, sunny, carefree lifestyle. Was that a thing to be bought?

A salesperson saw me staring at a red silk dress with turquoise trim and pink fringe on a mannequin. "That's our bestseller for the holidays," he said. "It'll look fabulous with your auburn hair."

I'd almost forgotten that my hair had a natural red hue. Melody took me to her salon, where Geylen went wild with scissors and colored over the gray. I emerged a new woman in an angled bob and short bangs. Melody said the cut was *très chic,* and I saw myself as funky and artistic and grown-up. I sent a photo to Octavia and the girls.

Dort: *Mom, you look like Edna from* The Incredibles.

I moved on to finger the baubles on a bright bracelet with pink, green, and yellow plastic beads. It was the kind of jewelry I would have loved when I was a little girl.

Grant stood next to me and said, "This place is a bit much, don't you think? Like a screaming bird."

"I don't know, I think it's fun."

He disappeared into the men's side of the store called Mr. Turk and returned holding a tiny pair of men's lemon-colored knit shorts embroidered with palm trees. "Honestly, could you see me in these? Grant of the jungle."

He'd never looked more out of place than he did in that store. From hiking he had a farmer's tan on his legs and arms. I swore he was the only person in Palm Springs who'd ever worn the color brown. And yet, I admired him. He was entirely comfortable with how he presented himself to the outside world. He didn't compare himself to other people.

"Put that down." I laughed.

"Three hundred dollars for a glorified banana hammock!"

"I actually love this," I said, fingering the bracelet, feeling that I needed it. Grant didn't dare buy jewelry for me because he knew I'd think it was wasteful.

"I don't know, that doesn't say 'Kim' to me."

"What *does* say 'Kim' to you?"

He seemed confused by this question. He disarmed me with his sweetness when he said, with complete sincerity, "What you're wearing right now. Gosh, I think you look beautiful in anything."

I smiled and held the bracelet up to the light.

"Let me buy that for you," Grant said, seeing the longing on my face.

"No, it's silly."

"So was the Jeep, but I can't tell you how much I love it. I know you're committed to your buy-nothing group, but that's in Madison."

Just then, the salesman approached with a bright cocktail dress that he said would "pair perfectly" with my new bracelet. Before I could protest, he led me to the fitting room. "Come on, let's see if I'm right that this is a great style for you."

Grant smiled. "Go for it. What's the harm?"

The harm wasn't in the dress—the harm was in *wanting* it. But I did. It fit like a dream. The silky lining was sensual against my skin, and the red brought out the bit of color in my cheeks from the sun. The pink fringe around the sleeves reminded me of Thomas's umbrellas. The salesman set a pair of gold wedge sandals at my feet. "Try these."

"Oh, I can't wear sandals, not with my—" Then I remembered, I didn't have a bunion anymore, and wedges were pretty safe. I slipped my feet into them, feeling like Cinderella. They fit perfectly. No pain. I walked into the showroom and stood in front of the mirror. "What do you think?" I turned, flounced the skirt, kicked up my foot. I hardly recognized myself.

Grant smiled appreciatively. "I love it."

The salesman put a pair of huge, vintage Chanel sunglasses on my face. "Voilà!"

I saw a woman about my age in the corner turn to look at us. Her husband was sitting in a chair, distracted by his phone, while Grant was focused entirely on me.

I went to change and looked for the salesperson to help me with the zipper, but he was busy charming a new customer. "Grant, can you come in here?"

He followed me into the dressing room, still holding the palm-tree bathing suit and a silky men's caftan. "Should I try?"

He slipped off his shorts and pulled the caftan on. He looked hilarious with his hairy, bare legs and his black socks and hiking boots. The caftan was so wrong for him that I started laughing uncontrollably. I had to wipe the tears from my eyes with the back of my hands. I'd almost forgotten how hard I could laugh with Grant. When we first got together, he'd always crack me up before we went to sleep, and I'd drift off with a smile on my face.

"What's going on in there, you two? Plenty of places in this town to get a room. You can head over to the swinger resorts in Warm Sands."

"We'll behave," I said.

"Oh, please don't! Nobody comes to Palm Springs to *behave*."

I took a photo of us in the mirror—what a pair we were. Grant said, "We still look like we come from a place where they salt the roads with cheese brine."

Grant held me from behind and nuzzled my neck. I could feel the beat of his heart on my back. He slowly eased the zipper down, kissing every knob of my spine as the dress fell to the floor. I stepped out of it, and he picked it up and threw it over his arm. "Let's go home, Kimmy," he said before exiting the changing room.

I walked into the showroom and saw Grant at the wrap stand. The salesman was chatting amiably and wrapping the dress in tissue paper. I whispered, "It's too expensive."

"I want you to have something nice, and besides, I'm buying myself a slick shirt, too. Didn't you say Melody is taking us out for Christmas dinner?"

Then, as if in slow motion, I watched the horror spread over the salesperson's face when Grant reached into his pocket and pulled out his makeshift wallet—a plastic Ziploc bag.

A few minutes later, *I* was the woman in a resort town emerging from a store with a bag filled with new purchases. Suddenly, the city that had seemed so empty before was filled with people. The restaurants were bustling with diners sitting outdoors. A bachelorette party of indistinguishable blond women in short dresses and cowboy boots walked by. The one in the middle sported a tiara and a pink sash across her chest with an image of a giant penis and the words TO HAVE AND TO HOLD. They were so young and lovely in the same way March is young and lovely. They giggled and chatted and swung their hips. They radiated hope and confidence, an assured optimism that their lives were only going to get better from here. Marriage meant something different at their age than it did at ours—or did it?

Chapter Thirty

Grant's Journal

January 1

Sometimes my age slaps me in the face.

More fatigued from my earlier hike than I should be. Legs are cement.

Daylight conservation is the name of the game. No time for breaks, but I'm taking one right now, I have to. I'm just going to lie down on this boulder to feel the sun. Close my eyes for a few minutes.

Woke up feeling like Rip Van Winkle. I must have been out for an hour at least. The sun was already behind the mountains. Harder to orient myself without it. Hadn't I been here before? I looked for the trail. How come it looked different? It was like I'd nodded off in one place and woke up in another. The only thing I knew was that I needed to go down. Simple enough, right? Too late to turn back to Morris Road, and what was there for me, anyway?

I was looking into my compass and lost my footing near the edge of a rock face and down I went . . . as in Chutes and Ladders down. I'm wearing my trail shoes instead of my hiking boots—another mistake. The bottoms are slippery from the snow.

Boy, did I slide. Bloodied up my hands, wiped them on my pants. My water bottle flew out of my pack with a clang, clang, clang. Did I drink as much water as I should have? No. I thought I was so smart, conserving what I had.

Wasted too much time looking for it. Now it's gone. Compass is gone, too. Apologies to my fellow leave-no-trace acolytes.

Bushwhacked through dense shrubs to find a clearing. Saw the lights of Cathedral City. Palm Springs will be north. So north I go.

Chapter Thirty-One

Palm Springs
January 4, 2023
2:00 P.M.

I took Brady's call in our bedroom so I could be out of earshot of Dort, March, and Octavia. Melody—bless her—had brought over some boxes of her old stuff for them to sort through, not so much to get rid of it, but to keep them preoccupied. They had their pick of vintage Pucci and Halston, plus some Hermès scarves.

"Well, we're up against some issues," Brady said. "The bloodhounds didn't last long. The cacti hurt their noses. We called them back, and I'm sorry to say, but it looks like we're going to have to wind down the search."

I'd read Grant's journal. I knew how much trouble he was in. It felt as if Brady were killing him. "Please—"

"The winds are already thirty knots. I'm sorry, but I can't send my guys up in that. We're going to have to sit on our hands until this storm passes. The search will change to a recovery instead of a rescue when we resume. I know this isn't the news you wanted to hear. We've done everything we can, Kim."

That's how I knew we were really in trouble: he used my first name, just as Grant's journal entries were addressed to me. Just beyond the door I heard March and Dort chatting with Melody. How could I possibly tell them? Should I?

"Can you try just a little more, a few more hours? What if he's—"

"I'm wishing the best for you and your family. I truly am sorry. I've got to keep these guys safe."

The shutters banged from the wind. I looked through the windows, already splattered with drizzle, and saw the mountains in the distance. How could I ever live in Palm Springs after this? What would it be like to look at the mountains all the time and know Grant was still up there?

But then again, how could I ever leave?

My mind used to wander every time Grant had ever left. I'd imagine all the trouble he could get into, the problems he could have. Never had I imagined this most horrible version of waiting, one that could stretch into and define all my remaining days.

Chapter Thirty-Two

Palm Springs
December 19, 2022

Thomas and Raul watched me say goodbye to Grant before he left for his hike. I returned to sweeping the dead leaves and palm tree skins that looked like abandoned prostheses that had gathered on the patio after the windstorm. "Want to come work out with us?"

"I don't know, I'm not in great shape these days."

"Believe me, that won't matter. Let us save you from your domestic follies. Let's all get changed. See you in ten minutes."

I tried not to laugh when we met in the courtyard. They had on tight, shimmery metallic bodysuits that zippered up the front.

"Like it?" Thomas asked. "We can run back and get one for you."

"Oh, trust me, that's not what you want to see. I'm not someone who likes to shimmer. I'd look like bratwurst in casing. A radioactive bratwurst."

"It's great for your vagina," Raul said.

I almost spit out the coffee in my thermal cup. "What do you know about vaginas?" I'd been in Palm Springs long enough to say that word out loud without cringing.

Raul said, "I teach physiology. That's how I met Thomas. He came to me for the science cred. And honestly, these suits are good for *everything*. This isn't clothing. It's like medicine you wear on your body. The fabric is grounding and earthing. It'll shield you from EMRs."

"From what?"

"Electromagnetic radiation. It neutralizes all the bad stuff."

"You can plug this part here into a grounding pole in your wall socket." Raul pointed at an attachment near the back.

I had many moments in California that made me feel as if I were late to the cultural party. There were phrases I'd never heard, foods I'd never eaten, lifestyles I'd thought only existed on television. I would sometimes feel as if the whole world had moved in a new direction without me. This was one of them.

Thomas said, "This is our business. We make clothing that reduces inflammation. And you know that inflammation is the mother source of all our problems. This is the marriage of fashion and function. It's made with real silver—"

"Well, we *thought* it was silver," Raul said. "We were working with a Chinese manufacturer until we found out they used recycled plastic instead."

"But the problem was solved! I found a prince in Saudi Arabia—I knew him from my days in Rome. Mohammed had a stockpile of silver—"

"—as one does!" Raul practically sang these words.

"—so we struck an agreement: I could use his silver if I also used his wool. But the wool was rank, from Turkish camels or whatever."

"It smelled like ass."

I loved how Thomas said the sentences and Raul provided the punctuation and color commentary.

"Now we've finally got the formula right. Feels great, smells good. We call it Silverwear, and trust me, it's about to be the next big thing. Go ahead." Thomas gestured for me to put my nose up to his underarm. "See? The only smell is me now."

"I can't believe you made this yourselves. I'm so impressed."

"It's what we do," Raul said. "Thomas is a designer. He doesn't like to brag, but he was most recently at Valentino in Italy."

This city was like a treasure hunt where I was always surprised by whom I'd meet. Just the day before, I learned that the person who owned the condo Gene and Jeanie rented was Madonna's architect.

Grant said he'd met Barry Manilow's gardener at the gym. One day I chatted with Bart, Melody's house cleaner, who used to be Elizabeth Taylor's personal assistant. And on a walk, I met a man who told me he had Frank Sinatra's pistol on his mantel. This didn't make Palm Springs better than Madison, where people were interesting for their own reasons, but it sure made it different.

Thomas said, "It was only a matter of time before I got burned-out at Valentino. I couldn't deal with all the drama and cocaine. And let's face it, nobody cares about the fashion houses anymore, not when you can buy surprisingly decent shorts at Walmart for twelve bucks."

"So, Kimmy," Raul said, putting his arm around me. "We saw the photos you took of Cassie last week—they were gorgeous. Could you bring your camera along today? We need some images to market our new business before we burn through our start-up funding. Of course, we'll pay you."

"But why me?"

"Because the other photographer we asked is busy with Michelle Obama! Why do you think? Come on, Kim. Don't hurt our feelings."

I put my hands on my hips. "Basil put you up to this, didn't he?"

"Why would you say that? You don't need Basil to pimp you out."

I could feel myself blushing. "I'm not a professional. You should get someone more qualified. But out of curiosity, how much did you have in mind?"

"Five hundred?"

I rolled my eyes.

"What, it's not enough?"

"It's too much! I'd do it for free, you know."

"So you *will* do it?"

"I didn't say that."

"No artist turns down a commission."

"They might suck."

"They won't! Where's that Kimmy we saw dropping it like it's hot on the dance floor? Show some of that confidence! Grab your gear. Let's go!"

* * *

We headed in the direction of downtown. Thomas turned onto Alejo. "That's Twin Palms, Frank Sinatra's house," he said. "The tour guides say that there's still a crack in the bathroom sink from when Frank threw a bottle of champagne at Ava Gardner. They tout it as 'local lore.' Like spousal abuse is so fabulous? That hothead could have killed her, and everyone acts like it's a quaint bit of local history."

Thomas then turned into a luxurious neighborhood with more tall gates, groomed hedges with Spanish tile roofs like Le Desert's peeking over the tops. The streets were filled with gardening trucks. "Welcome to Movie Colony," Raul said. "This is where Hollywood royalty lived. Marilyn Monroe, Cary Grant, Gary Cooper. When our designs take off and we make our fortune, Thomas and I will live here, too. It's on our vision board. This is where we can raise our baby."

"Doesn't cost a penny to dream," I said. That was what Polly used to say to me.

"A penny? Please. You have to take out a loan if you want to dream in Palm Springs."

Ruth Hardy Park was crowded with people walking their miniature designer dogs, elderly joggers speeding along the park's perimeter, and pickleball players already lining up to have a turn on the courts. On the playground I saw some kids—actual children. It hadn't occurred to me that I hadn't seen many until that very moment.

The workout participants spread out their beach towels and yoga mats to face the mountains, lit pink by the morning sun. I imagined Grant somewhere out there on his hike to who knows where.

I felt my phone buzz in my pocket; it was a text from Sally.

When is the last time you had a Roto-Rooter guy come by? There's a small sewage backup in the basement. Pretty gross. I've hired someone to take care of it. We'll send the bill.

I'd almost forgotten about our house, about our other life. I had a mortgage, doctors, dentists, yoga teachers, friends who needed me. A place to go back to. Was that "real life"?

All around me were people my own age and older stretching and chatting. They were a mix of gay and straight men and women, some in top-of-the-line clothing and expensive sunglasses and gear, others who, like me, wore baggy T-shirts and shorts. Everyone was happy and social. There were hugs and more hugs when we walked through the crowd. In Madison, Thomas and Raul would stand out like sore thumbs in their sparkling, body-hugging outfits; here, they were part of the milieu of tutus, wild leggings, neon socks, pink tennis shoes. and booty shorts. But just because Palm Springs was different from what I was used to didn't make the life I was building here any less real.

The silver-haired instructor with bulging biceps and thighs and su-pertight shorts adjusted his microphone and greeted us. Through the giant portable speakers, I heard the sound of new age flutes. He said, "Good morning, G-Force! Let's greet the morning, hakuna matata–style!" He encouraged everyone to face the mountains and wave their arms around. "Howl, go ahead. Let's hear you!"

Everyone began howling.

"Take a moment to appreciate the glorious sun that shines love and happiness on us all," the instructor said. I couldn't stop smiling and snapping photos. I loved being part of this emotive crowd. The song changed to Deee-Lite's "Power of Love"—we all knew it. The instruc-tor began to shift his weight from side to side before launching into a Richard Simmons–style workout.

Back at Basil's condo that afternoon, I went through the photos I'd taken, reliving the joy of the morning. I knew many of them were good, but one was the clear standout—Thomas and Raul, sparkling in the morning light, fierce, howling.

Chapter Thirty-Three

Grant's Journal

January 1

You know what they say: we plan, God laughs. He's laughing at me now. Cassie told me about a Sanskrit word, I can't remember it anymore. It means the thing inside you that can't be scratched. No matter what you go through in life, there's some true essence within you that is beyond anyone's or anything's reach.

I told her about the ship of Theseus paradox; If every part of a ship has been replaced, is it the same ship? Is there some essence of the ship that gives it an identity? Or are we really, as Hume would say, just a bundle of perceptions held together like a commonwealth?

The idea that there's some nugget of us, a magic bean, a diamond of the self that remains cradled and protected, free from all the slights—now that's an idea I can get behind.

I've found that part of me out here. I mean, I had it all along. I just didn't know about it. Even now, when everything has gone wrong—my feet are covered in blisters; I'm cold, tired, thirsty, hungry, lonely, lost—still, I know there's a part of me that's fine.

Everything, but despair.

They say that nine o'clock is hiking midnight. At least I think it's around nine.

It's impossible to hike in the dark. I tripped on a branch and introduced my face to a rock.

I'm no longer good for this day. I found a boulder with a crag underneath it to sleep under, ate my third-to-last protein bar, which got stuck in the back of my mouth, hunkered down, and still found beauty as I stared into the stars. Now for the best part: nothing. Not a darn thing.

I wish I'd spent my whole life knowing how deeply comforting it is to lie on my sleeping pad after a day of constant movement and feel gravity pull me to earth. I wish I'd always known what it's like to look at the stars and feel my heartbeat in my ears.

This is the real thing.

All these years, I never saw myself as part of the physical world, I was so caught up in the life of the mind. I do now. I have silence and the most amazing view; this right here is dinner and a movie.

It feels good to earn my exhaustion. My body is wrung like a wet rope. March called me the other day and said she was exhausted from work.

Exhausted? Work?

What have we ever taught our kids about real work? Young people get tired typing into their phones. Once, I saw some guys drive their Lexus out near Bodie, and they turned around when they came to a road that was impassable. The area was really nasty, with an embankment, a washout, and sharp rocks. You know what I did? I got out there and spent an hour moving rocks. Let's go, let's make a road.

When I sit down to eat, I'm hungry with a hunger I deserve.

Am I ever hungry now.

The old me would have thought this day had gone horribly wrong. This new me? I feel peace. I've ended up where I belong. Life didn't turn out the way I thought it would, but it led me to Kim. To the children we were meant to have. I have no regrets.

It led me to this moment in this place.

I've experienced the exultation of spending an entire day finding my own path, going where people don't go, of watching the color drain from the sky, of pushing my body to the limit. Past my fear.

And here I thought I'd spend the winter rotting away in a lounge chair.

January 2

Coffee should be added to Maslow's first level of the hierarchy of needs, along with food, safety, water. I'll never give up coffee again.

I'll bet Kim is pissed. She probably thinks I've pulled one of my disappearing acts, that I'm putting her through hell again. I'm the boy who cried wolf. It's possible—probable—she won't call for help. Talk about karma.

I can figure this out. I can figure this out!

I would love to let Kim know where I am. I want to tell her I'm OK. I want to tell the girls.

There's an element of this adventure that I enjoy, if I'm being honest. I mean, look at me. One day I'm grading papers, the next I'm man against nature, oldest story there is.

I'm certain I'll find my way today, absolutely certain. I feel rested. I was kept company by the pocket mice that crawled all over me to stay warm last night. My little buddies. In two, three hours, I'll be at the Trading Post if all goes well. I'll find my way back to phones, cars, Ubers.

Why am I in such a hurry to get back to that dirty, busy, insane world?

Before I left my little camp, I scored the tree, just like Hobie taught me. Adventure awaits, then home!

How is this possible? I'm back at the tree, back where I started. I've been hiking the whole damn day and I'm in the very spot where I slept last night, the same crevice under the boulder.

I don't even know up from down. It's cold, and it's getting dark again. Hobie told me that when he's on fire duty, he tries not to poop or pee because your full colon and bladder keep you warm. That's easier than it sounds.

Nietzsche said, "To live is to suffer, to survive is to find some meaning in the suffering." I'll find meaning in this someday. For now I can't do anything but slide under this rock and rest. I thought I was OK with my own company. I'm lonely, but I can pretend you're with me when I write to you here.

You? Whoa, Kim, this journal is starting to have some "if you read this, I'll be dead" vibes.

Plenty can go wrong when you don't know where you are. One bad decision has compounded to a thousand bad decisions, and I've made some bad decisions. Nuclear bad.

How often in life do we think we know where we are and we're dead wrong?

What an ugly situation I've gotten myself into.

Chapter Thirty-Four

Palm Springs
December 23, 2022

I now spend almost as much time with Melody in Smoke Tree Ranch as I spent in Le Desert. We'd have lunch, and then we would sort through some of her paperwork. I was making piles for taxes, Medicare, charitable giving, personal correspondence, and trash. I wrote a check to the funeral home that handled Vandyke's service. From what I could tell, her net worth was well upward of thirty million, and here she was being threatened with notices from collection agencies. Only someone with that much money could continue paying hundreds of thousands a year for a jet service she never used.

With the end of the year coming, she had piles of donation requests to sort through. I showed her a letter from the Hammer Museum in Los Angeles asking for her to contribute to their capital campaign. "Do you want to make a gift?"

Like an actress delivering a dramatic soliloquy, she said, "Art is not what you see, but what you make others see."

"Okay?"

"I borrowed that muscular Degas quote as the tagline for the Hammer in the midnineties, when I served on their board. We put it on everything advertising the museum: posters and brochures, even T-shirts. You won't see it there now. One day, without informing me, they just stopped using it. And that, my dear, is why you are going to write a letter to the twenty-year-old development director and tell her she will no longer see donations from the Underwood Foundation."

Every day was like show-and-tell. I would hand her an overdue bill or letter from an attorney or financial pro and ask her what to do with it, and she would direct me to a memory-laden item in her house. "Look up there"—she pointed at a large wooden box on a high shelf— "those are Vandyke's remains."

"Oh! Shouldn't you put them somewhere more . . . visible?"

"Why? I don't want to look at them all day long, do you? The urn is made of hand-turned ironwood. Native Americans believe ironwood binds together the spirits. Vandyke was a seeker near the end. He tried peyote and LSD. That didn't go well. The poor man was convinced that behind the mountains were dead horses, millions of dead horses. It was awful."

She picked up a glass cockatoo. "Mother thought it was hilarious that we have Swarovski crystal from 'Plastic Pat' Nixon. This was a gift from the First Lady, naturally."

To spend time with Melody was to feel as if I were part of Palm Springs history. I never got bored of her stories, and I could tell she loved having an audience. But we'd been at it for five weeks now and had barely made a dent in the sea of paperwork. "You should hire someone, Mel. There's no way I can get through all this while we're here."

"I'm glad you brought that up." She had a funny smile. "How about *you*?"

"Me? What do I know—"

"You can come with me when I meet with the lawyers and financial people and estate planners. They all think I've lost it, and I'm less likely to be taken advantage of if I have someone young and sharp with me. Look at you! You're much more presentable now, thanks to that haircut. We'll get you a few bossy outfits and we'll walk into meetings together like we run the world."

"But I'm not sure how much I can get done before we leave."

"Don't be an idiot. You aren't going anywhere." She put her hands on her hips and stared me down. "I'm suggesting you move here."

I almost spit out my lemonade. "To Palm Springs? I'm honored, but I can't. . . . We have a house. A home, in Wisconsin. Grant would never go for it. All my friends are in Madison."

"Haven't you made friends here?" She pointed at herself. "That's the problem with you, Kimberly. You're desperate for a change, but you don't have the gumption to take the leap. Sell your house! Isn't Madison one of those cities everyone wants to move to for some reason? It'll get snatched right up."

"But I'm not qualified to—"

"Who is actually qualified for work like this? It's the stuff of life. You're smarter than you think. Plus, you have the advantage of having worked for nonprofits. Vandyke gave money to charities I don't support."

"I noticed."

"See? I could use your help changing my giving strategy. Besides, you know how to talk to these people in a way that will make them listen." After years at nonprofits, the thought of "going client side" appealed to me immensely. Instead of begging for donations, I could hand over crisp checks with Melody's signature to all the causes I found worthy. What better way to change the world than with other people's money?

"You told me about that hedonist at your current job. Who needs him? I'll pay you a ridiculous salary, just name it."

"But I need benefits. Both Grant and I do."

"So, we'll get you benefits! Pick the best plan—free eyeglasses, dental, medical, zero co-pays, paid time off. I'll hire someone to come give you back massages. I'll install a slide in the office and a trampoline and you can pretend you work at Google."

"Melody—" The idea was actually starting to take hold.

"I'm asking you to be my . . . my what? We can come up with a title. How about president of the Underwood Foundation? Doesn't *president* sound nice?"

I stood and gathered some files, holding them in front of my chest like armor. Any normal person in my position would jump at an opportunity like the one Melody was offering me. So why was I so hesitant? I believed she was serious, and I knew she had ample funds.

But giving up my home and my life? I'd often thought about moving to Palm Springs since we'd arrived. What was a fun idea before, a flight of fancy, was serious now. I thought of all the things I love doing in Madison, the network of people I'd developed over the years. I knew where to vote, which doctor to see for which ailment, where to get my oil changed, the best restaurants for every craving or occasion. My life made sense back home; would it ever make as much sense here?

"Did Basil put you up to this?" I asked.

"Basil? Are you kidding? He'd have me institutionalized if he knew things had gotten this messy. This is *my* decision. I find you trustworthy. You married my son for love, even though you easily could have married for money. Your lack of shrewdness might be problematic in this new capacity, but we'll work on it. I know Basil asked you to take care of me, and you've been true to your word. Before you and Grant came along, I felt horribly alone and adrift. I know what you're made of, Kim. You're humble and sincere and, well, you are still utterly lacking in confidence and style, but I see you changing. Embrace it! Life is about change."

My mind was racing. "But where would we live? Palm Springs is expensive, in case you haven't noticed." My stomach twisted at the word *we*.

"Buy a place in *Le Depravity*. There's always something coming on the market."

"We can't just buy a condo."

"Why not? People buy condos every day. I'm not asking you to sacrifice your firstborn."

"But the girls—"

"—are living their own lives. It's time for you to live yours. Shake it up."

"What about Grant?"

Melody became warm, even motherly.

"You need to do what's right for you. I like Grant, but it's plain to see you're feeling uncertain about your relationship. The upside of never marrying is that you can extract yourself from it without lawyers and custody battles, but only if you so choose. If you were thinking of striking out on your own, you'd have a very soft landing here."

I looked through the sliding glass doors at the dirt, the cacti, the mountains. Could I really be part of this place? Was this my ecosystem? It was home for the winter, but could it be home all year long?

This job, this change . . . it felt like what I needed. But I needed Grant, too—and I didn't want to live apart anymore. I was already anticipating his arguments against the move. Would I have to choose between him and this job?

Melody reached for the folders I was holding and set them gently down on the desk. "If you decide to take me up on my offer, I'll pay you handsomely and make sure you find the work meaningful. Whatever you decide, don't think of this as a favor. I really do need to hire someone. Basil won't have the time to deal with it, and he's not good at this type of work, anyway. But I know you will be. You already are."

"Can I think about it? I need to talk to Grant."

"Think very, very hard, Kim, because I'm absolutely serious. But you'll need to let me know soon. My widow's veil is coming off. It's time for me to jump back into life and take charge of my affairs. And I dare say, it's time for you to take care of your own."

She was staring at my hand and I looked down and realized why: I was nervously yanking on my bare ring finger.

Chapter Thirty-Five

Grant's Journal

January 2

*T*hey're searching for me!
*   You called. Thank you, Kim. Thank you.*

I saw the lights, I heard the helicopter blades.

I scrambled out from under the rock and into the open area, my hands in the air. I must have looked like a prisoner of war. Hallelujah! Hey, hey, hey, it's me! Grant Duffy! Hey! Hey!

They missed me.

My throat is ripped up from screaming so loud.

Never in my life have I experienced a quiet more profound than the one I felt after the helicopter disappeared. That episode used up what little energy I had.

I ate my protein bar, and wouldn't you know I chipped my tooth from some dirt that got into it from my hands. Then I did something Hobie told me not to do: I drank from the stream. Let's hope a deer hasn't taken a dump in that water. I'll probably pay for this later.

I can't wait to be rescued in an open space, it's too cold and windy. I get it now. I get why you hate the cold. Me, too. I'd be happy to never see snow again.

I might never see anything again.

January 3

Hobie told me to follow the water. The only way to follow the water is to walk in it. I can't feel my feet, they're so cold. I've been collecting silver stones to give to you and the girls. My pockets are full of silver stones. That's what keeps me going.

I fell again. Trust me, you don't want to know what it feels like to hit your hip on a boulder with a bunch of stones in your pocket.

Remember when you found my journal and I said my writing would change if I knew you were reading?

I'm lost, Kim.

I am utterly, truly lost.

How many nights have I spent up here? Two? Three? I've heard more helicopters but they're gone by the time I run into the open to wave to them. I haven't heard one in a long while.

I'm so alone. My only company is Bob Hope's ghost.

And Nugget.

That's the name I gave the three-legged dog who followed me around for a while. People dump dogs like garbage in the mountains. Nugget could get around pretty good on three legs. He has icy-blue eyes. He talks to me with your mother's voice. He says keep going, you're fine. There are plenty of people with worse problems than yours.

I thought about asking you if we could keep the dog, but I don't even know if you want to keep me. You're having second thoughts, you said when we came out here. Where have those second thoughts led you? Look where they led me.

Chapter Thirty-Six

Palm Springs
December 25, 2022

Homesickness was a constant problem when I was a girl at the camp. Polly and Burl were often woken in the middle of the night to tend to kids who would literally vomit because they missed home so much. Spoiled babies, as far as Polly was concerned.

I wouldn't have thought that I'd experience my first bout of homesickness at my advanced age, and in sunny Palm Springs of all places. Yet, when I walked around Araby Commons and thought about Melody's job offer, I was struck by a painful longing for home, especially when I saw an elf inflatable emerge in someone's gravel yard, and decorative ornaments hanging from palm fronds.

The holidays pulled me to where my memories were. I couldn't believe it: I even longed for snow. I missed living somewhere where people still went caroling, where friends had cookie exchanges and white-elephant parties. Our neighbor Roseanne always left bottles of syrup she'd made from trees in her backyard next to our front door. I baked loaves of banana-and-cranberry bread for our friends and the elderly ladies at the senior center where I volunteered.

This year, the only thing on our Christmas Day agenda aside from a gift exchange and dinner with Melody was our family Zoom. When it was over, I said to Grant, "We could have done better."

"What do you mean?"

I wanted to cry. "I mean, now that it's just the two of us, we could have tried a little harder for each other for the holiday. Without the girls, we could start to make our own traditions. We could have at least put up a tree."

"You always complain trees are wasteful."

"We could make it more romantic."

"You hate romance. You think it's cheesy."

Hobie knocked on our door and entered before waiting for us to open it. He was holding a tin of the fudge that Jeanie had made for everyone in the complex. He wore a slim-fitting blue suit over a black T-shirt. He looked great. "Have you tried this stuff? I think Jeanie forgot to add sugar. Besides, it goes against my macro diet. You want it?"

"Nah," Grant said. Now he, too, was on a macrobiotic diet.

Grant took the tin into the kitchen and dumped the fudge into the garbage. While he was gone, Hobie lassoed me with his gaze. "It's hard to resist temptation when it's sitting right in front of you, know what I mean?" He winked.

"But you didn't resist. You tried it, and found it disgusting."

"You won't know if it's good unless you take a bite." He adjusted his collar and ran his palm over his hair. "I'm headed to a pool party at the Ace."

"A pool party?" Grant asked when he walked back into the living room. "On Christmas Day?"

"There's always a party somewhere in Palm Springs. The fun never stops."

Grant began getting his pack ready for the next day's adventure. He'd been going through a book on area hikes, and he hoped to get to as many as possible before we returned home. He even created a spreadsheet to log his stats, and a calendar with a schedule for the trails he planned to explore. He was especially excited about his New Year's hike to a place called Cedar Springs.

"Want to try this soul-gazing thing Cassie told me about?" I asked nervously. At last, I was "fully congruent with my yes." With Melody's job offer weighing on my mind, I needed to get a better, clearer sense of where I stood with Grant, and where he stood with me.

"Sure. Let's go full shaman for Christmas like the heretics we are."

"Okay, well, the point is to 'expose' ourselves, so I guess we're supposed to strip?"

"Well, fa la la la la!"

I locked the door, flipped down the California shades, and took off my clothes. Grant was incredibly comfortable with his body, although, without his glasses, he seemed especially naked and vulnerable.

"You're practically blind. You won't even see me."

"I see you when you let me." He stood in front of me. "Will you let me?"

"Do I have to?"

He nodded.

"Cassie says this helps us communicate on a deeper level, without words." We were just inches from each other. "Stand tall," I said. "We're supposed to put our shoulders back, arms down by our sides. Now turn your palms so they face out."

He stepped even closer to me. We were a hair apart.

"Now what? Because I'm getting kind of horny."

"Just hold on. We start with our eyes closed."

"For how long?"

"I don't know, as long as we need? It's not like we're baking something and need to follow the recipe. Clear your mind and close your eyes."

I tried to focus on Grant and forget about everything else. I felt my breathing begin to regulate, and I slowly became more aware of his heat and his breath. For the first time all day, I no longer felt homesick.

"We're supposed to step away and move closer to each other a few times."

We faltered, both of us self-conscious. This was like the start of meditation, when you think of your thoughts as visitors, inviting them in, and saying goodbye when it's time to go. I don't know how long we stood there like that; we slipped into our own private envelope of space, our own moment, and I did feel a connection forming—not a reconnection, but a powerful new one.

"And now," I said, "we're supposed to slowly open our eyes and look deep into each other's souls." I was terrified. What would I see when I looked at Grant? What would he see when he looked—really looked—at me?

He stepped closer and reached for my hands. It felt good to touch, to come together. I leaned in closer and pressed my forehead against his. Everything about his face was familiar to me, the angle of every bone, every line. I knew he was smiling, I could feel it. But his hazel eyes? I couldn't understand why I was nervous to look into them—when was the last time I'd really done that? After all this time, shouldn't this be easy? Why did I find it so frightening to connect, to see Grant instead of to think of him being a certain way—to really see him?

I decided that if we couldn't find each other once our gazes met, we might not have a chance. This little intimacy exercise Cassie had told me about in the laundry room had seemed so silly; now it felt like a do-or-die moment for us.

And when I opened my eyes, nothing happened. We didn't connect.

I was worried that I no longer had feelings for this man, that he was simply there, a companion. Someone I used to know. His eyes were like two question marks.

And then a wave of energy so intense it took my breath away washed over me. How was it possible to be with someone this long and never really see the person? And to not even know we weren't seeing each other? And to realize the man I fell in love with has been there all along?

It made me crack open, a sensation that was beyond words, a love so big I couldn't let myself want it because it terrified me—it has always terrified me.

"Do you feel what I'm feeling?" I asked.

It was as if a subway were rumbling below us. The glasses clattered in the cabinets. We pulled away from each other, shocked and terrified.

"Wait, is this is an earthquake? Is this what it feels like?"

"God, it is. I think we made it happen, Kimmy."

"We're naked! What do we do? Hide under the furniture? Run outside?"

Grant threw his hands up in the air. "I have no idea. I've never felt more midwestern."

"The earth *literally* moved." And then, just like that, it stopped.

Grant said, "I heard the rattling kind are no big deal. The worst are the ones that feel like a sudden shove."

I couldn't help but wonder if he was referring to this exact moment in our relationship.

If I hadn't been so shocked to experience my first earthquake, and so worried about getting dressed in case we had to go outside, I would have repeated my question: Do you feel what I'm feeling?

But I didn't. So I never had the chance to hear his answer.

Chapter Thirty-Seven

Grant's Journal

I'm not sure what day it is anymore.

"I'm lost!" I say to the man. "I'm lost!"
    I wave, I scream.
    A boulder, not a man.
    I'm screaming at boulders.

I'm done for.
    If not for you and Dort and March, I would be at peace. A funny saying.
    At peace.
    Peace is a place.

Chapter Thirty-Eight

Palm Springs
December 31, 2022

I refused to let Dort join a traveling soccer team in high school because I thought it was wasteful. Why trek all over creation to play a different group of girls when you could have a game right in Madison? But there the four of us were driving almost an hour from Palm Springs to lie down and listen to a bunch of noise. Cassie claimed the sound bath would rearrange every cell in our bodies, so maybe it would be worth it. She thought it would be a powerful way to welcome the New Year.

Cassie had struck up a conversation with Melody when she'd stopped by to pick up Grant and me for Christmas dinner at Melvyn's, and she invited Cassie to join us for the meal. As we sipped lemon drops and ate chicken potpies, I worried Melody would say something about the job offer. She didn't. That was when Cassie floated the idea of the New Year's Eve sound bath, and to my shock, Melody agreed to join us. She drew a hard line at the Jeep—Melody refused to be seen in or near it—which is how, a few days later, we all ended up in her silver Jaguar with shiny burled-wood paneling and white leather seats. I sat in the back with Grant so that Cassie could give directions. Compared to the Jeep, the car was so silent and smooth, I felt that I was floating.

"Nice ride, Queen," Cassie said.

"My husband bought this car shortly before he died. He called up his old friend at the dealership and had it delivered to the ranch sight unseen. A man in his condition had no business buying a car he couldn't drive more than a few months, but it made Vandyke—and the car dealer—very happy. When you're falling apart, the idea of possessing something perfect and new is very appealing. We'd get in this car and drive up to Idyllwild or the coast, Temecula, Death Valley, to Lake Havasu and back—it didn't matter. We drove and drove. This car is where we passed our last happy moments together." She started to cry; I'd gotten used to her fits of tears and passed her a Kleenex.

We floated up the San Bernardino Mountains and breezed past Yucca Valley, a town I now recognized from a day trip Grant and I had taken to Pioneertown, where all the westerns were filmed. Already there were destinations I'd visited *twice.* Now I could see where it sat in relation to other places. The map in my brain was filling in.

"These cures can backfire, you know," Melody said to Cassie. "I once saw a shaman in Putumayo who lived on a hill in a tent covered with jaguar pelts. He gave me some medicine that made me grow a whole new head of hair. What do you say we go to Two Bunch Palms for facials, instead? The manager is a friend. She'll let me show you the bullet in the mirror from the Al Capone days. It'll be my treat."

Cassie said, "I don't need old-dead-mobster energy today. I need androgynous vibrations."

"Good lord, young lady. The nonsense that comes out of your mouth."

Cassie stuck out her tongue.

We inched up the steep incline. Coming from the domesticated coolness of Palm Springs into the wild, instead of the other way around, was its own kind of whiplash. There was more of everything in the high desert: more cacti, more sagebrush, more brownness. The rocks here were bigger and bulbous, turd-like. Everywhere we looked we saw Joshua trees.

Cassie told Melody to pull into the lot near a sign that said INTE-GRATRON.

"What *is* this?" I asked, looking at the odd, white dome-shaped structure in the middle of nowhere. The parking lot was empty aside from a dilapidated school bus that said WE LOVE YOU TRACK across the side. Next to it was a courtyard filled with empty hammocks. "Looks like it's closed for the holiday," I said.

Cassie smiled. "Not for us. My friend Sienna works here. She's doing us a favor to get us in."

We were greeted by a rope-sandaled woman who was just as beautiful, young, and cool as Cassie. Never in my life had I seen as many beautiful people as I'd seen in California the past two months. Sienna turned to Grant. "Do you feel different already? Since you got here?"

He said, "I'm not sure what you mean by *different*."

"You're standing above a gathering of rivers deep underground. This is a geomagnetic vortex. You're part of a metaphysical connection with the earth."

Grant said, "Well, when you put it like that, sure. I feel like a new man."

We entered a round space with a ladder-style stairway off the center that led up to the dome. While Cassie and Sienna caught up, we fanned out to read the materials that were on display for the tourists who came here.

"This is definitely the sort of space that needs to be explained in order to be understood," Grant said. It was designed in the fifties by George Van Tassel, an eccentric engineer and inventor who claimed that aliens from Venus, "Venusians," took him on their spaceship and provided him with instructions to build a structure that could change human cells to make us live longer; in this way we would become wiser because, according to Venusians, humans don't get wise until we get very old.

"It's like we stumbled into a Kurt Vonnegut novel," Grant said. "Look at this." He pointed at a sign that said THE INTEGRATRON: A TIME MACHINE FOR BASIC RESEARCH ON REJUVENATION ANTI-GRAVITY TIME TRAVEL. "Is this for real?"

Sienna told us to take off our shoes and climb the ladder leading up to the domed space, where the sound bath was conducted. We entered a lofty room paneled with redwood from the Pacific Northwest. The space was amazing, both airy and cozy, almost like a church. Padded mats were spread out in semicircles around the perimeter, leaving room for the "stage," where there were massive crystal bowls and a gong.

Sienna explained that the structure, built without nails, was acoustically perfect. "If you stand by the beams on one side and say something, you'll hear it perfectly across the room. And in the very center there's an invisible chamber of sound. Go ahead." Sienna pointed at the tube of light coming from the opening in the center.

Cassie went first. She took a deep breath and let out a throaty scream. For all her lightness and love, I could see—even though I couldn't hear—that whatever she was releasing came from a dark and troubled place she didn't share on Instagram. To Cassie, the sound was amplified ten times.

Sienna told us to lie down. She sat in front of her bowls and picked up the mallet. She paused and locked eyes with Melody, a meaningful gaze. I waited for Melody to brush her off, tell her she was crazy, denounce the whole adventure as ridiculous. She didn't. "B is for the crown, connecting you to the divine," Sienna said. "This is for you, wise one."

She made a remarkably loud sound on her bowl that sliced through the air.

She moved on to me. She pointed at her neck. "And for you, G is for the throat. Communication. I sense blockages."

"And, Cassie, here's an F for your heart chakra. You're already inviting the right people into your life to help support your dreams."

"What about me?" Grant asked.

She paused and studied Grant. "Your sound is E for the solar plexus, for inner strength, autonomy, and personal power. You need it right now." She backed away. She had a concerned look on her face.

"What's wrong?" Grant asked.

"Your jinga."

"What's that?"

"Too much or too little energy. You have so much energy it *cuts* me."

"That's what all the girls say," he joked. She was dead serious.

Sienna told us to form a semicircle with our heads near each other and to close our eyes. She made the most unreal sound by rubbing the rim of the crystal bowl with her mallet.

The word *bath* had thrown me off. Baths are soothing; that's not what this was. The sound grew and grew, slicing through my entire body like a blade, a series of blades. It was almost too much. Then there were more sounds, and they didn't go anywhere. Instead, they seemed to gather and expand. The whole dome filled with echoes, vibrations, and humming.

I woke up, astounded that I could have fallen asleep through all that. Grant had fallen asleep, too, although that didn't surprise me— I've seen him sleep through everything. Our arms were effortlessly pressed together. I could tell the moment he woke up from the way his breathing changed.

I looked around the room and discovered we were alone. I was going to suggest that maybe Melody, Cassie, and Sienna had gone time traveling, but the silence felt too sacred to break. We stared up at the beautiful wood ceiling without saying a word. It was as though the sound bath had vibrated all my worries away and opened up a space inside me that I hadn't known existed. I felt open and clear for the first time in a long while, maybe ever. I knew I wanted to give Palm Springs a try. I turned my head and saw Grant grinning at me. He might as well have been the only person in the world, my singular focus. I looked into his eyes the way I had on Christmas Day.

I saw him not as my partner or future husband or future ex, not as our children's father, not as a professor or hiker. Not as the man who took off when times were hard, but as the man who came back. If we hadn't come here, would I have missed out on the opportunity to see him with these fresh eyes? Would he have been new to me again? New to himself?

It was time to tell him about Melody's job offer. I'd been thinking about it for a week, and I'd decided.

"Want to try that thing where we go on opposite sides and say something, like in Grand Central?" I asked.

"Sure," he said.

We walked to opposite sides of the room and sat at the base of the giant arced beams as far apart as we could get. Grant said, "*Tap tap tap*, is this thing on?"

"It really does sound like you're speaking into a microphone. Like you're sitting next to me."

"It's always been like that between us, Kim. For two people who've spent so much time apart, I've always felt you near."

"I need to talk to you about something."

"I need to talk to you about something, too." He was unusually serious. The sound bath had made space for this.

We talked over each other, me saying, "I have an opportunity to—" And Grant saying, "There's something I've been—"

"You go," I said.

"That job at Creighton? I had a Zoom interview a few weeks ago. It's just a visiting position, and not much money, but it's a chance to teach again. James says it's mine to lose."

"Omaha?" Our night in Nebraska seemed so far away—thousands of miles and weeks ago—that I'd almost forgotten the job was even a possibility. So much had changed since then. My heart sank.

"I'm not even sure I want it anymore, to be honest. But I'm not ready to retire, and I can't just hike all the time, even though I'd like that. I've spent my entire adult life building my career. And I miss being around young people."

"Melody offered me a job here. In Palm Springs. She needs my help. She offered me a salary that's frankly too much. And benefits. I've thought about it, and I really want to do this. I'm excited about the idea of trying something totally new."

"So, you've decided? Just like that, without even talking about it with me?"

"And have you? Without talking to me? I'm talking to you now. I've decided on a lot of things, not just the job. Grant, I've decided—"

I was about to tell him I wanted to get married when he said, "You're asking me to give up my career."

"I'm not *asking* you to do anything."

"No, why would you ever lean on me, need me, impose yourself?"

"God, Grant! Because I can't! You always run off."

"I haven't done that in years! I'm better, Kim. I lost my mom, my job, my community in Mounds, and I've been here this whole time. Instead of leaving, I've doubled down. You've been the one pushing me away, pushing us to change our lives, and I haven't gone anywhere. No wonder you wanted to snowbird. You can't commit fully to being with me any more than you can commit to being in one place. Relationships are about sacrifice, you know."

I began to shake with frustration. "I *did* sacrifice! I moved with you to Madison when I found out I was pregnant. I followed you for your postdoc and stayed in Wisconsin. I sacrificed my entire youth in order to be with you."

"You think you sacrificed your *youth*? Ouch. Here I thought you wanted to build a life with me. A life we'd chosen to spend together."

"Grant, I think—"

"You want sunshine and warmth? You want to live where everyone is on vacation? Fine. After you gave up your *youth* for me, I won't make you sacrifice your old age, that's for sure. You can ride that out alone."

Before I could say more, he stood, walked to the center of the room, and let out a scream in the sound tunnel that only he could hear. He thundered to the lobby on the first floor. I followed him down, careful not to break my ankle again. He put on his shoes; I slipped on my sandals and followed him outside into the thin air and the bright high-desert sun.

He stormed over to Melody's waiting car. "You just can't stand to be in the same place with me, can you?"

"That's exactly what I want! But being in the same place means weathering more storms. It means that we can't rely on the high of being reunited to keep us tied to each other. When you don't have another place to escape to, I need to know you'll stay and work things out. What are you going to do, Grant? Disappear again?"

That's the last thing I said to him: *What are you going to do, Grant? Disappear again?*

Chapter Thirty-Nine

Palm Springs
January 4, 2023
3:30 P.M.

The girls, Octavia, and I sat huddled under one blanket on the couch, sharing the silence. No television, no conversation. We were staring at the rain lashing the windows, watching the palm fronds pushed to the side. No horror movie could have made the scene feel more ominous. The room was heavy with the intensity of our shared sense of doom. It was one of the first times I'd let them see how worried I truly was. There was no way to pretend anymore, the situation was too dire.

A watched pot never boils, so of course my phone didn't light up until I'd left it on the coffee table, one of the first times in days that it hadn't been in my hand. I'd taken it everywhere with me, even into the bathroom.

Dort grabbed it, looked at the screen, bit her lip, and handed it to me. "It's Brady." She swiped to answer it and handed the phone to me. Whenever he called, I wondered what would be worse: hearing that Grant's body had been found, or for him to remain missing for days, months, years . . . forever?

Brady was a man of few words. "You won't believe this."

I felt all the blood drain from my face. "What? Believe what?"

"We were wrapping up when Hobie insisted on one last run, a real Hail Mary. I said no, it went against my better judgment. Winds were already getting bad. Fine, I told him. A quick up and down. Then we saw blue. The blue jacket. We found him. We put him in a screamer suit and hoisted him by helicopter off the mountain."

I took a deep breath to stop my lower lip from quivering. "Brady? Is he alive? You didn't say if he's alive."

The girls were glued to me, searching my expression for news. I couldn't exhale. Time stopped.

"Oh, sorry." I thought he meant he was sorry Grant wasn't alive. Then he said, "Yeah, he is. If he wasn't, I would have shown up at your door to tell you myself."

I let the phone drop out of my hands and into my lap. The girls hadn't looked at me with this much intensity since they were infants gazing at my face as I fed them. They must have thought it was bad. I was too shocked to even speak.

Octavia came to where I sat and put her arm around my shoulder, expecting the worst.

Finally, I came to, as if from a brief fainting spell. "Hobie did it. He found him. Grant is alive!"

Gene, who'd been like a watchdog since Grant had gone missing, heard us shrieking from his condo. He ran over to see if we were okay, followed by Jeanie, and his concern melted the minute he saw Dort and March smile. By then, the girls, Octavia, and I were jumping around, screaming. Never in my life had I felt such pure, ecstatic joy.

Jeanie walked into the room and clapped her hands. "Thank you for coming to my birthday party!"

After that, Le Desert, if seen from above, must have looked like a scene from a musical Basil would write the lyrics for, with every door swinging open at almost the exact same moment after Dort sent a text to the rescue group from my phone: *They found him! The bird is in the nest!*

Everyone rushed into the courtyard to celebrate in the wind and rain. We were soaked, and we didn't care.

Melody said she was on her way to pick us up. We had a few moments to hug Thomas and Raul, Coco, the couple from Minnesota, and two brothers from Winnipeg who'd just checked in to one of the units that day and had no idea what was going on, but joined in our celebration anyway.

It felt as if every bottled-up emotion, every worry, every bit of fear I'd felt all these years about losing Grant, had been relieved. I had to really lose him to know what I had. I threw my head back and laughed and wept at the same time. I hugged the girls over and over. Never in my life had I been so happy, or so sure that I wanted to be with Grant forever. I ran into the house and opened Grant's dresser drawer to find the engagement ring that I knew he kept hidden. It was my turn to see if Grant would say yes.

But it was missing. I tried to remember when I'd last seen it, my heart sinking at the possible implications, the vitriol of our fight on New Year's Eve hitting me all over again. Why would it now be gone?

The smell was the first thing that hit me. It was Grant's smell times a thousand; it was every dirty workout shirt, every smelly bathroom that I'd silently cursed over the last thirty years. I didn't care. It was Grant. The girls and I approached the gurney in the hallway where he was waiting to be scanned. His hair was shockingly dark against the white sheet. His face was drawn and sallow from dehydration, his lips were cracked. He had a black eye.

I hoisted myself onto the gurney and lay by his side. He was almost too wiped out to smile—almost. I kissed him on the cheek and began to cry. "I'm sorry," I said. "I never thought I'd be able to say I'm sorry. I'll go back to Madison with you. I'll go to Omaha. I'll go anywhere as long as you're there. I'm sorry, I'm sorry. I love you. I thought I might never be able to say those words to you."

"My pack." I didn't know if he couldn't talk because he was too thirsty or too tired.

"Your what?"

"My pack. I need my pack."

I figured he was delirious. "It's at home. Honestly, I thought about burning it."

He pointed at his legs. His hand was covered in scabs. "My pockets."

"What about them?"

His expensive pants had held up surprisingly well. I reached in and felt a bunch of rocks. I pulled them out—one, two, four, six. "These are beautiful."

Tears ran down the sides of his dirty cheeks. "For you. And you and you." He looked at March and Dort on either side of him. Never before had I felt more that we were a real family.

"Grant"—my eyes filled with tears—"will you marry me?"

He didn't answer. He was very still.

"Dad, oh my God," March said. "We can have a double wedding. Wouldn't that be nuts?"

We were all intently staring at Grant, waiting for his answer. He opened his mouth to speak, and then his skin paled and his eyes began to roll back in his head.

"Nurse?" March shrieked. "Nurse! My dad doesn't look right!"

"Come back to us, Grant," I said. I rubbed his hands, his cheeks. I kissed his forehead. The silver stones clattered on the hard tile floor. "Come back, please." I kissed him on the lips and tried to blow some life into him. "You can't do this, Grant. Not after what you've been through. Come on, we're all here, we all love you so much. We need you to come back. We need you."

"Dad!"

Before I knew it, a team of nurses and doctors told us to step aside. "Code blue!" one of the nurses said.

The last thing I saw were the bottoms of his bare feet, red, swollen, and covered in blisters. They pushed him into the emergency room, the doors swinging shut.

This time he wasn't missing or lost: he was gone.

Chapter Forty

Palm Springs
January 16, 2023

Grant had a steady stream of visitors in the hospital as he was re-covering from his embolism, giardia, broken shoulder, and torn muscle in his quad, so many problems that I didn't have an opportunity to ask him in his rare lucid moments if he remembered my proposal. His room filled up with everyone we'd met in Palm Springs after only two months.

It was therapeutic to go through the play-by-play of the events. I watched in real time as the most terrifying three days of our lives turned into a swashbuckling story. Everyone wanted to hear the nuts and bolts of how he'd survived. We recounted the heroics of his rescue—especially Hobie, who ate up the praise and attention. We knew that if he hadn't insisted on going up on one last helicopter ride, Grant wouldn't have made it.

"Talk about having your hill to die on," Grant said.

"Honestly, I thought you were a goner for sure," Brady said, his sunglasses propped on his head. Even away from the drama of the rescue, he still seemed serious and in charge.

"I wasn't worried," Grant said. "Not until the very last day. That's when I . . ." He looked at the girls, and at me, and his eyes filled with tears. "You know."

Brady said, "Not since Napoléon has someone made so many bad decisions. You should have had your phone with you, should have packed more gear, should have waited at Morris Road for someone to help you when your truck was lost. You should never have turned around and tried to hike all the way to Indian Canyons in the middle of the day. Should have checked the weather, should have packed more water and warmer clothes, should have bought a car from a reputable dealer, should have . . ."

Gene was sitting on the hospital room's little vinyl couch next to Jeanie. "Being a pessimistic philosopher doesn't help you much out in the real world, does it, Doc?"

Hobie said, "You were looking at Palm Springs when you thought you were looking at Cathedral City. So when you turned, you just went farther away. How'd you lose your pack, anyway?"

"I used it as a pillow. When I got up and started walking, I was so out of it, I guess I just left it there."

"Well, it saved your life. Helped us know generally where you were, and your journal led us to look for you in the stream."

Hobie hadn't worn anything but his orange search-and-rescue shirt since Grant had gone missing. Saving someone's life made it even easier to get laid, he joked (sort of), and it almost made him feel as important as he felt running the HOA. He pulled out his phone and pulled up a photo. "See these tracks in the snow?" He walked around the room and showed the photo of paw prints to everyone. "A mountain lion. I found the tracks behind Grant, after the chopper got him out. He had no idea he was being followed. Crazy, huh? If he'd turned right instead of left that last day, he would have walked right into her den."

"Too soon," I said, putting my hand up to block the image. "We've had too many near misses for me to process."

Finally, when everyone left, I sat on the edge of Grant's bed and stroked his arm where the IV kept him hydrated. "I know you didn't want me to read your journal, but what was the question you asked at Cedar Springs? What did you need clarity about?"

"You. I brought the engagement ring on the hike with me. It was in the inner pocket of the backpack. I wanted to hold it and meditate on it and really think about marriage. Not about whether or not I *wanted* to marry you. I needed to know if I could let go of my past and be there for you. Be the husband you deserve."

"And?"

"And I was going to throw the ring over the side of the mountain if I couldn't do it."

I shook my head. "What did you decide?"

He smiled. "The ring should still be there. Kimmy, I promise I'll never leave you again." He placed his hand on mine. "And then look what happened. I got lost. And when I got lost, I faced my fears and found myself."

"So did I."

"You proposed, Kim."

"You remembered." I kissed his hand.

"The whole time we've been here, I've been waiting for you to ask me again. And when you do, my answer is yes."

Chapter Forty-One

Palm Springs
June 24, 2023

It was easier to part with the Madison house after another family had lived in it. It felt less ours upon our return. My dishes, pots, and pans were in different places. I'd sweep and discover an earring under the bed, or a dog's chew toy between the cushions.

The girls came home to clean out their rooms. It was emotional to let go of the space that had provided us with so much comfort all these years, and it also felt right to transplant our remaining belongings into a little condo near the capitol with both of our names on the mortgage. We had a pied-à-terre of our own, one that would allow us to enjoy the glory of Madison summers and still leave for long stretches in Palm Springs, where we'd bought the condo Jeanie and Gene had rented. Poor Gene had passed away in March, and Jeanie was in a memory-care facility in Regina.

Now we were the ones complaining about emergency assessments for the roof, the heat in the hot tub not working, and the gardeners revving up their leaf blowers before eight in the morning.

It was official: we were snowbirds. Our winter in Palm Springs had been as much about finding each other as it was about moving into a new stage of life.

Grant splurged on a new car that he bought from a legitimate dealer: an EV truck that he could drive on the dirt paths to the hiking trails. Already, the bumper was filling up with stickers. In the middle, we placed one Dort bought for Grant that said PEOPLE TELL ME I'M CONDESCENDING. THAT MEANS I TALK DOWN TO PEOPLE. On the left was his old College of the Mounds sticker that he'd peeled off the Prius before it was towed away. He'd affixed it to the bumper with superglue. And on the right, a palm tree next to the words PS I LOVE YOU, right next to a sticker with Bucky Badger. The vanity plate said GNHKNG, "gone hiking."

Grant let the job in Omaha go, and we decided that I'd work for Melody in Palm Springs. While Grant recuperated, he worked part time at Revivals and began writing a book about finding a new life philosophy while hiking (although he was still banned from the Agua Caliente Reservation).

I was invited to be part of a show of amateur artists at the Desert Art Center. On display were paintings of Melody in her fur hat playing mah-jongg next to the mountain, Jeanie and Gene's gnarled feet in their matching rubber sandals, Cassie meditating, Hobie walking ahead on a hiking trail with Audrey staring back from his pack, Grant as Grambo, the Husbands stretching up to the sky in their metallic bodysuits (they were making a killing after being featured on Goop—alongside the photo I'd taken of them—and had bought a house in Movie Colony), Coco in the laundry room, smoking a cigarette.

At last, I'd allowed myself to see and capture what I found beautiful.

The ranch was the perfect place for a wedding. The sky was clear and bright, and the smoke trees had exploded into an opaque yet somehow neon-purple bloom as they always do around the summer solstice. The mountains in the background were steady and unchanged, nature's unconditional love.

A string quartet played Vivaldi, while behind them a dance floor was set up with the DJ from Streetbar with his trademark angel wings and KGAY hat, ready to spin some tunes. All were in the mood for a party as they milled around, waiting for the ceremony to begin.

Coco and Hobie held hands. March and Simeon cooed over Thomas and Raul's new baby, Crispin (the "littlest Arnold-Little"), while the Husbands and Octavia did what they do best: infuse the atmosphere with energy and make everyone feel special.

Cassie, resplendent in a flowy dress and halo made of pressed wildflowers, stood in the center of the guests. She rang some chimes, indicating that it was time for the ceremony to begin. "Please take off your shoes so we can connect with Mother Earth, and gather holding hands in a circle to unite in the present," Cassie said.

Basil kicked off his shoes. "You ready? Finally?" He smiled at me. "Not many men go from being a husband to best man."

I pointed at Sasha, holding a bouquet of wildflowers. "And not many ex-wives become the maid of honor."

"Symmetry."

I wore the dress I'd bought at Trina Turk. It was wrong for the season, but right for the occasion. Grant wore Melody's father's Smoke Tree Ranch insignia bolo tie. Grant was still thin, but he'd thankfully shaved his beard. March and Dort stood on either side of him.

"You know," I said to Grant, "I think everyone should wait thirty years before deciding to get married."

"You sure are sanguine about it."

"This is the most heteronormative moment of my life," Dort said.

We all fell quiet as Cassie began to walk around, smudging. "The sage is for cleansing. Let's begin by releasing what we don't need from our thoughts. Release what doesn't serve you. Create a space that is clear and uncluttered. Fresh and new."

Grant and I held hands.

Next, Cassie lit a stick and walked around us, waving it with intensity. "I ask that the plant spirit of palo santo infuse this space with blessing." The burning wood was sweet smelling, and it mingled with the scent of creosote. "Now I light the candles in the corners to call in the six directions: north, south, east, west, Mother Earth and Father Sky." Next, she walked around us with singing bowls. The sound was so true and clear that it was impossible not to be moved by it.

There was no question Cassie would officiate. After all, she'd helped us find each other again.

Some wild rabbits hopped around the shrubs. The mountains were golden now in the summer heat. I would never be able to look at them the way I did when we'd first arrived, as simply pretty and dramatic. Now I knew they were teeming with life, danger, and beauty, and they were a constant reminder of how quickly life can change.

I looked deep into Grant's eyes when I said, "I promise to show more emotion, relax, make myself vulnerable, look you in the eyes, be congruent with my yeses and always keep you close." Grant spoke of the wisdom he learned in the mountains, of the peace that comes when you stop thinking of what comes next, of ditching your entire operating system. He said, "I promise to stick around and never get lost. And I promise to love, honor, respect, and take care of you." He smiled. "And always make sure you are warm."

We exchanged rings and kissed, and Cassie declared us married with a final blessing.

"If you're not at home in your heart," she said, "then you're not at home anywhere."

Acknowledgments

I have so much gratitude for my editor, Sarah Cantin, the "Brady" of my writing life. It's easy to get lost while working on a novel, and when I do, she orients me in the story and helps me bushwhack through excessive plot. She's an incredibly hard worker and a constant source of clarity, insight, support, and wisdom. I appreciate and admire her so much.

I've been incredibly fortunate to work with Sarah and the same elite team of professionals at St. Martin's Press on all three of my novels. Many thanks to Jen Enderlin, Lisa Senz, Brant Janeway, Kim Ludlam, Katie Bassel, Erica Martirano, Erik Platt, and Drue VanDuker. Thanks also to Olga Grlic for selecting Kate Jansen's vivid artwork and for designing another truly delicious and evocative cover.

My agent, Marcy Posner at Folio Lit, has been my champion from the start. I love her, and so does my entire family—she's practically a Clancy. Her assistant, Jessica Macy, was also incredibly helpful.

As Thomas and Raul would say, my many sources for research put the "knowledge" in the acknowledgments (actually, they'd probably say they put the "edge" in). I learned about hiking and search efforts from Roger and Sheila Dannen's and Gord and Meldia Weisberger's firsthand accounts. Meldia also read my manuscript for accuracy. I'm so grateful for their time and generosity because I know it must have been hard to talk about such a harrowing experience. David Roe and

Greg Eiford were also very generous to share their hiking and outdoor adventure expertise.

Many thanks to the members of the Agua Caliente Band of Cahuilla Indians who keep Indian Canyons safe, and to the heroic volunteers with the Palm Springs Mounted Police. It's incredibly life-affirming to know there are so many people who will mobilize at a moment's notice to find you when you are lost. If only all of life could be like that.

I had to rely on a lot of people for insight into Palm Springs history, art, architecture, fashion, shamanism, difficult relationships, philosophy, stolen cars, medical conditions, social media influencing, etc. Thanks so much to Liz Cortez, Olivia Clancy, Jennifer Rosner, Tracy Conrad, Rick Baker, Don Parfet, Nelda Linsk, Caitlin Clancy, Julia Scoles, Sally Higginson, Matthew Tedesco, Deb Curry, Jeff Chaney, Linda Baehman, Breehan James, Sarah Miller, Ann Fitzpatrick, Erika Hanson, Britta Hansen, Valerie Del Perugia, Jane Townsend, Niels Mueller, Maggie Downs, the residents of our beloved Coco Cabana complex (the "coco nuts"), everyone in the Winter Dance Party, PoA, my book club, and the "Winettes." I truly couldn't have written this book without picking your brains. Josh Lieber, thanks for all your decades of friendship and promotional help.

I'm so grateful to fellow writers for talking me off the ledge on multiple occasions: Lauren Fox, Liam Callanan, Anuradha Rajurkar, Aims McGuinniss, Lynda Cohen Loigman, Ann Garvin, Amy Meyerson, A. H. Kim, Karen Dukess, Alison Hammer, Nicola Harrison, Steven Rowley, and Byron Lane.

Thanks to my cousin Cutie (Wendy Van Peenan) for providing feedback on an early version of the novel. My family members on both sides have been wonderfully supportive of my writing endeavors. I'm truly grateful.

I made a lot of progress on *The Snowbirds* during artist residencies at Good Hart in Northern Michigan, and at Write On in Door County. Thank you so much for the gift of glorious space and uninterrupted time to imagine and create.

Thanks also to all the many wonderful booksellers and librarians who have gotten behind my work and helped me find readers. As a lifelong book nerd, you are my people, and so are the readers who seek escape in stories.

Finally, thanks to my incredible family. Olivia and Tim, I'm so proud of the funny, smart, and thoughtful adults you've become. John, now that the book is done, I can thank you for making it so difficult for me to imagine a relationship in crisis. You're a constant source of steadiness, love, and support.

About the Author

Kate Berg

Christina Clancy is the author of *The Second Home* and *Shoulder Season*. Her work has also appeared in *The New York Times*, *The Washington Post*, the *Chicago Tribune*, *The Sun* magazine, and in various literary journals. She splits her time between Madison, Wisconsin, and Palm Springs.